TICKET TO RIDE

TICKET TO RIDE

JANET NEEL

 St. Martin's Minotaur ☎ New York

www.minotaurbooks.com

Library of Congress Cataloging-in-Publication Data

Neel, Janet.
    Ticket to ride / Janet Neel.—1st U.S. ed.
        p. cm.
    ISBN 0-312-34923-8
    EAN 978-0-312-34923-3
    1. Women lawyers—Fiction. 2. Illegal aliens—Crimes against—Fiction.
3. Attorney and client—Fiction. 4. London (England)—Fiction. 5. Serbs—England—Fiction. I. Title.

PR6064.E417T53 2005
823'.914—dc22   2005044458

First published in Great Britain by Allison & Busby Limited

First U.S. Edition: December 2005

10 9 8 7 6 5 4 3 2 1

For Prudence Fay
without whom there would
have been no book

JANET NEEL is the *nom de plume* of Baroness (Janet) Cohen of
Pimlico, who sits as a Labour peer in the House of Lords. She
started out as a solicitor, then went into the Board of Trade, then
to Charterhouse Bank. She now works at several places at once
including the London Stock Exchange. She has published several
crime novels. The first, *Death's Bright Angel,* won the John
Creasey Prize and the third, *Death of a Partner,* and fourth, *Death
Among the Dons,* were both shortlisted for the CWA Gold
Dagger.

TICKET TO RIDE

Chapter One

(Tuesday before Easter)

'Good morning, Lady Williams. I am looking for Lady Barlow.'

'You will have to coax her out from under that table.'

'I'll certainly try, milady.' The big man, dressed in long black frock coat and trousers, and a rosette at the back of his collar, bent, ponderously, to address a pair of long, trousered legs. 'Milady?'

'I am trying to repair the fax machine,' a voice said, crossly.

Beryl Williamson, anchored behind her desk, watched the scene thinking it would make an excellent puzzle picture, but one hardly becoming the dignity of the House of Lords. 'Anne, my dear, do give it up. It will get done while we are all away, and Mr Stubbs has come to say that your guests are here.'

'Damn.' The legs shook, and Anne, Baroness Barlow of Camden emerged, bottom first, coughing in the dust, while Mr Stubbs, as a well brought up ex-petty officer in the Royal Navy, gazed out of the window.

'Are you sure you're facing east, Anne?' Beryl enquired.

'Oh, very good, Beryl.' Anne sat back on her heels. 'Mr Stubbs, this is no longer a plug. It is dead. It is an ex-plug.'

'Give it to him, Anne, do. You seem to have picked up a lot of fluff. I have a clothes brush in my drawer there.' She gestured towards a bank of substantial filing cabinets. 'Now tell Mr Stubbs where your guests are to be directed.'

'They're in the Peers Lobby. I'll come and collect them.' She was brushing herself down, vigorously, as she spoke.

'Only you, my dear, would have decided to repair the plug on a fax machine while you were waiting for a large lunch party. I feel guilty for having mentioned it.'

'Well, I suppose it was a bit daft, but I, too, need to send several faxes.' Beryl watched, with affection while her friend finished brushing herself off, pulled open a filing drawer and extracted comb and lipstick and pushed her short, beautifully cut greying hair into place. She peered critically at her face, visibly deciding that a quick go with the lipstick would have to do. A decision that Beryl thoroughly supported, at nearly eighty years old she no longer bothered with make-up but, since she also no longer bothered about her weight, the clear pink skin and wide blue eyes that had always gained her more than her fair share of admirers, had endured.

'Right. *En avant*, Beryl.' Anne was stuffing things into her handbag. 'Can I carry anything?'

'No, I'm leaving it all here.' Beryl indicated her desk on which a pile of neatly annotated paper, and the draft of a speech sat. 'And you go on, I will catch you up.'

'They can wait and chat to each other. We'll go together.'

A courteous young woman, Beryl thought, for all she was on the other side, politically. And, of course, really not young anymore in any real sense, but in the House of Lords someone of nearly sixty, who could still get down on the floor to attack a plug, was young. Anne Barlow had been at the same Cambridge college as she had, just twenty years later, and over the years perhaps that mattered more than any political divide. She leant heavily on the stick without which she could walk nowhere and hauled herself out of the chair, envying momentarily the ease with which Anne was bending to tie a shoelace.

'Long arms,' Anne said, catching her eye, and she laughed and accompanied her friend through one of the heavy oak doors with which the House was so amply provided. She stopped to catch her breath; getting anywhere was a slow process these days.

'Remind me, Anne. Who are all your guests?'

'The child in whose honour the lunch is, Jules, who has just qualified as a solicitor. Then the boys, James and William, and Jules's employer Paul Jenkins and wife Sofia.'

'The immigration specialist?'

The Paul Jenkins Beryl knew of was one of the many thorns in the side of the police and the Home Office, representing as he did a tide of applicants for asylum.

'That's the one. You don't approve of him?' Beryl declined to be drawn, so Anne went on, 'And her...well, godfather, I suppose, Gwyn Jones and wife Sandra. A Welshman.'

'No!'

'I daresay, Beryl, there may be people called Gwyn Jones who are not Welshmen.'

'Not this one if he's the one I'm thinking of. A boyo from the valleys. Welsh-speaking. Social Services expert.'

'That's our man. At Hackney now, trying to cleanse the Augean stables.'

'Not the current stables so much, as the historical, surely, Anne?' Hackney had been run by Anne's party since time immemorial, and Beryl thought she should be reminded.

'The current situation isn't that great either. He's having to deal with the Mariott enquiry, and horrors are coming out from under stones.'

Hackney indeed was a blot on Labour's escutcheon and it was typical of Anne, a distinguished barrister, not to waste any time on a very weak point.

'Is your husband not here?' Beryl asked.

'No. Poor Henry is still doing a dam in Thailand and we decided not to wait. It could be three months before he gets back. It is a pity – we'd hoped he'd get home for Easter, but there it is. I don't think they have Easter in Thailand, and in any case both the boys are away for Easter. But he could have seen Jules – as the newest qualified she is on duty all over the weekend. *Darling!*'

Beryl watched her friend disappear into the embrace of a large young man, dressed in jeans, sandals with socks, a shirt with rolled-up sleeves and a hairy, brightly coloured waistcoat. Anne stepped back and surveyed him. 'Could we roll down the sleeves?' The young man who, Beryl observed, was startlingly good-looking and very much his mother's son, beamed down from his 6 ft 2 in. and obligingly started to do so. An improvement, but it still left the uneven black beard and the dark hair tied in a pony tail. The young man dug a battered tie from the pocket of his jeans and tied it on, smiling at her friend. It was a faded green and clashed with every colour in the ethnic waistcoat, but it was kindly meant and he beamed warmly at Beryl as he was introduced. Then came his brother, the eldest child, she knew, a total contrast, with his father's looks and the short haircut and sharp grey suit of the aspirant merchant banker, and his wife, a ferociously competent doctor. And behind them was a tall young woman with dark blonde hair gelled into fashionable spikes, and ridiculously like Anne. This must be the treasured child, the just qualified lawyer, looking unsmilingly round the assembled gathering. Her gaze rested for a moment on Beryl who sustained a small shock. A fierce young hawk, she thought, prospecting strange territory through green, widely opened eyes. She was watching a tall man who was calling greetings in Welsh across the lobby, gathering compatriots about him. Gwyn Jones of course, and as she fair-mindedly conceded, a sight to fill the eye, one of the fair Celts, quick-moving and crackling with energy.

'Jules, darling.'

The young woman removed her attention from Gwyn Jones and turned to be introduced, and Beryl saw that she was not really a beauty, except for the eyes, but she was a force, intelligence in every movement and she was attracting a lot of attention of which she seemed not to be conscious. The Senior Attendant in his improbable frock coat and tights could not take his eyes off her, and one of the small dark Welshmen was urgently asking Gwyn to introduce him. Beryl stood back obligingly while the Lord Williams clasped Jules hand, gazing into those amazing eyes. It took Gwyn some time before he could detach the good Lord and dispatch him to wherever he had been going before he had been struck by lightning.

'I think we're all here. Can we move down to drinks?' Anne was sounding just this side of harassed, and none of her guests were listening.

Beryl, being slow on her feet, decided to set off but was amused to see that it took even the efficient Anne a good ten minutes to get her party as far as the Peers' Guest Room, and finally sat down with champagne glasses in their hands. Beryl addressed herself to Sofia Jenkins and Sandra Jones, who were in danger of being left out. Anne's children were all talking to each other and both Gwyn Jones and Paul Jenkins were being hailed by acquaintances from all over the big room. The group finished three bottles of champagne between them, while the Barlow children remembered their manners and talked to the rest of her guests. Beryl was embroiled in a conversation about the decline of modern art with the number two son when she realised Anne was trying to attract her attention. 'I must get this lot to the dining-room. We're twenty minutes late. Will you change your mind and have lunch?'

'No, my dear, I have a speech. I will see you afterwards, and thank you so much. Very nice to meet all the young.'

One of Beryl's jobs in her distinguished retirement, had been to head the Cambridge college of which they were both alumnae and she missed being surrounded by people in their twenties and late teens.

'See you at tea then, if you are not on your feet.'

'Of course, my dear.'

Some two hours later, Beryl was making what she thought of as all convenient speed, which meant she was a little breathless. She needed to be in her seat at the beginning of the debate to hear her own front bench lead off, but she had been delayed by a phone call. It would be the more important to be conspicuously present today; the House was sitting close to Easter, thanks to an unpopular Criminal Justice Bill, but that had been finished the night before and only a few members of the House would be in their places. As she went through the lobby she saw Anne's group, evidently much flown with food and wine, saying their farewells. The artistic son had removed his tie, the neatly brushed son was looking a little less pulled together, and the lovely daughter, slightly flushed, was being teased by her brothers. The grown-ups were in only slightly better order, Gwyn Jones was talking rather too loudly in Welsh to an ageing cross bencher, and Paul Jenkins, dark and intense, was bending the ear of an arch-liberal of deeply fallible judgement from the Liberal Democrat benches. She ducked into the Chamber to avoid delaying the farewells further and, after a bit, with her frontbencher well into his swing, saw Anne, slightly unsteady on her feet, making her way to her usual place on the government benches, with all the other Labour subversives. True believers sat behind the government front bench in the eye of the cameras which recorded all business, but the more critical (and less ambitious for office) sat behind the Bishops. She got her speech over, waited for the next two, caught Anne's eye and rose to leave. By the time she regained the Lobby, with attendants hovering, Anne had come round from the other end and was waiting for her.

'Just as well you were there, Beryl. I was dropping off. Now if I were on *your* benches I would have had *two* sons in suits with short hair.'

Anne pushed open the unmarked back door of the Dining Room, a huge high-ceilinged room, into which the spring sun was streaming.

Beryl settled herself at a table, hooking her stick onto the chair and considered the point. 'Well, not necessarily. I have seen some of ours with some very wild children. Or grandchildren. Anyway, he seemed a lovely young man.'

'Yes, he is. But heaven knows when he is going to settle, or what as. I think just tea please, about a bucket of it.'

The hovering waiter grinned at her as he went to get her order and she closed her eyes. 'I'm afraid they'll remember us. Still, I left a huge tip – money must help, mustn't it?'

'What a very unsocialist view.'

'Yes, sorry about that. Don't tell the others.'

They drank tea, companionably.

'I needed that,' Anne said. 'I couldn't get rid of them, they were all having far too good a time. I even got James to sign in as Eldest Son of Peer.'

'You could have got your lovely Jules to sign as Eldest Unmarried Daughter of Peer,' Beryl pointed out. She checked, as her friend, hands trembling, missed the cup and poured tea into the saucer.

'Anne, my dear, shall I pour? Well, you certainly had something to celebrate today, with that child. Looks very like you.'

Anne Barlow was dabbing at the mess with a napkin. 'She is very like me,' she said to the table cloth. 'Which is odd because she is not my biological daughter.'

'No?'

Beryl had been in her time the close-mouthed recipient of every sort of confidence, public and personal. She handed Anne a sandwich to give her friend time to decide whether she really meant to go on with this conversation.

'She is the only child of my third cousin Flora and her husband Flynn, both now deceased.'

A lawyer's formulation, Beryl thought. 'You adopted her?' she said, cautiously, hoping her friend would relax.

'No. It's not…she doesn't want that. She keeps her given name of Jules Carlisle. Well, it isn't her given name even, her wretched parents christened her July Rain Carlisle.' Anne had started to dab at the mess again, head down, and Beryl signalled to a waiter, deciding that Anne did need to talk about the young woman, and she after all was a safe audience. She sat while the waiter cleared them up and gave them fresh tea.

Anne took a deep breath and a gulp of tea. 'Her mother Flora was at least ten years younger than me, but I knew her quite well because they lived in London. Flora was an only child. Her mother Muriel – second cousin to my mother – was a grim old bat. She's gone now, so I should not speak ill, but she wasn't a load of laughs. Flora was not clever but a nice little girl and very keen on me and my brothers and indeed the whole family.' She looked at her empty cup, distractedly, and Beryl took the pot firmly from her, and poured her another.

'So what happened to Flora?' she asked.

'She went to cookery school, then had a few jobs – I used to see her sometimes – then she went off with the raggle-taggle gypsies oh.'

'What?'

'She entered into a runaway marriage – she was by then of age – with a half Irish guitar player called Flynn Carlisle. One saw why – dramatically good-looking, black hair, long eye-lashes, and that lazy Irish charm which covers a deep reservoir of idleness.'

'There speaks the Protestant Scot.'

'In the event we Protestants were right. Cousin Muriel was distraught but in the grim Scots manner, she cut Flora out of her life, and it was *my* mother who persuaded me to take an extra day out of a business meeting in Ireland and see how Flora was getting on. Jules was about a year old.'

'And how did that go?' Beryl prompted, into the silence.

'They were living in a commune. Everyone was dirty, the kids had nits, and the women were doing all the work. Third World stuff.' She looked drearily over the bright river. 'I need hardly tell you that I was at that stage a sharp-suited, desperately ambitious barrister on the way up, with two children of my own, knocking myself and everyone else out just to keep the whole show on the road.'

'And not looking for any more responsibilities,' Beryl suggested.

Anne sighed but her shoulders relaxed a little. 'No, I thought I had quite enough second and third cousins living in damp bits of Scotland to visit, no one could expect me to visit cousins in damp Ireland as well. So I reported the facts to my Mum and she tried to persuade Cousin Muriel to go and see for herself, but she wouldn't, and then Cousin Muriel died. A stroke.'

'Did Flora come back then?'

'Yes, she did. Mum had persuaded Cousin Muriel at least not to leave her money away from her only child, so there was enough for a house in the Fens. I didn't go to see them there either, though Mum did, but I did get to Cousin Muriel's funeral if only because it was in London. Jules was about six then. And Flynn was drunk. I remember him walking unevenly up the aisle, bright red in the face, smelling none too clean, with Flora clinging to his arm to keep him in a straight line.' She sighed. 'I decided then and there not to have anything to do with any of it.'

'So you never – you didn't see Jules for some time.'

'Not for eight years after that. Not until the Tottenham Social Services department found me.'

'Why you? Or rather…'

'I know just what you mean. In the interval Flynn had died, having persuaded Flora to mortgage the house to finance his drinking. After he died, she sold up, moved to Tottenham and bought a very small flat with what was left. Then *she* got ill and died. And I never went near her through all of it.'

'You had two of your own,' Beryl said, patting her hand. 'And she was only a distant cousin.'

'Am I or am I not a member of the Labour Party? Do we not believe that we are all part of the main?' There were tears in her eyes and Beryl held her hand, delivering a basilisk look to a colleague wandering towards them, hopeful of company.

'Tell me about the Tottenham Social Services.'

Anne retrieved her hand and blew her nose. 'Ah, them. Represented by the boyo from the valleys, Gwyn Jones, then quite young, who had washed up there.'

'Ah. So that's why he was at the lunch today.'

'That's why, yes. A lively lad, then, and a very talented social worker. He took Jules home with him to his wife to give himself time to think and talk to the child. She was fourteen, and Flora, God forgive me, had told her to go to me as the best of her family if there was trouble. So she told Gwyn about me and he found me, which wasn't difficult as I was still living where we always had, maybe ten miles away, and reintroduced me to Jules without saying a word of reproach.'

'It must have been...well, it can't have been easy. For either of you.'

'I wanted her the minute I saw her.' Anne had recovered herself. 'But she didn't feel the same. I can see her now, bone thin, backed into a corner of Gwyn and Sandra's kitchen where she wanted to stay. Gwyn had to make her see that she couldn't – there was another baby coming and they had no room – and that I was the best of a poor set of choices. It would have been Care otherwise.' She hesitated and addressed herself to the cakes which Beryl had commanded. 'Jules had of course had a very bad time. There was a stepfather... It wouldn't have taken much effort by me.'

'But it worked? She's all right.' In Beryl's experience most of the stories behind the lives of apparently conventional colleagues were stranger than fiction, and this was turning out to be no exception.

'Well, yes. She loved our boys, who were just that much older that they were keen on her rather than jealous. And she and I and Henry reached détente. I cannot imagine what we would do if we lost her. As I might when she remembers that I lifted not a finger to help her or her mother for all those long years.'

Beryl gazed at her, momentarily not knowing what to do with the revelation of the depths behind the self-contained, cheerful exterior. 'I'm sure she has forgiven you long since. Does she live with you?'

'No. She did till she was out of university, but she has her own place now. The one thing I did manage to do for her was to clean up and let her mother's old flat, so that she could sell it for good money when she left university and started work in London. Of course she needed to be more central than Tottenham, so she has a mortgage but that's the same as the boys. They've got flats and mortgages too, even the dear hippy.' She blew her nose. 'Sorry, Beryl, I know you've got to get away.'

'Indeed.' Beryl was afraid that her friend was regretting telling her about the daughter who wasn't a daughter. She had been ten years in the House, long enough to know a lot about the lives of colleagues; they were all in each other's hands, but Anne might not yet have realised that. Seeking for a diversion, she picked up *The Times* she was carrying.

'Did you see the asylum seekers story?' She handed Anne the paper and watched her absorb it with the same swift concentration they all applied to digesting any written information, another *déformation professionelle* of a life spent absorbing policy papers or legal briefs. Beryl herself had been interested by the story, knowing something of the problems her ex-colleagues were facing.

It had been a dog that found them, *The Times* said, eight bodies in two shallow graves about a hundred yards apart. Hardly graves at all, indeed they lay in a natural indentation on the beach with a covering of sand. Eight bodies, all male, all young, all identifying papers removed. Whoever left them there had been in a hurry and had not had time to strip the bodies, so that the investigators could state with some confidence that their clothes had come from Former Yugoslavia. The men themselves, or some of them, were Serb, that much was clear, and in their twenties. They had all suffocated and the bodies had been dragged along the muddy sand to where they lay, west of King's Lynn. *The Times* was assuming that this was yet another batch of desperate would-be immigrants, squashed into a tiny airless cabin, who had died en route and been dumped by the people who were transporting them.

'What a horrible story,' Anne said, distracted, as Beryl had hoped. 'And what a peculiar route in by King's Lynn. Long way round from anywhere.'

'I suppose all the short routes are now guarded,' Beryl said, neutrally, getting a sharp considering look from her friend.

'Mm. Saving your background, Beryl. I doubt we're that efficient. But it is an awful story – the real villains are the organisers. What a business! I don't know what the potential immigrants think but they aren't getting much for their money, are they? No guarantees, just a ticket to ride.'

'That was ever so.'

'Indeed, yes. I'm always glad my Jules is doing decent domestic crime where she is. They do a lot of asylum work in the practice, but she's turned out to be a natural criminal lawyer. If you see what I mean.'

Beryl laughed, relieved to see her recovered. They went off to their various pursuits and it was an hour before she went down the plush-covered stairs to collect her coat from her peg in the darkened ground floor room which never failed to remind her of school, right down to the label, though now she was Bns Williams of Downham Market rather than Williams, B.

Chapter Two

(Maundy Thursday)

Jules Carlisle slid out of her bed, moving carefully so as not to disturb the man sleeping on the other side, and pattered down the stairs to the big kitchen/dining/living room cum office which was the reason she had bought the flat. The floor was uneven, and no two walls were at right angles, thanks to a nineteenth-century jerry builder who had made the joists too long and used unseasoned wood, but the ceilings were high and graceful and the light poured in. She put the kettle on and opened the big fridge to check she had milk and juice and bread. There was enough, there always was, but her hard childhood with alcoholic adults meant she never took a well-provisioned fridge for granted. She grinned to herself as she heard stirrings from the bedroom above; the noise of the kettle beginning to boil had always acted convulsively on the man in her bed. She listened, luxuriously, as he used the bathroom and then thumped down the stairs. A big man and not getting any smaller. He came up behind her and hugged her to him, his hands on her breasts.

'You don't really have to go, do you, cariad?'

She leaned back against him, infinitely comfortable and secure. 'I do, Gwyn. I am the only Qualified here.'

'Shame really.' You could still hear the valley in his voice, particularly at moments of tenderness, for all he had been away from Wales for twenty-five years.

'You have to go too,' she pointed out, disentangling herself to deal with the kettle.

'Yes, I do. It's all in twenty piles, waiting for me, and I need to get through it to keep ahead of those bastards.'

Those bastards, as she knew, were the Hackney officials who had managed to ignore (if you were feeling generous) or connive at (if you weren't) serious sexual abuse of children in Care, going back more years than anyone cared to contemplate. The real scandal was that monsters who had terrorised, beaten and sodomised the children in their care were not usually prosecuted, because what would be revealed was too uncomfortable for the various authorities whose responsibility the children had been. But Gwyn would change all that, she knew, and they were at one in their desire to see all these people in a badly run jail along with the negligent authorities, since hanging was no longer considered appropriate. Indeed, if opportunity had offered, she would gladly have seen her so-called stepfather staked out for the vultures to eat, but he had evaded her by dying of cirrhosis of the liver, six months after her mother.

'I have something to ask you.' Gwyn was sitting at the table, waiting, hopefully, for the solid bacon and egg breakfast she gave him on the rare occasions he could get away for a whole night.

'Ah,' she said, turning away from the pan and noticing, with a pang, that the thin spot in the centre of his thick, dark blond hair had spread again. 'So it wasn't my body you were after.'

He hugged her to him as she reached over to put his plate down. 'I hoped I'd proved it was.'

'You did, you did,' she said, laughing. Three times indeed, which was why they were both tired this morning. She sat down opposite him, watching the spring sun on his strong forearms. 'So what is it you want of me now, Mr Jones?'

'Well, not that, I'm afraid, I'm only human, girl.' He says 'yuman' still, she thought, with love. He looked at her, shiftily, as he swallowed the last bit of fried bread. 'I have them in my briefcase.' He hauled it up from the floor and extracted a thick envelope which he passed over. She opened it and looked over at him, reproachfully.

'Gwyn. *December*'s expenses?'

Gwyn was always behind with his expenses claims and being Director of Social Services did not seem to have improved the position.

'Yeah. Sorry. Trouble ahead if I don't get them in – I've spent half last week screaming at my staff about theirs.'

She looked at December, which was barely legible, added it up, cross cast, and found that the transposition in a mileage claim had thrown the calculation out.

'Where is January?'

'Underneath. I never understand how you *do* that, without using a calculator or writing anything down.'

'It's a trick.' They had had this conversation many times over the last twelve years. They had met when she was fourteen at her mother's bed in the Whittington hospital. Jules *soi-disant* stepfather had also been present, pissed out of his mind, Jules cold-sober and hungry, but both of them terrified. Her mother had been dying of breast cancer, diagnosed late, and inefficiently treated. Gwyn had taken her home that night and he and his wife Sandra had kept her for the awful weeks while her mother had finally died, and while he had found her distant family. She polished off January's accounts and looked at February's, finding immediately the point where Gwyn had claimed something twice. He was financially scrupulous and habitually underclaimed rather than the reverse. He must, as usual, have been tired.

'How is Sandra?' Sandra had taken the Jones children to see her mother which was why Gwyn had been able to spend the night.

'She's fine. Or she would be if Jake would leave home.'

The boy of four had now grown to a lumpen teenager terrorising his parents and his younger brother now a pleasant twelve-year-old waiting only, as Gwyn said, grimly, to turn into a monster like his sibling.

'When are you expected?'

March's expenses had added up and cross cast at the third attempt, and she handed them back to him.

'Not till about ten, but I must get there. Set an example to the idle buggers.'

The idle buggers referred to were the senior staff of the Social Services Department and the description of at least some of them was fully justified.

'So what are you doing today, my lovely?'

'Carrigan.'

'Guilty as hell,' Gwyn said, side-tracked. There was a certain amount of overlap in their work. 'You should be acting for the wife.'

'And so I would have been if the silly cow hadn't gone to the Law Centre, and got one of their volunteers.'

Jules had joined Jenkins Associates because it was a wholly professional operation. They were not council-funded, they did not use volunteers nor unqualified help, or people trained in other practices. They recruited two trainees a year from the best university law schools, and picked from their numerous applicants only the most persistent and the stroppiest, male or female. Jules had been, she knew, deeply fortunate to get taken on for Work Experience as a student, but she had capitalised on this piece of good fortune by working like a demon at every opportunity, so she got a traineeship when she graduated.

'What's wrong with the Law Centre?' Gwyn asked.

'You know what's wrong with it. They do social work, not law. They try to compromise with the Force, and that's what lands their clients in the nick.'

'Still not taking any prisoners, are you?' He smiled at her through a mouthful of bacon and toast.

'I haven't changed in the last couple of weeks, no.'

'Jules,' he said, having put the meal away at a speed that suggested he had few hopes for lunch. 'Come here.' He pulled her onto his knee and wrapped his arms round her.

'What?'

'You know I couldn't bear it if my most successful piece of social work came unstuck.'

She had understood long ago that she was his most successful rescue job. At fourteen, barely educated and sexually abused, seriously enough that a repair job and a course of antibiotics to get rid of persistent gonorrhoea were required, she looked like a loser, but here she was, twelve years later, a qualified solicitor and a light unto the nation, as Gwyn put it.

'I'm not going to come unstuck. Mr Carrigan is not stupid enough to attack a lawyer. He only does helpless women.'

'I suppose that's true.' She started to try and get up but he tightened his grip and she relaxed. 'This isn't fair on you,' he said, into her neck. 'I should never have started it.'

'You didn't start it,' she said, for this was an old argument.

'I didn't stop it, though, and I should have.'

'There isn't much point going on like this while you're cuddling up to me,' she said, angrily. It had been she who had started it; she had sought Gwyn out and it had been she who persisted. Not that he had been *that* reluctant on that evening nearly six years ago, but she knew that he felt permanently guilty about her.

He pushed her away so that he could look at her face. 'I suppose this isn't the time to talk about it, cariad, not when you've fucked me flat.'

He could always make her laugh, she thought, that was half the trouble. 'You just lay back and thought of Wales, Mr Jones?'

'Ah, Wales was never quite like that, what with the Chapel and the choir. It's why I came to sinful England, God bless it. Can I have a bath?'

'I think it would be wise,' she said, demurely, and the moment passed, while they got themselves together to go to their respective employment.

They did not have to fight for the bathroom because her flat had two, the second installed at hideous expense. A luxury, she had recognised, guiltily, but her need for it had made it seem an essential. She had got through much of her hard childhood by promising herself that one day she would be grown-up and would live properly. And take her mother with her, but that of course had not been possible. She was lying in the bath when Gwyn rattled at the door to say he was all but dressed and needed to go and she had to get out to unlock the door. Gwyn knew of course why she locked bathroom doors, as he had been the first person she had managed to tell about her mother's last man, who would push the door of the tiny caravan bathroom which did not lock, to catch her and look at her naked thirteen-year-old self. She had managed to frustrate him for a year but had had no way in the end of avoiding him once her mother fell ill and the long round of hospitals had started.

'When am I going to see you again?' she asked, wrapping herself in a towel in order not to drip down his shirt. He hesitated, looking down at her.

'Soon. When I can.' He kissed her and she stood in a patch of sunlight listening to him running downstairs.

Forty minutes later she was in her office, wearing the only shirt she could find that was both clean and ironed, which happened to be yellow, and a green trouser suit. She looked like a daffodil, and one of the plastic ones that came out of detergent packets at that, but there was no time to do anything different. She was, as befitted the most recently qualified member of Jenkins Associates, doing the Unsocial Hours, like the whole of Easter, while all the others rioted in Palma, Scotland or, in Paul's case, Slovakia and points east. She disposed easily of the two customers in the waiting-room and settled herself to get next week's paperwork in order for four court appearances. Being more efficient than anyone else, the police, the CPS (not difficult) or any rival firm was the least Paul expected of his people.

The buzzer rang, jerking her from deep concentration.

'Yes, Lou?'

'Got a customer.'

A typically laconic Caribbean approach, she thought crossly, then remembered that Lou was on her own out there, held in place by an edict that forbade the receptionist leaving the waiting-room unwatched ever since a customer had tried to set it and himself alight in protest against the Camden Housing Department.

'What sort of case? Broadly.'

'Asylum. Well, mostly. Excuse *me*, Sir, you go sit down.'

Louise, at full stretch could subdue a waiting-room full of distressed nutters, so Jules waited until the background noise had died away.

'Lou, you know I don't know anything about asylum. Give him an appointment with Paul or Anna on Tuesday, it'll save his time.'

'He say it urgent. It complicated. Better you see him.'

Arguing with Louise was not only exhausting but forbidden by the senior partner who pointed out that the firm would grind to a halt without a senior receptionist able, effortlessly, to sort sheep from goats and to subdue a stroppy client by the power of the eye alone.

'Half an hour on the Legal Aid then?'

Louise did the books in her spare moments, and all the lawyers checked with her before spending any time on anything. The practice was one step up from a Neighbourhood Law Centre housed in a decent modern block in the middle of Camden Town, next to a Halal butcher on one side and an estate agents on the other. A notice on the ground floor urged passers-by to come in and talk about their problems on payment of £50, which was payable by Legal Aid.

'Send him in then. Oh, hang on, what's his English like? I see.' She found a thick legal pad and sat up straight behind her desk. 'Good morning.'

He was a tall man, she saw, rising to greet him, at least six inches taller than her. Not old, perhaps thirty, and of the professional classes which was not that common in this practice. Intelligent-looking, excellent, hardly accented English.

'Please tell me your name,' she said, formally, when they had both sat down.

'Mirko Dragunović.'

She put the little squiggle under the c which all members of Jenkins Associates knew how to do, because the senior partner had been born Paul Jankowiç. 'I'm Jules Carlisle, a solicitor here. Your address?'

He hesitated, but the rules were clear; no address no advice. So he gave her a local address which looked familiar to her. A good-looking man too, she decided, with the snub nose and long eyelashes.

'And you are originally from where?'

'From Belgrade. In Serbia.'

Curiously enough she had been there, taken by Anne and Henry as a treat after her A-levels. Belgrade had not been a holiday for Henry, because he had been engineering something like a power station, but she and Anne had done cultural things together.

'So how can I help you, Mr Dragunović?'

He was clutching a newspaper, creased and dirty, and he spread it out on the desk between them, turned it round so that she could see. It was the *Daily Mail* for Tuesday, two days ago, the front page with a couple of pictures and an editorial calling for the police, MI5 and the Government to put an end to this tragic traffic in human lives. 'My brother.' He put a long forefinger on a picture of men in masks carrying away a covered stretcher.

'Sorry. What?'

'My brother. He was trying to come to England.'

Jules gazed at the smudgy picture; no one's face was on view except Commander somebody. 'Sorry, what makes you think…' She took a breath in, fearing that Lou's eye had failed this time and she had let in one of the nutters. The man clutched the desk and leant over.

'Please. I am not daft. I know my brother was coming by this way. He called me. Last week. He was in Holland and he said he will be here soon, and that he was coming by a boat to near King's Lynn. To *here*.'

'But surely…might he not still be in Holland?'

'No, no. He say he was coming on a boat on Saturday.'

Jules read the report again to give herself time to think, wishing that Paul, or indeed anyone else other than Lou were here. The police had found the bodies on Monday evening, and the paper said they were then a day old. That fitted with Mr Dragunoviç's story, but the world was full of lightly balanced individuals who rushed to the authorities claiming a share in any news.

'He never called again.' He was watching her anxiously, brown eyes fixed on her face. 'He would have.'

'Have you been to the police?' First port of call for those only ninety-five pence to the pound, she thought hopefully.

'I cannot go to them. I am illegal.'

She looked at him, her heart sinking. Not a nutter then. An illegal immigrant. 'You have not applied for asylum?'

'No.'

'How long have you been here?'

'Since three years.'

So he was an Economic Migrant, but did this help her at all? With everyone from Tony Blair down hassling the Home Office, she saw his difficulty. Whatever else happened he'd find deportation, prosecution and all sorts of bother if he went to the police and it would be better if Paul were in charge at that point. On the other hand, the man was desperate and four days was too long to wait if he did really think it was his brother who was lying in a morgue.

'Mr Dragunoviç, I – we – will only find out by going to the police. Have you a picture or anything to identify your brother?' She tried to stop herself speaking loudly and slowly; his English was perfectly fluent, just accented. He produced a picture from a wallet, so old that the leather was splitting, and a faded photograph, showing a young man laughing, his arms round an older woman, his mother, evidently. She thought of what the body might now look like. 'The same father and mother, both of you?'

'Yes.'

'Do you understand what DNA is?' She wrote the initials on the back of the nearest piece of paper.

'Deoxyribonucleic acid.' He smiled, wearily. 'I have Masters Degree in biochemistry.'

'Ah,' she said, taken aback. 'Have you been working in…in your field?'

'No. I am systems analyst.'

How, she wanted to ask, with what papers, but reminded herself that the man was in a high state of anxiety. And she still had no idea how to proceed.

'What are you thinking?' He was watching her like a hawk, she realised, and decided to come clean.

'I cannot think of a way to help you establish…well, whether your brother has…is…with the police…without exposing you. Which, since you are a client, I have no right nor obligation to do. Yet,' she added, remembering Paul's tirades against the Home Office.

'If I gave you a sample of my blood, *you* could give it to the police and if they say, yes, this is the family of…of someone we have…then you could tell me.'

She felt the ground abruptly firm up beneath her feet. 'I am – we all are – officers of the court, so formally I would be obliged to tell them who you are if…if they wanted to interview you. As they would.' She smiled at him apologetically. 'I specialise in crime, you see, so I know what I am talking about here.'

'I will take the risk. If none of them are my brother, then the police will not be so interested, I think.'

'That is probably true.'

'I have a sample with me.'

Oh, do you, she thought, grimly, so you had worked all this out. She sat back and thought. One point at least was clear.

'We have a doctor round the corner. He'll take a sample.'

Blood samples could be faked, and she was not going to risk the firm's credit with the hard men of the CID without ensuring that the sample of blood she handed over had definitely been taken from the man sitting in front of her.

She walked her client down to the local GP and sat in the small waiting-room reviewing her position. She had got into the law out of a need to see justice done to the dispossessed and dispirited for the sake of the child she had been and for what she had not been able to do for her own luckless, easily quelled mother. Paul, her senior partner, who trained her, had, however, dinned into her head the absolute necessity for a lawyer not to rush in but to know who and what his client was, where he came from, what he wanted and why, before moving one step away from a desk.

She reminded herself of all this while she waited for Mirko Dragunović. She took the sample from Dr Levy, checked the label, added her own signature and stuffed it in her briefcase along with everything else and took her client back to the office and sat him down.

'Now, Mr Dragunović, before I go to the police I need to know how you got here. You say you are an illegal. How did you come?'

The dark brown eyes shifted away from hers, and she waited until he understood that there was a price on her co-operation. 'I was a student,' he said, reluctantly.

'Of biology?'

'Of biochemistry. I was post-graduate.' He seemed stuck; he was looking fixedly at the desk.

'You overstayed a student visa? No? So how *did* you get to this country? And why?'

'I came originally to a farm. Legally. With your Home Office.'

The vision of bowler-hatted bureaucrats running farms in East Anglia convinced her his English had failed, but she persevered. Anyone familiar with immigration practice would have got it sooner, she thought, but she managed to collect that limited numbers of Eastern European students were allowed to come here under Home Office licence and work on farms for up to a year.

'What sort of farm?' She could not quite imagine how a Serbian PhD student was going to get on with sheep or cattle.

'Lettuce.'

'Just lettuce?'

'Yes. They need lots of hands – for planting, for picking, for packing.'

'This is outside, in the fields?'

'Yes. Except after October when we pick daffodils.'

'It sounds like hard work,' she said, scribbling to keep up.

'It was. And we are not…not accustomed. But I do it because what I earn in a year will buy much in our own country. Even an apartment.'

'So you entered legally,' she said, looking at her notes, bearing in mind that she would have to communicate all this to Paul. 'Then what? You overstayed?'

'I left the farm just before the end.'

She realised he was crying, and passed him the Kleenex, unembarrassed. Her criminal clients usually wept at some point. 'I met someone.'

'A girl?'

He looked at her sideways, impatiently, and she understood there was something else she had missed. 'A man?'

'Yes.'

A pity, in this context. If it had been a girl she might have been prepared to marry him and he could have stayed legally.

'Are you still together?'

'No. It was a…a mistake.'

'I'm sorry.' The man was plainly in agony.

'No. A terrible mistake. To stay. I should have gone back.' He was crying freely now.

'You mean you'd have been better off?'

'Oh that.' He found the Kleenex, blew his nose, gulping. 'No, but my brother…he could not come. Not as I did.'

She sat back. No, he couldn't, could he? she thought. If her prospective client had absconded from a Home Office limited scheme, there was no way his brother was going to be offered a place on the same deal. They kept records at the Home Office, if nothing else.

'So your brother came – he was trying to come – illegally?'

'Yes. He has done his service with the military.'

She extracted details of the brother Stefan, two years older than Mirko, the apple of all eyes in the family, clever and loved.

'If your brother turns out to have been one of that group?' She let the question hang, and Mirko sat staring drearily out of the window.

'If he is dead in this way I cannot go home to my family. So if…if, then I will help your police all I can.'

If his brother had died because Mirko had, for the sake of a gay lover, cut off the best line to legitimate cash, expiation and revenge could indeed be his only option.

'We are running ahead of ourselves,' she said, briskly, trying to shut out the tragedy that seemed to be filling her office. 'I will make sure that we find out.'

'I ring tomorrow? I can pay.'

'Tomorrow is too soon, I think, unless they can do – well unless the blood group tells them… Ring on Monday. I will have some news.'

She watched him from the window of her small second-floor office as he left. He had come in a car which she had not expected, something small and green, but he was into it and gone while she was still blinking in the sunlight.

She wrote up her notes, quickly, onto the computer as Paul trained all his people to do. Efficiency and communication were most of what was required of a lawyer, he insisted, and they all lived by his dicta. Wouldn't dare not to, even if he wasn't absolutely right. Paul in a Serbo-Croat rage was something no one wanted to face, or not a second time.

She sat and thought about Paul, in a rage, her general sense of unease and discomfort growing by the minute. If the blood sample in her case did show that one of the poor bodies was close kin to the man who had walked into her office, *then* what did she do? And how did she do it, whatever it was? She looked at the phone; Gwyn would by now be buried in documents and besides he had several despised assistants with him whose noses he would want to keep to the grindstone. She sighed and rang another familiar number.

'Darling, how nice. Can you come up for the night after all?'

A night being spoilt by Anne would have been a treat and she would have her to herself, because the boys and Henry were still away, but there was just the chance that Sandra would stay the extra night with her mother and that Gwyn could come back. 'No, sorry Anne, I can't. I have a date.'

'Oh good. Who with?'

'No one you know,' she lied.

'Oh, well, anyway. So…'

'So I have rung you because I need advice.' She recited her story and outlined her problem and listened – the wheels of Anne's mind could almost be heard turning.

'Well, you are all right so far, I think,' Anne said, slowly. 'But I think you'll run out of options pretty fast. You know a crime has been committed – people-smuggling *is* a crime. Your client wants you to give the sample to the police, you warned him about the possible consequences and he agreed to take the risk. Come to that, overstaying is a crime too.'

'Yes.'

'You're not sounding convinced? You were sorry for him of course. Well, so am I, but…well, Jules, you know, in life sometimes all you can do is the orthodox thing and let the chips fall.'

'Mm.'

'I suppose we could consult Beryl.'

'Beryl? The Beryl we had drinks with before lunch? Why her?'

'She was deputy head of MI5 twenty years ago – yes, I know, but she stays in touch and if they want someone to go on TV and explain something awkward they get her to do it, in a very judicial manner.'

'That nice old lady?'

'That nice old lady, yes. How long do I have, I ask myself, before you start saying that about me?'

'Not long at all.'

'You already do? I see. Well, I suppose I should be grateful to be thought a nice old lady as opposed to a nasty one. So. Would that – would you find that easier?'

'No. You're right, I'm a professional. I'll ring one of the CID people.'

'Now?'

'Very soon. And I could come and see you on Sunday for lunch.'

'That would be nice.'

She waited ten minutes to make the call, while she finished the preparation work for the case for next Tuesday that Mirko Dragunoviç's visit had interrupted. Her best CID contact was, like her, doing the Unsocial Hours and she found him quickly.

'Haven't got any of yours at the minute,' DI Jimmy Watt said, after about twenty seconds of civil preliminaries.

'Glad to hear. But I've got a difficult one.' She explained her problem and listened to the silence at the other end. 'I know it's not your subject, Jimmy, but you know who to go to.'

'Yeh. The motorway lads.'

She thought about it. 'MI5?'

'Yes.'

'Can I give you the sample?'

'No. No, I'll make a call. You there now? Till when?'

She confirmed she would be there, and occupied herself stuffing everything into the office dishwasher and wiping off a few surfaces in the staff kitchen. Then she settled back at her desk and had a look at her bank statement; the mortgage on her own, nice, clean little house fixed, capped, and carefully negotiated, was killing her. That and the bills still left from the second bathroom she had put in. She was just deciding that she'd have to advertise for a lodger, anything rather than take the help she knew Anne would offer, when the buzzer rang.

'You got visitors. Little Jimmy and a new friend.'

'Does the friend have a name?' She listened to Lou indicating with some clarity that no name, no entry.

'Richard Allenton. With reference to your call to DI Watt. He is with me.'

'Thank you, Lou. Please send them up.'

Paul had impressed on all of them the importance of maintaining formality when dealing with Authority. She rose to greet them. Richard Allenton was tall enough to make Jimmy Watt look small and square. A bit older than her, thin, dark and worn out, pale skin tending to grey. But a good-looking bloke, or would be with a week's sleep. He was like a detective she had read about somewhere, she thought, and remembered Henry reading *Bleak House*. Richard Allenton was like that, restless, his eyes moving, taking in everything before focusing on the tube of blood she had stuck on her desk.

'This is the evidence, then?'

'Yes.'

'You're sure it came from the bloke who came to your office?'

'I was with him at the doctor's.'

He nodded, eyes still everywhere. 'Tell me how he came to you.'

She told the whole story again, while he listened in critical silence. 'Did he say which farm he worked on?'

'No.' She was annoyed with herself for not thinking to ask. 'How many absconders are there from those Home Office schemes?'

'Not a lot.' He swallowed his coffee and put the cup down and she understood that he had already covered the point.

'My man's genuine then? He did work in this country.'

'A Mirko Dragunovič worked in Norfolk and absconded. If it

was the same man.' He looked over at her with bright brown unfriendly eyes. 'You're very cool about all this, Miss Carlisle.'

'Well, not really. I mean I don't usually do immigration cases. It's specialist work.'

'Tell me about it.' He looked around him, hungrily.

'I'll get you an ashtray.'

'Thanks.' He lit a cigarette, watching her through the smoke, Jimmy Watt silent in the background. 'So what did you think, Miss Carlisle, when he walked in?'

'I didn't, much,' she said, defensively. 'I was trying to clear my desk. He wasn't going to come forward to do any identifying of bodies. I thought a blood sample was the intelligent compromise.'

'It didn't occur to you to try and detain him. Or ring us – well, someone. What do you usually do if someone walks in and tells you he's committed a crime?'

'I warn him to keep his trap shut. Look, I had only Mr Dragunovič's word that he was who he said he was. So I got a blood sample.'

'Which could tell us what, precisely?'

'If it matches the DNA of one of the bodies it would prove that Mr Dragunovič was right. Very good clue, I'd have thought.'

Allenton stared at her. 'After you went to the doctor, Miss Carlisle, what did you do?'

'Went back to the office, said goodbye to Mr Dragunovič, and rang up Jimmy here.'

'But not quite immediately?'

She felt her neck prickle and go slowly scarlet. 'I called as soon as I had finished another important job. I'm sorry if this worries anyone. Why don't you take that fucking tube away and test it?' The blush had gone into her hair by now, she could feel it. The buzzer rang again, making her jump.

'Gentleman axing for Mr Allenton?'

He reached over for the tube and ran downstairs. From her window she could see a police car in the street, lights flashing. He handed the tube over, saying something furious and fast, then came back up the stairs.

'I didn't think it was that urgent.' She smiled at him, hopefully, but he wasn't having any.

'While he was having the blood test is when you should have called. There are eight people dead, and we need to find out who they are.'

'Nonsense,' she said, remembering Paul's rule of unyielding, courteous stroppiness when dealing with the police. 'It may not be a match at all.'

'No.'

'But you think it may be?'

He decided to unbend a little. 'Like it says in the newspapers: we know these people came from the Balkans.' He was sounding wearily patient. 'And the method of delivery is new and therefore interesting. There must have been a boat or a ship, but we've never had a landing in that part of the world. Something went wrong with this run, but there will have been others.'

'It doesn't sound a very good route. How do these theoretical people manage when they arrive on the beach? I mean, speaking not all that good English. What do they do?'

'A courier would meet them. Normally.'

The word hung between them. 'The papers said suffocated. *How*, on a boat? OK. Oh, I see, so you didn't publish the details.' She could feel her neck getting hot again, so she wrote the date on her pad. The phone rang and Richard Allenton picked it up before she could get to it.

'Yeh. AB? We've got one. Yeh. Give it to the labs, quick.' He put the phone down and looked across at her. 'So far, so good. The sample is AB, and so is one of the deceased.'

'So what do you do now?'

'Everything at once. The DNA tests. Get your friend Mr Dragunoviç in. He left you an address, I take it? We want that, now.'

'Indeed you shall have it.'

'And the interview tape?'

'We do not tape interviews without consent. And he'd have run if I had asked him.'

'I want your notes.'

She hesitated and he leaned on her desk. 'I'll have a warrant in half an hour if I need one.'

'I'm an officer of the court.' After a moment's hesitation she handed over a tape containing her notes, ready for Lou to audiotype.

He put her tape on the machine, not waiting for permission, and they all listened. When I am tired, she thought, you hear the North London in the slurred or missing consonants. 'Enda tape, fanks Lou,' it closed.

'Can I have it?'

'I have to have a copy.'

'Belgrade,' he said, thoughtfully. 'That where the family come from?'

'I assumed so.'

His hand moved to the phone and his fingers moved to tap in a number. 'Me. Look at the phone book for Belgrade, will you? Find Dragunoviç. A lot of them, are there? We want the one with two sons, Stefan and Mirko. I want to know where the sons are, right now. Yeh. Do that.' He put the phone down and pulled out another cigarette.

'But what if…if your body isn't Stefan?'

'Then they'll know where he is and not be worried, will they? We haven't got time to piss about, Miss Carlisle.' He punched a number when she gave him Mirko's address which looked phonier than ever, but Jimmy Watt went off with it without comment. She retreated to the cloakroom to have a wash, since Allenton was occupying her desk and her telephone, then emerged to find an empty waiting-room and sat down amid the two-year-old copies of *Hello!* and the neglected rubber plant with which the firm greeted its customers. A passing Jamaican, a client from time to time, checked in his tracks and waved to her and she smiled back at him, hoping that she had not somehow dropped the office into a mess, in a disastrous combination of the best possible intentions and downright inefficiency. She had better tell her senior partner all about it as quickly as possible. He had left a number, of course he had, but none of them had had any intention of using it. It was in the top right-hand drawer of her desk, along with a make-up kit and a packet of sanitary towels, and she was on her way to get it when the bell rang again and MI5 opened the door for his acolyte.

'It's a dry cleaner's, Sir.'

Something about that address had struck her as familiar and she gritted her teeth. It was the Pakistani-run cheapo dry cleaner By Appointment to the whole of the office. 'I heard that. I'm sorry.'

The men turned to consider her. 'Why'd he come here, Miss Carlisle?' Allenton asked.

'God knows.' I wish he hadn't, she thought, or I wish the whole thing would happen again, so I could do it right next time and these two suits would not be looking at me as if I was wearing a bunny outfit.

'A local, or had he heard of you?'

It was a sensible question and her brain snapped into gear. 'If you were an illegal immigrant, we'd be one of two firms in North London you'd come to.' Mirko Dragunović need not have known he was going to find the village idiot running the shop.

'It's been in the papers for forty-eight hours,' Allenton said, reflectively to Jimmy Watt.

'Yes,' she said, trying to get back into the conversation. 'Plenty of time to ask who he should see. And just his bad luck that our Paul wasn't here.'

'Your senior partner would *also* not have recognised a false address?'

Jimmy Watt winced, and she drew on a lot of training not to tell them both to fuck off. 'I have apologised, once.'

'You got a blood sample. That should help.' Allenton sounded as if his thumbs were being screwed. 'We can give you back your office now. Where can we find you over the weekend?'

He was speaking to her loudly and clearly and patiently, and it set up a resistance. 'Would the number of his car be useful?'

Both men stopped in their tracks, and Allenton swung round. 'Could be,' he said, the force of his need to know filling the room. 'What sort of car was it?'

'A green one. You wanted the number, did you?'

Allenton bit the inside of his cheeks. 'Please, Miss Carlisle. If by any chance you can remember any of it.'

'371 S1E.'

'Are you sure?'

'Yes. He was parked outside and I watched him go.'

'You didn't tell us this.'

'I've only just remembered. And I didn't realise I had noticed the number.'

He was standing very close to her, trying to get inside her brain, she thought, and she stepped back.

'Sorry. Tell me *how* you remember.'

'3,7,1 are prime numbers and the S looked like a 5, which is also a prime. Then you have another 1.' Both her auditors were staring at her fixedly. 'Neither of you know about prime numbers?'

'I'd forgotten, somehow.' Allenton's expression had a reluctant respect in it. 'How did you remember the E, I wonder?'

'I wouldn't swear to the E. And it might not have been his car.'

'I had thought of that. But if it is… Thank you, Miss Carlisle, that is useful.'

She and Jimmy Watt blinked at this outbreak of civility, and she meekly gave him her home number as well as the office number in case he wanted to contact her over the weekend. She watched them leave in a police car whose driver must have thought he was in a race, tyres squeaking as he conducted a U-turn and vanished up Camden Road, leaving her feeling distinctly flat, but she remembered she needed to talk to Paul. She looked at his schedule which made it clear that he was in a hut in the High Tatra, wherever that might be, and unobtainable before Monday. And by Monday, while she would still have to tell him, the whole thing might have turned out to be a mare's nest.

Chapter Three

(Good Friday)

'Darling? Jules? Sorry, I thought you'd be up. It's me, Anne.'

'What time is it?'

'Well, I suppose it's only nine o'clock but I thought...I'm sorry I forgot you had a date. How *was* your date?'

'A blast,' she lied. Sandra had brought the boys home when she had said she would, so Gwyn had not been able to join her. She had convinced herself that she would have him for an extra night and the disappointment had driven her, uncharacteristically, to kill a bottle of wine by herself.

'Well, good. Now did you go to the police? Yes? What happened?'

Jules, feeling shifty, offered her a carefully edited version of the day before.

'You did right, darling. And how clever to remember the car number.' There was a faint pause while Jules waited, gloomily, for the other shoe to drop. 'But should you...do you think, perhaps...call in some senior help?'

'They're all away.'

'Darling. Never tell me your senior partner is so lost to all sense of duty as to have left you without a number.'

'Oh no. I have one. It is a hut in Slovakia, and he gets there tonight.'

'I think you should call him tonight then, my love.'

Jules, feeling mutinous, let silence fall.

'Darling? Have you gone away? Don't be cross, you know it makes sense. Think how pissed off Mr Jenkins would be.'

'That's the bell. I have to go. I'll call you.' She put down the phone and went to the door and opened it to reveal Jimmy Watt.

'Jimmy! Come in.' She was conscious that her nightie came down only to mid-thigh and that her teeth were unbrushed. He was looking startled and she reflected that he was more used to getting an earful than a civil welcome from her or one of the band of brothers at Jenkins and Associates.

'I'm here to ask you down to the station,' he said, not moving off the doorstep.

'Why?'

'To identify Mr Dragunović.'

'You've found him.' He nodded, just perceptibly smug. 'How?'

'You gave us the car number.'

'It *was* his? Where did he live?'

'Stoke Newington.'

'Funny that. They've got lawyers in Stokey. What was he doing coming over to Camden?'

'My guv'nor thinks he knew about you. Well, not *you*, but Mr Paul Jenkins. The firm, know what I mean?'

She did know what he meant, but Jimmy wasn't asking a question, just providing a bit of punctuation. Anne had finally nagged her successfully into avoiding the use of 'know what I mean?' every other sentence, as everyone else in the Comprehensive in Tottenham had done.

'All I'm going to be able to do is tell you if the man who came to see me yesterday is the one you've got.'

'My guv'nor's ahead of you there. The farmer who employed Mirko Dragunović in Norfolk is also on his way.'

'Very efficient, but I have to have coffee.'

'Take your time. The other witness's train doesn't get in for another hour.'

'Come in and sit.' She didn't want him stuck on the doorstep giving the neighbours something to see. She had spent the first ten years of her childhood on caravan sites and the next four on one of the roughest estates in North London, and her mother had always worried about the neighbours. She put the kettle on, retreated upstairs and washed and dressed, and came down feeling more in control.

'Your guv'nor is this Allenton?'

'Yeh. For while this enquiry lasts. Nice place you've got here.'

Jimmy Watt was a bridge over to a part of her youth. His parents were Respectable; his Dad had worked for British Rail, and the possession of a working father had put him among the aristocracy at the William Snowden Comprehensive in

Tottenham they had both attended for three years. He had always been nice to her, whose family was not respectable, and she tried to repay the compliment where she could.

'This Allenton. He is MI5, right?' she asked, reappearing in the kitchen.

'Yeh.'

'What rank is he?' Jimmy stared at her. 'He's your guv'nor, you said.'

'They don't have ranks, them. He gets what he wants, though. My super didn't like it, but I was attached to this squad within...what...ten minutes of asking. What you going to do, Jules, file a complaint?'

On her home ground – her office – he called her Miss Carlisle, albeit in tones of heavy sarcasm. Somewhere, overnight, she had lost caste, she observed, sadly.

'If you've finished your coffee, Detective Constable, perhaps we could go to the station?' she said, sounding as snotty and long-suffering as she could. He swallowed a gulp too hot for him and was still blowing out his cheeks and licking his gums cautiously as they got into a car. Unmarked, she was pleased to see.

True to her training, when she got there she made a lawyerly fuss about not being allowed to see Mirko, who was, she reminded everyone in the station, Her Client. That fetched Jimmy's Superintendent, who had to call her Miss Carlisle and ask her nicely if she would mind waiting until Mr Allenton arrived. She found an old *Guardian* and was sat reasonably comfortably two thirds of the way through the Arts bit when Richard Allenton walked in with a big blond chap, built like the proverbial brick shit-house; Allenton looked thinner and more hyped up than ever, but he had on a clean pink shirt which was earning him some sideways looks, and he had shaved.

'Miss Carlisle, thank you for coming by. Mr Flowerdew, Miss Carlisle. She nodded, but the man had his hand out, all smiles, so she had to take it.

'It's a pleasure to meet you, Miss Carlisle.'

He wasn't actually wearing wellington boots but he stood

solidly on both feet as if he were. He had a big nose, peeling slightly, lots of dark blond hair and enormous hands. Not overweight, just big with square shoulders. She considered him, deciding she would rather have someone nearer her own size but he made everyone else in the room look consumptive.

But Allenton was fidgeting about, alerting her criminal lawyerly instincts. 'Mr Flowerdew. What have you been told?'

Allenton opened his mouth to snap at her, but the Flowerdew bloke was too big to shift in a hurry. 'That they have a lad here who worked for us three years ago and didn't go back when he should have.'

Boarding-school, she thought; an impression confirmed. No trace of local accent, as befitted the boss class. 'And why did they want you to come all the way to London?'

'To identify him. What is your position, Miss Carlisle?'

Oh, not so simple a gentleman farmer then. 'Assuming that the man they have detained is the one I saw yesterday, I act for him.'

'He told you his name?'

'He gave it as Mirko Dragunoviç.'

'Dark chap, over six feet, thin, or was when he came.'

'My man looked like that, yes. Did these various gentlemen tell you that he believes his brother may be one of the assumed illegal immigrants found dead on a beach in East Anglia?'

'Over to Lincolnshire. I know the place. Yes.'

Paul had taught her that it was always worth checking the police weren't keeping their cards inside their vests. She saw with pleasure that Richard Allenton was steaming like a kettle.

'Perhaps, Mr Flowerdew...?'

'Yes. Why not? You want Miss Carlisle first, I expect.'

Precedence is not normally given to women in this nick, she observed, which got her put in the lead down the familiar cell corridor which smelled of urine and was lit by hot overhead lights. She peered through the door of the interview room, noting the usual set-up, artificial light, a bottle of water and a tape recorder on a trestle table, the whole thing organised to look temporary and grudging.

The man she could see through the grill who sat opposite a

grey-faced CID man was Mirko Dragunoviç. Or at least the man who had so described himself to her.

'My client,' she confirmed. 'I'd better go in.'

'Can we let Mr Flowerdew have a look?'

Jules stood aside while he peered in and nodded. 'Thinner, but that's him.'

'Right.' It was Richard Allenton on an exhaled breath; interesting that he had been in some doubt. She observed that Andrew Flowerdew felt the same.

'Are you charging Mr Dragunoviç,' she asked, to get some structure into the scene.

'We will be, yes.'

'I need to see him. He may want to apply for asylum.' It really was not her subject and she had only the haziest idea whether he was eligible, but the same legal principles applied. 'You've had him for a bit.'

'Courts don't sit tomorrow,' Allenton snapped.

'Judges in chambers do,' she said, coldly.

'We'll see how we get on.' Richard Allenton wasn't even addressing himself to her, but Andrew Flowerdew lumbered into action.

'He's been a bloody nuisance and given me a lot of trouble with your lot, but he's got rights, hasn't he?'

Richard Allenton's face said not if he had anything to do with it but he managed a civil reply. 'He is here illegally, he can be kept in custody until he is deported. He may also be a material witness in a serious crime investigation.'

'Mr Flowerdew is correct in thinking Mr Dragunoviç has the right to a solicitor,' Jules said, warmly. Enlist the citizenry where possible when dealing with the Force, Paul had taught all his people, and that went double for MI5. Andrew Flowerdew patted her on the shoulder – like being saluted by a leg of lamb, she thought. Richard Allenton had been taught about the citizenry too, because, black-faced, he showed her into the interview room. Andrew Flowerdew followed her in, brushing off CID and MI5 like flies.

'Morning, Mirko. Sorry to see you here, but I thought I'd say hello. You'll be in good hands with Miss Carlisle here.'

Kindly meant but he wasn't convincing Mirko, who had given her one stony look.

'I'm sorry you've got this trouble with your brother.' Andrew had advanced and was standing close to Mirko while the rest of them hovered, uneasily.

'You found...' Mirko had gone white.

'No, no, there's no news yet.' Andrew pressed his hand, totally unselfconscious.

Jules glared at Richard Allenton, daring him to stay stumm.

'The blood. You are AB. So is one of the deceased, but that's all we know. So far.'

'Well,' Andrew Flowerdew said into a nasty silence, 'I think we should leave you to talk to Miss Carlisle. I'm staying the weekend in London, and I'll be by to see you again.'

Mirko reached out a hand to say goodbye, looking a better colour. Jules agreed with him, silently: the presence of this yeoman farmer was a very, very useful guarantee against anything untoward the Force or MI5 might try. The room cleared itself, Mirko's eyes following Andrew Flowerdew, and she sat down with her client.

'You told them.'

'You gave me a bum address,' she said, trying not to blush. 'I warned you they'd come after you, and you said you would take the risk in order to find out about your brother.'

Misery settled on the lines of his face and they sat in glum silence. She felt both guilty and inadequate, but reminded herself that his position was at the moment exactly that of many of the firm's clients: guilty of something, banged up while the Force try and get a case together. She asked him the usual things, did he need clothes? Cigarettes? A shaver? Lunch? Something to read? and collected a list. There wasn't a lot she could do for him until the DNA tests came through. She would go through the motions, but he wasn't going to be released, or charged, until they had the answer to that question. She could hardly ask for bail – another part of Paul's training was that you asked for bail only if you had a decent case for it and could say with some conviction that your client would not disappear. Which she hardly could, given Mr Dragunović's circumstances.

She stopped at the desk to make sure the sergeant understood his duties about food and showers, conscious of an approving audience in Andrew Flowerdew who was sitting in the waiting-room, looking exotic among the dark-skinned cast, large fair Anglo-Saxons not being common in Camden Town.

'I wondered if you'd like some lunch?'

She needed to talk to him, so she said yes, but she must just get some bits for Mirko. Mr Flowerdew didn't need telling where to eat, he'd done the groundwork and walked her to the expensive Indian, having made sure she liked the food.

It was a very good lunch; she had everything she wanted, having decided a man who owned thousands of lettuces in Norfolk could afford it. Andrew, as she was by now calling him, looked at home there too, against the elegant pale gold wallpaper – very upmarket for Camden Town, she thought, where mostly you would expect crimson flock. But perhaps they never were crimson flock people; as Paul always reminded them, most refugees were middle-class. In a pause, while she was urged to think about what else she could manage, she sat back and considered her host.

'Andrew. My client – Mirko – caused you a lot of grief, and you have two hundred of these people every year, yes? So what makes him special – I mean, why are you taking this much trouble?'

He blinked at her. 'I brought him to this country. I employed him.'

'Is the feudal system alive and well in East Anglia?'

He was looking puzzled and offended. 'No, but... You look after your people, and that goes double when they're a long way from home.'

No one, she thought, had felt like that about her or her mother. She looked across, defiantly. 'Well, it seems... Well, it's very good of you.'

'I don't see it that way.' There was an uncomfortable silence while both of them regrouped.

'Could you manage pudding?'

'Always,' she said, promptly, and he laughed, while she remembered her manners and turned the conversation to lettuce farming.

'It isn't very interesting now,' Andrew said, digging into an ice cream. 'In my father's day we grew lots of different things, but now it's nearly all iceberg.'

'Your father's day?' Of course this would be one of the bourgeoisie.

'My grandfather started the business. He did a lot of supply work for the MOD in the last war. Bought up odd bits of land, and cultivated it.' He caught her censorious look. 'We'd have lost the last war – or people would have been a lot worse off – without the food we grew in the Fens.'

She was full of excellent food, paid for by him, and decided she could have a rest from her usual confrontational style. 'Tell me about your farm. Drained peat? Canals.'

'Very rich drained marshland. The peat is running out, blown off the top or eaten by the clay. We grow on peat, but we've also got a lot of skirt land, where the peat is running thin but it's very fertile, mixed with the clay.'

Like much of the fens, she remembered, from her years on a bleak, dead flat caravan site, at Wisbech, the natives flat-faced and sullen. The incomers, like her parents, believed all Fen people had webbed feet and slept with their sisters as a matter of routine.

'It's very flat country. Cold in winter, the wind comes straight from Russia. But it grows stuff. Anything, not just iceberg. We've got 10,000 acres.'

And Mirko, she remembered, had worked on those flat cold fields, planting lettuces with the aid of a degree in biochemistry.

'Why do you…why do you bring people like Mirko over?'

'Can't get the local labour.'

'Because you don't pay enough?' A good lunch does not buy me, she thought.

'We pay the minimum wage. But it's field work, and people would rather be in a supermarket these days. We used to get local girls, they'd bring the kids, leave them in the sheds, but not any more. So then we had Poles or Czechs, but of course those are all coming into the EU and they can come in freely.'

'So you bring in Serbian students like Mirko.'

'Our basic wage is a fortune for them. They stay here just under a year, lettuces May till October.'

'Daffodils October to February. He told me.'

'They go home with a decent bit of cash, provided they don't blow it all in King's Lynn. It finances the rest of their degree, or buys them a flat. It's a good deal for them.'

'And for you.'

'And for us, which is why the Home Office runs these schemes. I have 180 to 200 of these kids a year, and without them...I'd grow cereals, I suppose, and they would go straight into EU warehouses. I do some of that already – and we'd import the lettuce from France.'

'What do the French use as labour?'

'Illegals. Moroccans.'

Achmed, the father of the family, came by to see they had everything. Jenkins Associates people got good treatment, because of Paul who sprung members and connections of the Achmed family from detention camps from time to time. Andrew, she saw, got it because he was a large white Anglo-Saxon man. With money. She was thinking about lettuces, grown all over Europe by people at the very bottom of the human rung, without rights or with very limited rights. Enough to put you off lettuce – except that this structure applied to a lot of things. Sneakers, jeans, tomatoes, to name but three.

'What took you into the law?'

She knew the real answer to that question but she did not give it; her early life was really not suitable for family viewing. She gave him the Authorised Version which started with A-levels at a good London school and progressed to Birmingham University and Law.

'Are your parents in London?'

No, she said, and did not expand. They were buried in London, where her father had acquired a plot in an unprecedented act of foresight. Probably won it in a bet.

'Are they both alive?'

Her expression must have given him a clue, so she said no, they both died young and a cousin had given her a home, without looking at him. But it put a damper on the conversation and he did not try and revive it, just paid the bill.

'I must go by the police station,' she said, as they reached the not very fresh air. 'That Allenton muttered something about wanting to question Mirko about his brother's route into the country. He ought not to do it without me, but MI5 doesn't go in for niceties.'

'They're at the front line of course.'

She reminded herself that a man who owned 10,000 acres would be Establishment. 'Do your temporary employees abscond much?'

'No. Mirko is the only one for five years. A few stay – three or four of the girls have married our drivers and settled. A couple of the boys married girls they met in King's Lynn. Mostly they go home. These are middle-class people with things to go home to.'

'But Mirko didn't want to go home.'

'I don't know how tolerant people are in Belgrade about gays.' She blinked at him, realising she was assuming no one in Norfolk would have known gay if it sat up in their soup, but Andrew was sounding perfectly relaxed. 'You know, then?'

'Yes. He made no particular secret of it. And no, he didn't have a particular friend among the pickers, but I understood there was someone in Wisbech.'

She couldn't imagine where in quiet, respectable Wisbech there was a place that gays could meet, but she had only been ten when she and her mother left there. They turned together into the station. Richard Allenton was lounging against the dusty counter, gazing out, ignoring the battered clientele on the benches. In a good light he struck her again as very fanciable, although she did not normally go for the thin, dark, shifty ones.

'Miss Carlisle. Glad you could get back. We intend to talk to Mr Dragunoviç about the route his brother might have taken, or be taking.'

'He isn't going to confide in you, is he, until he knows where his brother is?' Andrew Flowerdew saved her vocal cords. 'Why not wait till you have the test results?'

'Because if his brother is not among the dead, Mirko will keep stumm in case he's on his way.' Jules had thought about the point. 'While he doesn't know and is worrying himself silly he might just talk.'

She could see the muscles in Allenton's jaw move as he bit back whatever he was about to come out with. He beckoned them into one of the better interview rooms away from the gawpers. 'The way we see it, if we can get some information – quickly – we may be able to do something with it. So we don't find another load of bodies.'

'But is there any *profit* in delivering dead bodies?' Andrew asked her question.

'They'll have paid in advance. You're not buying any guarantees here, just a ticket to ride.'

Andrew blinked. 'Gets the firm a bad name, though, losing passengers. They'd avoid it if they could, surely?'

'Plenty more desperate customers where those came from.'

Andrew was plainly depressed by the global implications, but she was worrying about Mirko, not wanting him to start coughing before they had decided what deal to offer.

'I need to see my client.'

'Certainly, Miss Carlisle.' Allenton escorted her punctiliously down the corridor, leaving Andrew settled in the chair, and she headed in to reason with Mirko. Who was, to her relief, well ahead of them, and was not going to talk to anyone about anything until he knew about his brother. She emerged after a conscientious ten minutes to report failure to Richard Allenton, who nodded, sourly.

'Should have preliminary DNA results tomorrow afternoon.'

'Preliminary?'

'We get a rough match. Four points. Not conclusive, but a good start.'

'Nine or more if you want to take it to court,' she said, helpfully, as Allenton glared at her, so she left in good order, reminding him she would be back. Andrew Flowerdew left as well, leaving her his address in London.

She went home, buying some daffodils at a flower stall, and tidied up in a disaffected way. As she dumped the wet, cold stems in a vase, she thought of Mirko and his fellow students picking in cold Cornish fields. You tear off the whole thing, leaves and all, Andrew Flowerdew had told her in the intervals of lunch, so they keep better on the journey up to London. It doesn't matter what damage you've done to the bulbs because they get pulled up and replaced. She felt her lips pursing just like Anne's when she met wicked waste. She found she was restless, and decided to ring up Anne.

She knew perfectly well that her cousin felt guilty about the miseries she had undergone as a child, and occasionally and deliberately would play on that guilt to get something she wanted. But in her right mind she well understood what an undertaking it must have been for her cousin, at forty-nine with two sons, a husband and an exhausting career, to take on an underfed, abused, defiant fourteen-year-old girl as a daughter. And Anne had had a lot of work to do. She had been shaken but not daunted by the abuse Jules had suffered, and had seen her patiently through therapy, physical and emotional. What had worried her to the core was Jules's totally deficient education, and that she had set out to fix.

She had smartly removed Jules from her Tottenham comprehensive and enrolled her at a private tutorial college. Jules, on general principles, had been prepared to resist every minute of all of it, but the principal, a lively refugee from a tutor's job at Brasenose, had picked up her facility with numbers and encouraged her to do GCSE Maths a year early while everyone else on the staff struggled to bring her reading, writing and spelling up to scratch. After eighteen months of this, Jules had planted herself in front of Anne and said she knew what the college was costing and she was not prepared to be that much beholden. Anne, after a long moment in which she visibly discarded a lot of things she might have said – one of the most endearing things about Anne was the way every thought appeared in her face – had taken her to the fashionable local comprehensive and sorted through their staff until she found an excellent maths teacher and made quite sure his attention would be on Jules. The title had helped there; Anne was at the time newly in the Lords, appointed by an incoming Labour Government, but Jules had duly done her part and got two very good A-levels in Maths and two good ones in Economics and Statistics.

'Darling? How are you doing? How is your naughty overstayer?'

'He is in custody and I feel badly, but…'

Anne listened, interrupting only to check how long a reliable DNA test took. 'We did all this, of course, when one or other of the Criminal Justice Bills (there's at least two a year) was going through the House, but I've forgotten.'

'Two days, minimum.'

'They have to grow something, I think I remember.'

'No, Anne, they have to separate out the blood and do an analysis. It takes quite a long time.' DNA, she thought, was another thing that the oldies had not quite grasped.

'Did you talk to Mr Jenkins last night? No answer from the hut? Well, darling, did he leave no one else in the UK who knows about immigration cases? Surely not.'

Jules opened her mouth to defend Paul generally, and then remembered that he was in fact innocent on this count. She could have called in another partner, Jenni Patel (Indian father, English mother) and she wondered why she hadn't. Because I don't like her, she conceded, dourly. Jenni was thirty, a privileged beauty whose law degree was from Cambridge, and who appeared everywhere in perfectly cut little black suits and a superior manner.

'No. There is someone. Jenni Patel.'

'That very good-looking Indian girl? Where is she?'

'In Leicestershire.'

'Well, that's not far.'

'No, I know.'

They all had each other's home numbers, and Jenni had

correctly left the number where she could be reached at the weekend. It was time and beyond she brought Jenni in and stopped telling herself that the Duty Solicitor could and should do everything.

Chapter Four

(Saturday)

She waited to ring Jenni Patel, until lunchtime the next day. The weather had changed; a cold wind was blowing and as she gazed out of the window from her kitchen, hailstones bounced off the pavement below and rattled on the windows.

'What is our position, Jenni? Am I – or are we – likely to be able to make a deal for our client?'

'It will be very difficult. He is an overstayer from one of the specific Home Office schemes. It's the precedent they worry about. You see?'

Jules did see. Immigration was unpopular with the general public and therefore with politicians, and all the schemes which allow people to come in for specific purposes and limited terms were viewed with suspicion, as the thin edge of a very large wedge. Any suggestion that people could abscond, or overstay or whatever the term was, and *not* get sent home without their feet touching the floor, would be unacceptable.

And if we're being absolutely truthful, Jules thought, I'm with the general public here, rather than the rich, privileged liberals like Jenni. I've lived in a rotten flat on a poor council estate, and seen immigrant families put straight into the better houses, on the edge of the estate with a patch of garden. *And* I didn't believe – and nor did anyone else on the estate – that they'd had that bad a time where they came from.

She didn't share any of this with Jenni, but reminded herself that Mirko was a client, even if she didn't have much sympathy with him. He could have gone back, with a fistful of cash, instead of which the silly cuckoo had stayed and spoilt the rest of the family's chances.

'Jules, I will be happy to take over this case. The immigration issues are very difficult and it isn't your field, is it? Would he not get better service? I could come back for tomorrow.'

This was a concession; Jenni was at the family palace in Leicestershire and she was not famous for doing overtime unless

Paul was around to see.

'Tell you what, Jenni, I'll see if I can string it along over the weekend without doing any immigration. I'll ring you tomorrow.'

Jenni agreed but she sounded doubtful, so Jules rang off before she could argue further. I will call her in, she promised herself, the second I feel I am out of my depth. She was still restless; she had not managed to do any shopping or she might have done some cooking. There were other things she ought to have been doing, but in the end she turned on the TV and prepared to fall into a gentle sleep. Then the bell rang persistently and she had to haul herself to the door where she found Jimmy Watt, finger on the bell.

'My guv'nor wants you.'

'Why?'

'To accompany your client to identify a body.'

'Now, this minute he wants me? You've never got the DNA result?'

'No, but Mr Allenton has decided to try for identification of the body with the AB blood.'

'He knew there was one yesterday. What's biting him?'

'Dunno.' Jimmy, she reflected, always looked wooden when he was telling a porkie.

'Is Mirko ready to go?'

'Yes. He would have been OK to go without you, but...'

'Glad to know that your guv'nor has been properly trained. Let me get a coat.'

She thought about it in the car. *Something* must have happened to change Allenton's mind. The bodies would have been in a cooler since, what, Tuesday this week, so they weren't getting any more or less recognisable. This was not going to be pleasant, it had been two days before the bodies had been found. As they pulled into the nick, Richard Allenton nipped into the front seat beside the driver. He looked tired, his tie was twisted, there was a bit of breakfast on the suit, and his breath smelled. 'Glad you could make it, Miss Carlisle.'

'Why are we doing it now? You'll have a DNA test in, what,

another twenty-four hours, which will tell you conclusively whether my client has a relation among the departed.'

'New evidence has come to light.'

'What? Tell me, or I'll advise my client against it. Where is he, by the way?' Paul had always counselled against haste, particularly if it was the police doing it.

'In the other car.'

'Get him out, and I'll have a word. But before that you have to tell me why we're doing it now.'

'There is another case.' Richard Allenton ground his teeth, and looked out of the window. 'We decided it was worth a try to get some evidence of identity of these bodies now rather than wait twenty-four hours. We do know that one of them is the right blood group.'

'AB is what, ten per cent of the population?'

'There is some pressure for speed, from my bosses.'

It wasn't impressive but she would be on poor ground if she could be presented as delaying a murder investigation. Mirko was going to need all the help he could get from the authorities; no point antagonising them now. She resisted however until an exasperated Allenton got the driver and escort out of the other car and put her into it. Mirko was also not looking well.

'Did they feed you properly?'

'Yes. Yes, a good meal last night and breakfast, but I was not hungry.'

'This isn't going to be nice, Mr Dragunoviç. Even if this isn't your brother it'll still – well, I understand the bodies were not found for a couple of days.'

'I have to know. And one is of my same blood group.'

Very long eyelashes for a man, she noticed, as he looked down at his hands.

'OK. Now, Mr Dragunoviç...if it is your brother then they will want to know everything you know about how he got here. And if you want to stay you'll have to tell them. Sometime.'

'You will make a bargain first.'

'I will try. Don't talk without me in the room, whatever they offer you, and we'll just have to do the best we can to get you a licence, or whatever, to stay.'

Officialdom wanted her in the car with her client in handcuffs, and Richard Allenton, unfettered. She was prepared to warn Mirko not to talk with an MI5 man in the car, but he must have worked that one out for himself and just stared out of the window. She was doing the same, but Richard Allenton offered her a stick of gum which she turned down, then a Mars Bar which she couldn't resist.

'Have you been a solicitor long, Miss Carlisle?'

'Not very,' she said, deciding the truthful answer, which was that she had been qualified for just over a month, would be inadvisable. 'And you? Have you been in MI5 long?'

'Five years.'

'And before that?' Close up, with breath much improved by the gum she was conscious of a definite twitch of interest.

'I was in the Army.'

'In Military Intelligence?'

'Yes.'

'How did you get there?'

Richard Allenton shifted a bit in the front seat, looked fixedly at the side of the driver's head and decided he wasn't betraying any state secrets here. 'From university.'

'You were a clever lad?'

He grinned, suddenly, revealing good teeth, with a gap between the middle ones.

'I was good at languages.'

'Where did you serve?'

'Oh, various places. Northern Ireland. Germany. Bosnia, Kosovo.' He said Kosova, like the news readers did.

'You speak Serbo-Croat?' She had an eye on Mirko.

'I do.'

Mirko opened his eyes and shot something at him, and Allenton replied, his whole face changing shape to accommodate the consonants.

'Oi. No, you don't!'

'What, Miss Carlisle?'

'You must not speak to my client in a language I can't

understand. Mr Dragunovič, you too. Not a good idea.'

They both looked offended, but too bad. She had no reason to have a good opinion of Richard Allenton's integrity or of Mirko's intelligence. In any case, the car was turning and stopping outside huge gates, and a fat man was wandering out in a leisurely way. As Richard Allenton rolled down the window the man jerked into action and the gates opened.

'Pentonville,' Richard Allenton said.

'I know. Why?' Jules asked, meaning why a prison mortuary; none of the people they came to see were going anywhere.

'Security,' Richard Allenton said, as if she had asked a stupid question.

She felt Mirko go tense all over next to her as he peered out of the window, so she postponed sorting out MI5 and patted her client reassuringly. It was the usual square brick built, windowless building squatting at the side of high walls. Richard Allenton took the handcuffs off, moved either by compunction or the presence of Jimmy Watt and an escorting sergeant, unloading themselves from the other car, and rang the bell. The door opened on a neon-lit passage, dirty red tiles on the floor. It was as cold, well, as the tomb it was, and she wished she had worn more of everything. The group shuffled in and halted behind Richard Allenton who was being cringed to by an attendant. 'Thank you, Mr Ross. I appreciate it. Now, Mr Dragunovič, we are going to ask you to look at the body of one man who has the same blood group as you.'

'I will look at all.' She opened her mouth to protest, but her client was not listening, pale as death himself. These places all look much the same, she thought. Horrible. Walls lined with cabinets, steel tables at one end, kept at a temperature about five degrees above freezing. She got herself on Mirko's left side, but all his attention was fixed on the attendant who was waiting with his hand on a cabinet. The attendant looked at Richard Allenton who nodded and watched while he pulled open the cabinet, releasing a cloud of cold steam and pulled back the sheet from the face.

She had seen worse, she thought, stoically. As a trainee she had to escort the father of a six-year-old girl who had been missing for four days, to identify a likely body. She had tried to warn the man what to expect, but it wasn't any use. The police had been very good, two of them stationed to catch him as he fell, turning away in disbelief from a hideously swollen oversized human doll, cold air smoking round her. The man's head revealed here was not misshapen, but the skin of the face was swollen black and congested and the mouth open and swollen. She looked at the face, so did Jimmy Watt, and both drew in a breath simultaneously, and for a moment she could taste everything she had eaten that day. Richard Allenton never looked away from Mirko who swayed on his feet.

'My brother. Stefan.'

'Are you sure?'

'He has a ring. On his left hand.'

Richard Allenton looked enquiringly at the attendant.

'I will look,' Mirko said, from a great distance.

'It shouldn't be...they should have taken it off.'

Unless someone else did, the group thought, but the attendant arrived back, full of whispered apologies. There *was* a ring, it had come off the left hand. Plain gold. It had been cut through to get it off the finger.

'I think so. The fourth finger of the left hand.' The attendant nodded keenly and Jules watched her client, his face set like a stone mask. She reached out and put a hand on his arm. His shoulders lifted in one heave and he collapsed, taking them all by surprise. Richard Allenton got a hand to him but she was in the wrong place and sprained her wrist trying to help, and Mirko ended up sitting on the floor, shoulders heaving, making terrible groaning noises, between fighting for breath. The men of the party hauled him to his feet and put him on a chair and held him on it while he wailed and fought for breath. Jules hovered with a strained wrist and a pain in her chest. She hadn't, she realised, felt much sympathy for Mirko up to now. He had absconded for love or sex without thought of the consequences. But now he had seen his brother, a shapeless, swollen mess in a mortuary drawer, and had been felled by grief and remorse. And she had no right to be censorious. Stefan was dead and Mirko's life ruined, because

Mirko had exercised the basic human right to make a fool of himself over a lover.

The attendant brought tea, heavily sugared, and gave Mirko a cup, which he gulped down, still crying convulsively, his hand shaking so much that Jimmy Watt had to hold the cup for him. Jules sat down close to him, hoping to give comfort by proximity, but he was beyond all that. Then the attendant appeared with a blanket which Jimmy draped over him, and Jules realised she, too, was shivering. Richard Allenton jerked his head at her, over Mirko's huddled shape, and she went out with him, leaving Mirko to Jimmy Watt who was looking after him tenderly.

'You're cold,' Allenton said.

'Least of our troubles.'

'Perhaps. But one that we can fix. I've got an extra sweater in the car.'

'Thank you.' She was really cold, to the point where it was all she could think about. He got her tea as well, and she had taken a gulp and recovered enough to wonder if he fancied her when she noticed his expression. 'What?'

'I was just thinking we'd be better off in the office, but it's a bit cramped.'

The attendant had packed Stefan Dragunoviç away again, but however unconscious of his surroundings Mirko was, it was hardly suitable.

'I agree, though. Better to squash into an office.'

They went back into the room and applied themselves to getting Mirko on his feet. The escort took the tea away and they managed to get him up, bowed under the blanket like an old man. Jules heard a rattling noise and turned; so did Mirko, roused momentarily, and they both got a good look at another open drawer, with the covering slid back to show the head and shoulders. A blond, heavy bloke, not at all disfigured, looking as if he might be asleep until you saw how pale he was, the blood drained from the face. Jules had her left arm under Mirko's shoulder to hold him up, and felt his whole body go into spasm. She looked up into Richard Allenton's intent face. She'd seen this done before, the door left open so the man in custody catches a glimpse of his associate walking down the corridor, or the accidental-done-on-purpose meeting between suspect and victim. But only with live people, and not when the man in custody had just identified his brother's body. She shifted her grip on her client, who was still rigid, and looked Richard Allenton in the eye, outraged.

'My client is in shock and we need a doctor.'

He didn't like it, she saw, in fact he hated it, but there was not a lot he could do. They deposited Mirko in the office and she told them all to get out and come back with a doctor. She bent solicitously over her client and told him in a savage whisper to keep his mouth tight shut until she told him otherwise. He was shivering, but less rigid, and he heard what she'd said.

She made sure he was warm before she left him to the escort and went out into the corridor to parlay with MI5. Allenton greeted her with a hopeful smile which faded as she stripped off his sweater and handed it back to him. He couldn't think what to do with it, so he had to stand holding it.

'Miss Carlisle, we want to ask your client to look at another body.'

'You cannot be serious. In the state he's in.'

'We have reason to believe that…that the body we want him to identify was connected to his brother's arrival.'

'On what basis are you making this conjecture?' She was in a cold rage, and Allenton saw it.

'The body of a young male was found this morning a mile or so from the beach where the others were found. He'd been shot.'

'And why do you think there's a connection?'

'Information received.'

She waited in hostile silence.

'We think he may be the courier. And we'd like to know if Mr Dragunoviç can identify him.'

'Why would he be able to?'

'Oh, for fuck's sake, Miss Carlisle. He just saw him and knew him.' Yes, he did, she agreed, silently, and they'd all seen it, no point in bursting into indignant denials. 'Miss Carlisle, think about it. Your client helped to arrange the trip, didn't he? He is here in the UK, his brother wants to come over. Illegally, because that is now his only option, thanks to your client. Who does he ask to help?'

She was going to treat the question as rhetorical, but it also seemed a stupid one. 'Somebody right there in Belgrade.'

'Possibly.' Allenton was looking relieved to have got her to speak. 'Only the Dragunoviçes are Serb and the organisation and transport out of most places in the Balkans are Albanian. The Serbs have never trusted the Albanians, and with reason.'

'These the same brave and oppressed Albanians on whose behalf we went to war in Kosovo?'

He breathed out, carefully. 'It's a little more complicated than that, and just now it doesn't need explaining. Whoever got Stefan to Holland or Belgium, or wherever, the van is run from the UK, it has to be from Wisbech.'

'Wisbech. Where they grow lettuces.'

'Indeed. So you see why I want Mr Dragunoviç to have a proper look at this body and tell me who it is.'

She remembered her duty to her client. 'He is desperate to stay here, he tells me,' she said, to the air.

'So would I be. If I'd got my brother killed.'

'He would, I am sure, be more use to you if he could be somehow enabled to stay.'

'Given asylum, you're suggesting. On what grounds?'

They were alone in the corridor by now, the others had faded away. 'Your lot have been known to make deals when you needed help in Northern Ireland.'

'This is more difficult.'

'No, it isn't. It's like an informer getting immunity in return for giving evidence.'

They glared at each other.

'Let's see if he knows anything worth having, Miss Carlisle. *Then* we'll see what we can do. All right?'

'I need to talk to him privately. Not in that office.'

'There isn't anywhere else here. Unless you'd like the room...well, the room...'

'With the bodies in? What a wonderfully tasteful suggestion.

I'll talk to him outside, in the yard. You lot keep your distance.'

'If you must.'

Indeed I must, she thought, even if I freeze. The only truly secure place to talk to a client, who is under arrest, is in the open air, or curiously enough in the cells of any court. Given Mr Allenton's performance so far, she'd certainly expect the office to be bugged.

'You'll be cold, both of you.'

She ignored him and went back to find Mirko, who was drinking tea and she watched him for a minute, mentally adjusting her vision. It was indeed possible that he had been an active party in organising his brother's attempted landing, and it was stupid of her not to have seen it. It's because he came in as an immigration case, she told herself. We all know our criminal clients have something to hide, I just didn't translate this experience across to immigration clients.

'Mr Dragunović, if you are up to it I need a conference with you. In the yard, I'm afraid, because I don't want to be overheard.' He trailed after her, wrapped in his blanket, drenched in tears, looking like every refugee on the news. They stood and looked at each other, or rather Jules looked into his face and he looked at a point past her right shoulder.

'Tell me *what* you know,' she said, speaking slowly. 'They know you recognised the...other, well, the other dead man they showed you. No need to tell me who he is, save it. But what *else* do you know? We need to make a deal.'

'I know who is organising the cars that meet the boat,' he said, at last, from a long way away, while she shivered in the April wind.

'Good. Great.' She realised she was sounding like a cheerleader in an attempt to breathe some life into him. 'Was it the man...the man you saw in there? The other man?'

He didn't answer, his eyes had closed and he was shivering, his teeth clacking together.

'Mr Dragunović, listen. Are you hearing me?' She got a nod, and a momentary glance. 'I'll go on insisting on a doctor, so you can't be questioned till tomorrow. OK? Not a word till I get there in the morning.' She glanced over her shoulder to make sure the grim little group standing twenty feet away outside the mortuary couldn't hear. 'Do you understand?'

'I understand. I will not speak. Mr Flowerdew…' his voice trailed away.

'Who came to see you?'

'No. The brother.'

'The brother?' She remembered that Andrew had mentioned a brother, the one he was having dinner with at this moment.

'Ask him. You, not police.' The shivering had increased.

'Right,' she said, trying to sound more intelligent and in control than she felt. 'Tomorrow. And you don't speak.'

He nodded, lips clenched and she was enough satisfied that she had got her point across to signal to the watchers.

'My client will look at the man you want to identify,' she said, formally, and saw the tight lines in Allenton's face relax.

They took Mirko back across the yard, she and MI5 on either side of him and into the grim mortuary where, at a nod from Allenton, the other drawer was opened for them. Mirko looked down at the swollen face.

'He is called Kevin Roberts. He works – worked – as a driver.'

'Do you know where he lives?'

'In Wisbech, where I do not know. He lived at one time in a caravan.'

Jules felt her toes curl and started to shiver in the cold air. 'You are sure, Mr Dragunoviç? Did he have, to your knowledge, any distinguishing marks?'

'A tattoo. Of a snake.'

'Where?'

'His shoulder – the left one.'

Allenton glanced at the acolyte standing by the body with a clipboard, who nodded to him. 'Can we look?'

A gloved, overalled attendant heaved and through a cloud of dry steam they all saw the red curled dragon.

'A Welshman?' Allenton said, and looked at Mirko.

'I understand, yes. His father is.'

'There is other family?'

'Yes. But I do not know where they live.'

'Enough,' Jules said, her voice coming out husky. 'You have an identification.' She was trying to control violent shivering. Allenton nodded and the attendant pushed the drawer in again, and she put her arm through Mirko's to take him away from that dreadful room, but he would not move.

'Mr Dragunoviç, would you like to…to be…to see your brother again? To say goodbye.' Unbelievably, this was MI5 speaking. She felt Mirko's arm relax.

'Thank you. I could be alone?'

'Not entirely, I am afraid. There must be an attendant. But we will go.'

She moved to protest, but Mirko had dropped her arm and was waiting by himself like a statue, and she had nothing to do but to walk stiffly out of the room just ahead of Richard Allenton and Jimmy and the MI5 acolyte. 'Thank you.' She turned to Allenton, having had time to think, and he looked down at her, seriously.

'Would you like to put the sweater on again?'

'I would.' She was so cold she could not find one sleeve and he had to help her. His hands were warm, she noted, disbelievingly. Even with the sweater on she felt she might never be a normal temperature again. They waited ten minutes, drinking more tea, then the attendant came out with Mirko, who was juddering with the cold and coughing. He was still wearing the mortuary blanket, and she put her own cup of tea into his hands and wrapped the fingers round it. She looked at him, he was deathly pale and there was sweat round his hairline. The man was ill, she realised, alarmed, and looked around for help.

'Mr Allenton, I don't think my client should be in a cell tonight. He needs…'

'We'll take him back and he'll see the doctor.' Allenton was sounding unconvinced and she considered for a moment handing him back his sweater – again – but she was just too cold. Once back in the car, they put Mirko between them for warmth wrapped in all the blankets they could borrow, leaving none for her. Richard Allenton, who had accepted the fact that he could ask no more questions now, was in a foul temper and she was too cold to care about any of it.

She saw Mirko into a prison hospital bed, and made Jimmy Watt drive her home, responding with cold silence to any mitigating suggestion that his present guv'nor was a decent bloke with a very heavy job to do.

When she got home she gave herself a hot bath and a huge whisky and faced the facts. She was out of her depth and outnumbered; from the count of phone calls coming into the car, received monosyllabically by Richard Allenton, MI5 were mob-handed on this one. Ideally she needed Paul, but failing him, Jenni Patel as the immigration specialist would have to be rallied to the colours from darkest Leicestershire. It was a quarter past eleven, but the phone was making the noise like an arthritic police siren which meant there were messages. Three, as it turned out from Jenni, one to say she had left the Leicestershire house, the second to say she was on the train, and the third to say she had arrived at her London flat. And a fourth from Paul, apparently speaking from the middle of a storm, and promising to call again at 11.30 UK time. She decided it was legitimate to speak to the organ-grinder rather than the monkey, so she sat against the radiator sipping her whisky and waited until, punctual to the minute, the phone rang again.

'Jules. You were out all day.' The noise of rushing winds on the line failed to conceal the strong middle-European accent which Paul fell into when he was stressed.

'You said you couldn't be reached.' It was always well with Paul to get your retaliation in first.

'Jenni reached me. I never can not be found. I am on my way back, bloody hell, from where? Poland still, I suppose. Now, tell me, I know you are mixed with this case of the dead on this beach.'

'In this Norfolk,' she confirmed, flushed with whisky and pulling herself together to give him a coherent account of all that she had been doing, not helped by losing the connection twice.

'So. Jenni has come back, she will take over.'

'I need help on the immigration but my client – our client – is in danger of being charged with murder. I saw it in the MI5 man's eye. It's crime as much as immigration.'

There was a silence on the line and she assumed they had been cut off again. 'I myself will be back late on Tuesday night, or sooner perhaps, if I can leave the car and fly from, oh, Vienna, Cracow, somewhere. Talk with Jenni. Both of you, tell the client he must not talk at all.' Jules tried to say she'd done all that, but he swept on. 'Tell him to stay ill. Tell MI5 I am on my way. I will have a little word with this man's superior.' Jules spelt Allenton for him. 'But do nothing, Jules, you have understood? I will tell Jenni.'

'I'll do that, Paul. You just get on, you're having enough trouble with that phone.'

They said goodnight after a few civilities, shouted over the gale force winds, and she tried to ring Jenni, but had to wait a quarter of an hour. Her line had all too obviously been occupied by Paul, bending her ear on the absolute necessity of not letting Mirko speak, to anyone, until he got there.

Jenni was at her irritating best, and Jules had once more to relate every detail of her actions for the last two days, none of which seemed to meet with her approval, so that Jules was provoked into saying that of course what was really needed was the presence of Paul. That, satisfactorily, silenced Jenni; viewing Paul as the Angel Gabriel and staff as she did, she could hardly dispute this conclusion, and Jules went to bed feeling she had got one back.

Chapter Five

(Easter Sunday)

Easter Sunday was bright, if not warm by the time Jules got out of bed at 9 a.m. and she decided to make sure that Mirko was still safely tucked up and not talking to MI5. She went down to the nick and rousted out Jimmy Watt and bought him coffee and a doughnut round the corner.

'Your client's not too clever this morning. He's got a cold. Maybe worse than a cold, so he's under the doctor.'

'I told you he was poorly. A trip to the morgue won't have done a lot of good.'

'Having a conference with you in the cold didn't help either.'

'Jimmy, I know and you know that Mr Allenton probably wears enough equipment to receive the World Service, and is not a man to be trusted nearer than a courtyard away.'

Jimmy was unable to concede the point, so they let a pause elapse while they drank coffee.

'So there's nothing for you to do, Jules, with your guv'nor coming back.'

'How did you know he was? I was just going to tell you.' He looked at her, round-eyed and solemn, over his doughnut. 'Mr Allenton had a phone call.'

'Ah. But I'm on duty till Paul gets here.'

The closest Jimmy could get to a leer appeared around the doughnut.

'And Miss Patel is coming in at nine.'

Jenni has that effect on men, even policemen, Jules thought, crossly. They get very excited about her and they call her respectfully, Miss Patel.

'Oh, is she? Well, I'll go and see her. She'll be in the office. Can you finish that by yourself?'

He waved her off, mouth full of the second doughnut, and she regarded him with some affection. He tended to the stocky, and he would be one plump DC if his wife didn't take him in hand. He married at twenty-one, she remembered, and had three children in four years, two planned, one a surprise. She left him and let herself into the office calling hello so that Jenni would know she wasn't a burglar. The firm was based in a Victorian house, so people had small offices with redundant fireplaces and dado rails which got in the way of the filing cabinets. Jenni looked elegant, as usual, in a black trouser suit, perfectly fitted, worn with pearls and a black silk camisole, her black silky hair in a neat pony tail. A textbook illustration of how to dress for the office, Jules thought, regretfully, but on the other hand it alarmed the clients who were more comfortable with Jules's own varicoloured clothes and spiky hair.

'We must wait for Paul, of course,' Jenni said, without preamble. Jules explained that the client was in a hospital bed, unable to be interviewed – a sound career move, they were able to agree. Jules was a lot less pleased with Jenni's insistence on going with her to talk to Richard Allenton but she had abandoned her long weekend with family and it would be impossibly ungracious to refuse. Presumably, Jules thought, sourly, she hoped to stun MI5 with her looks and her professional ability and, following in her wake to the station, Jules had to concede she had done pretty well. The man Allenton actually stood up for her, mesmerised by her suit, her pearls and her upmarket bitchy manner. He offered coffee, but both refused, out of old acquaintance with CID coffee, and Jenni, in the manner of one announcing the imminent arrival of the Holy Ghost, explained that Paul was on his way home.

'I look forward to meeting Mr Jenkins,' Richard Allenton said, manfully, tearing his eyes away from Jenni's chest. 'Your client has pneumonia, by the way. Temperature of 103, getting antibiotics through a drip, in Pentonville's hospital.'

'We need to see him,' Jules and Jenni said, simultaneously. Paul had trained all his staff never ever to accept what police say about the welfare and comfort of anyone in their care.

'Both of you? He's not allowed to talk, even if he agrees to see you.'

'*I* must go,' Jenni said, firmly.

She needed to tell our Leader that she had seen the client with her own eyes, Jules understood. 'Fine with me,' she said, 'glad to have my day back.' She was not in any real doubt that the forces of law and order were looking after Mirko properly. They *needed* to keep him alive to answer questions.

'I could come with you, Miss Patel.' Richard Allenton glanced at Jules, and his neck just perceptibly reddened. He won't have any luck with Jenni, she thought, smiling at him. She and her parents have a Duke, or near offer, in mind for her, but it would do MI5 no harm to learn that there are some problems they couldn't get through by bribery, intimidation or hitting them with a blunt instrument.

'Miss Carlisle, Mr Flowerdew is in the waiting room. I don't know if you saw him? I told him that Mr Dragunoviç was too ill to talk, but he said he would like to wait and have a word with you.'

Jenni was looking interested but, since she'd commandeered Richard Allenton, Jules decided she would keep Andrew Flowerdew out of her clutches. Andrew was sitting, stolidly reading a torn copy of the *Daily Mail*.

'Andrew, was that all they could find you?'

The station sergeant, an old enemy, looked up. 'We're not a bleeding dentist's here, Miss Carlisle.'

'Glad to hear you've stopped pulling the customer's teeth, sergeant. Just recently, was it?' It raised a good laugh in the crowded waiting-room, and she and the sergeant bared their gums at each other. Jules got Andrew into the open air.

'We might as well both go home, Andrew. My colleague, Jenni Patel, who is an immigrant specialist is going to try and see Mirko, but I'm not sure it's worth it. He has pneumonia.'

Andrew Flowerdew nodded. 'Have you plans for today?'

'Well, since Jenni's here, I might go to Cambridge.'

'You wouldn't like to have lunch with me and my brother in Norfolk. It's not exactly on the way, but it's not that far. I'd hoped to see Mirko but since he isn't available I'd like to see Martin.'

Jules stared at him, thinking, and realised he was blushing. 'Yes, I would, if I can get to Cambridge for supper. And provided Jenni knows where I am.' Anne had installed in her the view that

men have a hard time because they always have to do the asking
and that therefore girls should answer yes or no at once, and
civilly, it's the least they can do. And in any case it would be
interesting to see Norfolk again from the safety of her
professional life. And chaperoned, apparently, by Andrew's
brother, how very old-fashioned.

'Can we go now? I've got the car and I'll just ring Martin and
tell him it's one more.' He fished out a mobile, one of the new
tiny thin ones. It looked ridiculous in his family-sized paw, which
reminded Jules that logically there should be a Mrs Flowerdew
somewhere. 'That's great,' he said, and beamed at her. 'Martin's
going to cook, and he is the best.'

'What should I wear?' Between her upbringing, when
assembling a reasonably clean set of clothes was her highest
aspiration, and Anne's view that a black trouser suit covered all
known social occasions, she had a hard job with clothes. She either
bought army surplus – which had seen her through university –
or spent far too much money, with about the same result.

'Well, I'm going to get out of this suit as soon as I get home. I
wore it to impress the police.'

'Will he mind jeans? Your brother.' She had confidence in her
Calvin Kleins which fitted where they touched and were hanging
clean in her wardrobe.

'He'll probably be wearing them.'

He drove her to her flat and waited in the car while she
changed. 'You'll need boots,' he said, brow furrowed, when she
came out of her flat five minutes later.

She had put on her special heavy thick-soled sneakers as a
concession to the countryside, but he rummaged in the boot of
the Range Rover to find oversize green wellingtons and an extra
pair of socks. They weren't, she thought, going to do much for
the Calvin Klein jeans, nor would the smelly green jacket,
constructed of oiled cardboard which Andrew said she would
need over her new sweater.

She followed him into the Range Rover – everything, like
Andrew, was a couple of sizes too big. The roads were clear –
everyone must have already been at their destination since Friday,

and it seemed no time until they were coming off the motorway into flat country which got even flatter. She could see for miles; there was nothing to get in the way, except an occasional, unexplained bank.

'The river,' Andrew said.

'Why are the banks so high?'

'The river runs higher than the land. There are steps here up to the lock. We're on our land here – would you like to stop and have a look?'

He slid out of the Range Rover and pulled on boots and another mildewed jacket over the good suit and they went up the steps, Jules's wellingtons slipping under her, blinking in the sun. At the top – maybe twelve feet above the surrounding country – the wind was blowing hard enough that she was glad of the jacket. And there was the river: wide and shallow, and dead straight, running a good eight feet above the level of land.

'It's a canal.'

'It's the old Bedford River, but all the Fen rivers are canalised in places. It would be marshland else. They run slowly because the land is flat and they carry a lot of earth with them.'

'Ah.' She remembered being told that – visions of meanders and ox-bow lakes and marshy deltas surfaced from primary school geography. 'Where does it come out? Into the sea, I mean?'

'At King's Lynn, this one. Here we pump non-stop to keep the land from flooding.'

Dazzled by the sun, she changed focus and looked down at the fields on the other side of the bank. They were covered with a sheet of water, not deep, maybe a foot or so.

'That's a wash. We let those fields flood; they dry up in summer and we – well, not me – a neighbour puts sheep and cattle on. It's good grazing.'

'But…you don't try and keep it dry.'

'No. You have to have a safety valve. Better the water in these washes than all over the fields.'

'The sky is reflected in the water, that's why it looks blue,' she said, a small problem solved, and Andrew laughed.

'You getting cold?'

'Just a bit.'

'It's warmer on the flat.'

It was much, and she was too hot in the oiled jacket. They stopped at the edge of a sheet of bright pale green, stretching half way to the horizon, with small figures concentrated in one patch. Like a picture out of the *National Geographic*, she thought as she followed Andrew towards a huge tent structure on wheels, the whole slightly on a slant in the thick mud. A dozen people were working there, taking lettuces out of the boxes brought to them, hacking off a few more outer leaves and packing them into plastic bags.

'Morning!' Andrew called, and the line looked up in acknowledgement, without stopping work. Three years ago, she thought, Mirko must have been one of this gang, all young, all bent double in backbreaking labour, but cheerful and self-respecting, sustained by a vision of the flats they would buy in Warsaw or Sarajevo, or Belgrade. And Mirko's brother might have been here this year as one of this gang rather than lying in a drawer in a London morgue.

'You use pesticides?' she asked, sternly, in order to distract herself.

'We do. One slug and the supermarkets or the processors send the whole truck back.'

'What about organic veg, then? Can you not sell that with added slugs?'

'Not really. We use nematodes on the organic stuff to get rid of slugs, but it's not reliable. We can't make it work for the quantities we're shifting commercially.'

'So we're all eating lettuces full of chemicals?'

'Yes. We plant a new crop every three weeks in this field.'

'Do your people get holidays?'

'They do. We roster them.'

So she was not inspecting a slave camp here, but it was still desperately hard work. Difficult to imagine the average British graduate being prepared to do it. A bright-eyed dark girl, in tight trousers and the inevitable cardboard jacket, came over, carrying a lettuce to show Andrew. He said something to her and she answered him, in a bristle of consonants, her face lighting up. She went reluctantly back to the line.

'What was that?'

'Serbo-Croat.'

'*You* speak Serbo-Croat?' She realised she was sounding incredulous.

'A bit. I was there with the Army. Martin, my brother who is a doctor was there too, but not in the same place. Took a year off after his houseman job. They wanted to keep him there of course, but...'

'But he wanted civilisation?'

'Yes, and decent kit. He used to say you were back in the nineteenth century in wartime Bosnia, and you lost people for stupid reasons.' He looked at his watch. 'I could use a drink before dinner. We need to get to the other side of Wisbech.' He said goodbye, bilingually, to his labour force and escorted her back to the car through the mud.

The Range Rover hurtled along the straight roads and as Wisbech came into view Jules wondered if anything about it was going to seem familiar. All she could recover was the look of the tattered, dirty beige caravan, which had been the family home, hooked up to the electricity which worked when there was money for the meter. She blinked at the 'Welcome to Wisbech' sign and suddenly saw the site, on the left.

'Could we stop?' she said, urgently.

'Here?'

'Yes.'

Andrew, credit to him, asked no questions, just drove to the edge of the site and pulled up. 'Are we getting out?'

'Just for a minute.' She slid out of the Range Rover and stood in her clumpy boots just looking. I was ten, nearly eleven, when I was here, she thought, fourteen years ago, but I remember exactly the place where our caravan had rested. The trees had grown and there was another van parked there, just as old and decrepit. Children ran and screamed and played round the water tap, same as she had, and she could feel the wet dirt between her bare feet again. Then a man came out of the caravan that stood where the family caravan once had.

'Jules?' Andrew came up to stand next to her, and the man turned his head. He stood, silhouetted against the caravan, staring.

'What you want?'

'Just visiting,' Andrew said, soothingly. The man stood where he was, scowling.

'Ray?' She hadn't meant to speak but it came out and his head jerked up.

'Do I know you?'

She took a deep breath. 'I used to live on this site. I went to the primary here. Jules Carlisle. I was in the same class as your sister.' Who had been the same terrifying mean bully as the older brother who now stood before them, older, but no less frightening. He'd grown but he was only her own height, dirty and slouching.

'What you doing here? This your husband?' He looked past Andrew to the shiny Range Rover.

'No. I came here for lunch and I thought I'd just...' I'd just what? for heaven's sake! Recover some childhood friends? This one had terrorised all the kids in the school, including his own sister, who passed it on with interest. I wish, she thought, oh I wish I could say I had stood up to him and his nasty friends, but for the three years she was in that school she tried only to stay out of their way. Whenever that tactic failed, she had done everything they had asked, however humiliating.

'Andrew Flowerdew,' her escort said, pleasantly, extending a hand.

'Ray Cardona, Andrew, sorry. We were at school together.' She was sounding like Jenni Patel, she realised, but couldn't help it. 'What are you doing now, Ray?'

A long dirty look. 'This and that. You?'

'I'm a solicitor. A lawyer.'

'Yeah?' He sounded incredulous. As well he might, she thought, proudly, since, when he had last seen her she had been living in a caravan with parents worse off and more feckless even than his.

'My Mum died, and I ended up living with a cousin.'

'Yeah?'

This wasn't going anywhere, but she couldn't seem to stop. 'How's your sister?'

He jerked his head towards the screaming children. 'She got four kids.'

The children were quiet now, all assembled round something, staring at a boy of about nine who was crouched on the ground. It would be an animal or a bug being tortured – it always had been when she was a child on this site.

'Is she here?'

'Down the shops.'

She tried not to sigh with relief; she wanted very much not to meet his sister Sharon again, but her feet seemed to be set in concrete. She was still, she understood, somewhere, the child wanting to ingratiate herself with the powerful bullies. 'Ah, pity,' she said, with effort. 'We need to get to lunch. Say hello to her, will you?'

'Yeah.'

'Nice to have met you,' Andrew said, punctiliously.

Ray mumbled something and watched them into the Land Rover. She could feel his eyes on her, and as Andrew turned the big car he was watching with that dark look of envy and intent to spoil or destroy that she remembered so well.

'I'm sorry.'

'Why?' Andrew was patiently letting a bent old woman walking as slowly as she could, rage and resentment in every step, get across the road.

'I just wanted to look, not…'

'Which school were you at?'

'Collingfield.' She had been at eight schools by the time she was ten.

'It's quite a difficult school.'

'I know just what you mean.'

'Cardona. I know the name. There's an extended family of them. Gypsies, in origin. Settled, as the social workers say.'

The notion of 'settling' gypsies – or tinkers, as Cousin Anne called them, was well-meaning but ridiculous, she thought, crossly. They may settle in an area but they don't integrate. Not even in London. She had several Ray Cardona clones on the books in Camden Town.

'I suppose you're a Justice of the Peace, then, Andrew?'

'Well, yes. And Wisbech is having a bad run at the moment,' he said, eyes on the road. 'Lots of crime. We've had problems at the farm.'

'People steal *lettuces?*' Visions of rural deprivation rose before her.

'Four men can clear a field in a few hours and have it sold a few hours after that. Here's the house.'

She had, she realised, been nursing a fantasy of something like Pemberley, Mr Darcy's house in *Pride and Prejudice*. What she saw was a house hardly bigger than her flat with a severe garden, laid to lawn as the estate agents said when they meant it had no flower borders in it. All around it, rather than a gracious park with well-grown trees, lay miles and miles of the same absolutely flat muddy land. She gazed at it sadly, but was distracted by a tall man emerging from the back gate, clad in immaculate khaki chinos, which fitted him perfectly. The brother Martin. He was a hair smaller than Andrew but about three stones lighter. He had the same dark blond hair but his was thick and curly. He had dark brown eyes where Andrew's were a washed-out blue, and long eyelashes and a straight nose.

He swept her in through the door of the unprepossessing house as if she were the person he had most wanted to meet today or any day. He gave them large glasses of beautiful white wine, chilled just right and put an arm round her to take her over to the window and show her the view from the back of the house which was, as he observed, exactly the same as the view from the front or the sides, give or take the odd farm building. He teased Andrew, who lost several years when he laughed, and whisked them into the kitchen to chat while he did complicated things with eggs and butter, long, strong hands which held pan and whisk exactly where he wanted them. He was, he had explained, a gynaecologist and Jules thought how reassuring a man with hands that good would be. He served them with a beautiful steak and a sauce Béarnaise, which tasted like nothing she had ever had before, even in respectable restaurants, light, buttery with the taste of something sharp underneath it, the whole dish mixed with red juice from the steak and complemented by a soft red wine. She ate it all, and the potatoes and the vegetables and asked for bread to mop up, which made both brothers laugh.

'I love a girl who cleans her plate,' Martin said, warmly, rising to clear, resting a hand easily on her shoulder, while she tried not to wriggle with pleasure. He put an exquisitely composed salad in front of them, several sorts of green, with sharp dark green chives on top. 'To clear the palate.'

'It looks wonderful,' she said, sincerely. 'Are these your own lettuces?'

'Well, no. Andrew grows iceberg. Fields and fields of tightly curled, tasteless green.'

'It's not that bad.' There was no hurt in Andrew's objection; this was an old joke between them. Martin raised a glass to him, and she saw that they really were brothers.

'Is – are your parents alive?'

'Oh, goodness, yes.'

'Do they live at the farm?'

'No. The lettuces come from our grandfather. Our mother's father. He only had girls, so he picked among the grandsons to run the farm. I was the only one really who wanted it. Our two cousins didn't, and Martin…'

'Martin doesn't. I'm much happier with my ladies. Jules would you like another piece of bread?'

'It's either that or tip up the plate and drink off it.'

He got her another slice of bread, laughing, and as he reached across to pour her some more of the beautiful wine, brushing her arm, she confirmed, regretfully that, lovely though he was, he was not at all sexually interested in her, or in any woman, all that physical charm and genuine warmth of personality notwithstanding. Andrew sat stolid and pleased opposite her; he was hetero all right, but he accepted his brother's tastes and was just happy to be there full of good food.

'That was terrific, Martin. Best meal I've had, well, since you last cooked for us.'

'Do you cook, Jules?' Martin asked, innocently, passing her some more coffee.

'Not like this.'

Thanks to Anne she could cook basic things like grilled chicken. But when she got home, around 8 p.m. from another day at the crime farm, what she actually did was to put a take-away in the microwave. She resolved to do better; that meal had been just as good as sex. Martin grinned at her leaving her with the uneasy feeling he had read her mind.

Andrew got up, loosening his belt unselfconsciously. 'A wonderful change from Mrs Harlow, that was,' he said.

'You could send her for lessons. There's a decent place in King's Lynn.'

'She'd be offended. This is my housekeeper, Jules, a good woman, but not the greatest cook. Take-aways heated up.'

'One of the sisterhood, then.'

Martin looked amused, so she asked for more coffee and another mint. He gave her a brandy as well, in a huge glass which she sniffed at cautiously, not being sure she could manage any more alcohol.

'We might ring up and see how Mirko is,' Andrew said, and suddenly there was tension in the room.

'He won't be much different from three hours ago, I wouldn't have thought,' Jules said, soothingly. 'Jenni – my colleague – has this number, anyway.'

'Was he ill before yesterday?' Martin was looking out of the window elegantly posed, but his back was rigid.

'He had a cold when he came to see me on Thursday. And he looked tired and thin. I'm sure he didn't actually have pneumonia.' None of this seemed to be helping the atmosphere, so she tried again. 'The police didn't sound worried. I mean, antibiotics cure pneumonia, don't they?'

'Yes. Yes, of course they do.' Martin turned from the window. 'Will you excuse me for a minute. I have to call and check on a patient.'

Jules excused herself to go to the lavatory – small, clean, décor from B&Q – and found that in her absence Andrew had fallen asleep in the long chair. Martin was reading the paper, so she addressed her question to him.

'Do all Andrew's lettuce pickers come from former Yugoslavia?'

'By no means. A lot come from Rumania, Bulgaria and Turkey. We used to get Poles and Hungarians but, of course, they can get unlimited work permits these days, being Accession countries.'

'How do you – does he – get them? Do you just take whatever the Home Office offers?'

'Some of that, yes. A lot of them ask to come to us. We both have contacts there.'

'He told me.'

'I was with *Médicins Sans Frontières*. He with the UN. I left after Sbreniça.' His voice changed and she hesitated about whether to carry on the conversation.

'The Serbs were the villains there of course?'

'Yes. I couldn't stand them. Murderers.' Martin got up in one swift elegant movement, and she thought again what a pity he wasn't straight.

'The Serbs are all right individually. I've employed a lot of them.' Andrew's eyes were still closed but he was shifting his feet experimentally.

'Hence Mirko.'

'Hence Mirko. I didn't know him but we'd had a distant cousin of his so he came recommended.'

'You knew Mirko too, didn't you, Martin? He told me.'

'Yes, I did.'

The tone in the room had changed again and she wondered what she had said.

'Come and see one of the pretty bits of Norfolk,' Andrew said, sitting up abruptly and feeling for his shoes. 'Can't have you thinking it is all fields of lettuce. We'll go and see a bit of King's Lynn, have tea up there and you can get the train to Cambridge from there.'

'Can we help with the washing-up?' Jules asked.

'Bless you, my children,' Martin said, benevolently. 'There's a machine, you can hear it gurgling to itself. You go and have a nice excursion.'

Chapter Six

(Easter Sunday Afternoon)

She was feeling sleepy from the huge meal, but the cold wind blowing through the streets of King's Lynn woke her up. A beautiful small town with handsome eighteen-century buildings and a sluggish river flowing imperceptibly through it. It was impossible not to be interested as Andrew took her round.

'They have to dredge all the time to keep it clear the silt brought down by the river,' Andrew said. 'Not on Easter Sunday perhaps, but every other day. You're looking cold. Is it tea time?'

She *was* cold, she realised, the stiff cardboard jacket seemed to let the wind in round the neck and sleeves. She glanced round for a café, but Andrew was leading her across the square to a substantial eighteenth-century building which housed what was obviously the best hotel in the town.

'Good tea you get here,' he observed, holding the door for her and nodding to the woman at the desk.

'Nice to see you, Mr Flowerdew,' she assured him, and came to take their coats and fuss over them. A bit more fitting for Mr Darcy than his house, Jules thought, amused.

They got sat down, and the tea ordered, and she could see in Andrew's eye that he was going to ask her something she didn't want to answer, so she got in first.

'MI5 says it's Wisbech people bringing in the illegals.' At least they had Richard Allenton in common.

'The chap they thought was the driver is a local man. Kevin Roberts.'

'How do you know that?'

'Richard Allenton told me. He thought I might have known of him.'

'And did you?'

'Yes. He'd appeared before us a couple of times.'

Jules thought about this while she poured tea for them both and decided she could not totally avoid some reference to the morning's visit, but it was difficult to decide what to say.

'I've been on that site before – where we were this morning – on a planning thing,' Andrew said, conversationally.

'You're a councillor as well?' He would be, wouldn't he? she thought, irritably. He must be pretty surprised to find himself buying lunch for an alumna of Water Lane caravan site and Collingfield Primary.

'MI5 really need Mirko to speak,' he said, after a pause. 'They're actually being quite patient. Of course he has a good solicitor who they have to be careful with.'

'Don't let's kid ourselves,' she said, grateful for the change of subject. 'It's Paul who *really* frightens them – I'm not sure I'll ever manage to do that.' She returned to the problem that was nagging at her. 'Mirko was working in London when they picked him up. How was he doing that *and* organising criminals up here? It's two hours on the train.'

'Mirko was just a customer, surely not an organiser? I remember him well, because of the trouble he caused us. Easily led.'

'So he met someone, somewhere, perhaps the same person who got him jobs, who imported people. And he kept in touch with them even though he didn't live here any more.'

'That, I understand, is what MI5 think.'

Richard Allenton seemed to have been sharing more with Mirko's ex-employer than with Mirko's lawyer. But then he needed Andrew's local knowledge; Jules and Jenkins Associates were just a nuisance to him. 'What do *you* think, Andrew?'

'As I told MI5, the Wisbech lot won't be doing the big ships. They aren't seamen. They do small boats in the Wash and they're all into cars, repairing them, driving them, stealing them. Kevin worked for a local minicab firm, when he worked. The real mystery is who is doing the organisation. I don't really see anyone here, including your old friends the Cardonas, doing the false papers and job-getting bit.'

'Ray Cardona and his sister were successful criminals at – what – eleven and ten years old, but I agree with you, the paperwork would have been beyond them. Ray couldn't read.'

'You went a funny colour when you saw him. Sorry. You don't

want to talk about it.'

A trolley swished over to them under the guidance of two women who rolled up the domed side of the silver cover to reveal an array of cakes, providing an instant distraction. She settled for an éclair, and Andrew for an enormous slice of chocolate cake.

'Speak of the devil. No, no, not Ray Cardona.' Andrew peered at her, concerned. 'Richard Allenton. Over in the corner.'

He was here to look for the organiser of course, she realised. Someone had to make the next slice of profit from the illegals once they were here.

'He appears to be by himself. It seems a bit...Jules, would you mind if he joined us?'

Men who are interested in me, she thought, do not usually invite other men over to share tea. But here, they were on Andrew's territory, and Richard Allenton was the stranger at his gates, entitled, presumably, to a straw pallet for the night and a go at the scraps. 'By all means.'

She had a good view of Richard Allenton's surprised face, and polite momentary demurral as Andrew went over to him. Two minutes later they were back, Richard's mouth expressing gratified surprise, but the dark eyes wary and suspicious.

'There's a story I can't quite remember,' she said, pleasantly, as Richard was seated and urged to cakes and sandwiches. 'It's mediaeval, about a man who meets Death, somewhere in Syria, and all he notices is that Death is looking surprised. The man – our hero – is terrified, so he rides as far and as fast as he can, killing horses beneath him, and arrives at Aleppo. There he meets Death again and cries out in terror: "But I saw you yesterday in wherever it was." "Yes," said Death, "and I *was* surprised, because I had expected to see you today, in Aleppo."'

Richard Allenton considered her with interest, but Andrew Flowerdew scowled at her reprovingly, and she found herself blushing. Well, she had meant to be rude but not to have Andrew disapprove. Richard's gaze flickered and he passed her the sandwiches.

'Our mutual customer is a bit better. I understand we'll be able to talk to him tomorrow.'

'Glad to hear it.' She looked over to the door in search of a Ladies Room to recover herself and her breath caught.

'Jules. What?' Andrew spat crumbs.

'Sorry. Nothing.'

'What nothing, Miss Carlisle?'

'Ray Cardona. Looked into the room, saw us, and fled.'

'Are you sure?'

'Yes.'

She picked up her cup. Andrew took it gently out of her hands, as Richard Allenton sat forward, alight with curiosity.

'Never trouble trouble,' she said, to her napkin.

'Lest trouble troubles you?' Andrew asked, interested. 'I haven't heard that for years. I'm sure it's nonsense.'

She looked at him, so big and calm, master of his substantial patch, and thought that there was a gulf a mile wide between people with normal childhoods and those like her. Despite a lot of therapy she felt defeated, dirty, and interior every time she thought of the child on the caravan site. I'm all right with Gwyn, she thought, painfully, because he's seen worse and sees worse every day, but civilians – men like Andrew and Richard – are appalled and repelled by my history. I should have saved the visits to my childhood for when I was by myself.

'I lived near here as a child,' she said to Richard Allenton, partly to make up for having been rude to him and because she had understood that he could look up anything about her he wanted to know and probably already had. 'So I got Andrew to stop off at…at the site where we lived for a bit and we met a horrible boy I was at school with. Now a horrible man. And I saw him again just now. And it's…what…twenty miles away from here.'

'What was his name?'

She had all Allenton's attention now, the dark eyes intent on her.

'Cardona. Ray Cardona. There was a whole clan of them. Tinkers, sorry, that's what Scots call them. Gypsies.'

Something, she saw, had rung a bell with him, but he wasn't saying. Andrew wordlessly poured her some more tea, which she refused in favour of a retreat to the Ladies where she collected herself. She arrived back at the table to find the men deep in conversation about farming and, mildly piqued, ate cakes while they discussed crop rotation and fertilisers.

'Sorry.' Andrew had noticed her expression. 'Richard's father is another of the brethren.'

So it is Richard now, she thought, and he is all right because you know his family or at least what his family is.

'Andrew, what are you and Miss Carlisle going to do now?'

Both of them blinked at him. 'I'm putting Jules on a train for Cambridge,' Andrew said.

'I have to go to Cambridge. I could drive you, Miss Carlisle.'

Jules hesitated. She really did not want to be shut up in a car for an hour with Richard Allenton, but Andrew was not helping her, apart from saying it was no trouble to get her to the station, but they ought to start now. She decided that it was childish and unnecessary to refuse a free ride from Richard Allenton, so she accepted with minimum grace.

'We'll meet you at the car then, Richard,' Andrew said, firmly. 'Are you in the car park?'

'Yes, but the driver will bring it round.'

And mine is bigger than yours, so nyaah, Jules thought, wishing Anne were here to see this. Andrew, she conceded, played a masterful return of serve by taking her by the hand to find her coat, leaving Richard to make his own arrangements, but there was a moment of awkwardness when they all three met on the steps of the hotel, with Allenton's chariot in the road below.

'I'll see you again very soon,' she said, warmly, to Andrew. 'Thank you for a wonderful lunch and tea.' He looked a bit like Gwyn, warm and solid, she thought, and he smelled good. He beat Richard Allenton to the car door and tucked her in the back, and she pressed the button to roll down the window and wave to him.

'Beautiful day,' Richard Allenton said, conversationally, as the car pulled away, and she agreed, politely, while considering her strategy. This was a policeman, no matter how courteous, and she organised herself to be civil and impenetrable and if necessary to go to sleep. He could hardly shine bright lights on her in a car.

'How long did you live in Norfolk?' he asked.

'About two years on that site.'

'With…with your parents?'

'I was eight when we came here, and not quite eleven when my father died, and Mum and I went to London. So, yes.'

'You've not been back since then?'

'You mean apart from the time I organised a couple of boatloads of illegals?' What happened to civil, she asked herself, crossly.

'Apart from that, of course.'

'No. I've hardly been out of London, except to university.'

'Funny you should walk into someone you knew on the site.'

'Not as funny as all that. His family were living there twelve years ago. They weren't exactly the upwardly mobile house-buying type.' She picked up the *Sunday Times*, making it clear she hoped that she had done polite conversation for the day.

'Miss Carlisle?' She looked at his profile, set in concentration. 'Could we not co-operate? There are eight dead – well, nine with the driver – and there'll be more if we don't stop the gangs. These aren't Scarlet Pimpernels, you know.'

'I have worked in one of London's more demanding criminal practices since I left law school and I really, really resent being patronised.'

She picked up the paper and flapped it to form a barrier between them.

'Bugger. Can we start again?'

She thought about it, then lowered the paper and indicated that he might address her.

'We're getting nowhere fast. We know – have known for months that people are being brought in by boat to this part of the country. We pick them up in ones and twos. Our information from the continent suggests the trade is in thousands. We think the gypsies – Cardona is a name we've met – are doing the transport for them at this end. So, you see, that when you turn out to have been at school here…and to know some of the Cardonas… You didn't remember the driver. In the morgue. Name of Kevin Roberts.'

She had been worrying away at the name since Mirko had identified the man, and suddenly a picture snapped in her head. 'I *knew* the name was familiar. But he was a mingy little redheaded thing three years down from me, a part Cardona – a cousin, but his father was Welsh. Ray didn't bully him – he tried it on once and Kevin's father half killed him.' Where had *that* come from? But the memory was clear; Ray had been off school for a week to her enormous relief. Not much gained really since he had needed to assert his authority when he did get back. She looked out of the window at the fleeting, dead flat countryside, but turned finally to look at Richard Allenton.

'Did Kevin have the tattoo then? When you were kids?'

'His father did,' she said, slowly. 'I remember now. But the man in the mortuary was too young, surely?'

'Oh yes. It would have been the son. We are looking for the rest of the family, who seem to have vanished from their usual place in the Fens. But you said he was a Cardona. Are you sure?'

She could see he was excited. 'Assuming the man in the morgue is the Kevin Roberts I knew, yes. A half Cardona which is just less awful than the pedigree version.'

'Excuse me.' He had his mobile out and was talking to someone in London, and she decided she would go to sleep.

'Miss Carlisle…your client. When we left him to say goodbye to his brother…'

'Yes,' she said, reluctantly but softened by the memory.

'He also asked the attendant to get Kevin Roberts out again.'

'Why? Was he not sure…?'

'He didn't say, of course. But I wondered if he was saying goodbye to him as well as to his brother.'

She tried not to gape at him. 'So you think he knew him well,' she said, idiotically.

'Well yes, we do.'

'You think my client – Mirko – was part of the transport system.' Paul, she thought, come home, now!

'Not necessarily part of the operating end, but he knew the people.'

Difficult to suggest otherwise indeed, she thought, grimly. The clouds were gathering over Mirko. 'I see. I will need to talk to him and to my senior partner. But thank you for sharing the information,' she added, courteously, and closed her eyes. She thought she had got away with it, but Allenton still seemed to be speaking.

'You've never seen Ray Cardona from when you were ten.'

'No.'

'But you knew *him* immediately? You went white when you saw him in the restaurant.'

She felt the back of her throat constrict. 'I was afraid of him when I was a child. And I still am.' She felt her throat ease as she squeezed out the unpalatable truth.

'I'm not surprised. A very nasty man.'

'Nasty?'

'Lot of form, mostly for GBH, several domestics.'

'For which I assume he wasn't charged.'

'That's right. The victims wouldn't give evidence. Two convictions for possession of Class A.'

'Is he a user?'

'The local force says not.' He looked at her enquiringly, and she nodded agreement. Ray had never liked losing control. 'The drug trade is in recession in this part of the world. And since the legislation, tobacco smuggling doesn't pay as well. Still goes on, but it's less profitable, so the practitioners have gone into transporting people.'

'But if you know all this…?

'No proof. Whoever's in charge doesn't leave things lying around. They kill when they need to destroy evidence. Kevin Roberts might have told us something, but he's gone.'

'So my client is very important to you.' No lawyer ever went wrong stating the obvious.

'Yes. He is. He might be able to give us a line on the group. It may not lead anywhere, but…'

'It may indeed be another dead end.' She winced as she replayed what she had said, but Richard Allenton hadn't noticed. She gathered herself. 'My client's aim in life is to stay here, as I've told you. You'll do better getting something out of him if we can help him stay.'

'We understand that.'

'He's going to need more than that.'

He glanced at her and she noticed how the dark hair curled above his ears.

'Or what?' he said.

'Or I guess he'll go on having pneumonia. It's not my game plan you're dealing with, it's his.' She had understood suddenly that Mirko had a plan, it was the rest of them who were being headless chickens. Not the pneumonia, presumably, he couldn't have managed that on demand, but the silence. She had been going on and on at him not to open his mouth without a lawyer present, and he must have thought her stupid.

Allenton nodded, logging the point. 'I was wondering if you could help in another way. Given your relationship with the Cardonas.'

'What *had* you in mind? Asking me to go underground? They know I'm on the side of the angels. Ray saw me with you.'

She thought despondently about Ray Cardona. A despised ghost from his past had unexpectedly turned up as a solicitor, an officer of the law, part of the engine of privilege that runs the country. Out of the blue after eighteen years. Ray would not believe it was a coincidence, and he would certainly want to know more about her. The best assumption was also that he knew who and what Richard Allenton was, so it didn't look like a good idea to visit Andrew Flowerdew's stately home again. Ray Cardona had always managed to spoil any quiet pleasure that anyone devised, and he had just done it again.

'Penny for them?'

She declined the offer, and closed her eyes.

'We're getting close to Cambridge, but I don't know quite where to go.' Richard Allenton was sounding tentative for the first time in their acquaintance and she sat up, dopily, and gave him instructions.

'Up here?'

'It's a private road but Anne lives at the end of it.'

The gates of the house were open and as the car nosed through them she saw Anne, crouched in a flower bed. She was tugging at some piece of vegetation, earphones clamped to her head, oblivious of them. Jules pressed the button to open the window and was arrested by a strange singing noise, a dimly familiar tune, and realised it was coming from Cousin Anne. She watched for a minute, affectionately, then turned to Richard Allenton to find him surveying the big house, set in its large garden.

'It's quite a sizeable weekend cottage. Is that your cousin?'

'Yes. That noise is her practising. She sings in the Parliament Choir.' She would, she realised, have to invite him in, rather than suggest he should get on with whatever he had been doing. Anne would never allow him away without tea and thanks.

'Does she work there? In Parliament?'

Anne had seen them and was getting up, waving enthusiastically and trying to tear off her headphones all at once, and Jules got out of the car to disentangle her.

'Anne, this is Richard Allenton who gave me a lift. Mr Allenton, my cousin Lady Barlow.' She sneaked a look at him; he was looking satisfactorily disconcerted.

'Baroness,' he said, only just not bowing. He had the title right, Jules saw, sourly, he knew Anne wasn't just married to a Lord Barlow.

'Come away in and have tea, my dears. You must be starving.' The traditional Barlow greeting but hardly, Jules thought, appropriate. Both of them had eaten an enormous tea an hour ago and she would be pushed to do more than a drink. Allenton, on the other hand, was eyeing up the biscuits hungrily and leaping around filling kettles.

An inner door opened and a presence leaning heavily on two sticks shuffled in.

'Beryl, I was just going to call you. Here is Jules, and Richard Allenton who has kindly brought her here.'

'He kidnapped me,' Jules protested, emboldened by her powerful female supporters. 'Lady Williams, Mr Allenton.'

There was a pause and she realised that Beryl Williams and Richard Allenton were both taken aback.

'We've met before,' Beryl said, settling herself.

'Indeed, Baroness. At a meeting in the MOD.'

'Yes, I remember now. I had been asked to come in because it was Bosnia. You are still serving?'

'Indeed. Yes.'

Anne's mind was on tea and counting biscuits, but Beryl, Jules realised, was waiting, courteous but implacable, for Richard to explain his presence in this kitchen. He had suddenly been reduced in age to about sixteen as he fidgeted by the kettle trying to take plates away from Anne and put them on the table.

'I am still involved with Bosnia,' he said, giving up the plates as a bad job but all too clearly unable to sit down while Anne was still on her feet. Jules took the plates and sat herself firmly down beside Beryl, and Anne put a pot of tea on the table.

'Indeed. And Jules has become in some way involved, I understand.'

Jules coughed on her tea, disconcerted by having the guns swing onto her. 'Well, sort of. As of Thursday I seem to be acting for a Serb who is on the run from the Home Office.'

'I didn't think Immigration was your subject.'

'It isn't.' Jules was also feeling about sixteen years old by now. 'But I was duty solicitor.'

'Your senior partner not being present.'

'Yes. How did you know he wasn't?'

'I told her,' Anne said, looking shifty. 'I was a bit worried about you taking on all this single-handed.'

Jules sat bolt-upright in reproach, and noticed that Richard Allenton had been unwise enough to grin. 'I was minding my own – or rather the firm's business – when a whole lot of new people came into my life. This is one of them. He isn't a friend, he works for MI5.'

'Have another biscuit, Richard.'

Anne, who was no good at conflict, could not bear to have anyone under her hospitable roof be uncomfortable. Beryl, Jules was startled to realise, understood that about her friend but was prepared to ignore it. The clear blue gaze rested on Richard Allenton, satisfactorily incapacitated by a large and crumbling biscuit.

'Is most of the firm's practice Immigration, Jules?' she asked.

'About half and half. I do crime, normally.'

'Interesting work, I expect.'

'Yes. And as I have just found, not unrelated to Immigration. This has turned into a murder case, somehow.'

'So Anne was saying. Of course, these people are here outside the law.'

'You're saying that violent crime is but a small step for the immigrant population?' Jules protested.

'As I am sure you know, most of the immigrants who are here without consent work long hours for rotten money and do not engage in crime. But the people who are bringing them in are criminals. Always were. People-transport just turns out to be a useful adjunct to other criminal enterprises.'

'I can't believe my pathetic client is one of the bad men.'

'He may well not be. But it might, I suggest, be better to let your senior partner handle this.'

Jules opened her mouth to protest, childishly, that she was fully qualified and capable of anything, but saw that Beryl had said all she was going to and had shifted her attention to Richard Allenton, who had managed to subdue his biscuit and was washing down the crumbs with tea. Her glance alone, Jules saw, got him to his feet, declaring his intention of leaving and shyly enquiring the whereabouts of the lavatory. Anne had sprung hospitably into action, finding a clean towel and agreeing that the garden was indeed looking wonderful but it was a lot of work. Left with Beryl, Jules eyed her uneasily.

'One of their rising stars, Jules. That young man.'

'Oh, is he? He thinks I'm an idiot.'

'Mm. I discern a gleam in his eye, however.'

Jules tried not to gape at her, but Beryl smiled serenely. She was prevented from any further elucidation by the return of Anne still fussing hospitably, followed by Richard.

'More comfortable, I hope?' Beryl enquired, and he assured her he was, much, thank you. Got the measure of her, Jules thought with respect, and saw the thought echoed in Beryl's small amused smile.

'Thank you very much for tea, Baroness Barlow. Very nice to see you again, Baroness Williams.' He cast one more awed look at Beryl and retreated in good order, followed by Jules, pulled to her feet by Anne's warning look. No guest, however unwelcome, left a Barlow house without being bade a courteous farewell.

'Most interesting,' he said, opening the car door. 'I'd no idea.'

'Your research failed.'

'You don't have the same name as your cousin, or I would have known. And of course Beryl Williams. A legend.'

Jules was feeling childish again. 'Why is she a legend?'

'They're waiting for you, but I'll tell you some time.'

'Was she very grand?' Jules asked, grudgingly.

'Oh yes. I met her at a liaison meeting. She was in to advise, although she'd retired. I was a bag carrier for my boss – this was just after MI5 inherited illegal immigration from MI6. I'm surprised she remembered me. I wasn't even allowed to sit at the table. But actually her reputation was that she remembers everyone. I must go. See you very soon.'

There *was* an unmistakable gleam of interest in his eye, Jules saw, and it would be wrong to say she did not in some way reciprocate. She waved him away and trudged thoughtfully across the gravel drive, deciding to have a walk round the garden.

'A lovely young woman,' Beryl Williams said to her friend, watching the long-legged Jules sniffing hopefully at a rose. 'I take it she is not short of admirers who do not work for MI5.'

'Well.' Anne was also watching, with love. 'No, she isn't, but none of them seem to stick. It's her, I think. She's just not interested enough in any of them. I don't know why.' She thought about it, as she had often before.

'Maybe she is just too interested in what she is doing,' Beryl suggested, but Anne, she could see, was unconvinced.

'I'm always afraid that her experiences as a child – well, a very young teenager – have put her off men. I suppose I mean "off sex".'

Beryl sat, not wanting to ask, but her friend sighed. 'She was abused – well, raped, not to put too fine a point – by the man who ended up living with her mother. Flora didn't know – she would, I am sure, never have put up with it – but Jules did not dare tell her. Flora was seriously ill by that time. And I could have prevented all this.' It was a cry of misery.

'You rescued her in the end,' Beryl offered, calmly.

'No. Gwyn Jones did. Sorry Beryl, I'm being a bore. This is old ground.'

'What happened, surely, is that her mother's death freed her to escape. She was then greatly fortunate to find both Gwyn and you, but she would have wanted above all to protect her sick mother from distress and that she managed to do.'

'That's true,' Anne said, slowly. 'But do you think…will she be able to move on?'

'Oh yes. She has great vitality. Young women like that do come through enormous difficulties, but perhaps by an unconventional route. And often with a man older than themselves. I see she has abandoned the roses, and I can hear my taxi. I must go too, Anne, and leave you with your treasured child.'

Chapter Seven

(Easter Monday and Easter Tuesday)

Easter Monday was a wonderful day, suddenly five degrees warmer, no wind and lots of sun. From the windows the trees looked fuzzy and just faintly green; a week of this and there would be leaves. Jules was in a first-class carriage on her way to London, having caught the 7.45 train with a minute to spare. Gwyn would say I was fortunate, she thought, that simple things like first-class travel make me content; many deprived children, however successful, can never get enough to achieve that effect. He was less right than he thought – while she was made happy by creature comforts the converse was also true in as much as she felt threatened by their absence. She had found she could not bear to live with only one bathroom and no central heating in her little house, and had put herself heavily into overdraft and credit card debt.

She shook herself out of this dispiriting line of thought and decided she would get a lodger, no problem, and in six…well…nine months she would be home free. Then she read the paper and then it was London and the tube to Camden Town and the office.

'Jules.'

'Ah, Paul. How did you get here?'

'An aeroplane, just now. And I am with Jenni. Can you join us?'

She was distracted by the sight of Louise, making tea, substantial hips switching angrily. This was unusual; Louise did not work hours of overtime nor Bank Holidays, unlike the obsessive lawyers who employed her.

'Hello, Louise.'

'I bin seeing the police.' Like all Paul's employees she was good at picking up unspoken sentences.

'Why?'

'They ax me about this Mr Dragunoviç.'

'What about him?'

'Did he ax for Paul, or did he juss walk in? I tell them he ax for Paul but he got you.'

'Was Mr Dragunoviç very disappointed at the time, Lou?'

'Oh yes. He nearly go away again.'

'But you persuaded him?'

A huge giggle shook the whole frame and she slapped the teapot down. 'Me? Make more people come here bringing trouble? No, I tell him you no good at *all* and he should come back for a *real* lawyer on Tuesday. He didn' like that so he stay.'

Given only minor editing, Louise would have said just that, so Mirko had come specifically recommended to Paul, as MI5 had assumed.

'What did you think of him, Louise?' She was the firm's front line and a better judge than most. She spoke immaculate English, she just didn't bother for her employers. But listen to her roughing up a local councillor – or chairing a staff committee – and you would think you were listening to Radio 4.

'Trouble is what I thought. Before him tell me anything. Him gayboy, and him ill.' Thereby, Jules acknowledged, noticing two important points both of which she herself had missed at first sight.

'You were right.'

'So now I stuck here on de Bank Holiday when I have a hot date.'

'How hot?'

'Him here.'

Jules had not seen the baby sleeping in the cot. A grandchild of course.

'Jules!' Paul was sitting at his enormous desk stabbing at a telephone, the wild hair in need of a cut. He was looking exhausted and more than usually theatrical. Lear, on a bad day. Jules had seen the play with Anne and had known at once that it was really Paul, moonlighting. Jenni was also in the office, gazing worshipfully at Paul, and trying to help him with the phone.

'Our client is ill,' he said, by way of greeting.

'I know. Stress, I assume.'

'No, really ill.' He dropped a paper and dived under the desk to get it. A corner of the huge desk heaved up and settled itself back with a thud. He emerged like a monster springing from the deep, black hair in his eyes, missing paper crushed in a large fist. 'That man Allenton tells me he is HIV positive.'

'Allenton?'

'Mirko Dragunoviç. Our client.'

'*That's* why he has pneumonia.'

'That, and because you interviewed him for some hours in a courtyard at Pentonville.'

Jules put him straight on that, not greatly bothered. It was Paul who had confirmed for her what she knew from childhood – that the police try to keep people who annoy them well off balance.

'Poor bugger.'

'Indeed, poor bugger, though your language is not becoming in a young woman, Jules. So they have him in a special bed and they are filling him with drugs, and denying him an interview with his legal representatives until tomorrow.'

'Is that OK?' Jules was startled because Paul would never have let *her* accept that position; she would probably have been posted to Mirko's bedside overnight to keep away the MI5 ghosts.

'Yes. They are desperate to question him but he is ill and they have other avenues to go down. I spoke to Allenton's superior. They are to call me at any time and I will be there.'

Jenni was watching Paul with the expression normally seen on the crowds in pictures greeting the Risen Christ, but Jules managed to concentrate on the issue.

'Paul, the police think he is part of the bad men. The people-smugglers.'

'They made that clear, thank you, Jules.'

'Do they think he organised the trip? Because he didn't strike me as up to it.'

'No. They think he knows but did not organise. But they do think he may have killed the courier. The man in the mortuary, whom you saw.'

'He's not up to murder. I don't believe it.'

Most of the clients were guilty of something, that's the nature of a criminal practice, but after four years of Work Experience and two months in practice, Jules thought, she had a feel for who is really capable of anything, and she couldn't see Mirko as a killer. On the other hand, he would have been revenging his brother and she was possibly taking too relaxed a view.

'I'll get to see him tomorrow, Jules. This will be my case. It is too...well, too involved and too much to do with immigration. Jenni will assist, now she is here.'

'But...but Paul, I mean I seem to be a bit involved. I haven't had time to tell you but I was with the Flowerdews – Mirko's old employers – yesterday, and the man Allenton drove me over to Cambridge, to Anne's.' And in any case, she thought, I may not be much of an immigration specialist but I was *here*, I am qualified.

Paul stopped hunting for papers and turned his full attention on her. 'You are not to be offended, Jules. This is not what we have trained you for. Of course you are welcome to become more...more expert in immigration, but you have never been much interested. No?'

No, she had to agree, she hadn't, and indeed had believed that much of the would-be immigrants the firm represented were shysters and liars, who could just as well go right back where they came from.

'And you are not entirely out of the case. I told your Mr Allenton that he should deal with me. He asks however that you should be there for the first meeting.' He was looking tired and cross. 'And since he is MI5 we have to do what it is he asks. But, Jules, you will, I know, tell me about any conversation you may have with him. Our position will be too difficult otherwise.'

It would, she saw, and she agreed. She still felt ruffled, but she had absolutely no legitimate cause for complaint. 'He's not *my* Mr Allenton. And...' She shut up. She was not timid, but it was Paul's firm. And she admitted he scared her like he scared the police and their most difficult clients. She had only seen him lose his temper once, but that was enough.

Paul got up restlessly; he was wearing one of his loose fitting Italianate suits, which were much more expensive than they looked. Armani, Jenni had said, and Jules had to concede that she would know. An attractive man, she observed, again, with all that wild dark hair and bright brown eyes. He just didn't affect her the same way as he did Jenni, or some of the female clients, but doubtless that was her loss. She fell in behind him and Jenni and they drove to Pentonville, finding Richard Allenton and Jimmy Watt waiting on the steps, arranged in attitudes of long-suffering patience.

'I will need a few minutes with Mr Dragunoviç first. And I would think that ten minutes would be enough for you, Mr Allenton.' That was Paul, methodically stating his position.

'Assuming, of course, that Mr Dragunoviç is prepared to tell us anything to the point.'

There were only two chairs in Mirko's room, so Jules elbowed her way to one of them, consigning Jenni to an awkward position against the wall. Paul had the chair at the other side of the bed. Jules saw, belatedly, that she would have been better off standing; she had a poor view of Mirko's profile and not much else. He didn't look like a man who had had a good night. He had a worrying pallor as if no blood was getting to the skin.

Jules did the introductions as the rest of the party settled itself.

'How are you feeling, Mr Dragunoviç? Let me say also, now, how very sorry I am that this tragedy should have come to you and your family.'

It sounded a bit theatrical, but Eastern Europe must have called to Eastern Europe, because Mirko nodded with regal dignity and expressed his gratitude.

'Now, Mr Allenton will not delay you long this morning. He has some questions he wishes you to answer, but you do not have to tell him anything, and if at any time you are doubtful you must say and we will have a private talk.' He paused to see if Mirko was going to speak. 'I have talked with Mr Allenton's superior. They expect to charge you with being an accessory to an illegal act. They may – I say only may – be prepared to come to some arrangement.'

'What arrangement?'

'Their powers are limited. I must tell you that at this stage, until we know more, you should tell them nothing that they could not find out for themselves by other means.'

'What do you mean?'

'You identified two young men in the mortuary. Your brother and Kevin Roberts. You knew Mr Roberts for a long time?'

'Yes.'

'For more than three years?' Paul asked.

Which would take us back to the time he was working with Andrew Flowerdew, Jules realised, and caught her breath.

'You knew him well?' Paul was persisting, steadily.

'Yes.'

Jules was trying to call to mind the seven-year-old Kevin Roberts, but what came up was the memory of his substantial, red-haired father, his face a clashing scarlet with rage as he methodically banged Ray Cardona's head against the wall of the school lavatories, roaring that he would learn Ray to lay a hand on his kid ever again. She finally recovered a faint vision of Kevin in another corner of the playground, staring with gratified interest and another weedy child with red-blond hair, a sister probably, weeping with terror.

'You knew him well, or only as an acquaintance?'

'He was my lover.'

Jules found she couldn't see over Mirko, so it was impossible to tell if Paul was surprised, but Jenni's mouth had dropped open and so had hers, as she wondered what the avenging Roberts father would have made of *that*.

'For how long?' Paul was sounding completely matter-of-fact, to Jules's admiration.

'Almost since we met. But it was no longer.'

Again silence, and Jules watched Mirko's eyelids close and a tear slowly seep through. It came to her, horrifyingly, that he might not know that this affair had left a deadly legacy.

'When did it stop?'

'Perhaps six months ago.' Mirko's hand fumbled on the bedclothes, looking for something, then he gave up and dabbed his eyes with the end of the sheet.

'Why?'

The thick silence again, and she could hear men's voices outside.

'I became ill. I had…I had to tell him.'

'Ill?'

'I found I was HIV positive.'

'Had you been seeing someone else?' Paul sounded completely matter-of-fact.

'I had, but Kevin also.'

There was a question needed asking, but Paul was there, so Jules stayed quiet, true to her training.

'So the relationship stopped, six months ago?'

'For sex, yes.'

'But you continued to see each other sometimes?' Jules had a hand on the edge of the bed and felt Mirko go tense. 'Did you have reason to think that Kevin was involved with people who brought in refugees?' Paul sounded, she thought, like I imagine the voice of God, devoid of all emotion. They waited and then she felt Mirko ease himself back onto the pillows.

'Of course I knew, but he was only sometimes involved. Mostly he drove a mini-cab – old ladies, schoolchildren for the schools.'

Schoolchildren who lived more than three miles from their school get free transport, she remembered. If they had stayed in Wisbech then she would have been picked up with the bigger children on the site and ferried to the Comprehensive in King's Lynn, probably by Kevin Roberts' father.

'But when your brother needed help, it was Kevin you asked to help. Not anyone else.'

'Stefan did not need help, he had arranged the trip but he told me he was arriving close to King's Lynn. So when…when he did not arrive, I went to ask Kevin because I thought he would know. I could not find him. So then I came to your firm.'

'Did you know anyone apart from Kevin, who was involved with helping people to come here?'

She felt the bed move beneath her hand. 'No. Often I hear that people may be…but I knew Kevin is part of this. So it is he I look for.'

'And you, yourself, were not involved? In helping to bring people here.'

'No. I am…I wanted only to stay, and work, I did not want to take risk.'

Now that rings true, Jules thought, and glanced at Paul to see if he agreed. He was expressionless, but she had the impression he was not entirely convinced, and he went through the routine again, Mirko fading before their eyes, before giving up with a just suppressed sigh. He advised Mirko to tell MI5 everything they wanted to know about him and Kevin Roberts, but to stick to facts, not to be led into speculation, to answer only the questions he was asked, and then briefly. Excellent advice, which he had trained all his people to give but, Jules thought, most clients can't stick to it, and there is where a lawyer comes in to deliver a swift kick to the client's shins or a sharp interruption to police questioning.

MI5, when admitted, weren't surprised, she noticed, or excited by anything Mirko had to tell them. They'd got it all already, and Richard Allenton was just confirming what they knew. She had given up her chair, all polite co-operation, to Jimmy Watt, so that she could watch Richard Allenton and Paul, who would be concentrating on keeping Mirko on the straight and narrow.

Allenton was just filling in the spaces in the crossword until close to the end of his allotted ten minutes when he asked in the same bored way whether Mirko had ever met any of Kevin's family?

'No. Or wait. Perhaps once or twice in a pub. There is a cousin who works for the same company. Ray Cardona.'

Richard Allenton seemed not to be particularly interested, though Jules practically stopped breathing.

'Kevin's parents?'

'No. His father is working away, near Sheffield, and his mother is dead.'

She could see now where Allenton was trying to go. The Cardona clan had strong tentacles; unless Kevin had been improbably discreet they must all have known he was having an affair with a male foreigner. She wondered how they felt about homosexuals and heard Gwyn say inside her head that in all societies that repress their women male homosexuality is an acceptable norm. Well, that fitted gypsy society all right, so perhaps nobody had minded.

Richard Allenton had decided he'd got all he was going to get. He announced, unsurprisingly, that he would be charging Mirko as an accessory to the crime of assisting an illegal entry to the country. A preliminary hearing by a magistrate would be held as soon as Mirko was fit to attend, and yes, the police would oppose bail. Mirko didn't seem to take in much of this; he was sagging on his pillows, having trouble keeping his eyes open, and Paul reached over him to press the buzzer for the medical help.

They all withdrew, leaving a brisk male nurse to bully Mirko into lying down again and swallowing another set of pills. Jules was impelled to look back and wished she hadn't; he was resisting being lowered onto his back, the dark brown eyes were fixed on her in anxious appeal, and she could not think what to do about any of it.

She joined the group outside, wondering whether she could get back for a private word with Mirko without making Paul very angry. From the way they were all looking at her, it was clear she had missed a question.

'Mr Allenton was asking if our client had said anything useful to you during your sojourn in the yard here.'

'Like I said, that client conference lasted about three minutes and consisted of me telling him to keep his mouth shut unless I was with him.' I do know, she reflected, uneasily, that telling a partial truth is as bad as telling a lie, but too bad.

'So he didn't tell you anything?' Richard Allenton raising the moral stakes, she thought, crossly.

'He never got a chance to speak.'

This raised a laugh but she wasn't sure she'd satisfied Mr Allenton. And she was in any case worrying about Martin Flowerdew. He had known Mirko but was uncomfortable with any reference to the fact he was gay. Had they had an affair and if so, oh horror, might the consequences have been similarly dreadful?

'Mr Allenton,' she said, noting Paul's warning scowl, 'is…was Kevin Roberts HIV positive?'

His eyebrows went up. 'No.'

So MI5 had thought of that too. 'So it was not from him...'

'No. Your client got it somewhere else.'

Paul was looking black and she did not dare ignore him any longer, but she felt as if she had the name Martin Flowerdew tattooed on her forehead.

'Time we went back, Jules. Now that Jenni and I are here there is no need for you to be in unless you have other work to do. You have? You would like lunch, no?'

She refused this treat on the grounds that the Carrigan case had got neglected because of the crisis with Mirko Dragunović, and took a taxi back to the office. She did not want to be alone with Paul and that sharp brain.

She found there that the Crown Prosecution Service, with a convulsive effort, had delivered itself of the outline case against her client, Winston Carrigan. This was typical of the CPS – they had been warned not to delay further and had got the papers to her over a holiday so that, if their luck was in, it would have been Jenkins Associates who had to ask for a delay, next time. They had the wrong firm to try that on, and this was not a very difficult case; they had got photographs of the damage and put enough backbone into her to give evidence. Mr Carrigan had been remanded two weeks ago to Pentonville where he sat, uttering threats against his wife and all her connections and cursing at Jules for failing to get him out. It was her job to read and digest this lot, go and see her unlovely client and put together the best defence she could before his appearance on Thursday. Bank Holiday Monday or not, she could get in to see him and clear her desk.

Three hours later, she trailed wearily back to the office. It had taken two hours to stop her awful client telling her that his wife was a filthy liar like all her family in West Cork, and to bring him to some sense of the peril in which he stood, of which the most immediate threat was a custodial sentence. He had brushed this aside, red-faced and sweating, and she had despaired of putting together any sort of defence for a minute. She had then remembered her *soi-disant* stepfather, and advised, smoothly, that he might be right that the courts would not sentence him to jail but what they would do would be to grant an injunction banning him from the marital home. The colour had drained from his face and she had then been able to work with him. Hopefully, she thought, the court would not believe a word of the defence they had cobbled together.

She realised she was exhausted but sat at her desk trying to remember what else she had meant to do over the Bank Holiday. The latest trainee, a plump girl with the top First in her year from the University of Newcastle, put her head in and Jules remembered what it was.

'Susie, have you got somewhere to live yet?'

'Oh yes. Thanks for remembering. I'm sharing a house up in Islington. Some friends from Newcastle had a place.'

'Ah. Well, good, I'm glad. I've just decided I'll have to…would like to…take someone in to share my house. I know you asked if I knew anywhere, but I wasn't thinking about it then.' She checked herself, deciding that this was coming out as less than gracious. 'Anyway, you gave me the idea.'

'I could ask around. Do you mind if it isn't a lawyer?'

'Not at all.'

Well, at least she had got the process started, she thought, wearily, and went home to put an instant meal in the microwave and slump on the sofa.

She woke tired on Tuesday, reckoning her chances of getting an extra day in lieu of the vanished Bank Holiday. *When* she would take that day presented the real problem; she had court appearances all week, and the next week was no better. And somehow, before she could go anywhere she had to find out what Mirko had been trying to tell her about Martin Flowerdew, all this without going against Paul's edict excluding her from the case.

Louise was in, also looking tired. 'The gay boy. Your fren.'

'We refer here to the firm's client, Mr Dragunovíç?'

'Him. He worse today. He have a relapse.' It sounded worse with the stress on the first syllable.

'How bad a relapse?'

'The message come from your friend Mr Watt, and that's all it said.'

It could be a true bill, she thought. Mirko's immune system must have been permanently sabotaged by being HIV positive, and he did have pneumonia. She checked, but neither Paul nor Jenni was in, nor expected, so she rang Jimmy Watt, telling herself it was her duty.

'How bad is he?'

'Had a bad night, temperature up a bit.'

Enough to make the MI5/CID team hesitate about trying to sweat him. Mirko was driving this particular bus, she thought, no doubt about it, and she needed to go and talk to him without upsetting Paul.

'We'd better take the poor sod some grapes, if that's alright with MI5.'

'Don't see why not, we'd be glad if he'd talk to anyone.'

'I think his lawyer is the only person who is going to visit him.'

'That's all *you* know. Mr Flowerdew rang up, wants to visit.'

'Andrew?'

'That's the only one I know.'

'I had lunch and tea with him in Norfolk day before yesterday,' she said, coldly. 'He didn't say he was coming down. Your guv'nor joined us for tea.'

'I heard. Anyway, Mr Flowerdew says he'd like to visit, tomorrow if your customer isn't well enough today.'

She breathed in, carefully. 'And why not? But no point dragging him down on the off-chance. I'll go over and if Mr Dragunoviç isn't well enough, at least he'll have got a care parcel and knows we're out there. Just tell Mr Allenton. I'm leaving now.'

She stopped off to get grapes, chocolate and a paper for Mirko. She sat in the car and skimmed the front page. A small paragraph saying police enquiries were continuing, nothing about having Mirko in Pentonville prison hospital, or Kevin Roberts in the morgue, so MI5 were playing their cards very close to their chest.

She drove up and told the guard who she was. He let her through, so she was able to walk into the hospital and get up in the lift unchallenged until she got to the second floor. 'I'm here again to see Mr Dragunoviç,' she said, briskly, to the willowy male nurse who was barring her passage.

'Not today. We did let Mr Allenton know. He's not well enough.'

'I'm his solicitor. I'm not going to upset him but he's…well, you know his history.' They usually do in prison hospitals. 'I'll just put my head round the door. If he's asleep I'll go away again.'

A noise from Mirko's room told her she had achieved her objective of letting him know she was here. The nurse, tut-tutting, opened the door, with her on his heels. Mirko was sitting up, eyes fixed on the door. He seemed to her to look no worse than the day before, but he promptly managed a coughing fit, and Jules did her best to flutter while the nurse propped him up and gave him sips of water.

'I see he's not at all well today,' she said, anxiously. 'If I just stay five minutes…?'

Mirko stopped coughing, smartly, and said, in a thread of a voice, that he would very much like just a short visit. The nurse hesitated but a voice could be heard through the walls, raised in incoherent noise, so he doubled out of the room, leaving Mirko and Jules looking at each other. Mirko beckoned her close to him, straining to speak, but she held up a hand and passed him a pad of paper.

'I'm sorry you're not too well today,' she said, in solicitor's sick-visiting tones, watching him as he scribbled. 'No, no, don't strain to talk. I've brought you *The Times* and the *Mirror* for light relief. And some chocolate,' she added. 'I'm sure the staff nurse is going to ask me to go soon, but is there anything else you would like? Bananas? I could get them sent in.'

Mirko handed her the pad and she put it back into her handbag, still babbling about fresh fruit. The door opened behind her to admit the nurse, looking harassed and suspicious, but she smiled at him anxiously from the bedside chair, and Mirko got his cough going again.

'I'll wait outside,' she said, as the nurse struggled with the pillows.

He came out, a long five minutes later, during which she had had to exercise enormous restraint not to look at the writing pad in her bag. He scowled when he saw her.

'I'm sorry,' she said, 'he isn't well, is he? He coughed and he couldn't really speak. I didn't know quite what to do. I was awfully relieved when you came back.'

The scowl eased. 'He really isn't able to receive visitors.'

'I see that. Oh. Oh, dear. I left grapes and chocolate. You don't think he'll choke on them.'

That drew a patronising smile and a pat on the arm. 'I'll make sure he only gets what he can manage, don't you worry. Now, can you find your way out?'

She confirmed she could probably do that, ran down the stairs and got into her car. She waited to be let out of the gates, her handbag tucked beneath her knees in dangerous proximity to the clutch, while the gate guard gave the interior a cursory look and waved her through.

Chapter Eight

She stopped the car at a chippie that the legal fraternity used when visiting Pentonville, and ordered the full breakfast. She took a cup of tea to strengthen herself before she read Mirko's message: 'Please, I must talk with Dr Flowerdew – Martin, now, soon, or get to him a letter, please. I can be ill...he will be able to help me.'

Well, that confirmed that as, she had thought, Mirko was controlling his present environment. She folded the note as the meal arrived and got herself outside it in record time. With breakfast inside her – and three calls on her phone – she realised she had to accept she was living on borrowed time. She had to work out, here and now, what to do about Martin Flowerdew who was involved somewhere in this mess. And she had to decide what to tell her governor, her mentor, Paul.

'Jules?'

She looked up from the pad and there, unbelievably, was Martin Flowerdew, all six feet two inches of him, immaculate in a sports jacket and blue shirt, a Westminster Hospital Trust pass clipped to the Gucci belt that held up a beautifully cut pair of grey trousers.

'What are *you* doing here?' they both asked, while she flipped the pad shut and put it back in her bag.

'I tried to visit Mirko,' he said. 'The people on the gate wouldn't let me in. I did leave him some grapes and a paper, and some chocolate. You're laughing. Do you think they won't get past the guards?'

'*I* left him grapes and chocolate and *The Times*.'

'Ah. Well, he got the *Telegraph* from me. So, did you see him? Yes, please, I'd *love* breakfast. Thank you so much.'

The ordinary customers in this place, she reflected, had to march up to the counter to put in an order and take the drinks themselves. The girl behind the counter had found the look of Martin irresistible and was standing by their table watching him indulgently, while he squinted at the menu on the wall and wondered aloud whether he would skip the mushrooms but have everything else. Something about this peacock display made a decision for Jules, and she took the pad from her bag and planted it in front of Martin.

'I saw Mirko, but I didn't let him speak. This is what he wrote.'

Martin read it, twice, his face gone into straight pulled down lines. He was still a good-looking man, but a different one, and she watched him with the food curdling in her stomach.

'Have you...what were you going to do if I hadn't walked in here?'

'I would have got hold of you. He asked me to find you before.'

'Did you tell anyone? Of course you did, you had to.'

'No, I didn't.'

His breakfast arrived and by the time the counter girl had found him the mustard, and the ketchup and the vinegar, and topped up his cup of tea, and as an afterthought offered Jules a top-up, he had collected himself.

'You think he can't talk without the police hearing, right?'

'It is the working assumption we at Jenkins Associates all make.'

'You're probably not wrong.'

'How well did...do...you know him?'

His head lifted but he didn't look at her until he had taken a mouthful of tea. 'Only quite.'

'He really wants to talk to you. He is faking sick, by the way.'

'Yes.'

She lost patience. 'Or you could tell me why you think Mirko wants to see you so urgently and I could tell you whether it sounded material to the case.'

'And if it did?'

'Yes, well, then you'd have to tell the police or I would. But lots of things people would rather not have publicised, have nothing to do with...well, with what the police are looking for.' He is going to tell me, she thought. He was looking at her very carefully, weighing it all up.

'Jules.' Paul, looking like a hungry and very angry bear with the wild hair standing out in a halo effect, had just taken in Martin Flowerdew, who had half risen in his chair, alarmed.

'Paul,' she said, quaking, 'meet Martin Flowerdew, brother of Andrew, Mirko Dragunoviç's last legal employer. Martin, Paul Jenkins, my senior partner. I met Martin here by chance, Paul. I only...I thought that someone ought just to see how bad Mr Dragunoviç was, and you and Jenni were not there...' She could feel her voice trailing off – he was plainly furious.

'I was hoping to visit your client.' Martin gathered himself to charm. 'On my brother's behalf.'

Paul waved at the girl behind the counter who came running with tea and a fried bread sandwich.

Jules gave her the slitty-eyed what-happened-to-*you*-sister look, which bounced off her. She stood, hands on hips the better to display the bosoms, all her energies bent on one heavily married bloke, and one bloke who wasn't interested, Jules observed. After a bit the girl went away reluctantly and Paul asked Jules, through a mouthful of fried bread, whether she'd got in to see Mirko.

'For about three minutes, long enough to see our client was alive, voiceless but not otherwise obviously worse than yesterday.' Jules, thanks to her upbringing was a good liar, swift, unhesitating and convincing, even with her closest associates.

Martin was making bill-paying gestures, and the counter girl beat her boss by a couple of yards to the table.

'I will buy,' Paul said, spitting crumbs and gesturing with his right hand. 'For the firm. Mr Flowerdew, give Jules a number so we can ring you as soon as Mr Dragunoviç can talk again, yes?'

Martin wrote down all his numbers for her; Paul, even stuffing his face with fried bread, was not usually ignored or disobeyed. She took the chance to give Martin all her numbers in the hope he would later tell her whatever he'd been going to when Paul arrived. He left, saying goodbye with his usual charm, but he was in flight and she knew it. She considered her boss cautiously: his temper seemed to have recovered.

'I frighten away your admirer?' Paul asked.

'Hardly.'

'No. You young women, so clever, so sophisticated. I am never sure what you know. So he is perhaps an admirer of Mirko?'

Right on the button, she thought, feeling chilled. 'Dunno,' she said, casually. 'Maybe he and Farmer Flowerdew just feel responsible for Mirko. In a feudal sort of way.'

Paul gave this serious consideration, the beautifully drawn eyebrows going up in a peak. 'Could be,' he conceded. 'You give me a ride back? I came by cab from the courts.'

Not wanting to risk this year's Mercedes saloon in this district, as he did not need to say. She wondered if Martin had found his posh Jaguar as he had left it.

They got in to find the usual post bank-holiday rush, the waiting-room full of the weekend's casualties some of whom needed to appear tomorrow to answer bail. Jenkins Associates' practice was to extract them from the cells if possible on a 24-hour-a-day basis, but the other newly qualified people on the criminal side had been doing the routine Easter duty and had got well behind. Jules worked like a dog till four o'clock, seeing people and getting the paperwork straight. She was just stacking files, tired out, when she heard a tap on the door and opened it to find Jenni Patel with a tray of coffee in her hands, a totally new experience. Other people brought Jenni coffee in her world. Jules managed not to gape at her.

'Thank you very much, Jenni. I was just trying to get tidied up before I go home and a coffee is just what I need. Do sit down,' she added, seeing that Jenni was showing no disposition to leave.

'I have a favour to ask of you,' Jenni said. 'My sister and her husband – they live in Canada – are coming over for two months next week. They had arranged to rent a flat but it has not worked out. Susie says you perhaps are wanting to let a room in your house?'

'Not to a couple,' Jules said, alarmed. 'Really not. The room is only just a double, and I...'

'No, no. They would have my flat. It is I who need a room, just while they are here.'

Jules tried not to look as staggered as she felt, but obviously failed. Jenni, colour showing in the perfect dark ivory skin, tried a merry laugh. 'It seemed, well, logical. We work at the same place, and it would be only for two months.'

'It is logical, and you would be welcome.' Jules was ashamed of herself. Anne had always been clear about the sacred laws of hospitality, and Jules felt she had been Unwelcoming, a cardinal sin.

'That's very good of you, Jules. If you are sure, it would be a great help to us all. I am not sure what the going rate is but I will be happy to pay it. I understand other people are paying £800 a month for a room in a shared house, but I could pay more, if...'

'£800 a month would be fine, Jenni.'

Two months of that would make a very useful contribution to the credit card debt, Jules reflected, and surely she could stand anyone for two months. If she liked the company then she could get someone else when Jenni left.

'But you need to see it. You'd have your own bathroom, but...'

'Would it be convenient if I came to see it now? When you are ready. I could drive you. I am sure I will like it, but I need to see how much space...so I don't bring too much.'

'Jenni, of course. In ten minutes?'

'That would be wonderful.'

With these standards of civility the next two months might even be pleasant as well as profitable, she thought. They took both cars, Jules thinking how shabby hers looked and felt the spirit of emulation stir. With all this rent perhaps she might get something a bit newer. She pulled herself up from this fantasy. Jenni's rent was spent already, and she realised as her eyes focused, that the familiar Volvo parked right outside her door contained Gwyn.

'I came by on the off-chance,' he said, a big grin all over his face, wiped smartly off as he saw Jenni.

'Wonderful,' Jules said, hastily, and introduced them, conscious of embarrassment. Gwyn had probably arrived wanting only her full attention in every sense of the word. She explained that Jenni might be coming to live with her, gave them both a drink and took her upstairs with her orange juice clutched in her hand. At least the spare bedroom was tidy, although she would have to snatch some of her clothes from the wardrobe, and the neat bathroom for which she was in hock to Barclaycard, was gleaming and immaculate. She suggested Jenni take a good look at the cupboard space and sprinted downstairs to explain to Gwyn, sitting gloomily at one end of the sofa, a large whisky two thirds empty in his hand, that this was only a temporary incursion.

'I need to go about eight.'

'No worries.'

Jenni's manners were *very* polished, Jules conceded. She emerged after five minutes, did the tour of the kitchen and living-room and garden, exclaiming with pleasure over every detail. She was clever with Gwyn too, while making it clear that she was about to go somewhere else she put him at his ease with a gentle flow of chat. Gwyn had relaxed and was turning on the charm, Jules saw, with affection.

'Another drink for you, Jenni?' he asked, hospitably. 'No? Jules, cariad, can I do you another whisky?'

She said no, on consideration, but Gwyn levered himself to his feet and got at the bottle and gave himself a double before returning to grill Jenni about her immigration work. This could go on, Jules thought, crossly, but Jenni was gracefully extricating herself and saying her goodbyes.

'Intelligent girl, that.' He was angry, she saw. 'You didn't tell me you were taking a lodger.'

'It just happened. I need to pay for the bathroom.' She looked at him, distressed. 'I didn't think about, well, us. She's only here for two months. Does it matter? I mean...'

'No, cariad, no, not really, I suppose. If she knows who I am, well...after all, we could just be friends with clients in common.' He was frowning, and she felt a cold chill. Why had she not thought this through?

'Sorry, my love, I really don't think I can say no, now. I'll just...well...explain enough so she isn't here when you come.' She burrowed into his chest, hoping that would ease the situation.

'It's…well, sorry cariad, it's your flat but we have to be careful. This case is putting a lot of pressure on the dugouts and jobsworths in the system. They hate me.'

Gwyn did not compromise with idleness or time-serving, or passing by on the other side of the road in people who were supposed to be looking after his kids, the ones like she had been.

'I'm sorry, but…well, it's only for a short time.' And, she thought, with a pang, I'm lucky to see you here once a month so we may not be missing that much.

'Cariad, don't look like that. Can we have tea?'

'Or better, take a cup upstairs,' she said, relieved.

He was tired and so was she, and for once they laboured in vain and finally she got him to agree that he would come even if she couldn't.

'I don't know why I can't today,' she said, as they lay in bed afterwards.

'You didn't expect me. I was an intrusion.'

'Yes. I guess. Sorry. You want food?'

'Stop apologising, and yes. Race you down there.'

She felt much better with a meal inside her, but saw that Gwyn didn't.

'Go,' she said, pulling his head down to kiss him. 'I'd like to keep you for a good night's sleep, but since that's not on, go home.'

'Yes.' He got to his feet, shoulders rounded in the way they did when he was really tired. 'Look after yourself. Your asylum case OK, is it? Sorry, I never asked.'

'It's reasonably OK. Off you go.'

She watched him leave, and when he'd gone she straightened up the kitchen, getting in practice for having Jenni as a lodger. She was restless, it was only 8.30 and there was nothing on the TV, so she was pleased when the phone rang.

'Richard Allenton.' She got her brains into action, smartly. 'I wondered if you'd like to come out for a drink.'

'Now?'

'I could pick you up.'

She had nothing better to do and she was worried about the

Dragunović case. She still felt that she had let Mirko down and, guiltily, that she was interfering to no purpose, but perhaps Richard Allenton was going to tell her she didn't need to, because clever old MI5 had done it all.

'I'll give you the address.'

'I have it. See you in ten minutes.'

So he was at Camden nick, she thought, running upstairs to comb her hair and getting a minimal make-up on. She looked at herself in the wide mirror above the basin – sex, even not wholly successful, had given her a glow. It was not however, she acknowledged, entirely sex with Gwyn but the prospect of time with Mr Allenton that was adding a bit of sparkle. She put on lipstick, pursed her lips censoriously at her reflection and fled downstairs as the bell rang.

He'd had a shower by the look of him. His shirt was clean and crisp, his hair washed and springy, and either he'd had his suit pressed or he had more than one in a tidy dark grey. They looked at each other with mutual interest, just as if this was a proper date, and all the way to the quiet pub in the backstreets of Kentish Town they made polite and somewhat stilted conversation.

'No one has told me if Mirko is any better this evening.'

'No worse.' Richard, for so he had asked her to call him, on the basis that when she called him Mr Allenton he looked round for his father, handed her a whisky. She had had one with Gwyn earlier and thought she would be safe to stay with it. 'Why do I think he is exaggerating his condition?'

The soda in the mouthful of whisky blew back through her nose, but she managed to stay cool. 'He was coughing his heart out this morning, so I stayed no time at all. Isn't a cough what pneumonia does?'

'Perhaps. His temperature's stable.'

'Well, I hope we're all pleased about that.'

'Yes. He'll have to talk to us sooner or later and we're getting on without him. But we need your help too.'

It sounded too much like help as in helping the police with their enquiries, and she prepared to lie if need be. Richard was looking awkward. 'We wondered…well, it's the Cardona clan. You knew them as a kid. Could you draw an organisation chart – who is related to who, that sort of thing?'

'What about the Education Authority?'

'We tried. They threw away the records up to 1990. Doesn't give us much to go on with your generation and the next one up.'

She was disposed to co-operate just as long as they stayed off the subject of her delinquent client, so she closed her eyes and thought. She had been in and out – more out than in – of the Wisbech school system for four years. She had moved from Falloden Primary – the name came back into her head, although she had not thought about the place for years, to Collingfield Primary.

'Have you paper and pencil?'

She started on the left-hand side of the middle of the pad with Ray and Sharon Cardona plus a couple of younger siblings called Peter and Eff. Eff was a girl, but she had no idea what Eff was short for. She moved over to the right-hand side and added Kevin Roberts, deceased, and his sisters Jeanie and Alice.

'Can you do dates of birth – I mean the year? Month, if possible?'

Falloden Primary had celebrated birthdays, no doubt, as a welcome change from trying to teach an intractable group of caravan dwellers and travellers, so she did better and got the months for the ones in her year and they estimated the years for the rest. She made a stab at the older Roberts and then remembered – she could not think how all this came up from some hidden reservoir in the brain – that there were three Cardona cousins called something very foreign which no one could spell. Caused a good deal of innocent merriment at the beginning of term among the limited numbers present.

'Kara,' she said, tentatively, then heard a sullen long-forgotten voice saying, bitterly, 'Karadic'. 'Peter,' she said, concentrating hard. 'Alex, errm, Joanna.' She had a shot at their years of birth, counting down and up from hers in 1972 and got as close as she could, although she was less confident as she said to Richard, who was staring at her, his drink forgotten. 'What?'

'Karadic. A Serb name. Were they in school for long?'

'Couple of years, must have been. The father came in and hit one of the teachers. The kids were excluded, I remember now.'

'They were – are cousins of your friend Ray?'

'Their mother and Ray's mother were sisters.'

'Ray's mother was a Roberts?'

'No. Ray's aunt – his father's sister, therefore a Cardona – married Kevin's father, as his second wife.' She was writing in names at the top of the page. She had been very interested in families having no one but a mother and a father, both orphans by the time she was born. And before she was ten it had been life and death to know who was related to whom and would bring down gang revenge if you tangled with them. Anyone with Cardona blood could call out the others like a swarm of wasps. She shared this thought with Richard as he took the paper from her and read it very carefully. 'Thank you very much, Jules.' He put it reverently into a plastic folder.

'You can have my fingerprints just by asking.'

He was a little slow to catch on, then he saw it and laughed. 'Very useful. I hope...well, I hope it didn't bring back bad memories.'

In fact this particular exercise had been like doing a crossword puzzle, she had enjoyed it and had been lifted by the unmistakable respect she was getting from MI5.

'What have you found, then, Richard? Fair's fair.'

'Indeed. We have a corner of a network. It's very large, as you must know.'

'Not really. Remember it's not my subject, I only got Mirko by accident.'

He turned in his chair and raised a hand and the man at the bar acknowledged. 'About 80,000 immigrants come in every year. Those are the ones we admit because they've got family or they've come to marry. We get another 80,000 odd as asylum seekers. Mostly economic migrants. Those are the ones in the camps and on food vouchers. They're not my worry however.'

'Yours are the illegals. The hidden ones.'

'Yes. We think there could be another 30-40,000 a year of

them. They're not coming in round the West coast nor through
Scotland. They come from the points on the Continent nearest
to us.'

'Dover?'

'We've virtually got *that* stopped. So they're coming all the way
up the east coast. We've probably got 30,000 illegals working
now in the eastern counties. And tens of thousands just across the
North Sea all the way back to the Balkans waiting to come. We've
found some of the agents in Norfolk and a lot of the employers
in the last few days, but we're only picking up the little ones. It's
a very tight organisation, run on the cell principle, like early
communists. Each person only knows two others.'

'Kinship networks,' she said, the whisky loosening her tongue.
Gwyn had taught her about them. 'No matter how rigid a
political or business structure, a kinship network is stronger.
That's why you wanted to get the Cardonas straight. You knew –
I take it you *really* knew – that Kevin Roberts was part of the
organisation.'

'We really knew. We have another member of his cell.' He was
watching her like her maths teacher used to when she was close
to getting an idea.

'The cells are discreet,' she said, remembering Gwyn, 'and self-
sealing, but kinship networks override any other organisation.
You may work for ICI or whatever this lot is called, but you are
a Cardona first, last and all the time. So telling a cousin, who is
like a brother in travelling circles, what you are up to doesn't
count.'

'Must be right.' He was unsmiling but impressed.

'So my chart may give you a link.' She looked into his face. 'It
has given you a link? Worth buying me a drink.'

'The chart was one hell of a bonus. I wanted to ask you out
anyway.'

He is MI5, she reminded herself. They do not deal in telling
the truth. A shrilling noise from his chest made them both jump,
and he fished out a phone and listened, his face setting into sharp
lines. 'Right. On my way.' He shut the phone off and looked at
her. 'Sorry, I have to go. I'll take you back.'

She could feel the whisky as she clicked on her safety belt, and she decided not to volunteer any more brilliant insights. They arrived, both of them silent, and Richard, she thought, already miles away. He came back to her as he opened the car door.

'Jules, thank you.' He hesitated, looking down at her. 'You know whatever it is your client doesn't want to share with us, we'll have to get it. Tomorrow, the next day, however sick he is.'

She looked up at him, deadpan. 'Goodnight, Richard. Drive carefully.'

Chapter Nine

(Wednesday after Easter)

Jules woke up very slowly, recollecting as she rolled painfully out of bed all the heroines who leapt into track suits and went for a run when they woke up with a hangover. All she seemed to be able to manage was to drink coffee, very slowly and incompetently, to have a shower and wash her hair with the wrong shampoo, the one she bought by mistake. Somehow it was two and a half hours later by the time she got out of the house, and then she had to go back because she had forgotten something. So it was 9.30 before she got into her office and by then the work had walked in off the street. She scurried through the waiting-room, head down, looking neither to right nor to left, like a waiter with too many tables to handle. But, like a good waiter, even when she wasn't looking, she found she had seen, and turned halfway up the stairs to greet Andrew Flowerdew.

'Andrew. You know Paul has taken over the case. And Jenni.'

'I do. It's not entirely about the case... And at any rate your receptionist says both Paul and Jenni are out.'

She looked to Louise who nodded in confirmation. So Paul really can't blame me for trying to help, she thought, and took Andrew up with her. She gave him the visitor's chair which, though not comfortable, was built to carry weight. He looked placid, as usual, but she could feel he was tense.

'I'm glad you are here, because I need to talk to you.' She had seen with the clarity that comes with a hangover that this was her best chance of clearing her lawyerly conscience. So before he could tell her anything other than how he took his coffee she told him about her visit to Mirko and his message to Martin.

'And Martin didn't get in to see him,' he said, thoughtfully. 'Do *you* know what it is?'

'I think Mirko is faking sick – well, faking some of it anyway – until he does talk to Martin.'

'And you told Martin that?'

'Yes.' She hesitated but ploughed on. 'I wondered if it might be a personal thing, which may be irrelevant to the case and very embarrassing for Martin.'

'Like what?' He seemed to have got bigger, sitting there, and he was redder in the face than when he first arrived.

'A sexual thing, I assumed.'

Andrew looked at her, tight-lipped, the colour rushing up his face. 'I don't believe it.'

'Better than a criminal thing.'

Andrew was extracting himself from the chair and she waited for him to storm out of the office, but all he did was walk over to the window. He seemed to be unable to speak, so she tried again. 'Martin can talk to Mirko, somehow. Or he can tell me, or his own lawyer. But he can't leave it as it is.'

'You want me to talk to Martin?'

'Yes. *I* can't leave it either, on the off-chance it is relevant. You're pissed off, I can see.'

'It's not you I'm cross with, Jules.' He turned again to the window and she opened her mouth to do something like reminding him that sex between consenting adults, whether hetero or homo, was not a crime. She thought better of it.

'Andrew,' she said, cautiously, having allowed what felt like several hours to pass, 'why did you come this morning? Did you have something you wanted to say or ask?'

A short unamused laugh. 'I was going to visit Mirko, just to see – well, that someone who had worked for us was all right. I thought it would be easier to get to see him through his lawyers.' Another long pause. 'Then I was going to ask you to have lunch.'

'And I blew it. Damn.'

He breathed out, his shoulders shifting. He looked very large in the tiny office, but he was a neat mover, avoiding the twin hazards of filing cabinet with a drawer open and awkwardly placed dusty fan. 'I enjoyed Sunday,' he said, addressing the window.'

'So did I. Very much.'

'But I must talk to Martin.' He made to sit in the visitor's chair, thought better of it, and put both hands on its back to lean over it and look at her. 'If I...well, if I can...well, if it works out, can we eat another meal together?'

'I'd love to. My turn to buy.'

He looked at her steadily, then grinned. 'It's only lunch.'

'It's the principle of the thing.' She was feeling a fool and had started to blush. 'Shall I ring and see if you can see Mirko?'

'I need to see Martin first.'

Yes, he did, she conceded, and took him downstairs. He slid into the car that was outside waiting for him. There was a woman in the driver's seat, very good-looking, and she felt a pang of disappointment for a minute. Then she realised that the woman was wearing a uniform, so her friend Andrew had a chauffeur. She watched them go; he was speaking into the car telephone before she had even pulled away into the traffic, leaving her revising her views on the profits available to gentlemen lettuce farmers.

She went upstairs deciding she had a phone call of her own to make before unleashing the floodgates, but Jenni was just arriving, collecting her first client, a woman in full downtrodden Muslim kit – dusty, black, long robe, topped by a depressing grey head-dress.

'Mirko is a bit worse today, Paul says. Paul is applying to have him moved to UCH.'

'Why?'

Jenni paused to make sure her customer was being fielded and made to sign forms by Louise. 'Paul feels that Pentonville may be out of their depth. There is a UCH specialist he wants him to see.'

'I bet UCH won't be keen. They don't want prison guards or policemen in the hospital.'

'No, quite right, they don't.' It was a bit like the voice of God in volume and omniscience, but she realised it was Paul coming in from the tiny car park. 'I wanted to get a specialist into Pentonville. That they have agreed, for today if the man can do it.' Which would, Jules thought, give Andrew Flowerdew time enough to find his brother and find out what was going on there.

'Jules. Are you there? Telephone.'

She made signs of apology but decided she need not have bothered. Jenni had seized her opportunity and was following

Paul to ask if she could have a word about a case. He's more patient with her than he is with me, she thought, crossly, but then I don't sit there lost in adoration while he speaks.

'Richard Allenton. You alone?'

'Hang on, I'll shut the door.'

'I'm in Norfolk.'

'Very flat, is it?'

'Not the bit where I am. I just want you to know that we are getting somewhere, thanks to your family tree. I'm on my way back. I wondered...can you come out to dinner tonight?'

She could hear police station noises around him, phones going and people talking to each other. 'I can.'

'Great. Wonderful. Look, I'll pick you up at 7.30 unless...well, if anything's holding us up I'll call you. OK?'

She put the telephone down, grinning. Her social life had always swung from feast to famine – and she assumed that to be true for everyone of her age. Two men keen at once was nice to have and for a moment she felt very cheerful. Not even the thought of Martin Flowerdew worried her. If he'd had it off with Mirko, she reasoned, perhaps it had predated Mirko acquiring HIV, or Martin, as a doctor, had practised safe sex like everyone was supposed to, and she always did, knowing all about sexually transmitted diseases. I was lucky, she thought, not for the first time, my stepfather could easily have been HIV positive, as well as nursing a persistent penicillin-resistant gonorrhoea.

She picked up the phone and told Louise she was free to take on whatever she had in the waiting-room, but she said Paul wanted a word. He was by himself, looking harassed, papers in piles all over his desk.

'Jules, I have problems today. The mother of Mirko is arriving at Gatwick, after lunch. She has telephoned. A man from the Home Office – that means MI5 of course – turned up to meet her.' Jules had forgotten that Mirko had parents, or at least a mother, and was momentarily pleased for him just before she remembered that she had another son too, in a drawer at the Pentonville mortuary. 'Yes. So. Exactly. I should go, because she should not confide in MI5 but, well, I am in Court on pleadings for Mrs Hastings, Jenni is also in Court, in Stevenage, and there is only Teresa...'

Teresa was the other Newly Qualified, but Mrs Hastings was up for murder and this preliminary hearing was critical. It would be practically Contempt, she conceded, for Paul to send a Newly Qualified instead of himself.

'I'm sort of free. If you don't mind me doing it.'

'I would rather not involve you again in this case, but I do not want her talking to all and sundry. So please, you will pick her up and bring her at once to me afterwards. She speaks very little English.'

'Of course. Is there a father Dragunovič?'

'He had a heart attack. No, he is alive in hospital.'

So it had fallen to Mrs Dragunovič to travel to a foreign country to visit one son in hospital and another in the morgue. The heart-attack option sounded more attractive.

'Do I have to go to Gatwick?'

'No. You meet at Pentonville.'

'They don't need her to identify the body, surely. Mirko did that.'

'No, no. She wishes to *see* the body.'

People usually do want to see their loved one, however dead or disfigured, as Jules well knew. At fourteen she had demanded that she be left with her mother's body and blessed Gwyn had insisted that she be allowed to. And they had both been right. Jules's mother had been in pain and frightened, and suddenly all that was over and she was resting. And an hour after she had died she wasn't there any more and Jules knew she need not worry about her ever again. But her Mum hadn't been lying on a beach for two days like Stefan Dragunovič.

'Jules, I am not happy with this case.' Paul managed to sound reproving which set up a resistance in her.

'Well, blimey, who would be? Our customer seriously ill in police custody, his brother dead and his aged mother arriving. That'll teach me to be here on Thursday before Easter.'

Paul's hands flew up to ward this off. 'I know, I know it is not your fault.' He paused. 'When he came, Jules, did he ask for a lawyer, or…'

'He asked for you, Louise says. You are well known. I could have said I couldn't take him on. I mean I nearly did. He obviously didn't trust me, did he, giving a false address.' Paul was silent, looking at his blotter which was annoying her. 'If you'd been here, Paul, and heard the same story, what would you have done differently?'

'The right thing would be to have told him to go straight to the police. Or to have taken him there at once.' She winced, but he went on. 'You see, Jules, I know this is not your work, but you will understand because it is the same with a criminal practice. We have to be very careful what we do. The police do not want these people, the refugees to be here, they are a nuisance, they are unpopular. You know the police are largely working-class with all the prejudices of the ignorant against the refugees.' Shared by me, she thought, mutinously, but Paul was in full flight. 'And the ones they hate more than the refugees are the lawyers, who insist that their clients be treated properly and in accordance with the law.' That *is* true of criminal lawyers, she conceded, silently: they were viewed by the police as an obstacle, part of the criminal fraternity. 'So in order to be able to do our work at all we must always be strictly within the law. We must not allow our clients to involve us in their illegal activities. And I begin to be afraid that this is happening here.'

And with reason, she thought, guiltily. She had given Andrew Flowerdew a few hours to sort out whatever it was between Mirko and his brother, but in the interests of her future, she decided to give Paul a clue. 'I'm sure Mirko is hiding something. It may or may not be relevant.'

To her relief he brushed this aside. 'Also, I am not happy with MI5.'

'No, well, I daresay others feel the same.'

'In *this* case and these MI5 people, Mr Allenton. You know that he is ex-army and was in Bosnia. Then in Kosovo.'

'But surely MI5 people have that sort of background?'

'Yes. But just as with the police who deal with criminals, always there are some who forget which side they are on.'

'What are you saying, Paul?'

'Just that...well, I have nothing I can tell you as proof. But, Jules, be careful. Remember there are wrong ones in MI5 as in the police, yes?' He looked at her. 'I say this to you particularly because you are the best, the most capable trainee I have ever had, and I want that you have the success you deserve.'

He waved her from the room and she went slowly upstairs torn between pleasure at the compliment and deep anxiety about the case.

Andrew Flowerdew did not ring, and two hours later, still burping from the cheese sandwich she had eaten too fast, she went off to Pentonville again and waited half an hour on the steps for Mrs Dragunoviç and an escorting MI5 man. Mrs Dragunoviç turned out to be enormous, wreathed in dusty black, but not old, in her fifties at best. She spoke very little English just as Paul had said, so in the end they fell silent until the MI5 man, receiving a signal from somewhere, indicated that it was time, and they proceeded solemnly into the mortuary.

Jules and the MI5 man stood either side of Mrs Dragunoviç as the drawer was trundled out, ready to support her. The MI5 man had warned her in Serbo-Croat what she was likely to see, but she turned even paler and swayed on her feet. She motioned them away sharply, eyes on the swollen, purple face, then, after a minute, bent slowly to kiss the awful head on the brow, steadying herself with a hand on his shoulder. The MI5 man took her arm as she straightened up, eyes slitted against the tears which were pouring down her face, and she staggered slightly as she turned to leave. Jules helped to support her from that dreadful room, banging into the furniture because she found she too was crying, but she managed to get the older woman to sit down in the little office and drink a cup of tea. Jules was trying to stop her nose running and her throat swelling like a blocked drain when Richard Allenton appeared in the doorway. He looked at them for a moment, then jerked his head at the MI5 man who followed him out.

'I would like to wash with water,' Mrs Dragunoviç said, carefully, through hiccuping sobs, so Jules took her teacup from her and called to the assembled forces of MI5 to tell her where to find the Ladies. She took Mama Dragunoviç there and leaned against the wall outside, blowing her nose. She had to *stop*, she told herself, this was someone else's tragedy and she was supposed to be a lawyer.

'Jules? There's another place if you'd like a wash,' Richard said.

'I'll wait. Thank you.' She might not be at her best, but Mrs Dragunoviç needed her. She managed a gigantic inelegant sniff which cleared her sinuses and fished out a comb so that she would look less like a refugee herself.

'I'll get you some more tea.'

She nodded, still unable to speak coherently and he went off. Waiting in the afternoon silence, she realised suddenly that she could no longer hear Mama Dragunoviç and knocked on the door, cautiously, calling her name with increasing urgency.

'Out of the way,' Richard was at her side with his attendant spirit. He knocked, calling in Serbo-Croat. 'Christ. Get some help, Mark.'

'Do you think she…?' Jules closed her mouth on whatever idiocy she was about to utter and Mark came running back with two men in white mortuary coats. It took a long time to get through the door; it had a bolt and no one had any heavy tools and the only window was tiny. Richard Allenton, wielding an inadequate screwdriver gashed his left hand to the bone but went on grimly trying, pouring blood. Jules kept getting pushed out of the way by increasing numbers of cursing men, and when finally the door yielded, Mrs Dragunoviç was found slumped sideways on the lavatory, skirts hitched up to show mottled thighs, her face purple, and congested, alive but not conscious. Stroke, the paramedic said, authoritatively, and Mark from MI5 went with her in an ambulance to UCH, leaving Jules with Richard Allenton nursing his hand and swearing steadily.

'I must see Mirko.' Jules had left his mother to the mercies of MI5 and the NHS on the basis that her duty was to her client and she was going to see him come what may. 'And I must ring Paul.'

'Yes. Fuck, that hurts.' Richard had been seized by one of the mortuary staff, armed with Dettol, who was presumably unused to working on live patients. 'Wait, will you?'

'All I'm going to do is to tell Mirko his mum won't be coming. And that I must do.'

He didn't like it, but the medic did something else to his hand, and he yelped and dug his teeth into his lip, so she escaped. She looked round for the male nurse; God alone knew what effect this latest disaster would have on a man who was definitely ill, even if not as ill as he had been pretending. And, she confessed to herself, she was dreading the interview to which a sense of duty had driven her, and she badly needed the presence of another human being.

It was not the same nurse as she had seen before and her heart sank. But he was young and Irish and sympathetic, and she explained what had happened and who she was, as quickly as she could, and he nodded intelligently.

'I wondered why the ambulance was using a siren, now. In the main, there's no, well…'

'No urgency?'

'Indeed not. Ah, dear…well…there's a terrible thing. I would be offering myself to tell your man, but I only came on last night. I'm a temp, well, I'm pretty regularly working here, but I'm not employed and I don't yet know him well. I'm Will by the way – William Cliffe.'

'William,' she said, 'that's very kind, but it wouldn't be right. I'm his solicitor and it is for me to break the news.'

'Just now?' He was looking ather, doubtfully, and she saw his point.

'Can I have a wet flannel?'

'Of *course*.' He found her one and she did what she could about her face.

'The great man was here today, so he was,' he said, watching her.

'What did he say?'

'Well, he was very kind. Said Mirko been well looked after but he thought it was worth giving him some blood. So we are.'

'Through a drip?'

'Yes. He is complaining about it.'

'Thank you for telling me.' She hesitated but she knew she had to go.

'I'll come with you.'

'I would be grateful,' she said, meaning it.

They went down the corridor together. Mirko was propped up, a drip running into his left arm, his eyes were closed and she felt her heart lurch, but they opened, slowly.

'My mother?'

She sat down beside him and told him, softening it as much as she could. 'In an hour, Mirko, I will ring up and we will let you know how she is.' She looked at him anxiously, his eyes closed and he started to shake and there were tears pouring down his face. 'I'm sorry, it's rotten luck,' she said, uselessly.'

'I'll get you some tea,' William Cliffe said, pressing his shoulder, leaving Jules to hold his hand. She remembered she needed to tell him something, and decided to take the risk. 'I passed on your message – to Martin himself,' she said, quietly, and he nodded to show her he had heard. They were sitting silently when William returned with a tray of tea and a grey-faced Richard Allenton, arm in a sling. In pain as he obviously was, he was gentle with Mirko, without getting into the trap of making things sound more hopeful than they were. Mirko listened unmoving, then said something sharp and interrogative in Serbo-Croat, to which Allenton replied in the same language. Jules looked at him reproachfully.

'I was confirming that Mrs Dragunoviç had visited…had seen Stefan's body.'

And keeled over at the sight, so now Mirko had a brother dead, a mother in hospital here and father incapacitated in Belgrade, all because he had fallen for a pretty face. She could think of nothing to say to anyone. Richard told her to go, he would follow. She sat outside, trying to work out what to say to him but was distracted by her phone buzzing. She had ignored it several times this afternoon, but Andrew Flowerdew might be trying to get through, and she still had an office and other clients. The reception was no good behind the high walls and she walked out into the courtyard.

'Jules.' Richard was dead-white and a bit short of breath as he arrived. 'Hang on. I was just asking that your client be put on suicide watch. Don't want to lose him.'

'No, I suppose that wouldn't help the investigation at all.'

He looked impatient and she thought of apologising but decided against it. His face, now she looked at him properly, was tight with pain.

'Richard, you're not in any shape to go out to dinner tonight, are you? Do it another day?'

His shoulders sagged, and she started to assure him that of course she would eat with him but was it actually sensible when what he needed was his own bed.

'I don't want…I want to have dinner with you. Even if it's a bit later. All this…' he looked round the policemen talking into mobile phones, 'is going to take a while to sort out. Fuck.' He wiggled the fingers of the injured hand and they both watched the bloodstain seeping through the bandage.

'That doesn't look right. Did they stitch it?'

'No, I wouldn't let them.' He looked at her. 'I was in a hurry. I am in a hurry.' He had turned so pale that she felt able to signal urgently to Jimmy Watt to come over and help her return his wounded superior, protesting to the medical help clustered at the mortuary.

'They're used to sewing people up, Richard.'

'Thank you so much. That's just what I was thinking about.' He clenched the good hand on her wrist. 'I still want to see you.'

'I have to run, I'm late. Call me.' She hovered anxiously as the medical help received him back, pulled on gloves and started to unwind the bandage. Then she decided to go, in case he felt unable to yell and scream and curse with her in the audience.

She got herself out of the gates and pulled out the mobile phone, ignoring the waiting messages in favour of finding Paul. For once he was there, with a client admittedly, but she told Lou to insist. She told her story in as few words as possible.

'She is conscious? No. She is…?'

'They don't know, Paul. They took her to UCH and I am sure you can convince them you're family.'

'Did you talk to her at all?'

'Her English is poor, like you said. No, I tried to be civil, but she only wanted to see her son.' The silence at the end of the phone rattled her. 'What else could I have...?'

'No, no, I wondered only what she was like.'

'Old. Very overweight. Dressed in black.'

'Most revealing, thank you, Jules. This case. It gets more confusing at every minute.'

Jules clenched her teeth, determined not to apologise yet again for involving the firm with the Dragunoviç clan.

'And Mirko?'

'Not at all well. Your man came by just after lunch and prescribed something new and different, which they are running into him through a drip. And he is being watched.'

'Watched?'

'In case he tops himself.'

'Yes. Yes, well, that is wise. I am surprised that your Mr Allenton is as compassionate – no, of course, he needs him perhaps to answer more questions.'

Jules managed not to rise to the description of Richard Allenton as hers, but noted that Paul was really angry with her over this case. Last time I even try to do immigration, she thought, but was brought up short by the recollection that she would not have met either of her two recent suitors had she rejected Mirko Dragunoviç.

She asked coldly if Paul had anything more and assured him she was on her way back to the office to finish up the work she had abandoned in order to help him with the problem of receiving Mrs Dragunoviç. She heard him laugh, and smiled to herself; Paul always recognised a fair point.

Once back in the office, she worked fast and sat back after an hour to think what else she could sensibly do about the Dragunoviçes for whom she seemed to be responsible. Anne would provide illumination or guidance, but at this hour she would be at the House of Lords and you could never find anyone there. Despite this she rang the House who assured her that a message would be left, and then Anne's mobile, which was answered in a hoarse whisper.

'Anne?' she said, shaking the phone.

'Shsh… We're not…hang on.'

She could hear voices, then silence, then Anne, still sounding like a burglar. 'Is this a bad time?'

'No, darling, we're not supposed to have our mobile phone on, and I was at a meeting in Bruce's office.'

'Who's Bruce?'

'The Chief Whip. Oh, the embarrassment. Not your fault, mine. I crept away because there were other people, but I must go back. What can I do?'

'It's just like school there, isn't it? Do you have to change into indoor shoes when you come in from the playground?'

'Not yet. But what a good idea, I must suggest it to the Committee.'

'What Committee?' Jules asked, rattled.

'House Administration of course, darling, do try.'

'Well, I wouldn't want to get you detention. Do you want to ring me back?'

'No. Tell me.'

Jules told her of the Mrs Dragunoviç saga, to satisfactory cries of distress and sympathy.

'Horrid for you. I suppose one has to say she is better with our own dear NHS than whatever they have in Belgrade. I wonder about that actually. Where is she? UCH, oh, well, they're good there. What else are you doing?'

Jules told her, comforted by the solid recital of decent Crime she was getting on with. 'But Paul isn't…well, very pleased.'

'Oh Paul. Look, darling, it won't be the first time he has had to deal with something nasty, one of his people dragged in over the doorstep. It goes with the territory he has chosen for himself. Immigration even more than crime.'

Anne's cheerful confidence was always infectious, Jules thought, admitting only a small treacherous thought that Anne dealt exclusively with very expensive commercial contracts rather than the Jenkins Associates workload and might just not know whereof she spoke in this case.

'How is that nice young man who brought you to Cambridge? Oh, I'm sorry to hear – I daresay he will be better soon. Darling, I ought to go back, but...'

Jules assured her she had just wanted to chat, and went back, soothed, to her caseload. Anne went back to the meeting and dealt as quickly as she could with the issue, volunteering for a job she had meant to avoid in order to get herself out of the room. She sat in front of a cooling cup of tea in the Bishop's Bar, a small room with a ridiculously high ceiling and too much dark furniture, tucked off the corridor to the library, and worried, and wished for her husband, still away with his dam. Henry would be able to tell her whether she was, once again, being burdensomely overprotective of the child, but Henry was not here and she could not readily imagine communicating her worries over an echoing radio telephone link at some strange hour of the night. She rose and went in search of an oracle, and ran it to earth in the far reaches of the Library, tripping over the outstretched legs of a slumbering fellow Peer. She apologised profusely and settled the man back to his afternoon sleep, watched sardonically by Beryl Williams.

'Beryl, have you had tea? Good. Please come and have some...oh, you're writing a speech.' She was, she realised, sounding like Jules.

'For tomorrow, my dear. I'll be glad of tea.'

They got themselves settled, Beryl patiently refusing the sandwiches and cakes pressed on her by Anne.

'Could you tell me about Yugoslavia, Beryl?'

'Known now as Former Yugoslavia. In how many words? And why me? Jamie Parten is the expert.'

Anne thought about Lord Parten, who had been in Dubrovnik training soldiers sometime in the 1930s, and still had the maps to prove it. 'It's the ear trumpet, Beryl. I can't quite cope with explaining what I want.'

Beryl sat, placidly, under a substantial oil painting of Pitt the

Younger, and indicated some further explanation would be needed. Anne, mentally agreeing with her, sought to get her enquiry into manageable form.

'I suddenly realised that when Jules speaks of her Serbian illegal immigrant client, that I really know not very much about the country, or what might have brought him here.'

'Mm. Her client comes from Belgrade, as I understood the matter. And is therefore probably Serbian.'

'That's right. As is her senior partner Paul.' Anne decided that the quick way was to expose the full extent of her ignorance. 'I have not, to my shame, quite understood who is who in Former Yugoslavia. Are all Bosnians Muslim, for instance? And why do they all go in for murdering each other? I mean, the country was peaceful for years, we all went there when we were young. Very cheap, very touristy. I suppose I never quite grasped where it all went so wrong.'

'That bit is easy. There have always been savage divisions inside what we used to call Yugoslavia, but after the Second World War until his death, President Tito held the whole country together. No one was allowed to murder anyone else on racial or religious grounds.'

'I remember, don't I, that the Serbs were on our side in both World Wars.'

'Indeed they were. And the Croats – who are also a Serb race but a different one, fought alongside the Axis powers, specifically the Germans.'

'But Tito still managed to make everyone get on after the war. A very strong man.'

Beryl drank tea, thoughtfully. 'Not quite strong enough to deal entirely with the underlying problem that in the end is the cause of all subsequent troubles. The Serbs who occupied much the biggest part of the country have for six-hundred years at least been under pressure from the Turks who wanted to spread east and were naturally acquisitive.'

'And who were – and are – Muslim.' Anne felt she was beginning to grasp the problem.

'Indeed. So Tito on the whole got them pushed back, and also kept the Croats in their place. But when he died in 1980,' she paused to wave to a colleague, 'the whole, forcefully held, country started to fall apart. Macedonia seceded. Croatia seceded, and the Muslim Albanians started to put pressure on the borders. So Serbia – that's where Belgrade is – began to feel isolated and surrounded by hostile forces. The precipitating problem was the secession of Bosnia which the UN supported.'

'Leading to war. But some Bosnians were Serbs.'

'About half of them, and they felt extremely threatened and appealed to their Serbian brethren over the border for help. The Serbians are aggressive and good soldiers and, as I say, they were threatened, so they retaliated and started to push the Muslim Bosnians out of the country.'

'Ethnic cleansing.'

'Just so. Culminating in a war, a ceasefire and then the tragedy of Srbrenica. The UN forces were there to keep the peace, although it could not be claimed that there was a peace to keep. At Srbrenica, this was proved finally and fatally; the UN forces ran for home ignominiously and the Serbian soldiery, aided by local Serbs, massacred probably 100,000 Muslims. It was a dreadful failure.'

'So that is who was in all the graves they keep digging up.'

Both women fell silent, Anne remembering the pictures she had seen recently on the BBC News of devoted forensic archaeologists picking through craters of skulls and bones, watched by a chorus of women in black head-dresses, weeping, their hands to their mouths in agonised anticipation.

'And that,' Beryl said, 'is why ex-president Milosevic is on trial at the Hague and why UN forces are struggling to find the rest of the offenders to bring them to trial.'

'Struggling? Yes, they are, aren't they? Why?'

'Because most of the Serbian people – and of course Milosevic himself – have never accepted Srbrenica as a war crime. They felt that their soldiery were fighting a war under orders and that they should not be tried for obedience to orders legitimately given. The Nuremberg defence.'

'Which we never accepted. I see. But Milosevic surrendered –

or as I remember thinking at the time, someone surrendered him.'

'Well, he went a bridge too far, in Kosovo. He set out – with the full support of his people – to push all the Muslims in Kosovo back where they came from. To Albania where indeed most of them had come from and which was a horrible, backward, murderous society from which anyone might have wished to flee.'

'But we stopped him,' Anne said, gripped now by the story.

'If by *we* you mean the Americans, yes, that's right. For not very creditable reasons. Refugees – Muslims – not wanting to go home to Albania were being pushed over all the other borders and threatening the stability of several neighbouring countries. The international community simply could not afford a refugee problem of that scale, so the UN doctrine of non-intervention in the internal affairs of any country unless it threatened people outside its borders was stretched to cover the case, and the Serbs were defeated and driven back, and heavily sanctioned. In the end, as you suggest, Anne, they gave up President Milosevic. But – you may not have noticed – the recent elections gave seats in the Serbian national parliament to a couple of people whom the UN forces are pursuing as war criminals.'

'There is no acceptance in Serbia of that particular judgement,' Anne said, slowly, and caught Beryl's considering eye.

'Classic of Jurisprudence,' she said, apologetically. 'Law has in the end to meet with general acceptance or it has to change.'

'In this case I do believe that it is the Serbian popular view rather than the law that will have to change, and indeed it is. But very slowly, and many of the worst criminals will probably not be brought to justice. Or not in my time.'

Beryl was in her early eighties, Anne knew, but she found it difficult to think of her as mortal.

'Ah,' she said, passing over the point. 'Thank you, Beryl. So – well, what happens now?'

'Difficult to tell, but the one sure answer is that all those countries wish to join the European Union by 2007, if possible. So far, the line is being held that countries must come to the table with clean hands so far as human rights are concerned, and

Serbia, at the moment, cannot be invited to join. Maybe over time they will give up the more conspicuous of their war criminals.'

'In order to get their feet under the EU dining-table.'

'Precisely so,' Beryl agreed. 'It is a poor country with very limited opportunities for their young which is always a dangerous position for politicians. That poverty of opportunity would certainly explain Jules's client.'

'It would. It does. Well, thank you, Beryl, I feel much better informed.'

'Is Jules involving herself with the young man we met last weekend?'

'She won't say, but then she never will. She keeps her cards very close to her chest, and I don't like to press. She isn't, when all is said and done, my daughter.'

Jules had got home from the office, and checked her phone to see if there was a message from Richard Allenton. None, and nothing on the mobile, so she stood, irresolute, trying to decide whether to give him up and heat up a battered packet of frozen macaroni cheese when the doorbell rang. She opened the door and Richard Allenton stood on the step. His arm was still in a sling and more blood had seeped through the bandage on his hand, he badly needed a shave, and he was in a filthy temper. He and Jules stared at each other, and she saw that Jimmy Watt, looking grim, was behind him.

'What?' she asked.

'Where have you been since I saw you?'

'In the office. Why? What's the matter?'

'Mirko Dragunoviç. He died suddenly, probably about an hour ago.' He was glaring at her, and she felt sick.

'How? I mean what of?'

'An embolism. A bubble of air from the tube in his arm.'

'The one he was getting blood down? Oh, God. His mother!'

'Still unconscious.'

'Why are you here?'

'The tube had been tampered with. Can we come in?'

'By somebody?' she said, giving ground and leading them to the kitchen. 'Are you sure? I mean don't tubes block themselves?'

'Very rarely. And the somebody used gloves. You were one of the people who were with him today.'

Jules who had automatically reached for the kettle, put it down again. 'Why on earth would I have wanted to hurt him? He's a client.'

'We are talking to everyone who saw him today. He was a witness, and my best lead. And he was lying like a flat-fish and I needed him to talk sense.'

They glared at each other.

'Sit *down*, Richard.' He was so pale, she thought he might collapse, and she was feeling terrible herself. 'You cannot seriously believe,' she said, holding the kettle under the tap, 'that I am in the business of murdering clients. Or anyone, indeed,' she added, thinking about it. 'I didn't notice the tube particularly, only that it was *there*. Could it have been put up wrongly? Sugar in your tea?'

'Yes. Yes, please, that would be good.' He had relaxed and was looking appallingly tired, so she put the macaroni cheese in the microwave and shared the result plus a few hastily boiled eggs between the three of them. Her visitors, she noted, ate like starving wolves and looked very much the better for this unedifying meal.

'You really think – you do believe he was murdered? I mean, might he not have committed suicide, what with his mother ill and brother dead.'

'We did think of that, and the nurse and one of our people were checking him every fifteen minutes.'

'Every fifteen minutes?' she echoed, thinking about it.

'Well,' Richard Allenton said, with a sigh that came from his boots. 'Almost every fifteen minutes. The male nurse checked him and went off shift, then our man checked him after fifteen minutes. Then his relief was late, so he nipped off to the canteen and when he got back after twenty minutes he thought Mirko was still asleep – he hadn't moved. The night nurse did the next check, but he was gone – had died, I mean. Then they found the tube had been interfered with.'

'So it could have been Mirko?'

'No. His prints weren't on the tube. He hadn't touched it. There were only smudges as of gloves.'

'Oh,' Jules said, inadequately. 'The nurse – that nice chap William. Would he have noticed anything?'

'He hasn't got home yet. We have a man waiting for him.' He looked at his watch. 'Thanks for the food, Jules. We need to go.' He looked at her and bit his lip. 'I'll catch you up, Jimmy.'

They waited, watching each other, while Jimmy Watt clumped off down the corridor.

'Not the dinner I intended,' Allenton said. 'Can we do it properly later in the week?'

'Yes. Yes, of course.' She paused. 'I just realised, I don't have a client any more. I must ring Paul. He doesn't know.' She rose, flustered, from the table and he caught her with the good hand. 'We'll ring him,' he said. 'You can if you want, of course, but we'll do it anyway.' His hand felt very warm on her arm. 'I'm glad in one way that…that you don't have a client. I mean it's less…' He stopped, colour showing under the dirt. 'You liked him, though.'

'I was very sorry for him. And I can't quite believe it.' She sat down, abruptly.

'Damn.' He hovered, irresolutely. 'I must go. Look at that.' Another set of lights was flashing in the road. 'Is your flatmate in? Or can you go to your…to Lady Barlow?'

'I'll ring Anne anyway.'

He let go of her arm and used the good hand to pull himself out of his chair. 'I'll call you,' he promised, and was gone, to join the flashing lights.

Chapter Ten

(Thursday after Easter)

Jules slept badly, although she lied, loyally, to Anne, who had rung her first thing to check that she was all right. She arrived in the office at 8 a.m., head aching, and Jimmy Watt followed her in.

'My guv'nor wants to talk to you.'

'What must I do?' She was unstable with tiredness and reaction. 'Get into a car with you, or wait here until he feels able to speak?'

'He said to check if you were here all morning, and he would come by. He's had a long night and he's getting his head down for a couple of hours.'

She looked at Jimmy and realised that, although he was tidy and shaved, he'd had a long night too. She found them coffee and emptied the biscuit tin in his honour. Watching him eat the best chocolate ones, she was painfully reminded of Martin, herself and Paul, all deluging poor Mirko with chocolate, grapes and papers. Only three days ago, and it was then it actually hit her in delayed reaction, that someone had killed Mirko. He hadn't died because he was ill. He'd been murdered.

'Who did it?'

'What, killed Mirko? Took you long enough to ask.' He looked at her and what he saw made him pour her some more coffee and put too much sugar in it. 'My guv'nor wants to talk to you himself, but…but we're no further on that than when we saw you.'

'You found Andrew Flowerdew?'

'We did. He says he went in about 5 p.m. – after you – never went near the tube, just looked at Mirko, who was asleep – really asleep – and went again. Mirko was asleep not dead, when the bloke on duty – not the nurse – looked at him at 7 p.m. He listened to him breathe.'

The door to the office banged open, and it was Paul; she could see him reflected in the glass.

'This is a tragedy,' he said, without preamble. 'Any news, Mr Watt?'

Jimmy, stolidly brushing off crumbs, explained that we awaited a call from Mr Allenton.

'And that poor woman. The mother.'

Indeed, the mother, and what was the matter with her that she had failed to ask, Jules wondered.

'No change. Still unconscious as of' – he looked at his watch '– an hour ago.'

'One hardly knows what to hope for there.' He considered Jimmy, still eating biscuits. 'Mr Watt, we are always glad to see you, but I would like to talk to my associate.'

Jimmy got up hastily, knocking the biscuit tin over. He was frightened of Paul, she noticed again as she picked up the tin and followed Paul into his office.

'You had a bad day yesterday, Jules.' Paul was not given to sympathy. The reason they all stuck to him like glue was not his charm of manner but because he supported them, right or wrong.

'I'm still having one. I'd forgotten about Mrs Dragunoviç. I'd only just remembered about Mirko. I don't know what's the matter with me.'

He looked at her across the desk, his brown eyes very wide under the broad forehead. 'You did not, I suppose, either kill Mirko or cause his mother to have a stroke?'

'No. No, I didn't, although for a while there, I think MI5 thought that I had.'

'Tell me.'

She recited the events of last night and he shook his head. 'I think I have said to you before that I am not very happy with Mr Allenton. Impulsive.'

'Well, perhaps. A bit.'

'And I thought also that he had taken a fancy to you.' She felt a slow, uncomfortable blush starting from the collarbones. 'I can see that Mr Allenton would be made bad-tempered by thinking a woman he...was beginning to like was involved in murder. I understand now why he was so angry when he spoke to me last night. Perhaps I forgive him.' He regarded her more benignly. 'And you are expecting to hear from him again?'

'This morning. About Mirko's death.'

'Ah, yes. Now that is what I wanted to talk to you about. We have of course no longer a client.' She nodded. 'We also have incurred expenses for which there will be no reimbursement.' He looked into her face. 'My dear Jules, we must think of these things.'

'Without feeling the need to send a bill to either of his smitten parents, I hope. What about *them*? Don't we act for Mrs Dragunoviç?'

'Not without instructions. And she is not conscious.' He looked at her. 'Of course we write all off. And, Jules, I am very sorry for the young man and his family, but if I am honest with you, I am glad that we should not be more involved. There are dirty waters around this case.'

'I know you'd rather we hadn't taken it on. You told me.'

'I'm sorry, Jules, I know you had become a little involved. You have lunch with me? Tomorrow?'

This was a treat, rarely bestowed, and then strictly in rotation, and it wasn't her turn. 'Well, I'd like that very much if you have time.'

'I make time. At one o'clock?' He sat down. 'We'll go to Mr Sen Gupta.' The posh local Indian, her favourite. Paul was the only person in the office who used his proper name, and she resolved to do better. As she got to the door he called her back. He was looking at the front page of *The Times*. 'Jules. Surely this is your friend. The social worker. Mr Jones.'

'Yes.' She felt herself blush.

'He is against some bad people there.'

'Hackney Councillors. Yes.'

'Perhaps them also, but I was thinking of others. The people not on the Council who protected these, these monsters. Some among the police.'

'Yes.' Three policemen had been allowed to retire as being ill, and Gwyn had told her there were others just as bad who were still serving.

'Mm. He is a brave man. Please give to him my congratulations when you should next see him.'

She went and sat in her office; it was just early enough for the customers to be still clustered outside. There were always a few outside the plate glass window, looking at their watches, peering hopefully in to see signs of movement. She had done it herself with Marks & Spencer when she was in a hurry, she thought, amused, as if one of the girls checking a till would open up early just for her. She was doing something just as daft at this moment, watching the telephone as if she could make it ring. She needed Andrew Flowerdew to phone, because unless he did, she would have to tell the first policeman she saw today about Martin Flowerdew. Mirko was dead; she could stall no longer.

The phone rang, obligingly, but it was Louise, and she had to ask her to say it all again.

'*Mister* Flowerdew – or rather two Mister Flowerdews – would like to see you now, Jules. I'll give them the coffee to bring up with them.'

'Where's Paul? On the phone? Damn.' She shot into Jenni's empty office to borrow her visitor's chair, nearly knocking Andrew back down the stairs as she came out backwards, lugging out the chair like an ant. Martin was three steps below him with the coffee tray. They sorted themselves out and she got behind her desk to take command of the meeting. The Flowerdews filled the spare space in her office.

'Gentlemen. What can I do for you?'

Martin was looking at his hands, and it was Andrew who spoke.

'I...we...think Martin needs a solicitor and we have come to ask you if you will act.'

She felt a deep chill. 'Why? Why will Martin need a solicitor?'

'We have a firm who does wills and conveyancing and all the company things of course. They don't seem very clued up on...on...crime.'

'Most commercial firms aren't.' She was too anxious to go on using the third person to conduct enquiries. 'Martin, why do you need us? What is it you are accused of?'

Martin managed to stop looking at his hands and considered the blotter instead. All the bounce had been taken out of him, he had shrunk into himself and looked wretched. 'They will think...I may...' He bit his lip and got his head up and looked at her. 'I may be accused of helping Mirko.'

'To do what?'

'To...to overstay.'

Well, it was what she had expected, but she felt as if a lump of lead had settled in her stomach and she could taste the Nescafé she had been absently drinking. 'Right. Stop. Don't tell me any more. I'm going to need to consult my senior partner.'

Andrew nodded. 'I nearly started with him, Jules, but I thought you...well, I thought we'd let you know first.'

So that she would have time to confess to Paul that she had been concealing something that might have been relevant, he meant. She gathered her forces. 'May I take you down to the waiting-room while I explain to Paul?'

'Certainly.' Andrew stood up and indicated to Martin he should do the same; it was as if the room had filled with trees. 'Jules. Whichever way – I mean whether you decide you can act or not, I intend to pay Mirko's legal costs here.'

'Why?'

'He worked for us.' Andrew simply sounded surprised, and it came to her that he was probably paying Mirko's mother's expenses too.

She would rather have been shot than face Paul at that moment, but she reminded herself that she might still have to deal with Richard Allenton and seeing Paul didn't seem so bad on a scale of one to ten. He was still on the phone so she had to wait a few minutes, but she stayed in the waiting-room to make sure Louise didn't sneak another phone call through to him. Andrew read the *Financial Times* which he must have brought with him. Martin just sat and looked at his hands. The rest of the clientèle didn't need any other entertainment – they looked at the Flowerdews, taking in their good clothes, their size and their colour, and sneaking the occasional look at Jules to see why she had involved herself with the White Anglo-Saxon Protestant ascendancy. She got in to see Paul, and explained, head down and brooking no interruption, wherein she had sinned, adding that she would have got Martin to see Mirko or told both him and the police about the whole thing this morning. Paul was, unusually, speechless.

'I'm sorry. I thought…' She closed her mouth. To her relief Paul had got his voice back.

'Jules. What has he now told you?'

'Nothing else, other than what I told you.' She managed to look at him, but he was looking at a pile of papers on his desk as if it could speak.

'I do not…I am not comfortable with this, Jules.' Nor her either, but the least she could do was stay silent. He was obviously going to say that they couldn't act, and she was working out which of the other firms in the business would be best for the Flowerdews. 'I had hoped we had seen the end of this case.' She sat up; Paul did not use the conditional carelessly. 'However, we are, as a firm, already much involved.'

'Because of me.'

'Yes, because of you and also because…well, I do not like to have a client die in police custody.'

'You don't think they did it?' She forgot she was rather lower than an earthworm this morning.

'Well, Jules, the consultant did not. Nor did you. I have met once the older Mr Flowerdew and I understand he was not by himself for more than a very short minute, nor is he very likely as a person. So who, then?'

'I've been thinking it was accidental – you know, a blockage in the tube, and air got through.'

'We must all hope so. Better than murder. So I will see the Messrs Flowerdew, but if we take them on it will be Jenni who assists me.'

She had seen this coming. 'I know you don't – you think it better that I should not be on the case, but this is crime, not immigration law you'll be dealing with. And you're busy, for hours of the day for the next few weeks with the Thompson case.'

Paul was doing that one as lead advocate, he thought that barristers were a waste of space; the solicitor had to be in court all the time anyway, why not do all the work ourselves and save the clients money? He was also very good at advocacy and he liked it, the showmanship, and he was physically impressive, with all that dark hair and commanding height. She watched him think – he was one of the rare people who was prepared to sit thinking his way through a problem while everyone waits. She was desperate to work with him on this one; she wanted to make up for whatever she had contributed to Mirko's death and she really, really didn't want Jenni to know how badly she'd slipped up.

'Yes. You have a point. And Jenni is not free. Well, at least you should take the notes. Ask them in.'

Andrew was still immersed in the *Financial Times*; Martin was distractedly flipping through *Woman's Realm*. Her ten o'clock customer, a small Somali woman, was there already, ten minutes early, rising hopefully from her seat, so she assured her that she would not be much delayed. It had started to rain and the day had turned grey; the trouble with a glass-fronted waiting-room was that the weather was right there with you, she thought, gloomily.

They had the firm's second best conference room – Jenni appeared to be conducting a mass meeting of some immigrant group in the best and biggest – and arranged themselves in pairs opposite each other at the table. Andrew opened the meeting by thanking them for what they had done for Mirko – not a lot, she thought, but still – and announced that he would be responsible for their costs. You could see, she thought, that he was used to dealing with professionals. Many of the clients treated the firm as if it were the Social, alternating between pleading and truculence.

'We were not instructed by you, Mr Flowerdew; what cannot be claimed from legal aid is our concern.' Paul equally was used to real clients, the sort who paid their own bills. One all. 'So. Tell me how we can assist you. Both of you.' To get the client to define what he wants was a sound rule for lawyers as well as for social workers.

'We – my brother and I – need representation and advice in

dealing with the police and MI5.'

'Of what are you accused?'

'Nothing, but he – we – are potentially involved.'

'In what?'

Jules was not contributing. In a difficult meeting lawyers operate in pairs, one to talk, one to watch and listen and take notes. Same with the police.

'As you know, I employed Mirko Dragunovič on my farm – along with 180 other young men and women – three years ago. This is a Home Office scheme under which they stay for eleven months. It is how we get two thirds of our labour. Many of them come from farming areas in Yugoslavia because we – Martin and I – had both spent time there and knew people there. Nearly all go back at the end of the year with a substantial nest egg.'

'And the others? The ones who do not go back?'

'There are only one or two a year. Until Mirko, these were young women who married men they had met here – our drivers, in fact – and were therefore able to stay.'

'But Mr Dragunovič stayed illegally.'

'Yes.'

'Were you in contact with him after his term here expired?' Paul, with a new or difficult client, withdrew his own personality, so that all his questions came out like something out of the air. They all tried to copy him, but Jules felt she came out like a speak-your-weight machine and made the clients anxious.

'*I* was,' Martin Flowerdew said, looking past both of them.

'You helped him to stay?'

'No I didn't. I'd met him when he was working for us, but I was as surprised as Andrew when he went AWOL.'

'But you helped him at a later stage?'

'Yes.'

'How?'

'With money – cash. I couldn't help with jobs, though that's what he wanted. He wanted a job in Addenbrookes. In Cambridge. At the time, I was working there as a houseman.'

'And Andrew, if I may, you knew about this?'

'Not then. Not at the beginning.'

'Martin. Why did you help Mirko at all?'

'I was sorry for him.' Andrew stirred in his seat, and Martin winced.

'Were you involved sexually with Mirko?' Jules's senior partner asked, still in that impersonal disembodied voice, and she braced herself for confession time.

'Briefly.' He was looking at the desk. Andrew's face was set like something off a tomb.

Jules felt quite sick, but her head cleared in time to hear Paul asking if Martin's employers were aware of his sexual orientation.

'Oh goodness, yes. Hospitals are full of us, Mr Jenkins.'

'So. You were aware that Mr Dragunoviç was HIV positive?'

'I am now.'

'And yourself?'

'I am a doctor, Mr Jenkins. I do not – I only engage in protected sex. And I am regularly checked – as all surgeons in the employ of the NHS are, these days.'

Paul was looking baffled, though you would have to know him well to realise that, and she felt the same. What was Martin doing here, in such a state?

'That isn't why I came to see you. It's another youthful idiocy. No. I don't feel like that. I'm just not sure I'd do it again, not that I can repeat that particular folly…'

Jules was watching Andrew who was looking exhausted, weighed down by old burdens. 'Martin,' he said, heavily.

'Yes. I was in Yugoslavia. In Bosnia, with *Médicins Sans Frontières* for a year in 1995. You've heard of them?'

They had heard of them, and Paul indicated as much to get him going again. 'I treated a woman, a Croatian girl. She was a student of seventeen years old. She'd been raped by…well, a number of Serbian soldiery and left pregnant, infected, in need of surgery… She got to us after, oh, six weeks. She was at Srbrenica.' He looked away, they all remembered the pictures on the news, the women crying for their husbands, the girls who had been raped, still dumb with shock and shame and anger, looking away from the cameras.

'I did what could be done for her but it was six weeks after the attack that we got to her and in the end the only thing to do was a hysterectomy.' He looked at us lawyers. 'There wasn't anything left for her – her father and three brothers were killed when…when she was left for dead. The mother had died long before, and the girl, Alyssia, just wanted to get away and make a new life for herself.'

'So you helped her?'

'I married her.' Jules felt her jaw drop, and even Paul looked startled. 'Well, I wasn't going to want to marry in the ordinary course of events, and I could get her into England that way. We shared a flat here for a couple of months, but I…found it difficult, and I think she did too, and nobody from the authorities had visited, so I moved out and she found someone to take my place. She is in the last year of a degree at Queen Mary College.'

It was just as well, Jules thought, that she had a non-speaking part.

'Who knows about this marriage?' Paul, on the other hand, was proceeding methodically.

'The Home Office knows, of course, but I don't believe they keep records, or not where they can find them. My employers know – I'm down as married but living apart, which doesn't cause any real surprise, given that they know I'm gay.'

Jules had managed to start thinking again and had the feeling she was missing something. Martin and this unknown, damaged girl had been legally married. She'd been here for, what, more than three years. It was a gallant action of which he had reason to be proud rather than otherwise, so what was the problem?

'Where is your wife now?' Paul asked.

'I don't know.'

All four of them knew he was lying and she waited for Paul to nail him.

'If the marriage was not a real one, you could be accused of aiding her to enter this country illegally. Could it be said that this is not a full marriage?'

'Yes. She, I fear, is never…is not going to be able perhaps… And I can't. It's not just being gay, I operated on her.'

'And you lived in the same house for only three months?'

'Yes. So Alyssia has got frightened and has moved, and I really need to find another way to help her.'

They sat, listening to Paul think.

'Mr Flowerdew, why is it now urgent to…to regularise your position? Is your wife being pursued in some way? Has something gone wrong?'

Oh, good question, Paul, Jules thought, with respect. He had disentangled effortlessly the Mirko plot which Martin had got off his conscience, and gone to the essential point.

'Yes. Well…yes.'

They waited for him.

'It goes back to Srbrenica. Where she was injured.'

'Yes, Mr Flowerdew?'

'They're arresting people for that now. There were survivors, there were witnesses, dead and alive.' There were indeed; mass graves seemed to be being found and opened every day, with terrible pictures in all the newspapers. 'And one of her friends from school who'd got out made enquiries for her and found her. We married there, you see, so the girl found Alyssia's married name. And suggested to the UN people that she would be a very useful witness.

'And Alyssia does not want to do this?'

'She is afraid.'

'Of what?'

'Oh, I thought I'd said. That she would have to go back. The Home Office seem to have lost touch with us, so we haven't had to prove we are living together as a couple. She thought if she became visible again, then…'

'I see. Also she might not wish to revisit the history again.'

Martin Flowerdew had obviously thought about this one and was shaking his head. 'No, that's not it. I wouldn't press her – I mean I couldn't, having seen what I saw. But she says she would know the faces of the soldiers who…well, I don't know whether she would or not, but she would give evidence if she could be assured that she could stay here, in the UK.'

Well, *that* made sense, Jules thought, deeply relieved. And why should the Home Office not want to help the UN and turn a blind eye to any irregularities in the marriage. She glanced at Paul who was looking as stone-faced as Andrew Flowerdew.

'Yes, I have to say…'

'You don't think it is as easy as that?' Andrew said, bluntly.

'No. But please, I will consider all the possibilities before I advise.' He sighed. 'I should see your wife, Mr Flowerdew. She is the real client; and for all sorts of reasons, mostly compliance, I have to see her. And I need to see her passport and some evidence of her address. Else I cannot act. I am sorry, this is bureaucracy and it is not sensible, but there it is.'

The money-laundering legislation of course, she recalled drearily. None of them could take on a client without knowing exactly the identity of the person seeking advice. She had got away with Mirko precisely because he hadn't become a client that Thursday; he was a walk-in who was entitled to receive a one-off piece of advice which is what he had got. And even then she was probably a bit close to the wind, not that anyone was going to care about it now.

'I can't do that.' Martin Flowerdew said, heavily. 'I promised her that she would not have to reveal her address.'

Paul spread his hands. 'I wish I could help more. Please. Talk to her. She cannot live in this worry. She is only a young woman.'

Martin sat, sunk in misery, and Jules caught Andrew's eye. He gave her a tiny nod which both she and Paul recognised as an acknowledgement and a declaration that he would try and talk sense into his brother and sister-in-law.

'You have met Alyssia of course?' Paul asked him, curiously.

'Yes indeed. Martin thought that I should know her in case – well, in case anything went wrong. A very brave girl.'

To whom he was not attracted, Jules noted with pleasure.

'I am sure she has nothing to fear if she has evidence of value,' Paul was addressing the top of Martin's head. 'Does she…did she…know, remember any names? No? Anything about the soldiers?'

Martin's head came up. 'Ah yes. She knows the battalion. And the platoon.'

'Oh really? But this…this must be valuable. How?'

'She remembers the cap badges and the number below them. They were drunk and they were in full uniform.'

A silence filled the room and Jules saw a hut in a camp with the soldiers, noisy, shouting and egging each other on, with the last of the UN forces – the Dutch, she remembered, hazily – scrambling for transport, hopelessly outnumbered.

'I could – well, we could find a way through channels if looking for some guarantee. On a conditional basis of course.'

Martin was watching him, looking hopeful. 'What do I need to do?'

'Best if she would come and see me, so I could know what. But also possible if you could get her to write a statement. Just for me – she is right, your wife, in not wanting to use the information too freely, until she has some guarantees.'

'I'm sure that's right,' Andrew said. He had relaxed and Jules understood that he had been saying much the same things to Martin and to Alyssia, presumably without getting any result.

The meeting rose, but Paul signalled her that he wanted her to stay behind. In any case, Andrew did not seem to want her company, and she realised that he intended to try and keep his brother on the course they had agreed, and wasn't going to let him out of his sight. She waved them off and went back to Paul.

'He knows of course where his wife is,' he said, sombrely.

'Oh yes, of course he does.'

'Please Jules, you do the note before you go home? I would like Jenni to see it. I am obliged to you for being here, but…'

'But it's not my case. I agree, I agree, I know bugger all about immigration.'

She finished the note, gave it to Paul, and did a couple more bits of urgent stuff, then decided to go home. It was one of the last days she would have the place to herself; Jenni would be moving in at the weekend. She parked the car in front of her own door and got out.

'Jules?'

She couldn't see him for a minute, because he was behind her in his ancient Volvo Estate. She went to kiss him.

'What are you doing here?' She slid into the front seat. 'Has the Inquiry stopped?'

'For the afternoon. The judge is talking to the lawyers.'

'No good can come of it.'

'I know. Look, my love, something's come up.'

'Come in and tell me.'

'I can't come in.' He wasn't looking at her and when she put a hand on his knee he jumped.

'What is it, Gwyn?'

'The press are all over this Inquiry.'

'Yes.'

'And they're looking for more evidence of abuse and scandal.'

'There's money in it. For the victims, I mean,' she pointed out. Jenkins Associates had had several graduates of the Hackney care homes come into the firm, asking about the possibilities of suing for compensation for their treatment. They had all been told to wait for the outcome of the Inquiry; it was clear already that Hackney were in for a tanking.

'Yes. So it's a fertile field.'

She realised that Gwyn, her capable, never flustered, infinitely competent Gwyn was having difficulty. 'What is it, really, Gwyn?'

'I had a call. From the *News of the World*. They say they had heard that there had been a complaint about me and a child in care, and would I be instructing solicitors.'

'You and a boy?' Boys was what the Hackney case was about.

'A girl. And eleven years ago.'

'What?'

'I wasn't that bothered at the time. I just told them it was nonsense, and of course I wasn't going to be instructing solicitors, having nothing to instruct them about. When I put the phone down I thought about it. The date is a bit…precise.'

She could see him now, eleven years younger, thinner than he was now, but looking as exhausted as he did now, standing in the relatives room at the hospital. It was just her. Her stepfather had gone to the pub, and her mother was dead. The hospital had called Gwyn who had taken her home with him to Sandra, rather than try and find a place of safety. It was the sort of thing the best social workers did in those days, rather than push a bewildered, bereaved kid into an institution while their parents were dying. 'Sandra was there too,' she pointed out.

'Oh, indeed. Yes, all of that. And I suppose I shouldn't be surprised. Nothing about this Inquiry should come as a surprise, but it still does. Anyway, my love, I thought I'd better warn you.'

'And Sandra?'

Gwyn and Sandra would invite her to lunch a couple of times a year and she had them to dinner irregularly. Gwyn and she had never discussed it but they both knew that Sandra would smell a rat if Gwyn saw her regularly and she never did. These occasions were not at all awkward, Jules enjoyed them and would forget that Gwyn and she were lovers and fall back into being a privileged child of the house.

'I thought I wouldn't. We all get funny phone calls. Judge Lawton does as well.' Gwyn was looking uncomfortable.

'Fair enough. I'll let you know if I get funny calls.' He wasn't done, she saw.

'My love, what with this…I think we'd better not see each other until the Inquiry is over.'

'Which is when?'

'Another six weeks.'

It seemed like eternity and she was upset but she agreed, reluctantly, she had the lawyer's horror of the Press. They said goodbye, but they didn't kiss. The thought of the *News of the World* hung over them both, and she went into her flat, feeling chilled, but reminding herself that the laws of libel protected them unless a paper had real proof which would not be forthcoming.

Chapter Eleven

(Friday and Saturday after Easter)

Her days seemed to be falling into a routine. Go to office, early, find Jimmy Watt hanging round in a car outside, give him coffee and biscuits, and wait for Richard Allenton to ring up.

'I'm not holding my breath, Jimmy,' she warned, but Richard had rung almost instantly. And an odd call it had been too. He had asked whether any of the half-Cardona Karadic cousins had retained any connection with Bosnia.

'I've no idea, Richard. I was *ten*, I don't think I knew about Bosnia. Why?'

'Just an idea we're following up.'

She gave up and waited for him to remind her that she had promised to have dinner with him, but he rang off without mentioning it, and she settled irritably down to work on decent, honest crime for a couple of hours. Then Andrew Flowerdew lifted her heart by asking if she would dine with him on the Monday. 'I'd like to see you before, but I have to stay here. The police are causing a terrific stir, turning us all over.' He was sounding irritated.

'Your farm? The one I saw?'

'No, the one on the coast.'

She had managed to let this passing red herring lie. There was no sign of Paul or of Jenni, no one she could ask about the case, so she went off for a quiet lunch. Louise accosted her as she came back.

'Call for you, five minutes ago. Mr Peter Mahoney.'

'Who's he, Louise?'

'One writing man. I ax who he and what he want. He did'n wan tell me but he from de *News of the World* and he wan talk about de Hackney Inquiry. What about de Inquiry I ax him, we not involved, and he say he unnerstan we have client who gonna sue.'

It would have been routine had this not been the *News of the World*. Paul's standing instructions to clients and associates alike were not to talk to those people, you can't win. And that it was the *News of the World* who had talked to Gwyn. She stood, thinking; she had once asked a friend who worked in a big firm what they did about newspapers. We have a Press Office of course, she had said, bewildered. The big firms did not live on the same planet, but it gave her an idea. 'Louise, use your posh voice and tell him that you're the Press Office and ask him how you can help. Don't help, of course, but offer to get back to him.'

The phone rang and they both looked at it suspiciously but Louise picked it up. 'Mr Allenton for you.'

'Jules. I have a favour to ask. Can you come up to Norfolk tomorrow, early, and look at some people for us?'

'Live people?'

'Indeed live people. We've got some dead ones too – that's not public by the way – but it's not them we want you for.'

'Where do I come?'

'We'll start in Wisbech.'

They agreed a car would pick her up at 7.30 the next day. She knew she ought to tell Paul she was going off with Richard Allenton, so she knocked on his door, but Louise said that he was gone for the day. She decided not to pursue him. Jenni would be moving in with her over the weekend, and if she told her that would do. She came back to Louise.

'Did you sort out the *News of the World*?'

She was using her educated accent, so she'd either just called or was just about to. 'He wouldn't tell me anything and no, I couldn't help him with his questions. It was you, personally, he wanted. I told him it was not policy for anyone other than the Senior Partner to speak to the Press, and he was not here.'

Jules felt cold; this was not routine business. She went back to her office and tried to call Gwyn, but he was locked in the Inquiry. She left a message asking him to call Miss Carlisle of Jenkins Associates but felt she had to add that Monday would be fine in order to make it sound like business. He would ring her at home, surely, so that they could confer. Or perhaps the *News of the World* man would be discouraged and go away. She glanced at the window to check that no pigs were flying past, and packed up her briefcase and went home, leaving the answerphone on to screen all calls.

The MI5 car was outside her door, bang on time, at 7.25 the next morning. Unable as she was to read in a car without being sick, she chatted to the driver until they turned off the motorway south of Peterborough to watch the flat unearthly Fen fields go past her, all livid green with new planting. It had been wet and water glistened everywhere. 'The River Nene,' the driver said, and she looked out to their left on a dead straight canal. River round here was a term of art.

They drove into the car park at the Regional Crime Centre, a five-storey red brick modern block. Crime must not have been happening that day; the car park was full to bursting but they set down in the space for VIP visitors. They meant Richard Allenton, whose car it was, she thought. It was just before ten, and the sun was out and the sky a brilliant blue and white, although there were pools of water in the car park. It took a few minutes to run Richard to earth as they tramped through grey corridors. They found him, finally, behind a door labelled 'Operation April Showers' which seemed a bit fanciful for this workaday place. Jimmy Watt was the only other familiar face among half a dozen solid, square men in plain clothes who shook her hand in varying degrees of unease. The meeting had just ended, that was clear, and everyone was in a purposeful hurry, switching on mobile phones as they left the room. Richard closed the door after them and looked across at her. He was looking bright-eyed and running on adrenalin. He had got rid of the sling, and his hand was neatly bandaged.

'Thanks for coming.'

'Not at all. I wouldn't mind a coffee.'

'Do you mind if we have it in the car?'

'Your driver has just driven all the way from here to London. What about him?'

'He gets a break. We're using a local car.'

It was a big green Range Rover with Jimmy Watt and a driver in the front and she with Richard and another man in the back.

The men were all disguised as countrymen, with the usual smelly green cardboard jackets and various types of corduroy trousers. And wellington boots. She was wearing climbing boots and an anorak and they decided those would do.

'You need flat caps and a dog,' she said, provocatively.

'A dog would be a nuisance,' Richard said, considering the point, but produced an authentic but unbecoming flat cap for himself and made his troops and her put on woolly hats. The Range Rover was too clean and well groomed and smelled of polish rather than of old wet dog, but they hit a substantial hole complete with thick mud inside the first mile and with the windows shut the cardboard jackets produced a powerful odour, so she felt they were pretty authentic by the time they reached where they were going. Which was about twenty miles north, down a set of roads which got smaller and rougher; until finally they ran out of road in a crude cement and gravel circle next to a sea of plastic in dead flat mud, with about a ten-foot bank to their left.

'We're on the coast,' Richard said, and she looked at the mud bank, blankly. 'Over the top.'

So over the top they went by the public footpath sign, leaving Jimmy Watt and the driver to guard the Range Rover, up the side of the bank where there were crude stone steps – well, small flat stones dug into the side of the bank, and there was not the sea, but a lot of grassy sand dunes. She gave Richard a 'Who, *me?*' look, but he put his head down and tramped on, slipping in his wellingtons while she followed him. She had better boots but Richard's legs were longer and she floundered after him for a quarter mile of heavy going and suddenly there was the North Sea, grey and misty and going on for ever. A large threatening cloud sat above their heads, waiting for its chance to dump on them. There was a thin, muddy strip of beach, totally deserted, at least for the half mile or so in each direction that she could see.

'Ah. The beautiful beaches of Norfolk.'

'We're in Lincolnshire.'

'Where Mirko's brother was found.' She had had time on the journey to work out where they were going if not why.

'Close to it.'

'There's a lot of coast round here then.'

'There is, and not a lot of people. Mostly birds.'

'Richard, why are we here, or is it a state secret?'

The attendant had withdrawn, tactfully.

'There was a landing somewhere along here very early yesterday morning. We'd had a tip-off and we were waiting on the roads back there. The information wasn't exact, but they were being dropped from a ship.'

'What, to swim?' She looked over a grey, oily sea.

'No, no, into a boat or boats. We're in the Wash and the sea's shallow, so a ship has to stay in the deep channel.'

The few drops had become many, and she put on the deeply unbecoming woolly hat she found in a pocket and pulled the hood of her anorak over it. 'Could you tell me in the car, or is there anything else here I need to see? I mean, did you find the boats?'

'No. Which is interesting in itself. The people we picked up yesterday aren't talking, they've all applied for asylum, but I am sure they have no idea where they landed.'

'Where did they come from originally?' They had turned back from the sea and were slipping and sliding through the stiff, spiky grass on the dunes.

'They're Serbs.'

'Yes, all right, but the ship didn't come straight from Serbia, did it?'

'No.' The rain was coming down hard and they were both huddled into jackets. 'We've been assuming they came in from Holland, on tankers.'

'But?'

'But not a tanker has moved out of Holland without customs or our people knowing for the last couple of weeks. This lot came in by sea. A container ship *did* come in, night before last, down the Ouse to King's Lynn. It's a regular, comes in every week. From Bosnia.'

'Ah, Bosnia.' That was why he had asked about the Karadic children. 'You...or someone, presumably searched her?'

'For the last month, yes, that would have been true but only when she gets into Lynn. I'm going to take you along to see her.' He raised a hand to Jimmy Watt who was standing on the top of the bank watching them labour along. She was having an interesting time, she thought, but hardly being helpful to the police. Had Richard got her up here because he didn't have time to take her out in the ordinary way? The rain slackened, and stopped as they reached the shelter of the Range Rover and she got her head out of the hood and shook off the worst. She looked across the acres of white plastic to a substantial metallic warehouse like a giant Nissen hut, a good half mile away, and thought about what she was being shown.

'You really think they came in here?'

'Or hereabouts. It's a long coast and we haven't found the boat.' Richard was standing beside her, looking across the curved roof of the warehouse.

'You're sure about the boat? I mean, they really didn't swim?'

'The shipping channel is a mile out. And the water's cold. And they weren't that wet. There was a boat.'

'How *many* people?'

'We've got twelve.'

'So is that one boat or more?' She was doing her best but she knew zilch about the sea and how you sail on her.

'Probably just the one. A big inflatable. Just a quick in and out.'

'So it could belong to the big boat. The ship?'

'Yes. There wasn't one on the *Gretel* though when she docked.'

'They could just have sunk the boat.' She could just see the driver's incredulous expression. Richard must have seen it too, because he asked the man to comment.

'They'd never – no one along this coast u'd ever. Cost a fortune that do.'

'What do they cost, Michael?'

'To buy? A good 'un. Six theousand up.'

'Nasty hole in the profits,' she observed.

'Against nature is what Michael is saying, isn't it?'

'Yessir. No'un 'ld do that. Not if they ever could help it.'

Local person reminds city idiots how real life is lived. She decided to leave the questions to Richard.

'Neow,' Michael said, glancing at her in the mirror as she drank boiling coffee from a tin cup. 'They'd bury it sooner. Plenny of spaces round this coast.'

She thought about the sand dunes, stretching endlessly, and tried to decide how big an inflatable boat capable of carrying twelve men not very far would have to be, and how much sand would be needed to bury it.

'Take eoff th'engine affore, wrap 'im up and bury 'un separate and yeo'ld be right.'

So the boat set out from shore at night and picked up ten or twelve men from a ship that was on its way into port at King's Lynn, one mile down the River Ouse. It landed its cargo, the man, or men, in charge of the boat, deflated it and hid it in the dunes to wait for the next delivery, burying the engine separately to deter the casual thief. But what happened to the passengers? How did they get collected? Where was the van driver? Waiting perhaps where they sat parked, a good half mile from the sea.

'Sorry, if I'm being slow,' she said, 'but wouldn't it be easier for the couriers – the people who collect the refugees – if you used a bit of the coast where the road, or a track, comes right down to the beach?'

The driver, fished under the seat and passed her a big *A to Z* atlas, and showed her where they were in the bottom of the U-shape called the Wash. The place was a network of little roads but all of them stopped well short of the sea. She looked at the surrounding area again; it was all called something Marsh, and little rivers ran through it, all the way up the left-hand side of the U as well. 'The sea is receding?' she said, cautiously.

'The land's pushing eout,' Michael agreed. 'They'un get a foot or so every year. Back of the dunes it's good growing land.'

Yes. Now she could see it. There was the bank, carrying a canalised river, then the sand dunes, then the sea. And back of the bank where they now sat in the Land Rover there was indeed good farming land, with something being grown intensively under the acres of heavy white plastic sheeting.

There was, she saw, no habitable dwelling here, just the magnified Nissen hut, with a couple of cars beside it, a big container and a pair of small figures engaged in unpacking it.

'Let's go down and have a word, Michael,' Richard Allenton said.

The Range Rover pushed smoothly off the concrete circle and bumped down the strip road, concrete laid straight on mud, with wickedly sharp edges. There were four men, and an ancient windowless van which had once been white, and a blue BMW. She got out for air but stayed in the background while Richard and Jimmy talked to them. Three of them were worker bees, with big dirty hands and one was more conventionally dressed but none of them had suspect foreign accents or trousers wet from sea water. Yes, they'd been here from eight to five on Thursday and the same on Friday, but no, no one stayed here at night, in the dark. You don't tend celery – which is what the plastic was covering – at night, their expressions said, and only a daft townee would even ask the question.

'What's in the container?'

'Kit to build another warehouse. We put all this plastic in it when it's empty. It gets recycled.' He waved his hand to indicate the field.

Richard nodded; this wasn't moving them on. He was watching the road and she turned to see a red car, impatiently driven, smacking off the bumps in the road. It slowed as it got close, but they were standing on the only turning point for half a mile, so he had to come on. Just one man in the car, dark, lightweight, eyes flicking over them all. Richard repeated his questions, the man looked blank and explained he'd come up to see the guv'nor, collect his pay for the week and bring the three men here back to Lynn. He was a driver and, no, he hadn't seen anything either in the last two days. His name was Artie Potton.

Richard gave it up and handed her and Jimmy into the Range Rover. Artie had to shift his car to let them get past; Michael having indicated with a single economic gesture that he was not going to risk the Range Rover's tyres on the jagged edges of the hard-standing, and they bumped, sedately, along the road.

'Richard. Two things.'

'What?'

'Artie's car. When we came out of Regional Crime it was in a side turning. It held back for them to get out.'

'Jules, are you sure?'

'I saw the number. I wasn't looking at the letters, but the number is 259. And it was a red car.'

'Are you quite sure?'

'Yes.' She could see her audience was not entirely convinced. 'It's a sequence, you see.'

'Run that by us again.'

'A three-number gap between 2 and 5, then a four-number gap between 5 and 9.'

There was a pause; she could see Michael's lips moving while he worked it out. Richard gave her a long, thoughtful look.

'What was the *other* thing?'

'Artie must be a Cardona.'

'Why must he?'

'They all look like that. Very dark, pointed ears, widow's peaks – you know, that bit in the hairline. Oh, and they're double-jointed. When he turned the car did you see his hand? The fingers go backwards.'

'We'll get you to look at some pictures. Quick as you like, Michael.' They had just reached a slightly better road and Michael got moving in earnest while Richard applied himself to the phone. He looked at her and shook his head. 'Are we going to have to round up all the suspects, see if they're double-jointed? And have widow's peaks?'

'Interesting to meet a man who doesn't believe in genetics.'

'I don't...yes, of course I bloody do. We don't have...I don't seem to...'

'We don't have them in London?'

She was laughing at him, so was Michael, and Jimmy Watt was doing all he knew not to. 'All right, all right. You never told me they were double-jointed, though.'

'You never asked,' she said, triumphantly.

They got back to Regional Crime quicker than they had come.

Jules was just pleased with herself but the men were working. Richard on the phone with acolyte taking notes, Jimmy on another phone, and Michael, as it turned out, doing two jobs. 'No bugger,' he said to Richard as they arrived back in Regional Crime's car park, 'I'd 'uv seen 'um neow I was watchin'.'

'Thanks.'

They trooped into Richard's office and she asked for coffee and took off as many wet clothes as decency permitted.

In the event they didn't have many photographs but they did have an MI5 man who knew about genetics and kinship networks among Travellers, who took out of her head everything else she knew about the Cardona clan and its ramifications. Richard left her with him and came back after an hour to report that a red Vauxhall Cavalier, number CJL 259, which was itself licensed as a hire car, was owned by Z Line Cars.

'A taxi firm,' she said, flown with success. 'Just what you'd need to distribute refugees.' She saw that this was something they'd all absorbed days ago. 'You might need a farmer too. Someone farming back of the dunes who would turn a blind eye and make sure Group 4 only came by at set times.'

'Yes,' Richard said, just not impatiently.

'You're so clever, why haven't you found the boat then?'

'We think they moved it rather than buried it after we picked up the cargo.'

'Over the dunes?'

'Well, no. They float quite well, so...' She gave him the withering look, and he grinned at her. 'It doesn't half help, though, that you recognised Artie. If you're right then we can get the list down to those places where Z Line taxis deliver people.'

'I wonder how many more of the clan were in it?' she said, thoughtfully.

'We're watching your friend Ray.'

'What about the travellers sites?'

'We hadn't got there. It'll take an army to watch them all.'

'You didn't look up the Karadic clan?'

'Only two of them in the book. Artie doesn't have an address, or not as Artie Potton. I wish we'd asked him where he lived.'

'As a lodger somewhere in a caravan. With one of the family,' she said, and he nodded, picked up the phone and issued some orders, and she wished jealously that she had staff at Jenkins Associates. She had a share of Louise, and a third of a secretary, and it was no good telling any of them to do things in a hurry.

'You want some lunch?'

'Only if you have time.'

'An hour or so. I haven't been eating regularly. There's a decent pub in Wisbech.'

'Just as long as none of the staff have bent-back thumbs.' She was not seriously concerned, she remembered from overheard adult conversation that restaurants wouldn't have Travellers, on the grounds that they'd feed their whole family out of the kitchen.

When they got themselves seated, in the bit with tablecloths, and got steaks ordered, he gave her a careful look, and she braced herself to stall any questions about her childhood.

'Why did you choose to go to Jenkins Associates?'

Taken off balance, she told him more than she had meant to about how she had fought to get in on Work Experience.

'Then I just clung to the walls so they couldn't get rid of me. Every time they needed something done in a hurry I came back from Birmingham and did it. So in the end they had to give me a training contract.'

'They're well respected, your firm. How many people do you have now?'

'Fifteen. Paul, five partners. Five associate partners, two Newly Qualified, one of which is me, and two trainees. Most of us are women. Paul didn't want another one when I applied for Work Experience. He wanted a man for a change.'

'But he took you.'

'Yes. He thought I had a practical approach.'

She remembered the interview well; she had found herself telling the big man with the mad hair and the bright brown eyes more about her history than anyone else except Gwyn or Cousin Anne knew. It was an intensely sympathetic personality and on song he made everyone else look a bit colourless. She could feel herself grinning as she thought about him. He had taken her out of ten people trying to beat down his door, because he thought she would know what the clients were on about.

'You work a lot with him?'

'Not all that much, but it's wonderful when I do.' They did not have to look at each other in a meeting to know exactly how to shepherd a client, or develop a line. It was surprising that, unlike Jenni Patel, she had not converted admiration and pleasure in a working relationship into unquestioning adoration.

'Do you see him much outside the office? I mean, do you socialise?'

'No,' she said, thinking about it. 'No. He buys me lunch sometimes, but only when it's my turn. He's got a wife but no children, and she may not be very sociable. He works very long hours.'

'Mm. Born in Belgrade?'

'Yes.' The tenor of the questioning suddenly struck her. 'Why? I mean, why do you ask?'

'He's very well known. Well, you know that. Even Mirko knew of him, you've told me.'

'He writes a lot on immigration law. He pushed for the policy we now have of admitting a certain number of ordinary non-refugees a year to work here. What the papers call economic migrants.'

'I agree with him.' He passed her the mustard as she cut into her steak. 'We are in a much easier moral position, internationally and domestically, with proper arrangements by which people can actually make their lives here rather than just be allowed in grudgingly to harvest lettuce.'

'Have you shared this view with MI5 colleagues?'

'Of course. Even the ones who can't be doing with foreigners see that enforcement is a bloody sight easier if we admit our share of immigrants in a formal way. And you get better co-operation in identifying the illegals.'

'Martin Flowerdew would agree with you too.'

'So does Andrew, stuffed shirt though he is.' He peeked at her round a mouthful of steak to see if she was going to react, but she chewed on, dead-pan. 'Your boss Paul, on the other hand, believes one should let them all in, whatever the social consequences.'

She finished her steak, trying to decide whether she should storm out in a rage. Hardly, Paul would not ask it of her and he was more than able to take care of himself. 'He's not your biggest fan either.'

'Is he not? I wasn't sure he was prepared to acknowledge my existence. Normally he speaks only to my bosses' boss.'

'Bor-ring.'

'Sorry,' he said, stiffly, and attacked his chips, while she finished hers. He poured her another drink after a while, still a bit tight-lipped. 'I really didn't bring you up here to rant at you.'

'Why *did* you bring me here?'

'I didn't...well, in the event it was brilliant, but I didn't really hope for...I thought you deserved to see what you were trying to deal with.'

'It was my education you were thinking of?'

'And I wanted to see you, anyway.'

'I enjoyed it.' She had found that being straightforward worked, when straightforward was what she meant to be.

'Good. Great. Thank you.' He stared at her over the table. 'Look, I've got to be here to cope with what's happening, or I'd take you back to London myself, but right now...well, right now I need to be in a meeting, and...'

'Put me on a train, Richard, don't worry about it.'

'Bugger that, least we can do is send you home with my driver. We'll pick him up at Regional Crime.'

It wasn't, in the event, quite as straightforward as that. Richard took her in with him so he could organise the car, but was waylaid by Jimmy Watt. They left her in a small, grimy waiting-room; she had finished the *Daily Mail* – and was deciding whether to tackle the *Sun* or the instructions for leaving the building in the event of fire, when he came back.

'Sorry. News.' He sat down. 'Your client – ex-client rather, Mirko. It really wasn't an accident.'

'You didn't think it was.'

'No. But I was short of suspects. The only prints were the male nurse's. And that you'd expect.'

'So now what?' she asked, when it seemed he had stopped.

'The nurse – William Cliffe – didn't report for duty yesterday. Nobody bothered to tell us when he rang saying he didn't feel well. He was due on tonight, so they rang up to check he was all right but got no answer. Then a bright lad there used his head, and decided he'd better go looking. Turns out Mr Cliffe, who lives with three other young men, had not been there or been heard from since the night Mirko died.'

She sat looking at him, trying to take it in. 'But…but if he did it, isn't it stupid to give himself away? And anyway…no surely, Richard, it couldn't have been *planned*. I talked to the lad, he's been working there for a few months. Perhaps he had a shock and has just gone off?'

Richard sat on the edge of the table. 'You're making sense, Jules, but I've got a bad feeling. I'd be glad to know where he is. And how he is.' He shifted his attention to her, and she saw, annoyingly, that he tried to decide how much to tell her.

'No need to bother this little woman with too much detail, Mr Allenton.'

'Get off. I don't know that I'm not disappearing up my own…up a sidetrack. But, you've been very helpful, though we haven't found anyone so far who looks or feels like a Directing Mind, an organiser. These – the drivers, the farmer – if we're right about what we think has happened – they're all foot-soldiers. Someone else is pulling the strings.'

'Someone abroad?'

'No. They've got to be *here* – this is an industry. The illegals get a full service, met off the boat, found papers and jobs. We've picked up a few.'

She thought around her clients to see if any of them would be Directing Minds. They were not that good. She acknowledged they were people who committed crimes and had a rudimentary support system, like someone who buys anything they've nicked. She acted for a few pushers, but they got their drugs in lots worth hundreds rather than thousands and sold them on in £40 packages.

'What would a Directing Mind look like?' she asked.

'The biggest villains I've met – the drugs barons and the smugglers – look like businessmen. Good suits, sober lives, members of Rotary. They don't get very near the action. They don't have to, there's plenty of cash to buy the soldiers at the sharp end.'

'Enough cash to pay for a murder?'

'Yes.' He was looking out of the window. 'Jules, I tell you...I...' He slid off the table and banged into the door. 'Damn. I shouldn't have brought you up here. Some of them have seen you.'

'I was much too muffled up for Artie to have seen me. And Ray Cardona *I* walked into, out of curiosity.'

'With any luck he thinks you're one of us.'

'And they don't touch MI5?'

'Not if they can help it. It's like policemen, we're more trouble than it's worth.' He was scratching a hole in the paintwork of the door and she coughed to get his attention. 'What are you doing tonight?' he asked.

'Washing my hair, I guess. Unless I get a better offer.'

'I can't leave. And I...well, I can't really... No.'

'What?'

'You're going to be offended if I ask the local CID to keep an eye on you.'

Incredulous was the word he wanted, she thought. They don't have the manpower to keep up with burglaries or battered women, never mind me. 'I won't speak to strange men, how about that?'

'It'll have to do. Anything funny, anything at all, you ring me, day or night. Can we have dinner when I can get down from here?'

She assured him they could, subject to contingency, and he put her into the car, with the driver who had brought her up. He was finding it difficult to say goodbye, so was she, but MI5 provided its usual reliable interruption. His mobile rang and he was gone, in long strides across the yard, with it held to his ear.

Chapter Twelve

(Sunday after Easter)

Jules woke late, with a bell ringing in her ears, and cursed as she rolled out of bed. It was of course Jenni, at precisely the agreed time. She rushed downstairs to admit Jenni who was looking as usual immaculate in designer jeans rather than the habitual trouser-suit. Jules, very conscious of her bird's nest hair, uncleaned teeth, and too short nightdress, unbolted the door, spoke words of welcome, and fled to her bathroom.

Twenty minutes later, feeling a great deal more human, she looked in to the spare room to find Jenni, industriously unpacking. She offered to help, cautiously, not wanting to seem invasive or proprietary. Jenni called her in however, and she gazed, enviously, at the contents of the wardrobe. Everything was in black, beige or white, with clever bits of coloured scarves and jewellery, and it was plain to see that Jenni would never have a moment's problem getting dressed for work or any occasion. Jules's own wardrobe came in a mad array of colours, so mostly she wore the same thing all week, give or take a clean shirt, because she had found the shoes and the handbag that went with it. When she was feeling more ambitious she would change outfits every day which meant changing shoes and handbags and invariably involved her leaving credit cards or other vital bits of kit in the one she was discarding. She shared this perception with Jenni, and wished she hadn't. With the light of battle in her eyes, Jenni stopped unpacking her stuff, followed Jules to her bedroom, laid all her clothes on the bed and bade her choose, here and now, one colour on which she wished to base her spring wardrobe. All else, she said, tactfully, must be put aside for another year. They fixed on beige and blue with three outfits in which Jules could go to work, one outfit in which she could go out, and two pairs of navy jeans. The problem turned out to be that Jules had precisely two pairs of down-at-heel navy shoes and one pair of navy sneakers, so she had to agree to buy more of each.

'You must have enough shoes to wear a different pair to work each day,' Jenni said, severely, and Jules agreed, meekly. She had plenty of shoes in several useless colours. Shoes to wear day in day out she did not have. She found herself thinking of Gwyn; he once said that the one problem for people with a disorganised childhood was that they didn't know what to buy or how to budget. Anne's standards had been strictly utilitarian, so that living with her had not much helped with this particular problem. She had provided Jules with uncompromisingly sensible school clothes and had given her a clothes allowance with which Jules had bought brightly coloured cheap rubbish. One way or another, she had never learned anything about planning for clothes.

She looked round to see that Jenni was turning out her knicker drawer and she had to snatch from her the less attractive items as they surfaced. Why, she wondered, do I have sixteen pairs of knickers, only two of which would do for company? She managed to hang onto a week's worth of white – well, off-white – against a promise that she would replace all at the earliest possible opportunity, then, warming to the task, helped Jenni to apply the same procedure to the rest of it, the ten misshapen, coloured T-shirts, the ten bras, five that had started white but which were now off-white and sagging, and five new ones in colours which showed straight through any light-coloured blouse, and uncounted pairs of laddered or snagged tights.

'I hope you don't feel…' Jenni said, over coffee in an unusual departure from her usual assurance, and Jules was able to say in all sincerity that no, she didn't, she was truly grateful, even though the replacement buying was going to do wholesale damage to the credit card.

'I'm not sure what there is for lunch,' she said, feeling it was the least that Jenni deserved.

The phone rang, just as Jenni was explaining that she would be eating a lettuce leaf or near offer, and it was Andrew Flowerdew. 'I have to come to London after all. Can we have dinner tonight? Wonderful. I'll pick you up.'

She hadn't, Jules thought afterwards, necessarily wanted him to meet Jenni who was looking particularly good in the Hermès jeans and silk blouse she had been wearing to move. And Jenni would tell Paul, immediately, that she was Fraternising, so she would have to remember to get her confession in first tomorrow. Well, at *least*, she thought, spirits lifting, she had a suitor. And a decent set of underwear to wear, even if not necessarily to display. She went for a walk after lunch, and had a sleep when she got back, so that Andrew arrived before she could get downstairs.

Jenni, meanwhile, had given him some of Gwyn's whisky and was prettily suggesting that he might help himself to it while she looked for the soda. She was going to be out of luck there, Jules thought, her food and grocery provisioning not being much better than her wardrobe planning, but Andrew settled for plain water and not very much of it.

'Busy day?' she asked.

'Yes.' He subsided into a kitchen chair with a handful of the cashew nuts that Jenni had unearthed from somewhere. 'I have police getting in our way on the coast farm.'

'Oh dear, Andrew. Are these going to be more clients for us?' Jenni asked, leaning over to give him a view down the silk shirt.

Up to that point Jules had been pleased with the plain, light wool, beige trouser suit she was wearing, but it immediately felt too severe. Andrew hesitated and flicked a look at her, and she feared she was looking as if she had eaten something sour. 'I do hope not.' He finished his whisky. 'Too soon to be sure. I'm booked down the road, Jules, we should go.' He turned back to Jenni and Jules willed him not to ask her if she had eaten, but he was saying goodbye and how nice to have seen her and he was sure their paths would cross again.

'Am I all right for wherever we are going?' she ventured, as they got outside.

'Absolutely. You look terrific. We're going to the Savoy.'

'Oh.' She had only been there with oldies like Anne and Henry. Well, she thought, you could not expect an East Anglican lettuce farmer to know about the latest London restaurants. Solid quality was what Andrew did, and she should shut up and enjoy it. She wondered where he was going to park the Range Rover, but all he did was hand the keys to the doorman who muttered something respectful and took it away to a secret resting place. Feeling distinctly princessy, she followed Andrew to the bar. And stopped in her tracks, because there was Anne sitting by herself at a table, gazing into space.

'Anne?'

'Darling. What are you doing here?'

'I might ask the same?' She bent to kiss her. 'I'm having dinner with a friend.'

Anne put on her glasses. 'Is that the lettuce farmer?' She beamed at Andrew who had turned back to look for Jules and was looking a little disconcerted. 'Do bring him over, darling, I misread my diary and arrived too early for the jolly.'

'What jolly?'

'The committee of the All Parliamentary Group on Energy Policy, since you ask. Hello there, how nice to see you.'

Jules introduced Andrew, seeing him blink as he assimilated the title. He had probably imagined a worthy social worker or teacher cousin rather than a Baroness, drinking whisky in the Savoy bar.

'How kind of you to take pity on me,' Anne said, cheerfully. 'I haven't brought anything to read and I am rather early. Jules has told me about your farm, Mr Flowerdew.'

'Andrew, please. Can I get you another drink?' He stood, smiling and comfortable now he knew who she was, secure in familiar territory.

'Better not. I am meeting some hard drinkers tonight. But do tell me more about your farm – I know a bit about the other end of the business from the MOD suppliers.'

Andrew's eyes widened. 'Which suppliers?'

'Well, 3663 are the big ones.'

Andrew sat down beside her, so that Jules was left to drink the gin and tonic that had appeared instantly while the answers to all the questions she had been too polite to ask poured out.

'It's a commodity business, iceberg of course,' Andrew was saying, taking a deliberate gulp of his gin and tonic, leaning forward in his desire to explain. 'The processors make the profit.'

'Really? I assumed it was made at the retail end. The likes of

3663 or the supermarkets.'

'Oh them too, of course. It is the primary producer who has a hard time maintaining margins.' He smiled at Anne. 'You know, when I was at school I was taught that primary producers get the short straw, so I wonder how I ended up as one.'

Not a very short straw, Jules thought, not if we can afford to eat at the Savoy.

'What else do you grow?' Anne was asking.

'Daffodils. Which are also a commodity crop. And specialist vegetables, for the Chinese and Indian restaurants and supermarkets. We get a decent margin there, because...'

Anne was nodding. 'You are only competing with air-freighted stuff. Yes. Are you expanding?'

'We are. We've just bought a couple of farms by the Wash. Mortgaged to the hilt, of course, and the buildings aren't worth keeping, so it's eating cash, but we have to do it.'

'Economies of scale?'

'Oh them, yes. But the peat is running out on some of the farms we've had for longer. Do you know the fens at all?'

'We have a house in Cambridge.'

'It's not really...you must come and see the farm.'

'I'd love to. Tell me about your labour. I know from Jules that you employ temporaries from Eastern Europe. Does everyone?'

'The smaller people are using a lot of illegals. Contract labour. Brought in on buses. Well, we use contract labour too, in the packing sheds. I don't like it much, I'd rather have my own people and I'd rather know that they weren't being paid £2 an hour and treated badly, but...' He broke off, having all too obviously remembered he was talking to one of the nation's legislators, but it seemed to have passed Anne by.

'Everyone on the site used to do a bit.' Jules was tired of being ignored. 'When I was a kid. They probably still do, but you can't pay native-born labour £2 an hour these days. They'll take you to a tribunal.'

Andrew was carefully not looking at Anne, whose Government chums had introduced the Minimum Wage legislation.

'And quite right too,' Anne said, firmly. 'So the real trick is to find something higher-margin to grow.'

'Which doesn't need much labour,' Andrew said, nodding.

'Cannabis,' Jules suggested, feeling the urge to disrupt this cosy conversation.

'There's some probably doing that,' Andrew said, seriously. 'Cash flow is a major problem for the smaller people. The banks have them by the throat. Well, us too of course – we'd all be bust if the banks called in their loans.'

'True of most sizeable businesses,' Anne observed. She looked up. 'Ah. I see colleagues – oh God, poor old Tim Foxcroft, he really doesn't see awfully well. No, it's alright, some kind young man has picked him up, but I'd better go and keep him company. I want a word anyhow, due to where he is Chairman.' Andrew and Jules gazed wonderingly at the very elderly gentleman being guided to the big central table and settled there by two minions. 'Lovely to meet you, Andrew. Come and talk to me. Invite me to your farm.' She returned Jules's glare with a look of innocence, and went to bend over the poor old gent at the table, pressing him back in his seat as he struggled to rise, knocking over a chair with a flailing walking stick.

'Chairman of what?' Andrew asked, and Jules had to admit she wasn't entirely sure, but it had to do with energy. Andrew shook his head. 'We'd better go and eat.'

They had managed to order and were drinking a delicious white wine by the time Anne and her committee were assembling themselves. They had managed to attract a lot of attention; Lord Foxcroft, despite the assistance of two able-bodied and recognisable Members of Parliament had managed to trip coming down the stairs on his return from the gents, and a large jovial woman was telling Anne, at a pitch audible to most in the River Room, the latest scandal in the electricity generation industry. Not quite what I would have chosen, Jules thought crossly, a romantic dinner in full view of my guardian and ten of her peculiar chums, but Andrew seemed to be taking it all in his stride.

'What brought you down today, rather than tomorrow?'

'Martin. He did, you'll be glad to know, promise to contact

Alyssia and talk to her about coming to see your boss. I thought…well, I thought…'

'That you would come down and see he has kept his word.'

'Yes. And deliver him – and her, if he can persuade her – to your boss tomorrow. But I'm afraid I ought to go back after that or I would…I was hoping we might do a theatre tomorrow, but I've got an appointment with the local Health and Safety. Not a day passes, I tell you. If it's not them, it's the rates inspectors or the local plod asking if I have seen any illegals.'

During the course of the beautiful meal she thought how much she liked him. There was a definite resemblance to her darling Gwyn. He had all Gwyn's sharpness of mind and sense of responsibility. He obviously felt strongly about the welfare of his kids, as he called them, although many of them could not have been more than a few years younger than himself. It was, she decided, amazing that some pretty competent Eastern European PhD had not swept him into marriage, thereby getting a wonderfully protective, rich husband and a British passport in one package.

On the way out, they had to pass Anne's table where some of the colleagues were well away, including the old boy who had tripped on the stairs. Anne had not noticed her so she was able to sneak past, but not before she had heard the old gent observe at top pitch that if we were going to cover the Isle of Lewis with bloody windmills then we might as well seal all the nuclear waste under there as well and tell the Scots they could lump it. Anne and the noisy plump woman, who she recognised as another Baroness, were both rocking with laughter and passing each other samples of their pudding. She hastened Andrew past, mentally shaking her head over the older generation, but he was grinning broadly.

'I'm never going to feel the same about the House of Lords,' he said, an arm companionably round her as they waited for the Range Rover to be brought round.

'No, it is pretty worrying.'

'I enjoyed it,' he said, seriously. 'I'll take you home, then go and see what Martin's managed to get done.'

Civilised, she thought, approvingly. Not assuming he would be asked in for coffee and whatever, making it clear he had other things to do, if not. Well, they did have time, the Flowerdew clan were going to be in and out of Jenkins Associates for some time yet. And a leisured courtship would be a rare luxury, and she might even enjoy it.

Chapter Thirteen

(Monday after Easter)

She slept badly on Sunday night and woke up late on the Monday. She scrambled through tea, strong and sweet, and cereal. Jenni, eating melon, orange juice and yoghurt, looked censorious but Jules forgave her, when she found she could get dressed in five minutes flat, from the hollowed-out contents of her wardrobe. Something about Jenni's expression made her look at her shoes and take them off to polish them. She had to settle for a rub-up with a duster since her navy Meltonian had dried and cracked beyond recovery. She promised herself she would buy navy polish and two new pairs of shoes, and shot out, impelled by the collection of Today's Must Do jobs.

'Phone call for you. Mr Jones. He ax you ring back.'

She ran up to her office and made the call. Gwyn was sounding very anxious.

'Can you meet me for a few minutes?' he asked urgently.

'Come here.'

An awkward pause. 'Better not,' he said, and she sat up, alarmed. 'Look, I haven't had breakfast. Could we meet at the caff?'

His obvious distress had brought out his Welsh lilt, she thought, as she got herself out of the office, trying and failing to say something to Louise.

Gwyn was there already, sitting at a table, looking harassed, and she did not dare kiss him. 'I've had the *News of the World* again,' he said, quietly.

'I did too, but I didn't return his call.'

'Patrick Mahoney,' he said, unhopefully.

'That's the one.'

'And you didn't talk to him?'

'No. We never do. I got Louise to call and be snotty.' She looked enquiringly at Gwyn who was looking tired and defeated, the bright hair flattened and in need of a wash.

'The bastard said he had talked to you. He's trying to say I seduced you when you were in my care.'

'Well, you didn't.' She was trying to decide what to eat; anxiety always took her that way.

'Jules. Stop fiddling with that menu.'

She understood then, with a chill, that it was serious, but the waitress had turned up, so she had to order breakfast. When the girl had gone, Gwyn explained, wearily, that being tired and stressed from the Inquiry, he had incautiously answered his phone and had found himself holding a conversation with Patrick Mahoney. And had obviously gone further than he should, she saw. He had confirmed to the man that she had lived with him and his wife for three months when she was fourteen, then gone to relations. And that, yes, he and his wife were still in touch with her. So far so fine, but the man had asked whether he ever saw her by himself, without his wife. Gwyn, no doubt still in giving Evidence to Inquiry mode had said that indeed yes, occasionally, since their fields of work sometimes overlapped. *That* had enabled the man to ring Sandra and ask poisonous and pointed questions which had naturally rattled and distressed her.

'It's very difficult to know what to do with those people,' Jules said, deeply dismayed.

'I didn't do it right.' Gwyn was always honest with himself. 'We need to work out what I should say next time, if anything. I could always threaten them with a libel action.'

She ate her breakfast, trying not to panic. They had been lovers since she was nineteen and she could see how easy it would be to imply that the affair had started earlier, when she was under age. Her stomach was churning uneasily.

'We do need a plan. What did Sandra say to him?'

'She said that she wasn't prepared to comment on this sort of nonsense.'

Good defensive stuff but, unfortunately, it was also the initial statement from every wife whose husband turned out to be addicted to hard drugs, three-in-a-bed sex, or little boys.

Gwyn finished his omelette, burped, and indicated that he could use another cup of tea. He was a better colour for the food, but he was still not looking at her.

'She was very unhappy about it.'

Yes. Sandra was the problem, Jules conceded, silently. Now she came to consider it – and why had she not before? – Sandra probably had her suspicions about Gwyn and her. Too much pressure and something would give.

'Who is doing this to you, Gwyn?' she said, having thought that if they could get a line on where this was coming from they could push right back.

'I've been thinking about that. It has to be connected to the Inquiry, but it doesn't make sense. They decided – I decided – weeks ago, to wash all the dirty linen in public. I didn't want anything left to come back and haunt us. So there's no point really in getting at me. He was sounding plaintive and ill-used and whiney, the pleasant voice rising to shrillness, which rattled her; Gwyn had taken every kind of knock in his stride in twenty years of social work.

'They might want to discredit you. As a person.'

'Who might?'

'Well, Gwyn…the Bastards?'

'If they get rid of me, the next one will be just as tough. Couldn't afford not to be.'

'That's true. Perhaps they'll remember that and stop. But look, Gwyn, we have to stick together – to the same story.'

'We do.' He sounded relieved. 'It's the only hope.'

Silence fell between them while they both thought about Sandra.

'I don't want her to know,' Gwyn said, baldly, into the air.

'I'd *hate* for her to know. Let's do the details,' she said, steadily. 'We meet rarely, on business, in each other's offices? No? I come to your house, you come to mine.'

They did the best they could in squaring their stories, but as she watched him drink a third cup of tea, which was all too obviously going to give him trouble later, she saw not her Gwyn, her saviour, her wonderful, kind lover, but a worried, overwrought, middle-aged man with guilt weighing him down.

'There's actually an answer,' she said, cutting him off in mid-worry. 'I'll get Paul on to their editor. No newspaper is going to go ahead unless they can stand the story up and they can't.' She looked round, carefully. 'You didn't seduce a minor in your care and if they say you did it's libel. They might not care with an ordinary person, but I'm a solicitor, and if Paul talks to them they will know that there is a legal firm at my back, and that we will sue. It doesn't cost lawyers a lot to sue, after all.'

She watched him think it through, and nod relieved. He, she saw painfully, would at this moment like to be anywhere else.

'I'll talk to Paul,' she said, pushing back her chair. 'And I'll ring you.'

She found Paul already in. She hesitated – he didn't much like being disturbed in the morning – like her he wanted to get half the day's work over by eleven. But it could not wait, so she knocked and went in. He didn't seem to be working; there were no papers in front of him, though the usual piles were ringed round the edge of the big desk. He was looking tired, the brown eyes set back in his head and the wild hair lacking its usual bounce.

'Jules.'

'I need to ask you something.'

'Tell me.'

She explained about Gwyn, trying not to blush. Paul listened, absolutely impassive.

'So I thought we could threaten Mr Mahoney with a libel action.'

Paul stirred in his chair and reached for a pad. 'They are alleging what, precisely? That Mr Jones seduced you when you were in his care at the age of fourteen.'

'But he didn't.'

He was drawing on his blotter, a sure sign of being not convinced by what he was being told.

'What is Mr Jones doing? Has he threatened a libel action?'

'Well – I'm not sure, I mean, I think he's been too busy.' It sounded hopelessly lame.

'You have talked to him? Yes? And to Mrs Jones?'

'No.' No, she hadn't, and Gwyn refused to do so. Both of them were too guilty to act innocent, even though they had not done precisely what was alleged.

'It would be a good idea, would it not?'

She felt the blush starting in her collarbones and could not move or prevent it, just sat there, slowly turning scarlet. Paul watched her, unmoving, until she felt tears in her eyes, then he pushed the Kleenex towards her, as she wished for death or an effortless translation to somewhere else. She blew her nose but realised she would have to go on.

'What they allege – specifically – is totally untrue. I was not in his care and I was not under age.'

'I see.'

She managed to stop crying by main force of will, and looked over at him. 'Maybe the journalist will go away,' she offered.

'This is Patrick Mahoney?'

'Yes.'

'He won't unless I speak to his editor. You must not speak to him.'

'But…'

'Nor indeed must you…talk with Mr Jones. This is a matter of the firm's reputation.' He wasn't looking at her, but out of the window and she had an excellent view of the hawk's profile, framed by the black hair just flecked with white. She was feeling sick. Paul had chosen her and trained her; he must now be wondering why he'd bothered.

'I would be grateful,' she said, simply. Paul could drive off the vultures, she had heard him do it before.

'Leave me please the number. And Jules, we meet with Mr Carrigan at twelve. Yes?'

'Yes,' she said and left, blindly, passing Jenni on the way out, her face shining with anticipation of an interview with her idol. Jules tried not to look at her but it was impossible to miss her change of expression to one of concern. She fled to an interview with one of the clients who had been caught with a van load of brand-new DVD players for which he had no explanation at all. Blessedly uncomplicated, and well within what was left of her competence that day.

When her delinquent customer had gone she sat and thought about herself. It was one of the few advantages of having been without responsible adult guidance until she was fourteen, that she knew how to think for herself. Gwyn had told her this is by no means the usual result; most fourteen-year-olds with chaotic childhoods would fall for the first leader they meet, and it was a matter of luck whether it was a drug dealer, a gang leader, or the Moonies. He must be thinking of boys, she had told him, scornfully, and he had said that indeed he was, now she mentioned it. She shut off Gwyn; in return for Paul beating up an editor, she understood she had committed herself to ensure there was nothing for them to find. She rang Gwyn's office and told him Paul's plan of action.

'Good. But...can we just discuss it?'

'That's not the deal.' She was feeling sick again. There was a long, weighted silence. 'You told him?'

'Not in words.'

'But he knows?'

'Nothing whatsoever was made explicit.'

They seemed both to be speaking as if they were under water, with long gaps between sentences. 'And he thinks it best if we don't communicate.'

'I see. He's probably right.'

Neither of them seemed able to get off the phone.

'It needn't be forever,' she said, trying not to cry.

'No. Perhaps not. I must go.'

The phone went down and she looked at it. He had never put the phone down on her.

She drank a coffee while contemplating the altered landscape of her life. No Gwyn for the moment. She pushed aside the thought that this moment might endure and reminded herself she did have suitors of varying reliability. She thought of Richard Allenton standing on a dyke in Norfolk, eyes narrowed against the wind. And there was Andrew Flowerdew.

She tidied herself up for the approaching meeting with Mr Carrigan – for once she had got make-up on, in Jenni's honour. Given a base to work on she conceded, reluctantly, it took no time to produce an efficient-looking young lawyer, smooth as paint, in contrast to the firm's founding genius who met her in the waiting-room, tie askew, hair uncombed and shoes unpolished. He should have got Jenni to do them, she thought, some spirit returning, she'd have been delirious. She did not dare ask him whether he had been able to subdue Mr Mahoney, and he did not say.

He used the time to go through the case and to check that she was doing the right things by the wife-beating Mr Carrigan. He had always told his staff that it was the clients you disliked who caught you out. You missed something obvious and you were left looking down the barrel of a Law Society Inquiry. Mind you, she thought, since the man's current defence rested on the proposition that his wife had provoked him into dismembering a chair and half killing her with it, there wasn't much the most conscientious lawyer could achieve. She was late with his lunch, you see, your Honour.

They arrived at the court and she was just wondering whether she dared ask Paul about the *News of the World* when he put a hand on her shoulder. 'I rang this editor. He was not there, which is typical, but he will ring back.' She thanked him and managed to act as an effective assistant, which made her feel a bit better.

She got back to her office well after lunch and sat, deciding that she would have to eat, little though she felt like it. The phone rang and she looked at it warily. She had asked Louise to screen all her calls but it was lunchtime. It went on ringing so she picked it up. 'Jenkin Associate here,' she said, in Louise's normal Caribbean lilt, which put the emphasis on the second syllable of Associate, and made it sound strangely exotic.

'May I speak to Miss Carlisle?'

'Andrew. It's me. What happened with Martin?'

'Ah. No news. He couldn't find Alyssia last night, or said he couldn't, so he is going to go round there today and leave a note if he can't find her. But I do have some news I thought you'd be glad to hear.'

'Please tell.' It came out heartfelt.

'Mama Dragunoviç has come back to us. Conscious, able to speak.'

'Wonderful.' It was too, she felt much less guilty about the poor old thing, but on second thoughts what was she coming round to? Stefan gone – if she remembered that – and Mirko dead as well.

'I got one of the daughters to come over,' Andrew said, cheerfully.

Jules had not given Mrs Dragunoviç more than a passing thought since Friday, but the good Andrew seemed to have made up for all of them.

'I have also some bad news. For me that is.'

'What?'

'I have to go back now, not just for the Health and Safety jobsworth. A group of illegals seem to have been living in an old shed on one of my farms.'

'Hardly your fault.'

'A couple of my students seem to have been feeding them. So the Home Office want to send them back at once. My students, that is.'

'So you're going back to help them resist? Can we do anything?'

'Not a thing. And I'm going back to do their packing. If the Home Office revoke my licence I'll have to plough the crop in. There's no spare labour anywhere in the Fens right now, with the police all over the place. I told you, Jules, remember?'

He had indeed. No one with a British passport wanted to stand ankle-deep in the East Anglian soil picking lettuces. 'All this pressure from the police must mean there will be a few farmers in trouble, then,' she said, relieved to have something other than the *News of the World* to think about.

'There are. And I'm not going to be one of them. I'm going to need to come back again later in the week. Can I take you to dinner when I do?'

'Yes. Thank you. I would like that.' There is a proverb having to do with eggs and baskets to which Anne was much attached. This looked to be a more reliable basket than any offered by

Richard Allenton.

'You couldn't do something for me? It ought to be Martin, but...'

'What?'

'Visit Mama Dragunoviç, assure her of my best services and tell her we'll see her right.'

'Break it to her that Mirko is dead? By an unknown agency?'

'No, no. The hospital have done that. I offered, but they did it. Second thing she asked.'

'I will of course,' she assured him, thinking that she would square it with Paul. Cheered, she went off for a quick lunch. Finding herself outside a shoe shop, she decided that, at least whatever mess her personal life was, she could be a person with enough shoes in the right colour to get through the week. They had the shape in navy, they had her size and she walked out twenty minutes later with three pairs of shoes, a lot of tights, and a feeling of having her life under better control.

She arrived back, laden down with bags unfortunately just as Paul walked in. He held the door for her and asked if she could spare him a moment. She stowed the bags beside Louise, who started immediately to unpack them in order to show them to the waiting clientele, and rushed into Paul's office, watching his face for news.

'We have not heard from Martin Flowerdew?'

'Ah.' Feeling better, she told him about Andrew's phone call. 'So Martin has actually gone round there.'

'When? Did Andrew say?'

She racked her brain. 'After five o'clock when his hospital shift finished.'

'Mm.' Paul was still looking bad-tempered. 'Well, I suppose we can do nothing but wait. Thank you, Jules.'

He was reaching for the phone as she left to recover her bags from the waiting-room, now full of Jamaican ladies who felt she ought to be buying something more fancy than the conventional leather she had bought, and she stopped to ask them what, precisely. They had reached the point of agreeing that she would look stunning in four-inch heels with sequins on them before the screams of laughter brought Jenni frowning out of her office, but Jules felt better. She would be six feet tall in four-inch heels, but both Andrew and Richard Allenton would still be tall enough.

The phone was ringing as she walked into her office, shedding badly rewrapped packages. She hoped it would be Richard or Andrew, but it was Gwyn in a panic, the Welsh accent very clear. 'It's OK, Gwyn, Paul is going to talk to the editor.'

'No. Listen. It's Sandra.'

'Why? What happened?'

'Mahoney got her this morning and nagged away. I was there, I shouted at her to put the phone down but she went on listening.'

'Then what, Gwyn?'

'Then she asked me, straight out, whether I had ever gone...well, whether we had ever... So I said, yes, but only when you were grown up and...and...'

'And only on alternate Thursdays in Lent... Idiot!'

'Jules!'

'It's not your secret only. You should never...'

'You don't understand. I couldn't...well, I couldn't lie, not when she asked me straight out.'

I bet they all say that, she thought, drearily, and with just that faint self-righteous tone. 'So what now?' She was feeling sick, trying not to acknowledge that this was the end, that Gwyn, darling Gwyn was not coming back, ever.

'I think she might come to you.'

The sickness was replaced momentarily by sheer terror. The prospect of talking to Sandra, who had never been other than good to her, made Jules want to crawl into a hole and die. 'I'll be here till six,' she said, miserably. 'Then I'm going home. If Sandra comes by' – she suppressed a gulp of panic – 'I'll ring you.'

She got through the rest of the afternoon somehow, telling herself she need not tell Paul about this latest development. Or not yet. Sandra would recover her temper – small blame to her for having lost it – and confine herself to giving Gwyn hell and she wouldn't have to talk to her. At 5.30 Paul put his head round the door. He was looking and sounding even less pleased than at lunchtime.

'We have heard nothing from Mr Flowerdew, Martin, I mean. His brother has not...? No?' She tried to get her mouth open to ask him about Mr Mahoney but she saw him remember. 'I have spoken to the editor. I think – and I hope – that there will be no more pressure on you, Jules.'

Now was not the time to tell Paul that there had been a complication; the only thing to do was to pray that Sandra would have the sense to help beat off the wolves at the *News of the World*. Her phone rang while Paul was still with her and she picked it up, apologetically. 'Mr Allenton. Him from MI5,' Louise announced. Jules saw that Paul had heard, and gave him a little helpless shrug. He left, looking furiously impatient.

'Can we have that dinner tonight by any happy chance? I have news.'

She was feeling so stressed and anxious that she very nearly invented a fictional date, but recalled that her alternative was to sit at home jumping every time the telephone rang in case it was Mr Mahoney or Sandra. Or go to the cinema. She could not go to Anne's in the present circumstances; her reaction to the news that her loved child and the trusted and admired Gwyn were lovers did not bear thinking about.

'Yes. That would be nice, if you don't mind me being a bit worn out. It's been a heavy day.'

'With my friend Mr Flowerdew?'

'Since you ask, no. He has gone back to Norfolk.'

'About time. His employees – him too for all we know – were nurturing illegal immigrants.'

'Dearie me. Say not so.'

'Alright, alright, we can do all this over dinner. Can we eat early?' To give him more time to seduce me? she wondered. 'I haven't eaten all day, that's why.'

'Certainly.'

'Can I pick you up from your flat?'

Yes, he could, she thought, Jenni would be there or at least her presence could be mentioned. It was not her day for new departures, fanciable though Richard Allenton might be in different circumstances, like when she was not being worried silly by what was going on in her lover's house. She put the phone down; she ought to tell Paul that she was having dinner with MI5, but perhaps it no longer mattered very much after Mirko's death. Yes, it did, of course, she told herself, sharply, go and tell him.

'Thank you for calling.'

She dragged down the stairs to see Paul to tell him she was dining with the enemy.

'Come in, Jules.'

She went in and sat down, warily, and told him about her date.

He looked exasperated. 'I would rather you did not become involved with the police, or MI5. We are involved in this case.'

'Well…well, I mean Mirko is no longer a client…I mean.'

'That is not the reason, Jules. This young man – this friend of yours, Mr Allenton. He has the reputation of a very ambitious man who will use any means to get where he wants to be. And if it were you he used, it would be bad for you and also not at all good for us here.' He sighed. 'Jules, my dear, if you could remember this, and remember that, well, you are perhaps a little vulnerable? A little, perhaps, pleased to be treated as a helpful insider? Yes?'

The subtext was all too clear and she could feel herself start to blush; would you please not be a silly girl again and involve yourself with men who ought to be off limits for you and involve me, again, in getting you out of the mire.

'I will be careful,' she said, with gritted teeth. 'And I will report anything significant. I promise.'

He waved her away, and she went wishing she had not agreed to go out with Richard Allenton. But when he arrived she found she was glad to see him. He had got himself shaved and into a clean shirt and tie, and while he was undoubtedly hungry – a plate of crisps and another of cheese biscuits vanished like snow in summer – he looked fresh. He sat and looked all round her big kitchen/dining-room, taking in everything in it, with the restless, observant look she had noticed when she first met him. Jenni was not there, and she was glad of it.

'Ready for off?'

'Absolutely.'

He had a driver with him which presumably made it even less likely he planned to seduce her that evening, unless this was a well-oiled routine, and the driver was told to drive round the block until Richard shone a light in the window or made some other unobtrusive signal.

'What's amusing you?'

'I couldn't possibly tell you.' The car drew up at a good steak restaurant where she ate on the days she felt she could afford it. They were expected, and menus put before them. She made her mind up swiftly, not wanting to stand between a hungry man and his dinner, but it took a little while to get the dark-skinned waiter, who appeared to speak no word of any known language, to understand what they wanted. The proprietor however, bustled over, dispatched his minion to the kitchen and got them drinks, so they were set.

'How are you doing?' she asked her escort, feeling a general enquiry could only be illuminating.

'Not very well. Oh, apart from the couple of boatloads we found living on your friend Andrew's land.' He glanced at her over his drink, but she just smiled at him and said she could not believe it was worth Andrew's while to jeopardise his perfectly sensible arrangement with the Home Office by importing a few more illegals.

'He has land on the coast,' Richard said, unsmiling. 'And he's quite heavily committed financially.' She gave him her best old-fashioned look. 'That's well known, locally. He would say so too.' He took a huge drink of his gin and tonic and at the moment the soup arrived, borne unsteadily on a tray by the waiter, so they were able to busy themselves passing each other the salt. Richard was eating with the concentrated speed of a man who hasn't eaten for a long time and she left him to it, deciding small talk could wait, or indeed not be indulged in if it was going to consist of sniping at Andrew Flowerdew.

He finished his soup and cleaned the plate with the bread and grinned at her.

'*Much* better now?' she asked, solicitously.

'Oh, ever so much, thank you.' He looked at her plate. 'Sorry, I must have slurped that down like a wolf. Nothing since breakfast and that wasn't much.' He yawned hugely. 'Sorry, sorry. Damn. I'd been looking forward to seeing you all day. What did you do today?'

She gave him the edited version, which missed out most of it.

'Tell me about your cousin Anne. Did she adopt you?'

'No. And of course now I'm of age. Gwyn – my social worker – wanted me to agree to be adopted, but somehow…' She hadn't meant to talk about Gwyn at all, but he was so much part of her life it was impossible to ignore him.

'That's Gwyn Jones, isn't it?'

'You know him?'

'Met him a couple of times. Over the Hackney saga.'

There had been two policemen involved, she remembered, among the suspects. The wretched children of Hackney had been far worse off than she had; if you cannot trust the police, where can you go? You'd truly have nowhere to turn.

'He must be very chuffed by you – I mean you must be one of his success stories. Do you keep in touch?'

Something about the question, even put between mouthfuls of the beautiful steaks that had now arrived, was making her uneasy.

'Yes, of course. I see them, him and Sandra, from time to time. And the children. If you can characterise the Jones offspring as children, that is.'

'Ah, like cobblers' children?'

'Exactly so. One fiendish eleven-year-old and a very difficult fifteen-year-old, both ripe for intervention by a good social worker.' Treacherous, but true, and Richard was laughing.

'If you had children, what would be the worst they could do to you?'

'Drink,' she said, instantly.

His hand, clasped round a fork with a lump of steak on it checked and she wished she had thought before she had spoken. He stuffed the contents of the fork into his mouth and gave her some more wine. 'My worst fears would be drugs. Same thing really.'

'Yes,' she said, gratefully, needing to get off this ground. 'Do you have brothers and sisters?'

'One of each. Both younger.'

Eldest children become policemen, just like serious Jimmy Watt. 'And parents?'

'And parents. Dad is a farmer, Mum is a teacher.'

'I remember your father farms.' It seemed a long time ago that she had found him and Andrew deep in farming chat.

He looked down at his plate, then across at hers. 'Sorry again. Please don't hurry, I'll sit and watch.'

What he was watching was her unfinished steak, not her, so she gave him half. He was bigger than her and, no doubt, his need was the greater. She declined pudding, then saw his face and urged him to have it for both of them. He considered it and decided against and smiled at her. She smiled back, conscious of a very definite frisson. His phone rang.

'Sorry,' he said, fighting with his jacket to find the phone. 'Allenton. Yes.' His face changed. 'How? No, don't *tell* me, I'm on my way.' He pressed the 'end' button, and looked at the phone, then remembered Jules, and the restaurant, and the anxiously hovering waiter. He called for the bill which removed the audience, then leant across to her. 'I have to go. You're not going to take me seriously.'

'No,' she agreed.

'Can we try Tuesday? No, damn. Wednesday?'

'It's a Law Society dinner.' She was consulting a Palm Pilot.

'Oh. Oh, well then. Thursday?'

'Yes. I'll cook. No, actually. I'll take you to an Italian.' She wasn't going to entertain Richard at home with Jenni Patel around. Even if she told her she was entertaining Richard as a prospective lover, she could see Jenni contriving to be there for drinks or coffee. This was emerging as another unforeseen problem about having a flatmate, even if, she thought with a stab of pain, it no longer mattered that Gwyn could not for the moment visit her.

He dropped her home and saw her to her door. She was both relieved and frustrated, and he saw it. 'I'm sorry about the job.'

'Men must work and women must weep.' Something had happened to her voice.

'Thursday.' He looked at her intently, and was gone.

The phone was ringing as she walked in and she looked at it waiting, and decided to let the answerphone take the strain. But it was Andrew Flowerdew, sounding harried and undecided about what message to leave, so she relented and picked up the phone.

'Oh, look, sorry to bother you this late... You weren't asleep? I wondered...well, you haven't seen Martin? He said he'd ring by 6 p.m. and I haven't heard anything.'

'I haven't seen him or heard from him, Andrew. You've called him, of course?'

'His mobile is switched off. And it's ten o'clock.'

My firm is the legal adviser for these people, she reminded herself. 'Are you worried enough to call the police?' This was Anne's test at any moment of anxiety, and it worked, as it always did.

'Yes.' Andrew sounded better. 'Yes, I am. And if the silly bastard has decided not to ring as we agreed...'

'Then he deserves any fuss that follows. Andrew, don't *you* know where Martin's wife lives? Between ourselves.'

'No. I *really* don't. Except that it is in South London. He was going over Vauxhall Bridge.'

'Give it till midnight – it's 10.30 now – then call the police.'

'Yes. Thank you, Jules. I wasn't making much sense.'

'Yes, you were. You're worried about him,' she said, kindly, and went off to make coffee and watch the TV, thinking no more of it.

But Andrew rang again twenty minutes later. Martin was in Hammersmith hospital. He had been mugged, found in the street and brought in unconscious. The police had found Andrew's number. Martin had a broken arm and concussion but was now conscious, Andrew said, sounding grim. 'I'm coming down as soon as I can. No, I'll get myself driven.'

'Andrew, what about his wife?'

'I don't know. You don't think…?'

Criminal lawyers are not anxious to import extra drama, there is usually quite enough to go round. 'Yes, I do,' she said, reluctantly. 'Were the police at the hospital?'

'Yes, but I suppose I should tell Richard Allenton.'

'You must tell Paul as well. No, hang on, that I can do for you. In fact, I can hear Jenni coming in now. You don't want to speak? No, all right, you get on, I'll tell her the facts and you can talk to her later.' It could surely not be a coincidence that Martin had been struck down when he was on his way to or from seeing his wife. Jenni came through the door. For once she was looking less than immaculate, with the collar of her neat suit turned up and a bit of the shiny dark hair escaping from its pony tail. She must have been working late, Jules thought, and made her a cup of tea while telling her about the events of the evening.

'What about the wife?'

'Andrew didn't know. I have his mobile number. You could call him. And Jenni, look.' She had had time to think. 'It's not my case, but shouldn't you tell Richard Allenton at MI5?'

Jenni had her back to her, looking for the herbal tea she preferred to the breakfast tea that Jules drank at any time of day.

'Why should we do that? It's not his business either. This has nothing to do with trafficking illegals. Martin Flowerdew contracted a legal marriage and brought his wife to this country as he was entitled to do.'

Jules was winded. 'You don't surely think it was just a mugging, do you?'

'Jules, until we know exactly what happened, I have no idea. Nor do you.' Jenni turned to look at her. 'I'll ring Paul just as soon as he could have reached his house.' She peered at her light, elegant gold watch which had been made by the sort of Swiss firm Jules had never heard of. 'I am sure he will say that we should not take action before we have some facts and before we commit ourselves or our clients to anything.'

Jules had to concede that all this made sense and sat down

again, refusing the herb flavoured hot water offered by Jenni.

'Paul always says we are like carpenters,' Jenni volunteered, her face softening as it always did at the mention of Paul's name. 'We must measure twice and cut only once.'

'Yes.' Jules had been the recipient of this dictum several times in her training and was annoyed by having His Master's Voice repeating it. But, she recollected fair-mindedly, if she had measured twice when Mirko Dragunoviç had walked into the office almost a week ago, then, most probably, none of this would have been happening. Or it would have been happening to a different set of people, so that she would not have met the Flowerdews, nor Richard Allenton, nor rediscovered Ray Cardona.

'Jules?'

'No, Jenni, it isn't my case and I am sure you are right to wait till you can talk to Paul. Particularly since you know where he is.' A somewhat underhand blow, she thought, seeing Jenni blush. 'I just – well, there may not be a connection, but the Flowerdews...'

She looked across at Jenni and understood that she was waiting for her to go to bed so that she could telephone Paul. At that moment the phone rang, and they both looked at it, and Jules let Jenni answer it.

'Lady Barlow. Oh dear, I'm so sorry. Jules is just here.'

'Darling.' Anne was sounding shaky. 'I'm so sorry to worry you. I got back and found I'd been burgled. I'm perfectly all right. It's just everything is such a mess, but it is not as bad as it looks.'

'I'm coming now. Did you call the police?'

'Indeed I did, and a kind sergeant is here. The trouble is, I can't remember what we have here, rather than in Cambridge, so I really don't know what has gone. They have a young woman PC who is being tactful with me.'

'Then you need me, at once. I'll get a taxi, and I'll leave the mobile on.' She called out the minicab service, turning down Jenni's offer to drive her – 'Since you have been out to dinner' – and in ten minutes was speeding over to the huge flat by Westminster Cathedral, which was the Barlow London home.

She checked her mobile was still on, paid the driver, and rang the bell. This was supposed to be a secure block, into which no one but an Authorised Visitor could get, but in practice the outer door needed a bang to close it and people in a hurry, or encumbered with parcels, would forget. And the closed circuit TV on which the porters in an office at the bottom of the street were supposed to watch comings and goings, depended for its value on a porter being available to do the watching.

Anne was waiting for her at the lift, looking pale and stressed. The flat however looked reasonably orderly.

'You've tidied up?' Jules said, hugging her.

'They didn't disturb this room much. Except for the books.'

The Barlow London home was in one of the old mansion flats facing onto one side of Westminster Cathedral, with three huge, high-ceilinged rooms at the front, two of them linked. The big room – all of forty feet long – which acted as dining-room and living-room looked all right except for the books which filled one end wall, and had been scattered all over the floor.

'Are the police still here?'

'Indeed. Two of them, in the bedroom, fingerprinting.'

'Really?'

The Met police was notoriously so overloaded that a burglary did not normally command much attention.

'I have to say that being in the House helped.'

'It would. And of course you do some work for the MOD.' Jules put the kettle on in the big kitchen which they had had moved, painfully, from the back of the flat where it formed part of the servants' quarters to the front where it was forty feet closer to the dining-room.

'The police asked about the MOD too. Most embarrassing. I had to explain that it is at the blunt edge that I advise: logistics, tents, boots, spare parts, food, uniforms. I wouldn't know a secret weapon if it stood up and saluted me.'

Anne was looking less tired, but Jules was not deceived. 'Could some Foreign Power not be interested?'

'In what, I ask myself? In the fact that we are keeping soap and lavatory paper in very expensive warehouses, because the military fear Tesco may run out of them. Is this going to terrify the enemy, even if we knew who they were? Al-Qaeda might be shaking in their boots, but it seems to me more likely that they would welcome having loo paper and soap dropped on them.'

'Is that the plan?' Jules asked, startled.

'No, of course not, darling, the soap is for the lads. Al-Qaeda do not stand still long enough to drop anything on, because if they did they would be dead, given the absolute overwhelming superiority of American air power.'

'Like in Iraq?'

'Yes.' She was feeling much, much better, Jules saw, with a pang. 'The only puzzle really is why the Iraqi army thought they had any chance at all in a pitched battle, or why the Serbs thought they did in Kosovo, or the Taliban in Afghanistan. It's no good just having ground troops. The modern army does not do much pushing forward in lines. If it meets serious resistance it quickly recovers and rings up for a plane to bomb the socks off whoever is firing at it. And if the other side doesn't *have* any planes, well, that's it really. The problems for us – the allies – will come afterwards, like in Afghanistan.'

'Or Kosovo.'

'Ah well now, that *is* interesting. Our win in Kosovo turned out to be the necessary sequel to Bosnia. After Srbrenica, the Serbs thought they could raise two fingers to the UN – and they had every reason to think so – so they tried it on again in Kosovo. But this time, the two biggest and ugliest of the Western Powers – us and the Americans – made it clear we were going in anyway, and while the UN was not much use, NATO was. So the refugees came back. Kosovo is settled, Milosevic fell, finally, and the murderers of Srbrenica are being hunted down. Much too slowly, but…'

'One of my new friends, Martin Flowerdew was at Srbrenica. Afterwards, I mean.'

'Farmer Flowerdew?' She had allowed herself to hope that this might be a suitable young man.

'No, his brother.' She grinned, wickedly. 'Who is gay. Hello?' She slid off the sofa, seeing a pair of strangers peering in at her.

'Ah, Sergeant Tewin.' Anne, even in distress, knew about the importance of remembering people's names. 'Any luck?'

'No, Baroness, I don't think so. He or they wore gloves. Would you like to come now and look at the bedroom and see what's missing?'

Anne turned pale, but Jules reached out a hand to pull her up and kept hold of it.

'There isn't any vandalism that we can see, Baroness. I mean everything's on the floor, but...'

'But no destruction. Thank you.'

Jules took her hand as they walked into the bedroom and urged her to start with the obvious, which Anne reluctantly did. 'My jewellery. They've left the box.'

'*Not* the Barlow diamonds?'

'No, not, they're in the bank. I never get them out, they cost too much to insure.'

'Not even for the State Opening? People wear tiaras there.' Jules was rushing to distract her.

'No, darling, you're thinking of Peeresses.' The police presence had obviously had the same thought and were looking baffled. 'They are wives of Peers, and they get to sit in the gallery in full evening dress and diamonds for the State Opening. But I am a Peer. One of the lads, only female, so I swelter in ermine stripes along with them on the floor of the house. The diamonds wouldn't show.'

'What about Henry? Could *he* sit in the gallery, in diamonds?'

'I don't see why not. Mind you he might occasion some remark in the tiara. And the necklace thingy, which is built for a very well endowed lady.'

The police were laughing too, Jules was glad to see. She had hated anyone seeing Anne so openly distressed.

'Baroness. Could we ask you to look at your office again?'

Oddly enough that was relatively undisturbed. The drawers of the big desk had been turned out onto the floor, but the three big filing cabinets, although unlocked, had not been disturbed, nor had the five labelled filing trays in which she kept current work.

'The MOD papers?' Sergeant Tewin had asked hopefully, but

Anne shook her head. She showed them the 48-page paper on Warehouse Reorganisation was in its place at the top of the stack, unread by the burglars, small blame to them.

Then she bent to look at the contents of the drawers. 'I don't keep anything valuable there and I won't find what is missing without sorting it.' She straightened up, feeling the blood rush to her head. 'Why didn't they take the computer? Now that would have been a tragedy.'

'You've got all your stuff backed up on disc, Anne, surely?' Jules said, shocked.

'Well, not terribly recently. Henry's not here, you see.'

Sergeant Tewin, cautiously pointed out that the computer was not the very latest, state of the art, such as normally is a target in a burglary. No indeed, Jules thought, and the TV was ten years old too. They agreed there was no point detaining the police further and parted with expressions of mutual goodwill at the end of which Jules steered her guardian to a kitchen chair, then searched all the cupboards for anything she could cook. They ate, and went on companionably to put all the books back, and sort out the bedroom. Jules left Anne in the study with the desk drawers to sort out, while she washed up.

'Jules!' It was Anne, sounding urgent, and she rushed to the study. 'Look, it's Gwyn.'

It was too, on the late news, looking weary, walking away from Hackney Town Hall, where the Inquiry was proceeding in the presence of the world's press. It had been a dreadful story of files destroyed and warnings suppressed or rubbished by Hackney's paedophile employees. Gwyn had been interviewed earlier in the evening and was reassuring the general public that the bad old days were gone, that children in the borough's foster homes and hostels were not being beaten and buggered. Or if they were, their complaints would this time be heard. He didn't raise his voice, he looked what he was: tough, uncompromising, and with no time for equivocation. At his best, Jules thought, her heart aching.

'He looks tired,' Anne said. 'How old will he be now? Forty?'

'Not quite, I think.'

'The poor chap looks older today.'

The Inquiry was the lead story and Peter Sissons moved on to the earthquake in Turkey from which bodies were still being recovered. Jules made sure that Anne went on sorting; the old envelope in which she kept the photographs waiting to go into albums was a mess, and it would upset her in the morning. Once sure that Anne was still working, she sat down at the computer.

'Jules?'

'I'm backing up your data onto a disc.'

'Darling, how very kind.'

'This ancient machine could pop its clogs any day, and you would have to remember all 900 addresses on its memory or reinvent all your correspondence for the last ten years. You *knew* that.'

'Well, sort of, I know, I've been very lazy and, I'm afraid, I rely on Henry. I tell you what *is* missing, or I think it is. I had two pictures of you in this – I was going to get them tastefully framed, along with the most recent ones of the boys.'

'Could they be in Cambridge?'

'No. It was the nice one you sent me of you at a dinner, and the little one Gwyn took when you were fourteen, and living with his family.'

'Oh dear. Well, I can get you the dinner one, and I expect I have another one of the kiddy one. That wasn't burglars, no one could have wanted those pictures. You must have lost them. Time we went to bed.'

'No, no darling,' Anne said, with an effort. 'I'm really all right. You go home.'

'Get off. I'm staying.'

Chapter Fourteen

(Tuesday after Easter)

Jules arrived back at her flat at 9 a.m. the next morning after breakfast with Anne to discover that Jenni had already left the house, but not without leaving a cheque for the first month's rent. She had difficulty in not picking it up and kissing it but did the next best thing which was putting it into a stamped addressed envelope for the bank. She arrived at work in good order, wearing a pair of her new shoes with some confidence now that she knew she could pay for them. Paul's door was closed, and Jenni's office empty, so they were presumably closeted together. She read Louise's appointments list upside down and saw, as she had expected, Andrew Flowerdew's name. He was expected at 10.30 and there was no reason she should not choose that moment to come downstairs and look for a coffee.

An hour and a half later she was just about to operate this plan when the phone rang. 'Mistah Jones.'

'Gwyn? Where are you?'

'On the pavement outside the Inquiry. Waiting to go in.'

'Are you alright?'

'Up to a point.' He had picked that up from Anne, she thought, painfully. It meant No. 'It's not good.'

'Is she…is she very angry with me?'

'Mostly with me, but you get a mention there too. More than one. No, we'll get by somehow. She knows I have to get through this bloody Inquiry or we're all in the soup.' A roaring noise extinguished conversation. 'Sorry. Bloody buses. I've had no more calls from the man Mahoney. What about you?'

'No. None.'

'Well, we've both of us got that to be thankful for. Cariad, I have to go.'

Damn him, she thought, he has no right to go on calling me cariad. She put the phone down, blew her nose and decided she could not hang around downstairs on the off-chance of seeing Andrew Flowerdew, comforting though that would be. She would just have to get on with her work —there was plenty of that – and let the day go as it would, and hope Jenni would be kind enough to tell her what was happening.

The phone rang again as she reached this conclusion. And it was Richard Allenton, against the usual background of twenty people all talking at once. 'I need a favour.'

'What?' She wasn't feeling sociable.

There was a pause, and the background noise died away. 'That's better. I'm on the fire escape.'

'Why?'

'Is there someone with you?'

'No. I'm just ratty. To what do I owe the honour?'

'It's business, much though I'd like to talk to you. Could you possibly meet me at Pentonville, if I send a car?'

'Why?'

'I like a girl who doesn't bother to chat. We have someone we want you to take a look at. Two someones.'

'Are they dead?'

'Yes. Both of them. But…but in reasonably good nick.'

'Apart from being dead. Not…not anyone.'

'Oh God, no. No one you could mind about, it's just that you are our best bet for a quick ID.'

'I am overwhelmed by the honour you do me but I do have a day job, which may today prevent me from moonlighting for MI5.'

There was a pause, while she could feel him trying to decide what to say. 'Your country needs you,' he said, finally.

'Are you making me an offer I cannot refuse?'

'No. No, I'm not, I can probably get them identified, just rather more slowly. I'm asking a favour.'

Satisfied to have got this established, she thought about it. The pile of work on her table was urgent but not desperate. Nor was it particularly interesting – Paul and Jenni seemed to be doing all that, and specifically did not want her to join them. And Richard Allenton was asking her nicely to do something interesting. It was really no contest but she waited another minute before agreeing to be collected in two hours which would, as she did not say, give her time to see Andrew Flowerdew if her colleagues were not going to bustle him out of the office in a cloak. Heartened by the conversation with Richard, she went downstairs to look for coffee and walked into Andrew Flowerdew, looking grim, and being escorted out by Jenni, who looked momentarily furious. Evidently, she had hoped to rush him off the premises.

'Have coffee with me?' Andrew said. 'Both of you?' Jenni hesitated and gave Jules a warning look which she decided to ignore. 'I need a friend,' Andrew said. Standing rocklike and substantial in the waiting-room, he was managing to look forlorn.

'I'll have a quick coffee with you. Can you come, Jenni?' She had observed that one of Jenni's enshrouded Muslim customers had risen and was surging across the room, so that she had to refuse, crossly.

'How is Martin?' Jules said, as they turned left out of the office.

'Lying.'

'Well...oh, I see. Lying.'

'He says he was on his way to see Alyssia when he was mugged.'

She considered this. 'Which bit is he lying about?'

'Oh, good question. He *is* injured, and he *was* robbed. I cancelled all his credit cards last night. But everything else is untrue.'

She thought about it as their cappuccinos arrived. 'What do *you* think happened?'

'Oh, that he and Alyssia were together and were attacked. And she got away somehow.'

'Did you tell Paul what you thought?'

'Of course I did. He is going to see Martin later today and see if he can get through to him how important it is that Alyssia comes to see him.'

'And to the police.'

'Oh yes, of course. They have been to see him of course, but he told them he was mugged and cannot produce a description. They were wearing motorcycle helmets, he says.'

'That bit is probably true.' The local gang, who specialised in mugging pensioners, all had motorcycles and therefore a legal reason for going round with their heads covered in plastic.

'Doesn't help, does it?'

'No. You're a bit stuck. What are you going to do now?'

'Get back to Norfolk again to sort out my students.'

'The ones who were abetting illegals? I thought they had been flung out of the country.'

'Not yet. MI5 have them. Your friend Allenton and his minions. No, they will be deported, but the whole thing has upset everyone else.'

'So you need to be at the bridge.' She smiled at him; dear Andrew, she could see that his employees would derive much comfort from his steady presence.

'Yes. And there is…I'm sure you haven't had time to look in on Mirko's mother.'

'Oh, Andrew. No. I am sorry.'

'No, no, no, I only asked you yesterday, but it's in the wrong direction and I wondered…'

'Count on me,' she said, deciding that MI5's driver could be diverted to do this chore. 'It shall be done.'

She met Paul on her way in and agreed that Andrew Flowerdew did seem very worried. Paul was looking harassed and she hesitated, but she did have to grasp this particular nettle, so she explained that she was being taken away in the next hour or so to help MI5 with their enquiries.

'Come into the office, Jules.'

He was, she saw, seriously displeased and braced herself to attack.

'I know it's not at all convenient, Paul, and I've no idea who they think it is, but do we want to make them get a subpoena? Or, look, would you like to talk to Mr Allenton, see if you can see a way round? I don't much want to trek off to Pentonville either,' she added, mendaciously.

He had started doodling with long, slashing lines. 'No,' he said, crossly. 'No. You have, I suppose, to go. Just remember, please, that this Allenton is on the other side. And that Mr

Flowerdew – both Messrs Flowerdews – are clients of the firm.'

Any minute now, she thought, teeth gritted, he is going to ask me if I could not find a nice young lawyer in some field where we are not. Or an accountant.

'You will tell me please what happens today? In as much, of course, as it relates to this firm,' he added, hastily, and she got herself out of his office, wishing she could lock herself up and get on with her job. Her 11 a.m. client came and went and then the MI5 driver came for her. His first bid was to refuse to divert to UCH to which Mrs Dragunoviç had been moved, but she dealt with this by ringing Richard Allenton and explaining that uncompleted work meant she would be a little late but less late if MI5 would agree to drive her. The car dropped her outside the main gate, apparently in the middle of a building site. She recalled, coughing in the dust, that this was a Private Finance Initiative, and that the whole hospital would be redone at great speed. She fought her way through to the reception and upstairs in a creaking lift which no Initiative, private or public, had yet reached. She checked with the Nursing Station and explained who she was.

'Some of the family are here.'

'Ah.' She hadn't thought of that, and Andrew, with all his troubles, had probably forgotten, but there was a daughter.

'Oh no, I tell a lie. Miss Dragunoviç went out to do some shopping. You could pop in.'

She went in, clutching the tulips she had acquired at the hospital gate. Mrs Dragunoviç was sitting up in bed, gazing out of the window. She didn't look good, a poor colour and bigger than ever. A collapsed mountain.

'You perhaps don't remember who I am. Jules Carlisle from Jenkins Associates.' Jules advanced as confidently as she could into that uncomprehending stare and laid the tulips before her. She touched them, uncertainly, with her left hand and Jules saw that her right arm lay unmoving on the bedspread. She said something and Jules strained to hear until she realised Mrs Dragunoviç wasn't speaking English. Jules apologised, loud and clear and slowly, for her lack of Serbo-Croat, wishing she hadn't come. Mrs Dragunoviç's face twisted with effort and she held out her left hand curled upwards like a claw.

'Money. You bring?'

Jules gaped at her. She was a guest of the NHS, dammit. Jules took a breath, trying to decide where to start, but the door banged open and a woman in her thirties, recognisably Mirko's sister, came through it at speed, jaw stuck out, trailing bags. She shot a stream of Serbo-Croat at her mother who replied sounding staccato and indignant, pointing her left hand at Jules. The only bit she got was the inconvenient collection of consonants which constituted Paul's original surname. The daughter bared a mouthful of teeth at Jules; close up she was much less good-looking than Mirko and an excess of crooked teeth didn't help either.

'I am Janina. And you are?'

Jules told her, adding the information that she had been with her mother at Pentonville when she had suffered the stroke that had put her into this hospital. Janina left the smile in place, but Jules could see furious calculations were going on behind it. She looked towards the bed.

'My mother asks why you have come.'

Social life in Former Yugoslavia must be very hard work, Jules thought, and explained slowly with gestures that Andrew Flowerdew had asked particularly that she came and saw that she had everything she needed. With a winning smile, for Andrew's sake.

Both women heard her out in silence, exchanging only one look. They watched her, obviously waiting for something else, but she could think of nothing more to say. She tried the interrogative mode, and asked Janina if there was anything that her mother lacked. A short burst of Serbo-Croat from the bed followed.

'She asks if Mr Jenkins will come to see her soon.'

Well, that much was clear, and, alas, Paul was going to be furious with her all over again. He had not wanted this client any more than he had wanted Mirko, and now she had enabled her to ask for him. And a right disagreeable old thing she was too.

She rose to go, only just leaving the flowers. 'Mr Jenkins is very busy, but I know Mr Flowerdew hoped that I would be able to tell him if there was anything that you needed.'

Another burst of Serbo-Croat from Mum, in which exasperation was clearly audible, and she looked enquiringly at Janina.

'My mother would like to see Mr Jenkins. Himself. Soon.'

Well, put like that, she thought, I really might as well not have bothered. She arrived in the corridor, still seething and holding a mental conversation with Paul in which she told him he could have this particular client without any interference from her when she recalled that Paul didn't want any more Dragunoviçes. He hadn't wanted the first one. The nurse who had let her in grinned at her.

'Give you a hard time?'

'Yes. Both of them.'

'They're very worried about money. They keep talking about it.'

'The NHS hasn't started to charge, has it?' She was thoroughly pissed off.

'No. But she has lost two sons, and her husband's in hospital. She must be worried about the future.'

An absolutely reasonable point which left Jules feeling six inches high. She said, feebly, that it wasn't that she was not sympathetic, but…

'But she's not an easy patient. And the daughter's very stressed.'

Assuming this to be nurse-speak for 'bloody disagreeable' she agreed and started back to tackle the groaning lift. Of course, the Dragunoviçes, mother and daughter, might be worried about money, but why should Paul provide it? Andrew Flowerdew as conscientious country employer was, she felt sure, contributing to their expenses. Well, Paul did a lot for Serbian charities – for free – and he probably did have access to a charity which would help. Andrew Flowerdew, however, or whatever Trust it was, could damn well do the next visit, since she had been about as welcome as a cup of cold sick. It was raining outside and the MI5 car had obviously been moved on, so there was nothing to do but wait in the rain. A cruising taxi slowed and looked at her, but she shook her head, regretfully; his hackney carriage licence plate number was a perfect numerial sequence – 13611, and she felt in need of some luck. Another cab, dropping off a flustered visitor, had a prime number as its DLVD number, which cheered her. Little things please little minds on a bad day, she thought, wishing she had a raincoat. But then the MI5 car arrived and she could get into it and relax.

The car had stopped for traffic lights and she sat up and looked around her.

'Pentonville.'

'Yes ma'am.'

So now she was an honorary member of the police force.

Richard was talking into his phone on the steps and waved but kept his distance, finishing his conversation, then ran down, Jimmy Watt behind him.

'Thank you for coming.'

'Not at all. It is a Public Duty I am performing.' Always remind the police that they owe you one.

'Well, it is. I hope.'

'Who do you think they are? The bodies?'

'I don't want to lead you. Could you just look?'

She thought – and hoped – that it would be Ray Cardona that was wheeled out for her, but it didn't turn out like that. She followed him into the familiar mortuary, a clutch of anxiety in her stomach. A drawer was opened for her. The face was young, stiff, mouth open and his neck arched back, as if he was fighting for breath.

'Artie,' she said, as steadily as she could, past the taste of bile in her throat.

'Are you sure? I wasn't myself, quite, although I'd seen him too.'

'Yes. Look at the widow's peak.' The deep V of hair over the forehead was particularly marked, with the head strained back.

'He's also got a mole or a wart, or something, just by his nose. When he…last week, I noticed it because he was self-conscious about it. I wondered why he hadn't done something about it. You can see.' She made a stagey gesture; she was not going to look again for fear of being sick.

'What about the other chap?' she asked, sucking in a blast of mortuary chill.

'We think we know who he is, but would you take a look?'

She had always had her fair share of curiosity, so she did as she was asked as the drawer rattled out. The face, half hidden, was scarlet and congested, but somehow familiar and after a minute she placed it. 'The nurse? From Pentonville? The Irish lad, William. You were looking for him…' Her voice tailed away.

'What was his second name again?' It seemed wrong that a young man should be lying in the mud, dead, and she had forgotten his name.

'William Cliffe.'

'Not an incomer then?'

'No. Born here. But his mother came from Belgrade. Married an Irishman. Lives in Bromley.'

She looked round the curious faces of the uniformed police, all of whom hastily looked away.

'Thank you, everybody,' Richard said. 'We're done.'

She was shivering by the time she got back to the car. Both young men had been alive, and she had talked to them only a few days ago. Richard came out to the car with her and looked at her, carefully, as she sat in the back seat.

'You've gone blue.'

'I'm cold.'

Richard felt in one of the jacket's pockets and fished out a flask. 'Get that down you. Have you enough clothes on? You're sitting on my old sweater, put it on.' He felt around her. 'What have you…Jules, your feet are freezing. Look, get them off.'

'What? Oh, my shoes!' She could see the driver's neck swelling with the effort to contain himself but she kicked them off and accepted in return a pair of socks which looked military, being made of unyielding, bristly wool.

'Move over.' He slid in the back and folded the military jacket around her. It was lined with something thermal and was still warm from his body and she relaxed into it, taking a healthy mouthful of the whisky-flavoured coffee, or coffee-flavoured whisky. He leaned forward to seize the car telephone, leaving his left arm round her shoulders, but she drank her coffee, sphinx-like. He would have to work harder than that to get a reaction from a person he had dragged out to do his dirty work. He was telling someone at the other end that he had an identification for Artie and confirmation on William Cliffe, and reorganising his schedule for the day, so she had to wait to ask her question.

'How did they die?'

'Different ways. Artie was shot in the chest, probably at the site. Cliffe was strangled and most likely dumped here.'

'Why?'

'We don't know?'

'We were looking for Cliffe as you know after Mirko's death. We'd talked, briefly, to Artie, then let him out, because we're holding three people we want more. And the judge was getting bolshie.' The police can hold a suspected terrorist for seven days without charge, but they have to go to a judge every forty-eight hours, so this was understandable. 'It looks as if someone is tidying up. Making sure they can't talk to us.'

'Cliffe murdered Mirko?'

'We think so. We would have tried to charge him, and I should have pulled Artie in, as soon as you led him to us. I was letting him run, but they got to him.'

'Who are *they*?' She didn't want to sit through a man replaying what he ought to have done.

'The people who are organising all this.'

'All what, precisely?' The whisky had got her mind into gear. 'Are there two different things going on? A standard economic migrant smuggling operation and then something else. Bringing in real criminals and terrorists. Two different customer bases are not usually served by the same operation.' She was watching his profile and saw his lips tighten. He took a swig of his coffee, giving himself time to think.

'The basic business brings in labour for the farmers and growers here. What seems to have happened is that a set of different – and more dangerous – people are infiltrating some of their own among the regular customers.'

'*Real* criminals?'

'The shippers are all real criminals. Most of the customers are not.'

'So were Artie and Cliffe part of the regular business, or involved with...well, with the terrorists or whatever they are?'

'Artie is a local, part of the basic business. Cliffe was another kettle of fish entirely. He has no history at all of political activity, so he seems to have been a sleeper. When someone asked him to, he killed a patient.'

'He did do that, did he? Or did he just let someone else in to do it, then run?'

They were still sharing much of his jacket and she could feel the muscles of his shoulder. 'It's possible, of course, but my guess is we'll never know.'

'What was our late client? I mean which category was Mirko?'

'We don't know. And he isn't here to be asked.'

She digested this. 'So what did he *do* exactly? Did he arrange passage for his brother?'

'No. We think his brother did that himself, just like Mirko told you. But he knew the network who were bringing in people who wanted to work here.'

So MI5 is scouring the country? Are you looking for...for the basic business network?'

'Yes. But I am specifically here to look at some of the people that are coming in.'

'So you are not interested in the ordinary economic migrant.'

'MI5 as a whole is, yes, because as you must know the level of illegal immigration is potentially destabilising. My particular interest lies elsewhere. I'm looking for individuals who are on our list for one reason or another, some of whom present a clear danger to the UK. Or are assembling here as a base to do something in another country. Or are running here to escape trial in their own country.'

'War criminals.'

'You all right, Jules?'

'Yes.'

She thought of Martin Flowerdew and his wife, and decided that Paul had not shared his information with MI5. It was more than her job was worth to go against Paul's expressed commands and tell Richard, but she would have, somehow, to make Paul tell him.

'Still a bit cold.' He huddled closer to her which was nice, but she was still shivering.

'Jules? We'll drive you back of course, but since we've ruined your day anyway, could we get you to look at some photographs?'

She thought about it and looked at her watch. 'I need some more coffee. And I need to make a call. In decent privacy.'

He looked at her, doubtfully, and offered an office, but she shook her head and took her mobile off to a corner of the car park and waited while the office found Paul and attached him to a telephone.

'Jules. You have finished with Mr Allenton? Yes? You were able to help him?'

'I recognised both of his bodies, yes.' She told him who they were and heard him sigh.

'Mirko's nurse? The man who killed him?'

'Either that or he let someone else in to do it.'

'Did Mr Allenton say anything of what he thinks?'

'Yes, he did.' She explained Richard's theory that Bad Men, war criminals or similar, were being brought in as part of a routine people-smuggling operation. She waited for his comment, hoping he would volunteer to talk to Richard. 'Paul? Are you still there?'

'Yes, yes. I am just...well, not believing, I suppose.'

'It does seem a tad elaborate, doesn't it? I thought Bad Men came in their own planes to unmarked airports.'

'Not so much since the Twin Towers.' Paul was sounding cold and far away, and she pushed the phone more firmly against her ear. 'So, Jules, where did our late client meet these people? What does Mr Allenton think? And what people?'

'He was professionally mysterious about all of that.'

'You are coming back? Good. Ring me if you think...I am

concerned about this, Jules.'

Well, me too, she thought, particularly since I seem to be piggy in the middle. She walked over to Richard Allenton, scowling, but he smiled at her with evident affection.

'What?' she said, ungraciously.

'It's just…well, you don't look quite like the smart London lawyer I first met.'

She reached for her handbag and combed her hair. 'Better?'

'You look fine.'

Just as I feared, she thought, but the hell with it. 'Lead on.'

He reached to open the door and, as she passed him, he touched her shoulder and just for a moment the world stopped turning. Then there was a knock on the door, and Jimmy Watt's voice was saying that the room was ready, sir.

'Right.' Richard was sounding husky. He stood back, erasing all human expression as he held the door open for her.

'Thank you, sergeant. Miss Carlisle. Sergeant Franks, who is in charge of Exhibits.'

She was given a chair and a large album of photographs. She picked Ray Cardona, Artie Potton, and Kevin Roberts and then sat back, hesitant.

'I haven't seen the rest of the Cardonas since I was ten. Fourteen years ago.'

'Do you recognise anyone else?'

'Well, I think so. This could be Kevin Robert's younger brother Pat.' She looked up but Richard and his sergeant were professionally deadpan. 'Alright, I'll just bash on. This here is one of Ray's brothers – younger, and I can't remember his name. And *this* is another one.' A curious sameness in the format of the photographs struck her. 'These are all taken with the same…at the same…?'

'They were photographed at a police station, yes.'

'Are they all still with you, as it were? I mean I know Artie Potton is…but I suppose I could look at the originals for you if it would help.'

There was a pause, and she saw that the sergeant was watching Richard. 'None of them are currently in custody. Could you go on Jules, we have a few more?' They gave her another book, this time the photographs were a more mixed bag.

'Heavens!'

'What?'

'I would say that had to be Sharon Cardona, but she's got very fat.'

'It is,' Richard said.

'She isn't a suspect? You put her in to keep me on my toes.'

'Not quite.' Richard was frowning, and she returned to considering Sharon. Not a pretty woman, but recognisable by the dark hair pulled lightly off her forehead, the Cardona widow's peak very marked, and the small eyes very bright above the lardy cheeks. She turned the page. 'Mirko. No, not *Mirko*! I mean I have seen the picture before. He had it with him the day he came in to see me. It's Stefan, or he said it was.' She looked up. 'And another one – oh, it's the same one blown up.'

'Not blown up, just with more background. It was with Mirko's stuff.'

'It's still Stefan. Look at the bones in the face.' She glanced up at Richard, but he was looking at the photograph, intently, so there was something she had missed. She looked at it more carefully; Stefan was in uniform, and younger. Not much but this was not someone of twenty-eight, she'd been right about that, more like twenty-three. It was now to be seen that he was sitting at a desk and to his right was a cap, with a gold leaf badge. She peered at it.

'An oak leaf,' Richard said. 'He was an officer.'

'I'll take your word for it.' Next to the cap was a piece of metal work, and as she looked at it she recognised Roman numerals VIII/IX.

'Anything?'

'Just gave me a bit of a turn. The body in the mortuary. I'm not sure I would have known the man in the photograph was the same… It was him of course. Stefan, I mean.'

'Oh yes. The DNA proved that.'

She turned the pages, recognising no one in the parade of faces. Probably half of them were Regional CID or people's brothers put in to make sure she wasn't being overeager. She stopped at a picture of a very pretty girl, very young with an aureole of blonde hair. She stared at it, puzzled, and became aware that both men in the room were tense. 'I don't know her, I'm sorry. There's something though. Oh, wait a minute. She's not English.'

'But you don't know her?'

She looked again at the bright young face. 'No. No, really not.'

'Turn over a page.'

There was another photo, smaller, and she looked at it for some time. 'The same girl. I still don't know her but she's older. Is she…was she…dead?'

'No, no, she isn't.'

They seemed to have run out of photographs, and she looked up. 'Any more? Or can I go home?'

They were both looking doubtful and she felt that she had disappointed them somehow. 'I'm sorry if I haven't been helpful, but it's no good my making things up, is it?'

'No, none at all. All right. We'll get you a car.' Richard opened the door into the corridor. 'Sarn't!'

He escorted her to the car and thanked her punctiliously for her help.

'Go carefully,' he said, and they rolled out of the car park.

Chapter Fifteen

(Wednesday, the week after Easter)

She woke to hear the phone ringing and reached for it.

'Darling?'

'Anne.'

'Did I wake you? I *am* sorry, only it's eight o'clock and I thought…'

'Oh God. Eight o'clock!' She sat up, which was a mistake, and flopped back against the pillows. 'I am usually…I mean I am awake. I shouldn't drink.'

'Were you on the razzle?'

MI5's car had delivered her at eight the night before and she had eaten the not very much she had found in the fridge. Then Jenni had come in and they had had a drink together. Several drinks. 'No, but I had a hard day. Can I ring you later? I'm already terribly late. Are you all right, though? No more burglars.'

'Of course. I only wanted to square a date – I was hoping to lure you to dinner.'

'Who with?' Anne had taken to inviting her with the sons of her oldie friends at the Lords. With very mixed results.

'Tell you later. Are you alright? Apart from the drink, I mean.'

'I'm fine,' she said, feeling suddenly and surprisingly weepy. 'A bit tired perhaps.'

It took her forty-five minutes to get herself ready to go out, clean, fed and reasonably coherent. Thanks to Jenni's wardrobe clearance she got dressed without the usual morning agony, but by the time she had eaten breakfast, slowly and cautiously, there was no time to put on make-up. But her hair was washed and, apart from looking washed-out, she thought she would do.

The waiting-room was full, she saw, mostly with teenage boys, and she scuttled in, head down, making for the stairs. There had been a drugs bust at the local Comprehensive and Peter, one of the partners, had got landed with representing all the customers as opposed to the pushers. She was still ten minutes ahead of her first customer, she saw, as she sat down, gratefully. Her phone rang and she reached across for it.

'Mr Jones to see you.'

Her heart thumped. 'Mr Gwyn Jones?'

'Mr Jake Jones.'

Jake, Gwyn's eldest, who had been four years old when she had joined his family, ten years before. Fifteen now, as tall as his mother and not that much smaller than his father when last seen. She felt cold, then hot, and could not think for a minute. Then she rang Gwyn, but he was in the Inquiry of course and could not be got out. She called Louise. 'I'm coming down.'

It took her a minute to pick Jake out. All the partnership's male teenage clients, black or white, had shaven heads, earrings and huge baggy trousers, and all of them seemed to be in the waiting-room. Jake solved the problem by standing up – or rather getting up into a half crouch, clawing at his trousers to prevent them getting entangled with the vast, unlaced trainers.

'He bin here since 8.30,' Louise reported, dourly. Her 10 a.m. client had also risen, hopefully, but since it was only five to, she managed to indicate she would be with her shortly. She took Jake up to a conference room.

'So, Jake,' she said, unhopefully. 'Nice to see you.'

He looked at her and she felt guilt and responsibility like a huge bird settling its claws on her shoulders and pressing down. He looked terrible, pale and red-eyed. She had never, she realised, given a thought to Gwyn's children, but here before her was a living, breathing reproach. He had been crying, the tear tracks marked on his dirty face, which in the manner of the teenage boy he had wiped with the cuff of his oversize sweat-shirt.

'My Mum,' he said, to the desk. 'She's gone away.'

Jules sat, frozen, watching Jake. He picked at the edge of the table with nails chewed down to the quick. She made an enormous effort and got her mouth open. 'What about your Dad?'

'Oh, *he's* still here. Well, he isn't, he's at work.'

The consoling social worker wasn't going to play in this scene; this boy knew she had something to do with the loss of his mother and was not going to leave.

'Why did she go?' Jules asked, understanding she had to head into the storm.

'They had a big fight. Her and Dad. It's bin going on for days.' He was looking out of the window in order not to look at Jules, or cry, and her heart clenched in pity. 'It was about you,' he said, to the windowsill. 'And there's this man from the newspapers who rings up. I don't know why.'

'Did your father not tell you?'

'No. I want to know.' He turned his head and looked at her boldly, and she thought wildly that she didn't know much about child psychology, but this wasn't a child and he needed an answer.

'He wanted to...well, to smear your father. So he was trying to say that your father had abused a child in his care. Me.'

He absorbed this, slowly. 'Why would the paper want to do that?'

'Your father is very important to this Inquiry, and to Hackney, in the future. If he can be shown to have done anything like what some of these men did then...'

'But he didn't.' It was an appeal.

'No, he didn't, Jake.' Safe ground at last. 'Of course he didn't. You probably don't remember anything about that time. You were four years old. I was in your house for three months, both your parents were very good to me and then I went to live with Anne. Someone is trying to make trouble to prevent your father getting at all the monsters who have been beating and bullying and abusing children in Hackney's care all these years.'

'But if it isn't true, then why does this man say it? And what's the matter with Mum? She must know that Dad wouldn't...'

'I would think so,' Jules said, the ground turning to quagmire beneath her feet.

'So they can't...I mean they quarrelled about something else.' He looked at her directly, so like his mother, that she caught her breath.

'Well, it's very upsetting,' she said, lamely. 'But I'm sure she'll come back. She won't...well, she may be cross with your father, but...'

But she had. She had been so angry that she left her treasured sons. Jake, even bewildered as he was, knew that it must have taken something very serious indeed to make her do that.

'Did you talk to her?'

'I should have, but I had no idea she was so upset.' Jules felt sick, her ability to lie, flat-footed, was deserting her.

'Will you talk to my father? Today?'

This was going to be a formidable man, she saw. As clever as his father but with Sandra's strong will.

'I will, later today. I promise,' she said, wanting only to get him out of the office so that she could find Gwyn and agree what was to be said.

They said goodbye on the doorstep and Jake shook her hand awkwardly, deploying his left hand to hold up his trousers and loped out into the traffic, missing a motor-bike by inches. The Belloc couplet 'Do not adultery commit/Advantage rarely comes of it' came into her mind from nowhere, but she thought drearily that until now she had believed that all the disadvantage fell to the parties engaged in the activity. She had not understood what collateral damage might be caused, but watching that thin, distressed boy dodging traffic in Camden High Street, she felt real shame.

She saw two clients, taking notes automatically but with her mind not engaged, then around 12.30, Gwyn rang and she was able to tell him what had happened. 'He knows,' she finished, baldly. 'He knows he isn't being told all there is.'

'Christ.' There was a long, miserable pause. 'Right. Yes. I'll go straight home when the Inquiry rises. About five o'clock.' Gwyn was good at recognising when he can't control a situation, she reflected, drearily. He always said that social workers had to be or they'd all have nervous breakdowns. 'You're right. I told both boys what the paper was alleging and that it wasn't true. But then Sandra went off to her mother.'

'Yes.' They listened to each other breathe.

'Hard to blame her, but…it's a bugger all right.'

'Is he…well, she won't ever want to see me again, but will she…will you be all right?' Her voice wobbled, and she felt like fourteen again.

'Don't cry, Jules. This is my fault.'

'Oh nonsense.' She was shocked out of tears. 'I was there too.'

'I was in *loco parentis*, morally if not legally. I ought not to be in social work. I'd better go and work in a bank.'

'Don't you dare. Think of the Hackney children.' She took in a breath.

'We'll get through this. you'll have to confess to your kids and I'll have to cringe to Sandra if that's what's wanted. And we'll all go on marching forward.' But he and she would not be able to see each other again.

'Oh God, I hope so.' He wasn't thinking about her at all, only of the wife on whom he was utterly dependent. Jules felt the old chill of exclusion and misery. Well, at least the *News of the World* had been beaten back.

That thought led straight to Paul who had done the deed for her and she rang down to see if he was available. She had told him about the events of yesterday inasmuch as they involved MI5, but she had forgotten, totally, to tell him about Mrs Dragunoviç. He was free, so she went down and told him the facts. She had not expected him to be pleased with her and he wasn't, but she was bent on getting this particular *histoire* out of the way.

'The thing I do not understand, Jules, is why you took it upon yourself to visit her.'

'I thought I'd said. Andrew Flowerdew asked me. He didn't want her lying there, worrying. After all she's old' – too late, she recalled, that Mrs Dragunoviç was perhaps five years older than Paul, but she ploughed on – 'and her husband's ill and both sons are dead.'

'I am aware of all these things. And as soon as there was time, perhaps even today, I intended to go and see her myself.'

'I didn't know that, Paul. I thought you didn't want her as a client?'

'I do not, but like your friend, Mr Flowerdew, I would not leave her penniless and alone in a foreign land. You should have consulted me.'

She decided not to apologise, not again, but to go and do some work. There were clients who needed her. She looked across at him to see if it was safe to go, but he was looking at her as if she had missed something out.

'You say she was asking for me?'

'Well, she was asking for money. I didn't commit you, Paul – I know you run these charities, but I promise I didn't offer anything.'

He nodded, wearily. 'That at least was sensible. I may be able to find some assistance for her from one of the funds, but she will have to apply… She will want to go back of course… Now, Jules, please leave all this with me to deal with when I have the time, and if Mr Flowerdew wishes anything else he should ask *me*.' He looked at her, carefully. 'Is anything else the matter?'

'No,' she lied, stolidly. 'I'm tired and I've got behind – no don't worry, Paul, I will catch up.' She rose to go and he nodded at her, eclipsing himself instantly in his papers.

She hurled herself at an afternoon of wall to wall clients, each one opening up a sea of troubles. Criminal work can be very straightforward, she knew, but not one of the cases she saw was going to be. She found herself longing for a customer who had been caught in the act, clasping incriminating evidence to him, by a policeman who had cautioned him by the book, leaving a lawyer nothing to do but work out the plea in mitigation. By 6 p.m. she was sitting holding her head, trying to disentangle her notes of the four o'clock appointment which had involved a history of betrayal, misunderstanding and possible corruption on the part of the arresting officer which could have been set to music. She had no idea if any of it was true.

The phone rang and she reached for it; whatever trouble it brought could not be more demanding than what she was tackling. It was Anne, sounding mildly miffed, and she apologised for having forgotten all about her and the putative date with the son – no the grandson – of one of Anne's peculiar chums. They chatted for a bit, Jules soothed by Anne's cheerful flow of chatter. Jules agreed she would go to lunch on Saturday, and put the phone down feeling better, and more competent. This feeling evaporated as she looked round her office. Lawyers try to run paperless offices, where all notes live in the electronic bowels of the computer system, but Jenkins Associates' customers communicated, if at all, on lined paper for page after page. The Courts also sent out pages of actual paper and Jules had found that if she were ever to establish what she had done, and how, the quick thing was to add her bit of paper to the file.

The phone rang, and she trampled over paper to reach it. 'Jules? Are you by yourself?'

'I am, yes.' She felt hunted all over again. Gwyn was sounding grim.

'I had to tell Jake. He said he knew from seeing you this morning. I had to tell him the truth, so he would know that…that the other wasn't true.'

'Oh Christ.' Her heart was thumping and she sank down on the edge of the desk, dislodging a couple of files which fell splat on the floor. 'Was he…?'

'Yes. Yes. He hit me. And I hit him back.'

'Oh, Gwyn.' No hand had ever been lifted to a child in the Jones's household.

'I told him that…that you and I were not…' She let him struggle, she was too miserable to help. He took a breath she could feel over the line. 'I said I wanted Sandra back desperately, because I wanted to live with her for the rest of our lives.' He was crying, she realised, and felt sick.

'So, did he feel better?' she asked, when she could.

'He was furious with me but less frightened. He is making supper.' Gwyn knew, how should he not, how terrified children are of having their homes break up over their heads. 'And we are going to ring up Sandra after that.' She could not speak, but it did not seem to matter. 'I thought you'd better know, so you don't worry.'

'Thank you.' She rang off and sat in the echoing silence of her office, unable to get up and do anything sensible like clear up the floor. She found she was remembering, clear as a film, a cold grey day in November when she was fourteen. She was in a hospital bed, still dopey from a general anaesthetic, after the first operation to repair an internal tear caused by her stepfather. She had been deposited there by Gwyn on his way into work and he had promised, as she had clung to his hand, that he'd be there again at tea-time. But it wasn't Gwyn she had seen when her eyes focused but Sandra, enormously pregnant, bent over the four-year-old Jake, who wanted to be let out of his pushchair. Seeing Jules's face, Sandra had gone straight into a weary explanation of Gwyn's absence, stuck in a court room somewhere. Jules had not been able to stop her mouth turning down and had begun to cry, ungratefully, when the ward sister arrived to check her pulse. The sister had stopped in her tracks, ignoring Jules, peeled Jake off Sandra and placed her firmly in a chair. Then she had reached across the bed for the buzzer with Jake wriggling in her grip, chatting to Sandra, watching her face with that comprehensive nursey look. Jules had, she remembered, wincing, gone on crying, feeling that it was unfair that Sandra was getting all the attention, but she had not actually thrown herself out of bed nor made herself sick, while they whisked Sandra away to a bed in a ward two floors down. Sandra had used three different buses to come and see her, it turned out, dragging Jake, because her mother was away and her neighbour ill. The hospital must have kept Jake too because Gwyn had him on his shoulder, drooping and boneless in sleep, when he came up to see her briefly later that night, worried silly about Sandra and the damned baby who arrived in perfect order two months later and turned into Mark. Gwyn had stayed only a couple of minutes and she had cried herself to sleep, feeling deserted all over again. Of course, she thought, she had never come close to being equal to Sandra in his affections, then or now, however much she had tried, but she was being frozen out, and it was her own fault for trying to take something that she was never going to get.

The stairs, being wooden, creaked and reverberated, so she had time to arrange herself in an attitude of work before Paul walked through the door. He didn't knock, unless he knew there was a client with her.

'Are you all right?'

'Just trying to catch up.'

'I looked in only to say I have just talked to Andrew

Flowerdew. He is having a most difficult time with the police, because of his students' behaviour. I may have to go up there myself or, indeed, send Jenni to help.' She felt a prickle of jealousy but decided that Jenni would hate the house and the flat fields.

Paul was looking out of the window, fidgeting and she could see he wanted to walk about, but there were too many papers on the floor. 'Come down and have a drink with me, Jules.' As always with Paul, it was a command not an invitation and she said she would follow him down, relieved to think she had been forgiven. She made a half-hearted attempt to tidy up then decided it was too late and too difficult and she would shut the door on the whole mess and get up early tomorrow to cope. Paul had a fridge and cupboard in his office and there were bottles displayed on his sideboard. He gave her a whisky and she drank it rather fast, so he gave her another one and the second best armchair, and she sank into it.

'Louise tells me that Mr Jones's son Jake was here this morning.'

She swallowed a gulp of whisky. She always forgot that Paul was omniscient, it was how he worked. He looked at all their diaries on the system, he knew exactly who was where. He was rubbing his right eyebrow vigorously, which is what he did when he was going to say something unpopular.

'You told me that that particular situation was over, Jules.'

'It is.'

'The boy came to see you why, then?'

She could not tell him to mind his own business, given he had agreed earlier to help her keep the *News of the World* at bay. 'To say that his parents had been quarrelling and his mother had gone to stay with her mother, taking Jake's younger brother with her.'

'He came to tell you this?'

She was not going to cry. She put the glass down. 'He knew – he had listened enough to the rows – to understand I was in this somewhere.'

'You told him what?'

'Nothing, since it was not my story alone to tell. His father has now told him the truth so that he can at least understand that Gwyn had done nothing illegal. Jake is fifteen, a girl of nineteen would seem like a grown-up to him.' She looked across the table, exhausted but relieved to have told someone the full strength. Paul, she realised, with a convulsive clutch of the stomach, was looking horrified.

'Jules…my dear. I did not tell you because…well because you are enough distracted…but my contact at the *News of the World* rang…when?' He scrabbled for a piece of paper and held it at arm's length to read it. 'Late yesterday to say he wondered if I had been giving him a wrong direction.' He looked at her stricken face. 'No, no, Jules, I spoke with him, it was only a question that his reporter had heard something, so I told him of course that there was nothing he could write. But… Well, perhaps it is alright; you say the boy and his father have had an explanation? Then the boy will not – could not talk to anyone.'

She could taste the whisky, sour in her mouth. 'I never thought…I never thought of the kids.'

'No. Now, do not look *so*, Jules, no one has rung me up today. You are tired and perhaps you need some time off.' He raised a hand to stop her speaking. 'We cannot spare you, of course, that goes without saying, but the world will not end in a week. Think about it. We'll talk tomorrow, yes?' He rose, indicating, unmistakably, that it was time to go and she was out of his office before she could formulate a response. He'd be proposing counselling next, she thought, in despair, and she wouldn't blame him. She sat, limply, behind her own desk and tried to gather herself, wondering if food would help, it usually did. The phone rang and she looked at it, then remembered its function and picked it up.

'It's Wednesday. We still on for dinner? I left a message earlier.'

'Richard.' She scrabbled in the pile left for her by Louise as she went home. 'I'm sorry, I've had a bad day. I'm exhausted.'

'I'm no better, but we both need to eat. I'll pick you up.'

'No.' Paul was still here, she could hear him moving about. 'I'll meet you somewhere.'

'Casa Luigi,' he said, promptly, naming the best of the local Italians. 'I'll get a table. Twenty minutes.'

'Half an hour.' Her hands were filthy, her hair all over the place, and she was wearing one of the less good bras and a pair of the greying knickers, having agreed with herself to wait for the weekend to buy replacements. There was no time to go home to change.

She got to Luigi's only five minutes after she had said she would to find that Richard had been given one of the booths. He got up to kiss her, formally. He had made an effort; clean shirt, clean shave, smell of toothpaste mixed with Campari.

'I ordered you a Campari too. I hope that's ok.'

It went down without touching the sides as one of her building labourer clients said of the beer at the end of the day. Richard raised a hand and another one appeared. 'You look as if you were being pursued by the Furies.'

'I am,' she said, before she could stop, but Luigi himself appeared, with menus, so they both had to concentrate and get their orders in. Jimmy Watt, in order to impress her, had told her Richard's rank, which hadn't meant a lot, and the size of his salary, which had, so she felt no need to offer to go Dutch. She was probably on MI5 expenses as a paid auxiliary anyway, she thought, sourly.

'Wine, Jules?'

'No thanks. I've been drinking.' Two whiskies and two Camparis were already making her head spin. Food would help, but she was at risk of telling Richard about the Jones family and her role as Chief Homewrecker. She sought for another conversational opening, but nothing came and Richard seemed quite content to sit quietly drinking, so she felt free to watch him. He, too, looked as if he had escaped from something, and she was reminded, suddenly and sharply, of Gwyn. 'Are you married, Richard?' She was habitually direct, but not *that* direct and she couldn't believe she had spoken those words.

'I'm separated.'

That's what married men on the pull say, she knew, either that or that they live in the same house but they never go to bed with her. That was him off the list, and she should have asked the question before.

'Caroline and I separated almost two years ago.' He finished his drink in one gulp and took a handful of olives, not looking at her. 'She left, in fact. She didn't like my job.'

It's not the job women object to, she knew. It was the man's obsessive attachment to it. 'I wouldn't mind some of those olives.'

'God, I'm sorry.' He looked at the bowl, confused. 'There are only three left – I'll get some more.' He waved the bowl at Luigi, and a minion arrived to exchange it for a full one. 'She – Caroline – and I have agreed to go for a divorce as quickly as possible.'

'What does she do?' She wasn't sure she believed any of this, but the details could be interesting.

'Lives with a chap in the Foreign Office.'

'Ah.'

'She needs the divorce because she's pregnant.'

That was quite a lot of detail and a very elaborate lie if it was one. 'I just decided to give up married men, you see,' she said, flatly.

'Is that why you looked so ill when you arrived?'

'Yes.' She bit her lip in order to keep herself from saying another word, and buried her nose in the second Campari.

'I could go away and come back in two months with a decree nisi,' Richard offered as he took the glass away from her and covered her hands with his. 'Jules, I've not been a pillar of virtue, but I've never not told the truth about…about where I was at.' He'd gone pink all round the cheek-bones and his mouth was set. 'What about you, Jules?'

Well, she had asked him first. 'A long-standing relationship has come to a close.'

'He's married? And going back to his wife?'

'He never left.' She pulled her hands away as two plates of beautiful Parma ham and melon were put before them by Luigi himself, with many a nod and beck and wreathed smile. 'I don't want to talk about it.'

Richard nodded and they wolfed the contents of their plates, ending at the same time.

'Maybe we should talk about work?' She was feeling not exactly better, but less awful. She had said to another human being that the little piece of Gwyn she had was gone for ever.

'Why not? How was your day?' He saw her face. 'Sorry. I'll tell you about *my* day. I spent part of it with Andrew Flowerdew. A complex man, that.'

'A sober, careful farmer, surely?'

Richard gave her a careful, measuring look. 'Yes. With the odd kick in his gallop. He had a long relationship with an animal-rights activist.' She raised her eyebrows at him, and he sighed. 'Jules, there's a file on anyone who has a Home Office permit to employ people from Eastern Europe, you must see that.'

'Yes.' It was not unreasonable but like everything about MI5 it made her uneasy. 'How serious an animal-rights person?'

'A suspect in one of the attacks on Huntington Life Sciences. And no, we never proved it.'

'And Andrew knew? Knows?'

'Stood bail for her, what, a year ago.' He was watching her without quite looking at her. 'You should ask him.'

'I will,' she said. 'I intend to have all my relationships straightforward for the future.'

Richard looked meaningfully towards the kitchen and Luigi burst out, carrying two giant plates of veal al limone which prevented them having to speak for at least ten minutes. Richard had quietly ordered some wine and she was having her fair share of it

'Not that I'm necessarily planning a relationship with Andrew Flowerdew.' She saw from Richard's face that in the conversation she had been holding with herself these were the first words she had spoken aloud. He edged the wine over to his side of the table and poured her some more water.

'What about with me then?'

'I'd decided not.'

'Why? I mean why not?'

'MI5,' she said, noticing that the edges of the room seemed to be moving.

'Well, I can't give that up, Jules.' He gave her a worried look.

'You're looking very pale. Is it time I took you home? Right.' He got the bill with impressive speed and led her carefully downstairs.

'I'm alright, Richard. Just tired.'

His phone rang, and he swore, then muttered into it urgently. He snapped it shut and peeled her off the shop window. 'I shouldn't have given you so much to drink. Shall we walk back?'

'Where's your car?'

'I've just called it. It's the usual bloody...well, I need to go, I'm sorry.'

They walked in silence, his arm round her, then a car drew up beside them, keeping pace with them, and she turned to deliver her usual message to kerb crawlers, but saw that the man getting out was Scottie, Richard's driver. They got in and Richard looked at her anxiously. 'Will your flatmate be there?'

'Dunno.'

'If she isn't I'm coming in, I'm warning you now, just to see you're all right.'

'I'm in no shape to do anything, anyway.' She saw, from a distance, that Scottie appeared to be choking. She combed through her handbag for the keys.

'Your flatmate's in,' Richard noted.

'Really?'

'Light's just gone on. I'll take you up to the door.'

'No, don't.' She ached all over and wanted only to be alone, but she summoned her best smile. 'I know you have to go.'

'I'll ring you,' he said, anxiously, and was gone.

Chapter Sixteen

(Thursday after Easter)

Jenni was tidying up the kitchen when Jules managed to get down to breakfast the next day. Not that it was that untidy; Jules had refused even a cup of tea the night before in favour of falling into bed, having only just managed to remove her make-up. She had, she knew, been a disappointment to Jenni, who had been wanting to talk, but the day had been going on for too long by then. She exerted herself to think of something to say of general interest, as indeed anything at all, and failed.

'Paul is very worried about you, Jules. He says he has suggested you should take some time off.'

'And what would I do with this time off?'

'Oh, Jules. What other people do. Go to the gym. Go shopping. Have a facial. Be good to yourself. Relax.' People always suggest as panaceas the things that they would like for themselves, she thought, and absolutely nothing on this list rang a bell for her. 'We could talk about it later, Jules. I have a nine o'clock. But we could do something together this evening. Better not to drink by yourself.'

Jules opened her mouth and closed it again and waited as Jenni left, neat as a new pin, in her nice clean car, then sat slumped over tea and dry oatcakes for another ten minutes until she felt ready to move. She rang the office and found her morning had cleared, which seemed like a miracle. She asked why the eleven o'clock and twelve o'clock new customers had cancelled and discovered they hadn't; Jenni had taken one, and another of the partners the other. She was being given a pretty unequivocal message and she might better find a convenient rest home for a week from where she could bounce back rather better than new. She thought about all this while she got dressed and cleaned her shoes, just to show Jenni she was still in control. That gave her an idea; she would use the unexpected free morning to buy new underwear so that she could impress Jenni with her poise and ability to organise her life. She got to the local Marks and did the lot – bras, knickers, socks, a couple of scarves, a new belt and two blouses in an hour and a half, and she did feel better. The credit card had lasted out too. Sitting over a coffee and a Danish, she switched on her mobile. There were three messages, the first from Richard, hoping she was all right, and she smiled at the phone. But the next two were both alarming. One from Gwyn, sounding exhausted and angry and very Welsh; he had been pursued by Patrick Mahoney who had found out somehow that Sandra had gone away. The third was from Jake and asked only that she ring him. Her real preference would have been to get back into bed and pull the blankets over her head, but the memory of the thin, anxious boy fighting through the Camden traffic stopped her, and she rang him on his mobile.

'Hello. Oh, Jules, it's my fault.' He was sounding desperate.

'Jake, calm down. What is?'

'I talked to that reporter. I told him Mum had gone. You see, I thought...I thought if she saw it all in the papers...'

'That she would come back?'

'Yes.'

'She will, Jake. Don't worry.'

'Yes, but now Dad is furious. He told me not to talk to them but it was before. Yesterday.'

'After you had seen me.'

'Yes. There was someone – this man – there, outside school.'

It was iniquitous, she thought, to pester a boy of fifteen but she wasn't going to worry Jake further. She could hear heavy breathing on the line.

There was a long, painful pause. 'I liked you.' Loud sniffle. 'So did Mark.'

'Oh, Jake.' She slumped. 'I am sorry. There isn't any explaining that's going to help, but... Well, I wasn't thinking about you and Mark.'

'No. You weren't.'

Enough already, she thought, stung. 'So you think about him. If you don't want to talk to horrid insinuating Mr Mahoney, tell him to talk to your father. And put the phone down on him. They try to keep you talking, you know.'

'What does insinuating mean?'

'Telling you things he's making up as if they were true.' What has happened to the children of the educated middle-class? she wondered.

'Oh, OK. Ya. I see. That's what he did. I won't talk to him next time.' She waited out the long pause. 'Look. OK. Catch you later.'

Utterly disheartened, she decided to go back home and deposit her parcels before going to the office where she seemed to have not a lot to do all of a sudden. She would have lunch, she thought, and go in, virtuous, calm and dressed in new knickers, not that they were going to be visible. She rang the familiar number. 'Anyone wanting to take me out?'

Louise's rolling belly-laugh which cheered whole waiting-rooms of dispirited clients made her feel better too.

'Mr Flowerdew called. Any good? Inspector Jimmy Watt. Oh. And Mr Patrick Mahoney – three times. They all left you their numbers, girl, you take your pick.'

She wished she hadn't asked, but she was being hunted again. Poor Jake, in anger, had given Mr Mahoney a fresh lead and trouble was coming her way. She asked Louise to put her through to Paul; she would need his help, but he turned out to be on the phone, so Louise told her to give up, she'd make sure he called her.

She dragged her feet going back into the flat. She could hear the answerphone bleeping and knew it could not be a good sign. It wasn't; there was a hurried call from Richard, asking could she ring, business not pleasure, and three from Patrick Mahoney. She erased the messages, as if that would cause Mr Mahoney to go away or drop dead, hid the phone under a pile of cushions and shut the door on it. Then she remembered that Paul was going to ring, extracted the phone from the cushions again and made a cup of tea, dropping a cup, which she normally never did.

The bell rang, and she went to the street door. She opened it, and lights blinked in her face and a small fat man stepped onto the threshold.

'Jules Carlisle? Patrick Mahoney.'

She kicked him just under the kneecap, accurately and hard. She had not kicked or hit anyone since she was fourteen, but the reflexes were still there as practised as if she had done it every day for the last year. He howled and clasped his knee and she pushed him and he fell off the step and she slammed the door and put the chain on. She could hear him hopping around, effing and blinding, and threatening to sue, then he stopped quite suddenly. She nipped upstairs and knelt below the sightline in her bedroom, peering over the window sill. Mahoney, still crouched, clasping his knee, was shouting at a tall man who was taking down his car number. The tall figure resolved itself into her senior partner, sweeping Mr Mahoney and his photographer before him. They got into their car, Mahoney shouting imprecations and the photographer dropping bits of kit, and took off gunning the engine furiously. She rushed downstairs to let Paul in, deeply grateful that Jenni's unseen influence had caused her to tidy the place up before she had left that morning.

'My dear Jules. How did Mr Mahoney get your address?'

That did give her pause. Everyone in the firm was ex-directory and they never gave the clients their home numbers, but people like Mahoney presumably corrupted someone in the council or the electricity board or the mobile phone companies.

'Can you – would you, dear Paul, ring his editor?'

'I did, when I saw all those calls for you. I would very much like a cup of tea.'

She flew into action, sat him at her big kitchen table and even managed to find some biscuits. Paul was looking tired, she saw, conscience-stricken, no doubt worn out by having such unreliable help.

'Thank you. Now, sit down, Jules, it is not good news I have for you.'

She sat, stiffly, her knees going. Surely she had not been bad enough for him to fire her? She was so appalled that she did not hear what he was saying for a minute and had to ask him to start again.

'They are going to run a story tomorrow, Jules. It would have been a better story – for them that is – if they could have got you to talk, but the editor is content that even without your comments the story will...will attract a lot of attention.' He looked at her to see if she was with him. 'They have talked to your Mr Jones. Or rather to the boy.'

'Jake?'

'Yes, to him.'

Her mouth had gone dry and the headache that had nagged all morning moved down and to the right so that the whole of that side of her face hurt. 'They can't say that Gwyn seduced me when I lived with them. I'll sue.'

'They understand that, Jules.' Paul was sounding weary. 'No. They will say only that you remained very close, and that Mrs Jones was upset. And so was her son, who has, I fear, said more than was sensible.'

'He's only fifteen, poor kid.'

'Indeed.'

'At least I did Mr Mahoney's kneecap.'

Paul winced. 'That may not have been wise.' He saw her face. 'No, Jules, do not worry, I would doubt that he would sue. He was trying to get into the house, yes?'

'Yes,' she said, seeing her way clear. 'He sought to push me aside. He placed his hands on my breasts and made a suggestion.'

'While doubled up from the pain of his kneecap? Jules, if you have here a whisky I could drink it.'

'I do. I'll just get it.' It was Gwyn's, of course, but she decided not to share the thought with him. The smell of the drink made her feel sick, and she sat down as far away from it as she could. 'When is he – are they – going to print this story?'

'Tomorrow. I want you away from here, Jules.'

She felt bile in her throat as she tried not to think what might happen if Sandra also talked to them.

'I have advised Mr Jones also to send his son away.'

'You talked to Gwyn?' she said, stupidly. 'How was he?'

Paul stared into his whisky, thinking about the question. He had had a haircut and the high cheek-bones looked very prominent. He is a very good-looking man, she thought, it is not surprising that Jenni is so smitten. 'He was distressed, of course, particularly for his sons, but I had the impression that his principal concern was for his wife. If this is painful for you, Jules, I am sorry.'

'No. No, I know – have always known – that Sandra is the only woman who matters to him.'

'This will be unpleasant, however, and you need to leave here. You may have discouraged Mr Mahoney, but others will be on your doorstep. Where can you go?'

Where indeed? She thought, gazing at him. Cousin Anne? She shut her mind to the conversation she would have to have, and started to think round her old university friends. The phone rang and she stared at it. Paul reached out a long hand and picked it up, and listened for a moment, his eyebrows going up like triangles.

'She is here, yes. When did you hear this, Mr Flowerdew? I see.' He handed me the phone. 'Mr Andrew Flowerdew.'

Andrew's voice on the phone was deeper than when he was there in person and he was speaking slowly. 'Jules, I know you're being done over by a newspaper. I wondered if you'd like to come here to escape? I'll ask Mrs Cole to come and stay. Or Jenni could come too.'

'How did you know?'

'Richard Allenton told me.'

She opened her mouth to ask how the hell *he*'d known, and closed it again. MI5, like the tabloids, did not live by the ordinary rules as she was beginning to understand. She looked at Paul, who was openly listening.

'Andrew, it's a very kind offer. I must, whatever I do, see Cousin Anne first.'

'Now why didn't I think of that? Would she come with you? Then I don't need Mrs Cole.'

'She may be too cross with me to come.'

'No, she won't. She'll want to help.'

By chaperoning her, so Andrew could not have his wicked way with her, she supposed.

'You can get the 3.15 if you hurry. Or the 4.15. I'll meet you at the station.'

'If…if there is a story I should go round to Cousin Anne's

now…' She could hear her voice droop.

'Look, Jules, love, it's not the end of the world. My father always says if no one's dead and no one's seriously ill, then whatever it is will pass. Lady Barlow will forgive you, you'll see.'

He was right, she realised with a tiny lift of the heart, whatever she had done, Cousin Anne would see her through.

Two hours later she was wondering about that conclusion, as she watched Cousin Anne, summoned from Chambers in a hurry, pour out tea, her hands trembling so that the spout knocked the rim of the mug. Jules had rung to warn her of trouble, unspecified, then left Paul answering the telephone for her while she packed. A tabloid journalist had rung, hoping to get the material for a spoiler, then Mr Mahoney, foaming at the mouth but instantly deflated by Paul in best Rottweiler mode. Paul had offered his own weekend cottage, but as she pointed out that was an even more readily traceable connection. She stuck with plan A, refusing also the offer of sanctuary in the family palace in Leicestershire made by Jenni who had arrived in the middle of all this and made Paul a fast omelette because he had unwisely said he had missed lunch.

Getting herself out of the house might have presented some difficulty since there were two men lurking outside, one carrying several cameras and the other speaking urgently into a telephone, but Jimmy Watt arrived, in a real police car, which caused them to retreat to a safe distance. He had brought an envelope from Richard with a compliments slip with a wholly illegible scrawl attached to a draft of page four of tomorrow's *News of the World*. They spread it out on the kitchen table and read it, *en groupe*. It was worse even than her worst fears. Paul read professionally, finger stubbed on the points that might be libellous. Jules just stared at it, letting bits of it into her brain as and when she could bear to. It was just this side of libel, she judged, and she could see from the way his mouth tightened that Paul thought so too. Jules looked past him to Jenni, and saw that she was not even reading, she was watching Paul's profile with concentrated longing. Give it up, Jenni, she thought, or you'll find yourself where I am one day.

Jimmy Watt, who had read it, put an arm round her and said sorry, but Mr Allenton had thought forewarned might be forearmed, and the photograph of her was very good. It was one of the few really good ones of her ever taken, she thought, sadly, and it ran across three columns. There was also one of Gwyn looking windblown and tired, emerging from the Inquiry, and a nice one of Sandra taken with some of the girls she taught. They hadn't got one of Jake, or perhaps some residual respect for the Press Commission had prevented them splashing a hapless fifteen-year-old all over the paper. Jules peered at the last photograph and recognised herself again, as a thin wide-eyed teenager, grinning at the camera. Gwyn had taken it in his office when she was fourteen, apologising for the necessity but explaining they had to put photographs in the files to make sure that colleagues in the future were dealing with the right kid. Jules had laughed and Gwyn had taken the picture at that moment, and had lots of copies done because both of them had liked it. Jake had presumably given it to Mr Mahoney at some stage, knowing no better. I looked, Jules thought, a much more bold and robust proposition than I remembered, well capable of seducing anyone who fancied fourteen-year-olds.

They had finally managed to unglue themselves from the paper. Richard had sent two copies, so Paul took one away with him and left her with one which she had handed, wordlessly, to Anne as she arrived in the big flat. It would have been better to have talked first, she thought, watching Anne turn scarlet with suppressed emotion as she read.

Anne put the mug down, and they managed to look at each other.

'Is it true?'

'Yes,' Jules said, steadily feeling herself blush all over.

'Gwyn.' Anne looked as if she had woken up in a different world.

'Yes. I'm sorry, I'm sorry. It is my fault.'

'It cannot have been. Gwyn is, what, fourteen years older, and in a position of trust.' She was white with rage and Jules quailed momentarily.

'Oh, Anne. That's a cliché. I seduced *him*, when I was nineteen. It hadn't entered his head.'

'The whole wretched story is a cliché. I suppose he is your lost father, never mind Henry, or the boys, who love you so much.'

This was worse even than Jules had feared and she bowed her head, feeling tears of rage and grief not far away. Anne put down her mug and picked up the offending article again. 'Well, we certainly need to get out of here. The Press will be down like locusts, since I'm in it too.'

'I'm sorry.'

'Oh Jules, do stop apologising, it's far too late for any of that. It's damage limitation time. For you.'

'And Gwyn,' she said, teeth gritted.

'He can bloody well look after himself. Are you packed, Jules? I'm not yet.'

The boys always said, Jules remembered, through a haze of misery, that Anne, faced with trouble flew into a passion, then settled down to sort it out, while Henry was always instantly supportive and flew into a passion a week later when everyone else had forgotten about it.

'Yes. You don't need to come with me.'

'Yes I do. I've talked to that admirable young man who was about to import a chaperone for you until I offered. I had assumed, I suppose, much too hopefully that you and he were heading for a serious relationship.'

'No.'

'Because of Gwyn?'

'No. I've dated other people besides Gwyn.'

'Well, thank God for *that* at least.'

Jules rose to her feet, buoyed by rage, to leave but recalled that she had nowhere immediately to go, and flung herself into the kitchen. She was staring out of the window, choking back tears when she felt Anne's arms round her.

'You gave me a terrible *shock*. It's not you I'm furious with. One for all and all for one?'

She turned in Anne's arms and they hugged each other, ignoring the ringing phones.

'A drink, do you think? We've got time, I've got a driver coming in fifteen minutes.'

'A *driver*?' Anne and Henry were not given to extravagance.

'It didn't seem the moment for a train, Andrew and I agreed. He would have come himself. He's lovely. Why aren't you interested? Not gay, is he?'

'No, it's not that. It's just too early to tell. I don't want to jump into anything. And there's the added complication at work too.'

Anne's hand paused over the whisky glass. 'I didn't know anyone of your age said things like that.'

'You're out of date.' They were over the worst, Jules understood, as Anne took up the paper and read the article again, slowly.

'Where did they get the photographs?'

'Oh. From the boy, I imagine. Jake.'

Anne put the cutting down and went off to her study, and Jules waited, thinking about nothing, the headache that was still sitting over her right eye trying to make up its mind to go away or push harder. Anne came back, her colour still high.

'I thought so. These pictures in the paper are the ones that were taken when I was burgled.'

'So they are,' Jules confirmed. She blinked. 'You don't think...no, I mean how...'

'I think we should find out, now, where the newspaper got them from. Do you still have copies?'

'No. Yes.' The headache tightened over her eye. 'Yes. Yes, I do.'

'What about the boy Jake? Would *he* have provided them?'

They looked at each other.

'It's possible, I suppose,' Jules said, heavily. 'I could ask Gwyn to ask him.'

'I would rather...no, if I speak to Gwyn I will have to say what is in my mind. You ring him.'

Jules had to leave a message on his mobile, explaining what she wanted, but he rang back, a minute later.

'Your solicitor got me a copy of the article. He said you'd left town.'

'Not quite yet. Anne and I are being driven up tonight.'

'Can you talk? No? I imagine she is – and rightly – angry with me.'

'Yes.'

His sigh came from his socks. 'Well. I daresay it will all come right some day. I'll ask Jake. Wait a second.' She could hear the conversation in the background. 'Jules? They asked him for photographs of himself and of me but, thank God, he had the sense to say no. He and Mark will have a bad enough time at school as it is. They didn't even ask him for photos of you.' He stopped. 'We have the one of you – the one I took – in an album. But it's still there, I checked.'

'They never even *asked* for a photograph of me? Jake was sure?'

'Yes. That's odd, isn't it?'

'Yes.'

'And you of course didn't…?'

'No.'

'Right. Sorry, I must go – that's the other phone.'

'I hope…' but he had gone before she could say whatever it was that she hoped, and she was left with the ringing tone.

The bell rang and she let Anne interrogate the intercom. An elegant young woman – trust Anne to have found a female chauffeur – trotted up the stairs and captured their suitcases and they were in the car, rugged up and gliding through the City about five minutes later.

'Ring up your policeman friend.' Anne, though plainly exhausted, was not going to go to sleep until Jules had done as she was told. Jules thought about calling Jimmy Watt and decided to go for the organ grinder; she owed Richard a call anyway, and this time miraculously he answered. She thanked him for the clipping and told him, feeling less confident by the minute, about the small mystery of the photographs. He got the dates of the burglary and the name of the attending CID which she had forgotten, but which Anne had written down methodically in her diary.

'Were there a lot of copies of both photos around?'

'The recent one, yes. There were a few copies of the older one but I couldn't find one.'

'I'll talk to the editor.'

'He won't – oh, I see. You're going to ask him where he got the photos from. He won't tell, surely, if they were…'

'He won't have a choice.' That was what she found chilling and sneakily attractive about Richard and MI5. If they want to they could make people tell. 'Where are you, by the way?'

'On our way to stay with Andrew Flowerdew. Anne is with me.' There was a fractional silence on the line.

'Enterprising chap, Mr Flowerdew.'

'He offered because you had told him I was in trouble.'

'He certainly wasted no time. Clank, clank, on with the armour, off to the rescue. Was Lady Barlow your idea or his?'

'None of your business.'

'I'll get back to you about these pictures. How long are you going to stay with Mr Flowerdew?'

'I expect we will have worn out our welcome early next week.'

'I'll be round to see you there.' She felt her eyebrows go up. 'Jules? You still there? Look, I have wondered whether we have exposed you to some…well, risk…and this business with the newspapers looks a bit odd.'

'It's Gwyn they're out to get.'

'You didn't read the article carefully enough. Sorry, Peter, yes, give it to the CID, get them onto it, here's the number in London.'

'But Richard, why didn't they burgle *me* to get the pictures?'

'This is all a bit hypothetical, but if they'd burgled you it would have been obvious, wouldn't it? This way it isn't. Look, don't worry your head, I know where you're going. Flowerdew's got Group 4 to look after you both and I'll get the local CID to concentrate as well. I'll talk to you later…'

He rang off, abruptly, as he usually did, and she relayed the conversation to Anne.

'How old is Richard?'

'About thirty. And more or less single, as you did not ask. And he isn't gay either.' The pretty chauffeuse's ears twitched perceptibly.

'He's obviously worried for you. Let me read that dreadful

article again.'

They excavated her handbag and they both read it again. Richard was right, Jules thought, dully; *she* was the villain of this piece, Gwyn had come out as a devoted social worker who had been targeted by a neurotic teenager. There was a strong implication that she, not Gwyn, had told Sandra all about it in order to force his hand. She looked helplessly at Anne, who was looking just perceptibly smug.

'I read it more carefully than you and I agree with Mr Allenton. Have a little sleep. There is nothing else for you to do.'

Chapter Seventeen

Jules slept badly, tossing and turning, due, no doubt, to the combined effects of stress and being fed cheese sandwiches and red wine by a concerned Andrew Flowerdew when they had finally arrived around ten o'clock the night before. By five o'clock she could stand it no longer and crept downstairs, wearing Anne's spare dressing-gown, which Anne had insisted she bring, and a pair of socks for warmth. She pushed the kitchen door open and let out a yell of sheer terror as she walked into a man with a gun.

'Andrew!'

He stared back at her. 'I was doing some work, then I heard footsteps. I was just coming to see whether on top of everything else we had a burglar.' He put the gun back, carefully, in the bread bin. 'Sit down, Jules, you've gone a funny colour. Here. The tea's fresh.'

'Were you going to shoot me if I'd been a burglar?'

'If I needed to.'

'One day I shall be defending you in court.' Her heart was still thumping.

He sat down opposite her and put bread in a huge, old, clumsy toaster that looked as if it ought to be powered by steam. One slice of toast sprang out, the other didn't and started to burn. With one practised gesture he reached over and switched the toaster off, then started excavation with a knife, jabbing at it with more force than could have been productive. He was looking hunted, she realised, his normal pink-faced placidity gone. Something was getting to him.

'I'm sorry we had to come and stay – well, like this, in a hurry.'

'No, no, that's a pleasure. I'm really pleased to have you. And Lady Barlow. It's just all this with the police and the stupid idiots among my students. If the Home Office stop the scheme we can't go on.'

'So you couldn't sleep?' she said.

'Well, nor could you. Do you want some more toast?'

'Yes, I do, but will it be the last straw for that ancient machine?'

He looked at the toaster, seeing it properly. 'It is rather old. My mother had it.'

'And her mother?'

'Oh, come on Jules, it's not that bad. Well, perhaps it is. I'll get a new one. It's the time, not the money. So why are you awake?'

'Too much going on, I guess. Couple of heavy days.'

'With Mr Allenton?'

Cold and tired though she was, she felt a small warm glow. 'The day before yesterday I was, literally, assisting the police with their enquiries. Identifying bodies.'

'Anyone I would know?'

She told him, since she could see no harm in doing so, and he was shaken. 'The nurse! No wonder Martin's uneasy.'

'Would you have known the traveller? The taxi driver?'

'Oh, probably. If he's one of that family he would probably have been up before us at some point.' The 'us' was the magistrates of course, she understood. 'He was murdered?'

'Or fell on a bullet, yes.'

'Bloody hell. Nasty people about.'

'Well, that's why the police are harassing you and your students.'

'I suppose. But the forecast's good for today, and I need…well, I just hope they won't all be too upset to do a decent day's work. You're not eating your toast.'

'I'm wondering if you've got any jam.'

'Sorry, of course I have.' He opened a cupboard and found a jar and passed it over to her, unable to stop a single, longing look at the bits of paper he'd been working on.

'Go on with whatever it is, Andrew, do.'

'It's the factory returns and I can't make them add up. Probably the wrong time of day.'

She stretched out a hand and after a moment's hesitation he gave them to her. She saw one mistake – a simple inversion – very quickly, but the second one took longer. A number had got repeated across two columns, but once it was in the right column she got the numbers added and cross-cast and gave them back. Andrew put his jaw back in the right place and looked at her hungrily, and she saw her six bedrooms with *en suite* bathrooms move a step nearer. She could see, she thought, smugly, where someone who could add three columns in their head would be useful to a lettuce farmer.

'You're a genius!'

'No,' she said, regretfully. 'It's a limited facility.'

'God bless you.' He looked as if he would like to take her in his arms. It must be like being a good cook, men always react the same way, she thought, and smiled encouragingly.

The phone rang.

'At quarter to six in the morning?' she asked, faintly.

'Probably one of my drivers. Wanting to know if he's working. I was going to wait till seven to call them.' Andrew picked up the phone and she watched him, covertly, then openly when it became clear she might as well not be there.

'At Harwich. But...you have his passport. Or the Home Office does. Another one?' He'd lost weight, she saw, and the round pleasant face was looking square and formidable. 'Yes, I see. No, I don't see how I could have known that. He just slipped through the screening, I suppose. Yes, of course you have to. I'll be here.' He put the phone down and sat looking at it. 'Fuck. And fuck again. Excuse me, Jules. One of mine, armed with false passport, picked up at Harwich. And Allenton is on his way, just to make this morning quite perfect.'

Fifteen minutes later, they came through the back door, fearing, as they said, to disturb the house further, Richard Allenton, Jimmy Watt and a couple of DCs. Richard looked like the Grim Reaper, very pale, eyes narrowed in concentration, hair standing up at the back of his head.

'We've been up for some time,' Andrew said, challenging Richard to make of that what he would. He offered breakfast or at least tea and toast, and Jules put herself in charge of the toaster while he and Richard conferred in hushed tones. She decided she wasn't bothered; one of them would tell her later. Andrew went heavily off to find some piece of paper, and Richard sat down and looked hungrily at the toaster which rose to its usual standards.

'I see. One slice hits you in the eye and the other burns. Very practical.'

'Please turn that switch off beside you,' she sid, not wishing to join in any implied criticism of her host. 'Butter, jam, marge on the table. Who is he? The chap you caught.'

'No idea yet. But not good news. Either he's a ringer or he's a sleeper – someone none of us know about, wanting to be activated. Classic terrorist stuff.' He had managed to get jam all over his chin, she saw, as she gave Jimmy the burnt slice of toast with the worst bit cut off to take out with him to join Andrew in the big shed next-door.

'Well, I'm sure Andrew didn't know,' she said, furiously. Richard was looking professionally non-committal which annoyed her. 'We do try not to act for terrorists at Jenkins Associates.'

'I'm sure I hope you succeed,' he said, coldly.

'What are you suggesting?'

'I'm not sure your beloved boss is on our side.'

'Paul wouldn't be prepared to act for anyone doubtful. He was very unhappy about Mirko. If he'd been there that day I don't think we'd ever have been involved.'

They were sitting in hostile silence when Andrew and Jimmy came back with the papers Andrew had hunted up.

'No, I agree,' Richard said, through a mouthful of toast as he flipped through the papers. 'Nothing to show. I'm not surprised we missed him.'

'Was that an apology?' Jules asked, brightly, and Richard looked up at her.

'I'm sure Mr Flowerdew understands the necessity.' Mr Flowerdew, looking like a statue, nodded to show that he did just about, but wasn't going to move anywhere. 'OK, we're off. Can I have a word, Jules?' His glance flicked over Andrew. 'See me to the car?'

It would, she told herself, be ungracious to refuse, so she put on an oversize pair of wellington boots and clumped into the bright dawn, huddled into Anne's second-best dressing-gown which had been constructed out of a blanket by some deserving Scot in the Outer Hebrides. 'What?' she asked, managing to stand on the toe of one boot with the heel of the other.

'I called the editor at the *News of the World*. He's pulled the article.'

She gaped at him. 'How did you do that? Oh, I suppose you threatened him.'

'Didn't have to. I told him the photographs had been stolen. They're not idiots, they don't want to be accused of receiving, especially when the story isn't *that* good.'

'In what sense?' she asked, off balance but offended.

'Neither you nor Mr Jones appear in *Coronation Street* or play football. They were very upset at losing two pages but they will have something in reserve. Or rather someone.'

She pulled the cord of Anne's dressing-gown tighter, understanding slowly that the black cloud over her future – and over Gwyn's – had suddenly lifted and that they could all go back to living their lives. She could not see Gwyn again, or not by herself and not for years, but he could go on being the best thing that had happened to the London children in his charge, and she could go on with her career without everyone feeling she was stupid or vulnerable or oversexed.

'Thank you, Richard.' She was going to behave like a grown-up and not cry or fling herself into his arms.

'You're most welcome.'

'I could go home.'

'You could, but it would be a terrible disappointment for Mr Flowerdew.'

She managed a quelling look which seemed to have no effect at all on Richard who was frowning, plainly thinking of something else.

'Actually, I would rather have you back in London. I'm a bit...well, at least you're not all over the papers but I feel we have exposed you a bit more than I'd like. Too many loose ends up here. But you need a bit of a break, good fresh air, get over it all a bit.'

She felt a deep, resentful blush come up from her neck. 'That could take a little longer than a weekend.'

'I'm sorry.' She had disconcerted him, she saw. 'You...you were very fond of him? Of course you were...are,' he added, hastily.

'Yes. I loved him, if you want to know.'

'He shouldn't have...sorry, Jules, none of my business. I just...' He stopped and looked away towards the horizon where the sun was flooding the flat land. 'I'm going to stop digging myself in any deeper. I just wanted to say I'm sorry, it must all be bloody painful.'

Yes, it was, she thought, remembering Gwyn in the early days, just after her mother had died, his arm round her in the doctor's surgery, gently coaxing her: 'come on now, cariad, away you go, she's a good friend this doctor, she knows what's happened and she'll see you fixed up.'

'Oh Christ, I've made it worse. Don't cry, Jules.' She could hear men behind her. 'I need to go. I'll call you. I'll be back. Look after yourself.' He cast a hunted look towards Jimmy and the driver who were gazing with apparent interest at the distant sun. 'You're pissed off with me now.'

'A bit,' she admitted.

'Don't be. Please. Go back to bed. Get some more sleep. I'll call you.'

Andrew was bent over the accounts a little too pointedly when she got back, so she volunteered to look at the rest for him. It took her about ten minutes and he was touchingly impressed and grateful, so she went back to bed with a gratifying sense of having been a good guest.

When she woke at half past ten and looked out of the window, the first thing she saw was Sharon Cardona, or her double, several stone heavier and six inches taller than when last seen, but unmistakably Sharon. She was dropping out of a van in the yard with a clutch of other women in trousers and wellingtons, dyed hair and loud voices. She had turned the corner before Jules could get a second look and she wondered if she were still asleep. She got dressed, thoughtfully, and went downstairs to find nobody at all, not even Anne, but the wherewithal for breakfast laid in a neat row in the kitchen. She ate the cereal and drank orange juice, decided not to tackle the toaster, and was making tea when she saw the Range Rover pull in at the side of the house.

Just past it, through the trees and an unadorned wire-fenced yard she could see the van that had brought the Sharon Cardona look-alike, but she forgot about her at the sight of Anne, in wellington boots and a Barbour over her good trouser suit, beaming with pleasure. She and Andrew had been on his eight o'clock round, checking that everyone was out either planting or picking lettuces. Anne was still fully occupied with extracting enough facts about Fen horticulture to be able to speak in the House.

Jules waited for a gap in the conversation before telling them, shyly, that she was no longer to be pilloried in the *News of the World*, expecting an outpouring of joy, but the announcement fell flat. Richard Allenton had rung Anne in order, no doubt, to put himself in credit with her.

She waited, rather cross, until Anne had gone to de-layer herself. 'Andrew, there's a van out in the yard which brought a gang of women in first thing this morning. The thing is, I think one of them was Sharon Cardona, Ray's sister.'

'I'm sure we don't have anyone on the books of that name... The van, that's an agency. Called Spare Hands, you ring them up, they send you whatever they've got and invoice us for N bodies. It's run from Wisbech.'

'So it could be her. She lives on the site there.'

'Yes. I'm not quite sure what...'

'What you can do about it?'

'Does it...she...make you uneasy?'

'A bit. Look, I may be seeing visions. Is there a way – sorry, can we take a tour round the plant?'

'How long since you saw her?'

'Mm – fourteen years. But I knew her straight away. Like Ray. Only I just want to check.'

He took a drink of tea. 'I've been in the factory once this morning, but...'

She ignored his reservations and pulled on one of the ownerless jackets in the hall and her own wellingtons. Andrew resignedly got back into his jacket and, pausing only to install Anne in the living-room with a fire and the morning paper, led her out.

'She'll go to sleep.'

'Lady Barlow? She ran me off my feet this morning.'

'And just when you were going to sit down with the paper yourself.'

'That's all right. I want you to be comfortable.'

But it *was* Sharon Cardona. They walked in through a small entrance at the side of the huge doors which opened to let in trucks carrying lettuces from the fields, and Jules saw her straightaway, dyed blonde hair pulled back from her face by the blue hair nets they all wear, the widow's peak sharply defined, and the same mean, tight mouth as the rest of the family. She glanced up and Jules shrank behind Andrew as they turned away from her line. The stopped briefly in the office while Andrew invented a reason for his second visit within two hours, then they were out in the bright day, the sky high and blue above them.

'You're sure?'

'Yes.'

And what would you like me to do about it? hung unspoken in the air and she didn't know the answer. Sharon Cardona was entitled to work where she wanted, and Andrew was short of hands. But her skin crawled.

'Let's go and have a read of the papers,' Andrew suggested.

The *Telegraph* and the *Daily Mail*, she assumed, but actually he had *The Times*, and the *Independent* as well. She read *The Times* and drank coffee and chatted to Andrew about the farm and managed to forget about Sharon Cardona. Until she looked out of the window, across to the yard, and there Sharon was again, by herself, hurrying across towards a black cab. She was wearing a scarf but it slipped back as she heaved herself into the taxi, straining her head back as she said something to the driver. In profile, the face was a fatter version of her brother's, and Jules stepped back from the window, wondering how a shift worker afforded a taxi. Well, probably she didn't – it would have been driven by another member of the Cardona clan. The taxi swung round to go out of the gates and she dropped her cup.

'Andrew!'

'What? Don't worry, it's only a mug.'

'Sorry. Can't think what's the matter with me.' She was scared silly, her mouth had gone dry and all power had gone out of her hands. The taxi bearing Sharon Cardona away had the same hackney carriage licence number as the one she had seen parked outside the hospital where Mrs Dragunoviç lay in bed. She tried to tell herself she was suffering from delusions, brought on by stress and alcohol, but drunk or sober she knew she could not mistake that numerical sequence. The taxi she had just seen had 13611 on its hackney carriage licence plate, same as the one in London. She checked her bag to see that her mobile was with her.

'I have a boring phone call to make, Andrew, and I'm going to head out to the garden for it.'

'We've got phones. One in the hall.'

'It is of a personal nature. I need to talk to Gwyn. My partner in sin.'

'Of course,' he said, instantly, blushing. '*I* could go out in the garden.'

'No, I need the air. It's a lovely day.' She couldn't get very far from the house without meeting a fence, but she did her best. Richard wasn't answering his mobile and Jimmy Watt wasn't at his desk at Camden nick, but she left a message on Richard's mobile. It was a bit garbled, because she was rattled, but she explained about the licence number, because surely he would know that she had to be right about it.

She walked back into the house, trying to look unconcerned. She was having trouble breathing. Andrew Flowerdew's offered hospitality had looked like a haven, but Sharon Cardona worked here and the taxi that had picked her up, in the middle of a shift, had been outside the hospital in London. And she had brought Anne with her into this trouble.

In her second year at Birmingham, there had been a spate of attacks on women students by attackers the police did not seem able to identify, and the University Administration had laid on a series of classes in self defence, run by an erstwhile sergeant in the Special Air Services, called Lofty. Jules had gone to a lecture, urged to it by Anne and found herself both interested and informed. The difference between the SAS and the citizenry (apart from a foot in height and a couple of stones) turned out to be that they were Prepared, they knew where the fire exits were, they were Aware At All Times, and they could always improvise a weapon. Sod improvisation, Lofty, she thought, what we need here is an actual weapon in the shape of something sharp from the kitchen. She headed that way, but Andrew met her at the kitchen door. 'I have rung the agency. They sent me a Mrs Sharon Fowler this morning. I suppose Cardona was her maiden name.'

'Look, I'm sorry, I was being silly. She can't do me any harm. I mean we're not children any more. She's got a living to earn.' Her voice sounded unnaturally loud, and Andrew looked at her curiously.

'It has upset you. I'm sorry. Come and have some coffee.' He made it and ushered her out of the kitchen, so she had no chance to abstract anything sharp. Anne was gently asleep on the sofa and Jules wondered anxiously how she was going to wake her and share her worries in private, but the phone rang and Andrew went into the hall to answer it so that Jules was able to explain the problem.

'Mm.' Anne had obviously been well under water and, Jules realised desperately, was being slow to catch up. 'Mm. Have you told Andrew?'

'He might be in on it,' Jules hissed, furiously, and Anne woke up sharply.

'Mm. Right. We're going for a walk, with your phone. Both of us.' They looked up, startled, as Andrew Flowerdew came back in.

'That was Martin. My brother.' He looked at them both, plainly embarrassed. 'Look, he was being very mysterious, he wouldn't say what it was about on the phone, but he hoped you would both be here when he came.'

Jules sat bolt upright. 'Why wouldn't he say?'

'Jules.' Anne put a hand on her knee. 'How far away was he, Andrew?'

'Half an hour, he says.'

'Then I have time to make a phone call?'

'Of course. There's a phone in the study.'

Jules, feeling hunted, followed her into the small, clustered hall. 'Anne, he…'

'Darling. Andrew is inviting us to use the phone. This is hardly the action of a man with something to hide.'

No, it isn't, is it? Jules agreed, feeling foolish, and sat on the edge of the big cluttered desk while Anne picked up the phone and jabbed at it. 'Darling?'

'What?'

'I'm being stupid, I'm sure, but I can't get a line.'

Jules leaned over and pressed 9, assuming that it was a switchboard, but there was no sound at all. She slid round and tried again and understood slowly that there was not even a dialling tone. 'No,' she said, huskily, 'it doesn't work.'

They stared at each other. 'Have you your phone? Get a number for me, quickly. Then go and waylay Andrew. Take him for a walk. Quickly.'

Jules shot out of the study and found Andrew in the hall, looking thoughtful. She could hear Anne's voice but the words were not distinct. 'Can we look at the garden?'

'Well. Yes. You pretty much see it all from the living-room.' Andrew was sounding disconcerted.

'I thought I saw a viburnum round the side.'

'I wouldn't be absolutely sure but I don't think so.' He took her back into the living-room and peered doubtfully out, and she was just working out how to insist on going to view the viburnum, what ever that was, when Anne joined them, rather pale but composed.

'Did you get your phone call?'

'Yes, thank you.'

There was an awkward pause, while they all looked at each other, then Anne asked Jules to fetch something from the study which turned out to be the mobile phone. Jules seized it and slipped out of the back door, taking advantage of the very limited cover. She could not reach Richard, nor Jimmy, so she left messages, asking either, or both, to ring urgently. Then she tried Paul but he wasn't answering either, so in desperation she rang Jenni and told her about the black cab.

'Are you sure?' Jenni asked, doubtfully. 'You are a bit stressed, naturally.'

'Jenni, it's a *number*. Please, pass the message, OK? I can't find any of the police.' She heard voices coming towards her and snapped the mobile off. The voices faded and she could hear the roar of a highly powered car which pulled to a halt just outside and she saw Andrew go out to meet it and Martin unroll himself, agitation in every movement. It's true, she thought, slipping back in through the door, breathing short, the hairs on the back of the neck do prickle when you are frightened. She went swiftly to the kitchen; there was a small knife on the table beside the delinquent toaster and she pushed it into her pocket just before Martin and Andrew entered, followed by Anne.

'Jules,' Andrew said, 'could you…could we talk? Something odd has happened.'

She straightened to her full five feet and eight inches and looked at both brothers. They really were much bigger than her. She made sure her feet were on firm ground – Lofty had been very keen on that too – and waited for them to come up to her. They both looked anxious and not at all menacing, and she relaxed a little.

'Martin came up in a hurry, you see.'

'Yes.'

'I'll tell her, Andrew. Alyssia – my wife – went to the police, finally, after I was attacked. They were going to bring her up here when she had talked to them, so she and I could decide what to do.' It wasn't a cold day, but Martin, in a fashionable padded jacket, was shivering, the handsome face looking pinched. He looked at Andrew and it was plain they had had an argument. 'They told her she could ring me but not Paul, even though he had agreed to act for her.'

'They didn't want her to ring her solicitors?'

'Yes.'

'Why?' Jules had forgotten to be frightened, she was so outraged by this piece of MI5 high-handedness. 'Did she say?'

'They told her that information was leaking from somewhere and it seemed likely that…'

'Bloody hell. I've had the local force try to keep information from the lawyers on spurious grounds of security, but I didn't expect it...'

'That's what I thought,' Andrew said, calmly. 'So I thought – we thought – we'd come and talk about it and warn you that that's what they think.'

The 'we' had not included Martin, that was obvious. He was avoiding her eye, and fidgeting with his feet. Anne, perched on a table, was watching him carefully. 'Thank you. I'll call... No, I'll have a think, then I'll call someone.' Jules realised she had lost her audience. Andrew was looking past her, frowning slightly, so she turned to look too. In the flat distance there was something coming down the road, at a good clip, dust rising round it. As it got closer it turned into a dark-coloured van, with its left indicator winking as it slowed, and she waited for it to turn into the yard. Only it didn't, it came to a halt beside the house and a man got out slowly, slight, small, dark and with the distinctive widow's peak. Jules managed a strangled squawk, the man heard her and looked up, then there was a crash as the back doors of the van flew open and there were men, masked and carrying pick-axe handles, everywhere, running into the house. Two men grabbed Anne, and Jules rushed to help, but something hit her head and then there was only darkness.

It was the engine noise that woke her, that and the uneven bump you get from a loose exhaust system. She had driven one around all one winter in her first car. She was lying face down on the floor which was moving and her right cheek was being rubbed raw by some coarse and hairy material, but she could breathe, though her throat hurt and so did the rest of her. She made some sort of noise and tried to move to ease the pain in her back.

'Jules?' It was Anne, sounding dreadfully anxious.

'I'm OK.' Pain shot through everywhere as she turned her head. She seemed to be wet, and she realised she had peed herself.

'Let her sit up at once, you stupid men. Do you want to be in real trouble?' Through the pain her heart lifted. If Anne was in action all might not be lost.

'Can't breave,' she croaked, obligingly, and someone turned

her over, roughly, so that she yelled, but she was hauled up against Anne's knees, and the object covering her face was whipped off. She could see nothing, then a dot of light widened and moved. Someone was smoking and she started to cough. 'Put it out, you silly bugger, you'll suffocate us all.' The voice of command was unmistakable, and the cigarette went out. 'Lady Barlow, are you all right?' Andrew's voice, she realised, with a lift of the heart.

'Thank you, yes. How is Martin?'

'Unconscious still.' Andrew was sounding grim, but Jules felt infinitely better. It seemed that they were after all on the same side.

'Shut up talking.' A voice she did not know, edgy but with the flat Fen accent. Not Ray Cardona, who was presumably driving them to wherever they were going. Jules checked herself over, piece by piece. Her throat was sore and swollen, so her voice wasn't going to be much use. Her head and her back were in agony, but her toes would wiggle and one knee was hurting, so her legs were still with her. Her hands were tied behind her back and one wrist was very sore against the tie. She wasn't, she thought, much of a fighting unit, and Anne was sixty this year. Andrew seemed to be awake and in control of himself, but Martin was out of it. Anne's arms were round her, holding her in place and for a moment she felt warm and comfortable. Then she thought about what these people might want and how they would get it and found herself shivering quite uncontrollably, teeth chattering.

'Jules, Jules? Look, gentlemen, she's in shock, she needs to be warm, or you'll have a real problem.'

A torch went on, at the end of the van, and she could see Andrew, blood on his face, head hanging down. Then her mouth was forced open and a stinging but warming liquid poured into it. She spluttered, shuddered, and went on doing both long enough to get a look at the interior of the van. Lofty had emphasised that information was the key in a hostile situation and that one must collect and store every tiny piece of information that comes one's way. For weeks after the lecture indeed she had found herself looking round lecture halls for the exits, counting people and their exact disposition in meetings and assessing refreshment trays in the canteen for their potential as weapons.

She didn't have much time before the light went out again but she had arrived at a total of six men in balaclavas, sitting in the back with them. Anne and Andrew sitting up, and what she feared must be Martin, head in a sack, lying on the floor. Anne had her hands free, Andrew's were strained behind his back. And there could be two more men in the front, one driving, one being on the look-out. They were going more slowly, bumping on a bad road, then they slowed definitively and stopped, the engine still running. She could hear feet, and voices, then the engine went off, leaving a blessed silence and the back of the van opened up a crack, letting in a shaft of sunlight, a damp smell and the noise of gulls crying. Darkness descended again as someone dropped a sack over her head. As she spat and cursed she heard Anne protest then cry out and fall silent; then they were out in the air, even the light through the sacking making her screw up her eyes, then they were indoors again being rushed through an echoing space.

Another one of Lofty's maxims came back to her through the pain: you need to muddle your enemy, he had said, not let his plans go smoothly. She managed a cry of pain – not difficult, with all of her hurting – and slumped, making herself as heavy as she could, so as to slow down the man pulling her along. He tried to hold her up and drag her along, but he was small, so he called for assistance. She didn't have a plan, she was just trying to disrupt whatever their plan was, as Lofty would have wished, so she lay, loglike, trying to pretend she was unconscious. Someone took the hood off her head again and she saw grey light, and the corner of Anne's good jacket.

'Get her up.' Two sets of hands seized her arms and lifted, and she hung, heavy and silent between them.

'Let her go!' She heard a curse and a cry and a thud. The men who were dragging her dropped her again, and she lay, one cheek turned so she could see Anne who was sitting on the ground, jaw clenched in pain, holding her head.

Someone took off, feet thumping on the cement. The men near her took off too, but she managed to trip the third by kicking up one leg backwards. He got up, kicked her and took off after the others and she rolled over, almost into Anne who took her face in her hands.

'What's happening?'

'Andrew managed to get away…no, they're chasing him still.'

'Can you untie my hands?' She rolled over on her face and she tugged at the ropes.

'No.' Anne was sounding bleak. 'Hang on, I may have something in my bag. Oh *fuck*, no scissors.'

'I've got a knife!'

'Darling. Where?'

'Pocket.'

'Got it.'

She felt the tie loosen and an agonising pain in her wrists and she dug her forehead into the concrete in order not to cry, felt the ties part and rolled over into a foetal ball, hands pressed against her stomach.

'They're coming back. They have Andrew! No, wait. No, Oh, God.'

She got her head up, six inches off the floor, screened by Anne. The six men were gathered round a screaming shape on the floor, and she felt sick. Two of them glanced over but she was on the wrong side of Anne. She looked around, frantically and found she could see the shape of a door on the wall on the opposite side. 'I'm going for that door.'

'Jules, no. They could kill you.'

'I think they mean to anyway.' She could hear the shake in her voice and felt Anne's hand stilled on her cheek. 'What's happening now?'

'Four of them are holding Andrew. The other two are watching them.'

'Right. Good. You get up and hobble over to them and make a fuss, demanding a doctor for Andrew. I'll go for the door.'

'But if it's locked…'

'Have you a credit card?' One of Lofty's minions, who'd taken a fancy to her, had shown her how to get a door open with a credit card. It wasn't at all difficult, particularly if it was a Yale or a single bolt, assuming her agonisingly painful hands would work at all. Anne put a credit card into Jules's hands, then got to her knees, then her feet and started to totter towards the enemy who, as Jules had hoped, stood and waited for her. She shuffled along at the speed of a woman twenty years her senior, uttering cries of distress, and Jules waited, watching her close the gap. Anne had reached the group and Jules got up in two ungainly staggers and ran, her wrists so painful she thought she might pass out again and heard shouts echoing behind her. It was only a single bolt lock, but her fingers would not work and she nearly dropped the card, so one man was only about ten yards away when she pulled the door back and was out and away, running for a dark green Jaguar with a number she knew parked broadside across the track. She could hear pounding feet behind her but she was going to get there first, and reach her dear Paul who had got out of the car and was standing waiting with a very businesslike-looking gun trained on the path. She threw herself on the ground so he could get a clear shot at her pursuers, but she had forgotten about her hands, so she screamed as she touched down. She spat out a mouthful of the black Fen peat and sat up, cradling her useless hands to find she was looking down the barrel of the gun, still in Paul's hands. He was very pale and still, his black hair lifting off his face in the wind, his hands absolutely steady.

'Paul?' It came out as a high-pitched croak.

'You silly girl.' She watched his hands clench on the gun. 'Get up.'

She did, supporting herself on the car. She could feel her jaw start to shake and she gritted her teeth. 'Paul?' she said, meaning what has happened, why are you here, why am I silly? The angle of the gun changed sharply so it pointed past her and she turned to look at Anne who was hobbling over to the car with another man as escort. She hobbled on, ignoring the gun and came to put a supporting arm round Jules, who could not seem to manage intelligent speech. She just leaned on Anne achingly, looking at Paul's classic profile against the wide, blue sky. Behind him she could see the Nissen hut and the fields of plastic which covered the celery crop. and the container into which the plastic would go to be recycled.

'Cardona,' said Paul authoritatively. Ray stepped forward and she felt everything tighten. 'What does she know?' her boss asked.

'We was just going to ask.'

'No problem,' Jules said, managing to get the throat muscles into action. 'I know absolutely damn all. Perhaps someone could tell me? Presumably you are working with Richard Allenton, Paul? I thought I was too.'

Paul turned his head sharply, in order to think. I have watched him do that forever, Jules thought, painfully.

'When did you last speak to Allenton?'

'I've lost track of the time.' Her good watch, a present from Anne for her twenty-first birthday had gone. 'Around eleven o'clock this morning.' She had made a mistake, she saw, and all the lines in Paul's face had set hard, making something ugly out of the beautiful bones.

'Where are the others, Ray?'

'In the shed.'

'Lady Barlow. I'd like you to join them.'

'I will not leave Jules.'

Ray Cardona made a muffled incredulous noise which Paul ignored. He stood looking at them both, the brown eyes narrowed in calculation. 'They'll have to go on the ship,' he said, turning his head to Ray. 'All of them.' He looked across at Jules. 'Better for you and Lady Barlow not to make a fuss.'

It had been Paul himself who had taught her that if your natural opponents, like the police, ever suggest that you should not make waves the time has come to move very fast before they bury you. So as he walked round the bonnet, she jabbed at him as hard as she could with the tiny knife. But she only managed to scrape him on the throat and he staggered but recovered himself and seized Anne forcing the gun into her mouth so she cried out.

'Mum!' Jules called, agonised, and Anne's eyes turned to her. 'Stop, Paul, I'll be quiet.'

'Drop the knife.' She dropped it onto the concrete where it lay. 'This is all a mess,' he said, furiously. 'None of this...' He pulled the gun away, roughly, and Jules saw, agonised, that Anne was bleeding freely round the mouth.

'Darling,' Anne said, warningly, 'calm, calm. May I go to her, Paul?'

'Just keep her quiet.' He turned to Ray Cardona. 'Put them into the container now. With the others!'

'Paul. Wait,' Jules said, desperately. 'Richard knows. He's told Alyssia not to talk to you. He knows where we are. I told him.'

'You didn't know about this place.'

They had worked together for nearly three years, she thought, disbelieving still, and I was his best and cleverest trainee. 'Richard does,' she said, and watched his face change.

He waved his hand to the men in dismissal. The other hand, she was glad to see was occupied holding a handkerchief to his neck. They tied her hands again and she yelled, stopping instantly when she saw Anne's agonised face. They walked Jules and Anne, two men for each, across the huge shed, past the plastic-covered fields, Jules sucking in air, steadying herself in the hope of being able to do something – anything. Never give up, Lofty had said, the SAS never do.

They were hustled across the concrete and into the container. As she fell over something on the floor, the light went out and a door slammed with a solid heavy clunk. She started to shiver.

'Jules.'

'Here, Mum. Andrew?'

'Yeah.'

'You OK?'

'Lotht teeth.' He spat in the darkness.

'Martin?'

'He's thstill out. He's breathing. We're in a chiller container. We won't freeth.'

Jules was shuddering now with cold and shock, and Anne was shivering too. But she still had her hands free and she managed to free Jules and Martin, both of them yelping, unhelpfully. They huddled together, shivering. 'I rang Richard Allenton from the farm,' Jules said, when she could. 'He'll come.'

'Would he know where we were?'

Well, Jules thought. He could start at the farm and he would undoubtedly comb the coast, but all of them and the ship would be away. Jules shut her mouth; the least she could do was spare Anne this knowledge. Then she thought of something more hopeful. 'Paul must know he'll be caught if he does anything to us.' No one spoke for a minute.

'Darling, he is leaving himself. He's on his way out.'

Yes, of course none of it mattered any more. That's why he was so angry with her and that was why it would matter not at all whether she and darling Anne, or Andrew, or Martin were alive or dead. Paul just needed the time to get clean away. Indeed, he would have less to worry about if they were all dead.

For something to do they started to tour the walls to see if they could find anything to help. It didn't take long; they were in a space only about twice the length of Martin's unconscious body and rather less across. They had just established this when there was a deafening roar and the floor shifted, throwing them in a heap on top of each other. Jules fell on Martin's legs and hung on as the floor lurched and rose. They were being lifted, and they were jolted again as they settled on a surface. They started again going round the walls, tugging at every protuberance in the hope it would come off and yield something – a door, a weapon, a chink of light.

The transport moved, then checked, then started again with a roar, then stopped and they all fell on each other again. Then there were voices shouting at them to keep back from the door and then a space swung open and they shrank back, dazzled by the sun which was, unbelievably, still bright in the sky.

'Miss Carlisle? Lady Barlow?' It was a man very like Lofty, wearing camouflage kit, and there were others, much the same size, who surged past them to collect Martin.

'Mum.' She seemed to be unable to move.

'Darling? See, it's all right, it's the Seventh Cavalry.'

'I peed my knickers,' she hissed, painfully.

'Oh, *darling*, this is the SAS or near offer. They are trained to live on frogs and strangle people with their bare hands. Wet knickers is nothing to them.'

The nearest man managed to contain himself long enough to assure them both that that was the case, and Jules let herself swing into his outstretched arms to be handed over like a parcel to the group below, one of whom was Richard Allenton.

'Jules.' He wrapped his arms round her, oblivious to the curious looks from his colleagues.

'When did *you* get here?' she asked.

He was deathly pale and he wasn't looking at her. She squared her elbows to break his grip. Jimmy Watt appeared, making tutting noises, put a blanket round Anne and gave her a box to sit on while Richard and Jules stared at each other.

'You were here already.'

'No, no. I promise you, Jules. It was a fuck up. We lost you. We tried another place we've been watching, then we came here. You and Lady Barlow were being marched into the barn.'

'You didn't take them when they took us.' She could feel Anne's cold hand in hers. 'You could have...they were going to drown us.'

'Jules, I told you. We were slow. We didn't have enough people with us. We could have got you killed.'

He was shaking, she saw. 'You needed a bit more proof, didn't you?'

There was a long silence, and honest, stupid Jimmy Watt turned slowly pink and Richard took his hands away. 'Yes. But I was sure...I thought we had the operation tied up.' There was a very long pause. 'I'd have killed him – Jenkins – myself, if...I ought to resign over this.'

'Mr Allenton. You have Mr Jenkins?' Anne interrupted.

He bent to Anne. 'Yes. We shot his tyres out and the car went off the road, into a ditch. Upside down.'

Jimmy had a mobile clamped to the side of his head, and handed it over to Richard, wordlessly, who listened, mouth tightening. He was in a suit under the camouflage jacket and silly hat, and his face was patchily blackened. 'We need him. Make sure they know that.' He snapped the phone shut. 'Jimmy, get over there, will you? Wisbech General, and stay there until I come.'

'Is that about Martin?' Anne asked.

Richard looked at her, rattled. 'Christ. No. I'll just find out about him. That one was about Mr Jenkins. He's alive, but only just.'

'But you need him so that you don't have to resign. Too bad if Martin dies.'

'No, Jules, that's really not...'

Anne toppled sideways off the box with a little cry, and Richard, moving with the speed of a striking snake, managed to catch her before her head hit the concrete. He shouted for a doctor and some confused time later they were in an ambulance, Jules wrapped in a blanket, with Jimmy Watt holding onto her, and Anne in an oxygen mask with a young man holding her wrist, and police cars fore and aft of them, all their sirens blaring as they blasted along the Fen roads.

Chapter Eighteen

(Two weeks later)

'So how is dear Jules?'

'Oh dear.' The sun was burning off the river in the bright May sun and a passing tourist boat was lined with people who waved to them enthusiastically. Both women inclined their heads, regally, in return.

'We are *snots*,' Anne Barlow said. 'We ought to wave back, so they could say that England's ruling classes waved to them.'

'You must be thinking of the House of Commons.' Beryl was one to acknowledge the realities of power. 'Is Jules still very upset?'

'Upset isn't quite the word I'd use. Furious. Fit to be tied, perhaps. Alternating with desperate attacks of guilt, because poor Martin Flowerdew is still extremely ill. Of course she has some justification; the firm – Jenkins Associates – has collapsed. The money was in a muddle apparently, apart from...well...'

'The founder in custody together with one of his principal assistants.'

'Yes. That hasn't helped. At least Jules wasn't on the immigration side, though it's a difficult point to make when she was also the person who started the landslide. And then she feels she has been made a fool of. By Paul and Jenni Patel, of course, and by MI5, in the person of Richard Allenton.'

'She – and you, my dear Anne – were extremely lucky, but I suppose she is in no mood to acknowledge that.'

'No, I'm afraid not.' Anne drank a gulp of coffee and frowned at a friend bearing towards them, who changed tack with a nod. 'She is however prepared to listen to you...oh dear, how awful that sounds, but she is in that frame of mind because she believes it was you who got us rescued.'

'She is quite wrong. I went straight to the DG when I got your call, but they were already in hot pursuit.'

'It would be nice if she would believe that. The other young man – Andrew Flowerdew – is naturally totally preoccupied with his brother, and of course Gwyn has troubles of his own, and she's taken against young Allenton, so…'

'So, on top of everything else she is a bit short of admirers.'

'Exactly so. So if she is…well, less than herself…you will forgive her?'

'My dear, I had a college full of young women in my later years.'

'So you did, I'm sorry, my brain must be a bit scattered not to have remembered. There she is.'

They both looked across to the door where Jules had been waylaid by one of the more dashing hereditary peers.

'Oh good, she's done her hair.' Jules's bright hair was done in spikes, and she was wearing make-up which failed to hide a row of stitches running down one cheek. 'She has been too cross to do any of that.'

'A beautiful girl. Look at Francis Winslow going through his routine.'

'Is she being reasonably civil?' Anne asked, nervously. 'I daren't look.'

'Perfectly. Treating him as her grandfather.'

'Poor Francis.'

'He won't have noticed. Here she comes.'

They watched as Jules picked her way through the chairs. She was much too pale and too thin, Beryl thought, but life coursed through her veins all right and she would recover. There was a small flurry while Anne anxiously ordered biscuits and suggested a glass of milk, earning herself a look of withering impatience.

'Beryl is kindly going to explain it all, darling,' Anne said, bravely, to the averted face of her adoptive daughter who was sitting hunched and miserable, picking at her fingernails.

'Only if Jules would like,' Beryl Williams said, comfortably, putting more sugar into her coffee.

'Oh, I'd be more than grateful for anyone telling me anything truthful.'

'Darling, I'm sure they…'

'They nearly got us killed. All of us. And Martin is still very ill.'

'You need to stop blaming yourself, Jules,' Beryl Williams said, calmly. 'You did very well. And actually so did Mr Allenton, taken all in all.'

Jules hunched her shoulders, radiating rage and disbelief, and Anne and Beryl exchanged a small involuntary smile. 'So,' Beryl said, taking silence for assent. 'I need to start at the beginning, with the Dragunoviç family. It was Mirko Dragunoviç who came to see you, but it was Stefan Dragunoviç who caused the whole thing to unravel.'

'*Stefan* Dragunoviç?' Jules repeated, rudely. The trouble was, Anne thought, that the poor child had been quite badly concussed and had not managed to take in much of what was being said to her for three days in hospital and ten days being nursed at home. Still, much more of this sullen behaviour and she might be tempted to hit Jules over the head on her own behalf. She sighed, running her tongue over two temporary replacement caps on her front teeth, where expensive dentistry was pending. A gun forced into the soft palate, she and her dentist had agreed, did no good at all to ageing teeth.

'Stefan?' Jules repeated. 'The treasured son! The one from whose backside the sun shone! Sorry, I mean the one of whom great things were expected.'

'It's the definition of great things you need to think about. Stefan was the breadwinner, that's the point of him. It's how he won the bread that was the problem and what he'd done to get started...'

'Beryl, tell me it as a story, please. I keep snatching bits from the air and I'm getting confused.'

'It *is* confusing,' Beryl agreed. 'This part of the story starts with the massacre at Srbrenica. A massive political failure which left the UN forces hopelessly exposed, and they would all have got killed if they had stayed. Everyone knew a massacre would follow if they left, if only because the British had told them so.'

'But no one believed us.'

'It's worse than that. They believed us – well, the Serbs had already massacred thousands – but they didn't – they being the UN – have enough clout or money or grasp of the politics to keep an adequate force there.'

'Please go on, Beryl,' Anne said, hopefully.

'In 1995, a year before Srbrenica, Stefan had gone off to do his army service, having finished at Belgrade university. He was a Captain in the Serb Army by 1996. Mirko was doing a post-doctoral stint at university, so he never had Stefan's opportunities.'

'There were opportunities there?' Anne asked.

'For many more killings and massacres in the years after Srbrenica, yes. They'd got away with it once and all the international community had done was complain. And the people they killed had savings, and treasures in their houses, for the taking. Stefan was an officer in the Serbian army. He got his share.'

'How do you know that? Oh, wait a minute. What did he *do* with it?' Jules, to Anne's relief, seemed to have woken up.

'Drugs, I understand. He'd acquired cash, and he had all his army connections, so he set up in business. He wasn't the only one, but he was a sizeable fish. But he didn't get started until 1998 and by then Mirko had gone to England.'

'To dig lettuces for £6 an hour,' Jules objected, rudely. 'Why didn't Stefan give him some money?'

'I don't think we'll ever know. It is clear that Mirko did not then know Stefan was a criminal, and they may have decided to leave him in ignorance. A lot of their cash was here and a fluent English speaker was always going to be useful. And then, when Mirko absconded it was already 1999 and they decided to leave him here, in case.'

'In case of what?'

'In case their worst fears were realised, and the Serbian army lost another war. As they did, in Kosovo.'

'Why did Kosovo make the difference?' Anne asked.

'Because we won this time – or rather the Americans won – and that was the beginning of the end for Milosevic and for the lesser people who had flourished in his shadow. Like Stefan Dragunoviç.'

Anne saw to her relief that her adoptive daughter was sitting up properly, and was concentrating. 'But Stefan must have made money by then,' Jules objected. 'He could have bought a big house and sat there, with his invalid father, ageing mother and sisters in the spare bedrooms. Why did he want to risk a journey here?'

Alas, poor Jules, Anne thought, still trying to fight the truth.

'Because he had committed dreadful crimes, and as the Milosevic empire crumbled, real evidence was being collected, graves were being dug up and, in Stefan's case, survivors were coming forward with evidence against platoons if not individuals. Survivors like Alyssia Flowerdew. She is only one of many.'

'Stefan was afraid. He saw the writing on the wall, in short,' Jules said, slowly.

'That's right. He had a bit of time to read it, he's not one of the biggest fish, but the UN mills were grinding slowly but thoroughly. Assisted by MI5.'

'So he ran,' Jules said. 'His parents weren't war criminals and he'd hidden the money, so he left them behind and came himself, and got in touch with Mirko?'

Anne felt rather than saw Beryl's considering look. 'Well, not only Mirko.' There was a long pause but Beryl went on steadily. 'Paul Jenkins was holding cash for him and others and Paul had been running a people-carrying business, end to end, from Serbia for several years. He used to run them via Holland, but it got too difficult there, so he switched to taking them through Latvia to East Anglia.'

It was hard, Anne thought, but Jules needed to hear this. The admired Paul was a major league criminal, not a hapless immigrant lawyer who got pulled into criminality by his clients. She risked a look at her child who had gone even paler than normal.

'Did he know…that Stefan was a war criminal?' Jules asked.

'In fairness to him, Jules, he would have taken the line that Stefan was a soldier who had tried to defend his country and was now going to be a victim of winner's justice. He would not have defined him as a war criminal.' They watched Jules think about the point.

'Did Paul know Mirko?' Jules asked, miserably.

'No. Stefan made his own arrangements via Paul. He told Mirko he was coming and who the organiser was in case anything went wrong. This is speculation of course. Mirko is dead and Mr Jenkins is not talking.'

'So it really *was* Paul, Mirko wanted to see. He just got me instead.'

'Yes. And you led MI5 to Mr Jenkins. They got lucky. I am told that the Division actually had an eye on him but I would guess only half an eye. They are now having a very good look at all the firms who do immigrant work.'

'And Jenni Patel?' Anne decided to take a hand.

'As Mr Jenkins' lover, she knew about the network. If she'd been there on Maundy Thursday instead of you, she would have hung on to Mirko and got Paul back from Pale – which is where he was – to cope.'

'She did get him back,' Jules said, stonily.

'But too late. MI5 had Mirko by then.'

'And Stefan's body? How did they…? What went wrong? They died of suffocation, or was that another MI5 fiction?' Jules asked.

'No, it was an accident. Like the Chinese case. The illegals came over in containers, but small ones.'

'Like the one that we were in?'

'Yes.' Beryl's gaze took in both of them. 'Yes. The ship – it's a twice weekly run in from Latvia – comes in through the Wash and heads for the Ouse at King's Lynn. When it was about two miles off shore, a boat would meet them – or rather run along beside them, they can't stop. The boat goes off with a dozen passengers, the ship steams on, and there you are.'

'The boat comes out from the shore?' Jules said.

'Yes. They found three boats. One buried, two under tarpaulins in various sheds.'

'So, what happened to the run which Stefan was on?'

'The assumption is that the people on the ship found the contents of that particular container dead, or dying, and they could not, of course, take them into King's Lynn. The boat crew wouldn't have wanted to take them either but they had to. The courier, who was Kevin Roberts, was probably made to do it at gunpoint, and also to bury them. Then they shot him, to tidy away the evidence.'

'Who are "they", Beryl?' Jules asked.

'Your old friend Ray Cardona and his associates, who had been summoned. They're all safely tucked up and they'll all be away for some time. Forever in Mr Cardona's case.'

'He's dead?' Jules asked, hopefully.

'No, but he killed his cousin Kevin Roberts, and Artie Potton and William Cliffe. He was still carrying the gun.'

'He was always stupid.' Jules drew in a deep breath, and Anne watched her, aching with sympathy. 'So it was me and Mirko, innocent idiots both, who drew MI5's attention.'

'You did better than that. You gave MI5 the Cardonas, and then they were able to link up the parts of the operation, thanks to you and your gift for numbers. Don't cry, my dear.'

'How can I not cry?' Jules said, snuffling. Anne scrabbled in her handbag to find a clean handkerchief which she pressed into her hand. 'Martin is still unconscious, and Andrew blames me, of course he does. And I haven't got a job any more, the firm is collapsing. And...well...' Tears were rolling down her cheeks, and Anne looked over her head, anxiously, to Beryl.

'Of course it was *very* bad luck for Mr Jones,' she observed.

Jules looked up at her, tears arrested by astonishment. 'Bad *luck*? On Gwyn?'

'Well, Jules, Mr Jones just got caught in the middle. You were getting very close even if you didn't know you were and the scandal totally unsighted you, and gave Mr Jenkins a chance to get you away, out of action. He must have been overjoyed when Miss Patel, whom he had planted on you, told him about you and Mr Jones.'

'But we didn't...I suppose it must have been...'

'People are very observant about matters of sex.'

The three of them sat considering this judgement while the table was cleared about them.

'You were a threat to Paul from the very first, Jules. While he was away for that critical three days you had exposed his firm to an awful lot of MI5 attention. You are an observant, highly intelligent lawyer. Mr Jenkins knew he would need to put you out of action, and he naturally preferred to involve you in a scandal rather than…well, something more drastic.'

'Am not I the lucky one?' Jules said, bitterly. 'So it was – oh, hell – it was Paul who organised the burglary, in order, I suppose, that it could be a fully illustrated scandal. And tipped off the *News of the World.*'

'That's right, Jules, but you kept your head and it looked as if there would be no story, since neither you nor Mr Jones would comment. Mr Jenkins must have been getting very anxious.'

'I don't see why he was anxious,' Jules said, her shoulders sagging with self-pity. 'I was so *slow*. Old mother Dragunoviç must have thought me impossibly *stupid*. She thought I had come to bring her money. And I went back and told Paul all about it without for one moment understanding what I was telling him. I'd probably never have understood.'

Beryl considered her. 'You are exaggerating your mistakes, Jules, which is always a bad idea. You had worked for Mr Jenkins since you were a teenager and you had every reason to trust him. Nor should you blame yourself unduly for what has happened to Mr Jones; had Mrs Jones not involved the whole family in her outrage there would not have been a good enough story for Mr Mahoney to bother with. But once she had flung out of the house and upset her son so much that he talked to Mr Mahoney, well, then there was a story. Silly woman.'

Anne, in total agreement with Beryl's views, just managed not to say so, and saw with deep pleasure that Jules was looking shocked.

'Well, Beryl…I mean…I'd have been very angry if my man had…well…had done what Gwyn did.'

'It is to be hoped that, assuming you loved him and wished to keep the relationship, you would not have exposed him to the *News of the World*, and destroyed his image in the eyes of his children,' Beryl said, with a snap.

Anne was reminded that Beryl had never married despite unmistakable evidence that there had been devoted men in her past, some of them now colleagues in this place. She sneaked a glance at Jules who was looking shocked but less frail.

'Beryl,' Jules said, slowly.

'Yes, my dear.'

'What about Richard Allenton. Was I a decoy? Because if so it was unforgivable.'

'Indeed it would have been. But as in most dramatic happenings, this was cock-up not conspiracy. The farm was being watched by Mr Allenton's forces, because they assumed Mr Jenkins was going to have to come after you, but there was only one of them on duty at the time, the other four having been diverted by a landing of more illegals. Mr Jenkins' people drove straight past the sole watcher and snatched the four of you, and it took the poor chap forty minutes to assemble a posse. He followed of course, and had already rung in, frantic, by the time I got through to the DG, your intelligent mother having rung me.' Anne breathed in sharply, but Jules had not reacted. 'I understand Mr Allenton offered his resignation. Which was not accepted. They have high hopes of him.' She regarded Jules kindly. 'You had a bad fright.'

'I thought they were going to kill us. Me and Mum.' Tears stood in her eyes, and Anne dared to reach for her hand.

'Oh they were,' Beryl agreed. 'And you two and Andrew Flowerdew did very well to delay them as you did.'

'But the cavalry arrived,' Anne said, irresistibly patting Jules as she looked out at the sun on the river. 'And we are all alive and I still have most of my choppers, though I thought for a while I would end up with a nice stainless steel set.' She looked hopefully at Jules.

'There's still Martin,' Jules said, stonily.

Jules had stayed for lunch at the House in the end, because she felt she owed it to Anne. She knew she had been pretty difficult company. Various nice old things, friends of Anne's, had stopped by the table and said hello. There had not been a lot in the papers but as Anne said, many-tongued rumour had been operating and most of the colleagues seemed to know that there had been a major breakthrough in the war on people-smuggling, even if they were hazy on the detail. But after lunch, there was no escaping the grim task of going to see Martin, brought low on her account.

'I'm coming with you,' Anne said, firmly. 'You are not quite able for this one, not yet.'

She agreed, feeling guiltily that she ought not, but deeply grateful for Anne's company. A taxi appeared, summoned by one of the sturdy policemen at the Peers' Entrance, and as he turned she saw with a small shock that he was carrying a gun.

'Needs must,' Anne said, following her gaze. 'Lots of Bad Men about.' She stopped, stock-still, in the sunlight and clasped a hand over her mouth, and Jules found herself able to laugh and push her respected relation into the taxi.

At the hospital, Anne talked them past the guards to Martin's bedside, the nurse in charge casting a respectful professional look at Jules's cheek. Her make-up must have worn off, she realised, but Martin was unconscious and Andrew nowhere to be seen.

'How is he?' she heard Anne say, quietly.

'A little more active. You were with him when...'

'Yes, we were. We were luckier.'

'What do you think?' Jules knew she was being stupid but could not stop herself asking.

Martin looked totally different from his conscious, active self, pale as death, frowning slightly, and still as an effigy, tubes attached to various parts of him. The nurse, a brisk woman in her forties, gave Jules the considering look with which she had become all too familiar in the last ten days, and motioned them outside the room.

'You can't tell with these cases. He may recover completely.'

'Or?' Jules could not help herself.

'Or there may be some residual damage.'

Jules felt sick, and something must have happened to her face, because the nurse was by her side, making her sit down, and dispatching Anne to find that great medical standby, a nice cup of tea. She was gulping it down, when she realised Anne was smiling at someone over her head. She looked up and it was Andrew, broken arm in a sling, pale in the spring sun which was illuminating the horrible brown floor, accompanied by a thin pale girl, with washed-out blond colouring. She was the girl in the photograph that Richard had shown her days ago, only older and much less pretty.

'Jules, you haven't met my sister-in-law. Alyssia.'

She was small, tired and ordinary with flattened blonde hair and wide-set eyes; and Jules could only gape at her.

'He is the same?' she said to Anne, ignoring Jules.

'Yes, my dear. Did you get a good lunch?'

The girl smiled at her, gratefully. 'We did. Andrew ate a lot.'

They all looked at Andrew who was standing in a patch of sun, looking as if he needed to be in a hospital bed himself.

'I am sorry, Andrew. I brought trouble on your house.' Jules had to speak or evaporate through the floorboards.

He blinked and looked across at her and she saw him remember that he had fancied her and hoped something might come of it. 'No. I employed Mirko.' He'd been going over this, she saw, just as she had done. 'It started there.'

Yes, Jules thought, but I ran to the farm and brought the trouble after me. Without me, Andrew would have been a bystander whom they wouldn't have wanted or needed to tackle and Martin might have been safe.

'Jules.' Anne put a hand on her arm. There was, after all, nothing to be said. Anne took Andrew with her, back into that silent room, leaving Jules with the pale unremarkable Alyssia, whose husband and sole support had been severely beaten in trying to protect another woman.

'It is I who have brought the trouble.'

Jules was so surprised she dropped her briefcase which she was carrying as armour. 'You?'

'Yes. I did not know the men who hurt me – I do not know that I would be able to recognise them, but I remembered the numbers of the units. And Mr Jenkins knew this.'

'Martin told him,' Jules said, remembering. 'And you would not have been wrong.'

'No. I am a person who remembers numbers.'

Like me, Jules thought. 'Stefan Dragunoviç was there,

when...when...' She stopped, unable to finish the sentence.

'Hm, yes, but others too.'

She had been seventeen, Jules remembered, aching with pity and horror.

'I wrote down numbers and kept them in my mind. But when...when I came here, I did not want at all to remember all these things and give evidence. If I had...told your police straightaway, none of this would have happened. So you see, it is my fault that Martin...'

That was true, Jules thought, feeling ill with relief. Alyssia had been a very real danger if not to Paul personally, to people he believed had been engaged in defence of their country. Had MI5 not snatched her into protective custody she, too, might have been a body in the Fens.

'Because I was hidden they followed Martin. To the farm.'

'It was Martin then, that brought them?' Jules asked, just to confirm that she was not solely responsible for the shambles. 'Oh, I'm sorry.'

Tears were pouring down Alyssia's cheeks. Jules led her down the corridor, urging handkerchiefs on her, hoping to find a nurse. What she found was Richard Allenton, looking gaunt but energised and purposeful.

'Jules. We need you again. To help disentangle the money.'

'You can't have me.' She indicated Alyssia and watched, jealously, as he put an arm round her and mopped her face and soothed her in Serbo-Croat. You saw a different man, she thought, when he spoke another language. He shook his head, emphatically, at something Alyssia said and made a gesture towards Jules. She didn't need a translation, the sense of relief evaporated instantly.

'It *was* my fault,' she said, cutting through the Serbo-Croat crooning. 'It was me they came after.' She wasn't going to cry.

'One group was following Martin, yes. But what brought Mr Jenkins himself was the knowledge that you, Jules, had recognised the cab that picked up Sharon Cardona as the same one that was waiting at UCH for Janina Dragunovič. It made the link.'

'I didn't tell him. I couldn't get through.'

'You told Jenni Patel.'

Of course, Jenni. She was being held under the provisions of the Anti-Terrorism Act. The Patel family had bought the best lawyer in London who was making no impact at all on a series of judges with their appeals to get her out. With Paul refusing to speak, she was MI5's best hope of unravelling the rest of it and getting a conviction. But still, Jules thought, I was not entirely responsible for the injuries to Martin Flowerdew. He was being followed, and by people who would not have hesitated to murder him if they thought it would lead them to Alyssia. And, no doubt, had all the party quietly submitted to being trussed up and stuffed in a container no one would have got hurt, and the SAS would have uncased them in good time. I'll know for *next* time, she thought, furiously.

Richard gave Alyssia a final mop-up, and a few more kind words in Serbo-Croat, while Jules collected her briefcase and had a word with Anne. The Flowerdew clan appeared to have adopted her as a relation; she was sending Andrew off to do some therapeutic errand for her and he was obeying with the exasperated docility of a son or nephew. Jules gazed after him, finally understanding that what was between them was liking and mutual pleasure in each other's company but not what she reluctantly felt for the delinquent, careless, exhausted Richard Allenton. Anne seemed to have acquired him as well; he was being told to take himself off and get a shower and have a break, and he too seemed to be receiving these instructions meekly. Anne herself had a sparkle in her eye and a spring in her step, and if Martin had not been so ill, Jules thought, she would have been enjoying the whole thing.

'Jules, where are you going? We need you.' Richard looked at her face. 'If, that is, you can spare…I'll drive you.'

To make sure she didn't get beyond the reach of his forensic accountants, presumably. 'No, thank you.'

'Jules. Do let Richard take you; it is on his way,' Anne said.

And just when had she started calling him Richard, when he had nearly got both of them killed, she wondered.

The driver took them through the park, and she wound down

the window, breathing in the fresh air and looking around her, at the children playing, the women with dogs, and in line skaters with their headsets darting among them all.

'Can I buy you tea?'

'No.'

'Can we walk a bit, then?'

'Why?'

'I have something to say to you.'

She didn't actually want anyone to say anything to her ever again, but she supposed she might as well get it out of the way, so she indicated he might speak.

'It's an apology. I wasn't careful enough with you. I did think we had the operation under full control when...when we didn't. I let it go on because...because I had to get Paul.'

Nothing new here then, except, she supposed, the apology. 'You were risking the Flowerdews. And Anne.'

'I'd never dare to do *that* again. I have made my apologies to her.'

'Did she accept them?'

'Up to a point. I think I am, at best, on probation with her.'

She could feel him looking sideways at her; they were marching purposefully along by the lake.

'It isn't a good enough excuse, Jules, but I was there, I...we...let Srbrenica happen. I needed to do different this time.'

'No matter what' hung unspoken between them, and Jules stopped walking in order to think. 'You would have wasted a lot of time and resources if you'd lost Paul.'

'Yes. But, Jules, you don't – please look at me – you can't really think that was what I minded about. I thought we'd get there sooner, I have never been so thankful, ever, as when we saw the lorry just coming out with the container on top. And then I found you weren't hurt, or not much...'

He looked scruffy and hangdog, and he was desperate for understanding. If Anne was prepared to put him on probation then so perhaps should she be. They stood and looked at each other, and it was he who broke the silence.

'Could we have lunch tomorrow? Not dinner, because – well,

there are a lot of things to do.'

There were always going to be a lot of things to do, but she had commitments too, and it was time she grew up and learned to form sensible relationships with men. And there was some promising material here to hand. 'Yes. I would like that.'

His whole face relaxed and he took a half step forward, then checked respectfully, so it fell to her to kiss him chastely on the cheek. She didn't step back and his arms went round her and he held her with the walkers and cyclists and skaters parting around them. Then his mobile went off, and his car slid into the side of the road, a discreet twenty yards away. He took her back to the car, one arm firmly round her, the other reaching for the phone.